THE
STRANGER
IN CENTRAL PARK

Photo by: edtorro/Shutterstock

THE
STRANGER
IN CENTRAL PARK

James Patrick Dillon

ENLIGHTENED
LITTLE SOULS, INC. ™

CLEARWATER, FLORIDA

An Enlightened Little Souls Book

This is a work of fiction. Names, characters, places, and incidents either are products of the author's imagination or are used fictitiously. Any resemblance to actual events, locales, or persons, living or dead, is coincidental.

Published by: Enlightened Little Souls, Inc.

Clearwater, Florida, USA

Edited by Susan DeFreitas, Collaborative Editor, Indigo: Editing, Design, and More

Cover compositing/design execution by Sasa Bralic for Enlightened Little Souls, Inc.

Enlightened Little Souls, Inc. and the Enlightened Little Souls, Inc. logo are trademarks of Enlightened Little Souls, Inc. Registration pending.

Production by Indigo: Editing, Design, and More

Printed in the United States of America

ISBN: 978-0-9998335-0-6

Library of Congress Control Number: 2017951675

For my Julia…

"I have found the one whom my soul loves."
—Song of Solomon 3:4

"No longer two, but one."
—Mark 10:8

Truth, like gold,
is to be obtained
not by its growth,
but by washing away from it
all that is not gold.

—Leo Tolstoy

CHAPTER 1

"I am not my body."

Shocked by the sight of it, bruised and bloody, curled and nearly naked in the dewy turf beside a weeping willow, she thought, am I spirit now?

A ghost?

A fascinating cacophony arose. It reminded her of a buzzing cloud of fireflies she'd run through as a child while on her first twilight picnic. She decided to focus on the individual sounds that made up the grand noise and immediately realized the cacophony actually consisted of voices. Tens of thousands of individual, human voices. And she knew what each voice was saying or had said or would ever say. Though in her new, disembodied state of being, there seemed no difference between what any of them had said, were saying, or would someday say.

Past, present, and future are one here, she thought. Wherever "here" is.

And now she realized that by tuning her awareness like one might tune an old radio—slowly, deliberately—she could dial in her new, special ability to not only hear but also to see anything: The sudden caw of a crow protesting the presence of a solitary hiker on the

Appalachian Trail. A gleeful child giggling on a playground swing in Houston, the swing chains in need of oiling. Pachelbel's Canon streaming from a radio on a London kitchen counter where a pie cooled, the curtains pillowed in the summer breeze, and dusty sunbeams struck a flare on a checkered tile floor.

Anything.

And with this discovery came a deep and abiding conviction she could choose to go anywhere she wanted. To some far-off world. To one of the magical realms she'd floated through in vivid dreams.

Anywhere.

Below, in her field of conscious awareness, the fog parted and two more trees emerged beside her petite corpse. The edge of a lake revealed itself, and a statue appeared: a grand bronze angel, wings wide. The angel stood upon a pedestal at the center of a circular pool on a red brick terrace beside the foggy lake.

Two staircases.

A boathouse obscured by the fog.

Now hills. Treetops. Streets. An entire city.

I am leaving the Earth, she thought. Ascending.

She sensed the desperate need to pick some new life to live, to settle on some new dimension or destination for her spirit or soul, her nonphysical self or whatever it was that she had become. She somehow knew she had to do this immediately or she would leave life on Earth permanently, become one with the light of creation itself, and fly through the vastness of timeless space before "receding again into the endless sea of divine consciousness out of which the experience of 'I'—like a wave—has arisen."

What? Where did those words come from?

Recalling her contempt, when in her body, for people who thought communicating as cryptically as possible was the same thing as being intelligent, she knew these could not be *her* words.

So whose were they?

And again, that other question arose: If I am not that lifeless young woman down there on the lawn, who am I?

What am I?

An answer as swollen with terror as a tsunami came flooding in: She was still an "I"—an individual—but one without an identity, without a name, and surely without a physical form, and if this "she" had arisen, perhaps it really would recede. Permanently.

But, into what?

My God, she thought. Am I really about to disappear into the eternal anonymity of some vast "sea of divine consciousness" and be gone forever, just because I do not know where else to go or who else to be?

She somehow knew the answer.

It was yes.

Yes!

And the city lights became a distant twinkle. And a sort of sleep began to overtake her.

No. I am not leaving.

I'm not ready.

I must think. I must solve this.

Yet she could do nothing, could be nothing new because she felt she was no one if not the dead woman. So only one course of action presented itself: That body down there, broken and bloody and undeniably lifeless as it was, would have to be hers again. It would have to live again if she was going to "be" again.

It will have to be me again.

Now!

And so she dove, by sheer force of will, through the clouds and fog toward the lifeless corpse, but when she emerged from the mist, the world was upside down.

No, she realized. The moon is not below me now. It's just a reflection on the lake. The real moon still hovers above me, full and bright.

It's just a false perception.

That's it, she realized. That's the key! Just as the reflected image of the moon had passed for the real thing, my body had always merely passed for the real "me" because I had perceived it as such, and believed it was me. And during the assault, the struggle that had claimed the life of my body, I fought so hard *because* I believed I was it.

As in dreams, one does not know one is dreaming until one reaches a higher state of consciousness, until one awakens, I did not know that I merely *believed* I was my body until now. And now…now I am awake. Truly, spiritually awake.

I did not believe in a spirit or a soul or God or Heaven or life after death. But now I realize this consciousness is the real me. The essential me. I am unbound consciousness. Eternal Spirit!

A bright light flashed, and a deafening roar shook her with the force of creation itself. She exploded, scattered, and dissolved into a profound, empty, and ever-silent stillness.

She became one with the plenum out of which every thing that exists arises.

Like water poured out of the cup that held it, poured into an endless sea, she departed and yet somehow remained. One without any other.

One with God.

Two hours earlier

"Please hold for the president."

New York City Mayor Jack Molinaro shot out of bed and began to pace. Heart racing, he pressed his cell phone hard against his ear and waited for what seemed an eternity.

4

"Jack," RJ finally said.

"Mr. President," Jack replied, stiffening to a sort of involuntary attention.

"They've retaliated. Shahab-3 missile took out our embassy in Tel Aviv, Jack. Leveled ten square blocks."

"My God," Jack said.

The day before, the Israelis had launched a preemptive strike against Iranian nuclear facilities. RJ had denied foreknowledge. However, no one believed him. Not even Jack. "Casualties?" he asked.

"The vice president is dead. Our ambassador. Most of the staff. God knows how many Israelis."

War, Jack thought, knowing this meant that the president would launch a full retaliatory strike and then send ground troops to defend Israel. Much of the Muslim world would join against them this time, and the Russians and Chinese had already made it clear they wouldn't tolerate another US occupation of the Middle East.

Global conflagration. It's coming.

Suddenly, Jack's mind turned to pure selfish interest. Some shame for this arose in him, given the situation. However, a thought had intruded, as if on its own, and he couldn't ignore it: The number-two spot in the administration had just opened up, and in the musical chairs of the political world, whenever someone got promoted or died, a dozen asses immediately scrambled to take the one new empty seat.

With a potential global apocalypse on the horizon, this particular empty seat would have to be filled, and quickly.

Is this the real reason for the call? Jack wondered.

"Could have been you that died over there tonight, Jack," RJ said.

"Yes," Jack replied. He had been vetted, had made the short list of potential running mates when RJ won the nomination. But he'd been passed over. My own fault, he confessed to himself. I blew it. "Terrible tragedy, Mr. President."

"I'm afraid there's more, Jack. We have reliable intel that an attack on New York may be imminent."

Jack stared at the white-sheet emptiness of his king bed. Its vastness reminded him that his wife had left him, and Abbey, their five-year-old daughter, who had so loved to squeeze between them in the middle of the night for a family snuggle, was gone now too.

But they are still in the city, he thought. And now this.

"Homeland Security, FBI, and the rest are on their way to brief you."

"I understand," Jack said. He checked the time. Nearly 4:00 a.m.

"Godspeed, my friend."

"Thank you for the call, Mr. President," Jack said. He hung up, set the phone on the nightstand.

A personal call, he thought. That *did* mean something.

The empty seat could be mine this time.

Should be mine.

I felt so disappointed when I wasn't chosen as number two. Now I'm alive because I was passed over. That would have been me in Tel Aviv. Talk about irony. I'm alive because of a scandal, because my wife publicly left me.

It still hurt, politically. And definitely personally. But he'd earned the pain. In spite of two decades in politics, he had enough integrity to admit that much, at least.

He went to the window, drew back the curtain. The moon, full and bright, and haloed like a prison searchlight in the predawn fog, cast shadows everywhere.

And now there's an active terrorist cell, he thought. In my city. But where?

Jack clicked the remote and turned on the TV. CNN was reporting the "breaking news" and had footage from Tel Aviv. Jack muted the sound, sat on the bed, and called Becka Ramirez from his cell.

Officially, Becka served as his press secretary, but she had been much more than that.

Her cell phone rang.

No answer.

Why? She always took his calls, anytime, day or night.

Now CNN cut to footage of a "UFO" flashing in the sky over Manhattan. Onscreen the graphic screamed: *Breaking News: Unidentified Object burns up over NYC. Possible missile attack against U.S. fails.*

"What?"

Jack got dressed and descended the stairs.

As RJ had promised, Homeland Security, the FBI, and a parade of others who had also been sent by the president—the CIA, the NSA, even the assistant commerce secretary—arrived in short order and briefed him about the coming war, what they characterized as most likely "a suicide bomber," and the need to redouble security. The feds had now officially classified the UFO event as "unidentified space debris" or a "small meteor" but definitely not a missile.

Jack conferred by phone with the governor and both of his state's US senators, and gave the order to have his people coordinate an emergency-response protocol designed to secure key municipal and commercial buildings, Wall Street, major hospitals, and the city's most famous landmarks.

Next he met with the deputy mayor, the city council president, and his police commissioner, Karl Kastleman. Karl called in a dozen of his own top brass and staffers, and notified the director of the NYC Office of Emergency Management to mobilize his team.

"If there's a suicide bomber in this city, we'll find him, Jack," Karl promised.

As they were wrapping up, the governor's office called to advise Jack that they'd put the National Guard on its highest alert status, and he in turn ordered every cop, firefighter, and trauma-center MD in the five boroughs on emergency standby. The official word was, "We're on high alert because we are at war." No mention of the bomber.

So they were ready for anything. As ready as they could be.

Jack dismissed the last of his team and trudged up the stairs.

He stood at his bedroom window again and looked out without actually seeing.

Damn fog, he thought. Weird for this time of year.

He intended to shower but crashed on his bed instead.

Take ten minutes, he told himself. Just ten…

His cell phone rang again, startling him. He lifted it from the nightstand. The caller ID said *Katie*.

He picked it up.

"Sis?"

"Jack. She's missing."

On hearing the voice, Jack realized the call had been made *from* his kid sister's phone, but not *by* her. Dee Weiss, the "psychic" liberal nut job who had moved in with Katie two years ago and turned her against him, had called from his sister's cell.

"What do you mean, missing?" Jack asked.

"She left just before dawn. Said she was going running."

"She always goes running."

"This is different. I can feel it. Something evil has her. And there's something else. Something good—"

"How long has she been gone?"

There was a brief delay before Dee responded, and in the gap—because of it, in fact—Jack came to a definite conclusion regarding the nature of this call. A conclusion based on the history between his sister and Dee, and on the fact that Katie always went jogging well before dawn and sometimes stopped at Starbucks for a chai afterward—or used to, before the so-called "psychic seer" had disallowed it, for reasons she claimed were metaphysical. This was just more of Dee's "telepathic" bullshit. "How long?"

"Of course," Dee said.

"Of course what?"

"You don't believe me. You need to do something, you self-absorbed son-of-a—"

"That's enough!"

The phone went dead.

"Hello?" Jack said. "You hung up on me? Really?" He tossed his cell on the bed and began to pace again. "Fine!" He grabbed a tumbler on the nightstand, downed a puddle of Jameson, flopped on top of the covers, and stared at the ceiling.

Dee's desperate tone had shaken him. True. But her hysterics had a kind of contagious power. Not just over him. Over everyone.

"She could incite a riot at a Buddhist monastery," he said aloud.

That's all it is, he thought.

That and the uncontrollable emotional response Dee's contempt for him always provoked. And the still-open wounds from Dee's all-too-frequent public proclamations of complete and utter disrespect for Jack and "his Republican ilk." Yeah, and the fact that she'd tried to force Jack to switch his views on gay marriage by arranging to have his two closest male friends' wedding ceremony on the steps of City Hall.

Dee had stood up as their "best man," in front of every news camera she could gather, *while* Jack was being considered as RJ's vice presidential running mate.

And his own sister had stood at Dee's side.

No one in Jack's position would have given Dee the time of day. No one.

He pulled two big, soft Gracie Mansion down pillows over his head and muffled a deep, guttural scream.

CHAPTER 2

THE EYES OF THE BROKEN AND BLOODY BODY BENEATH THE WEEPING willow flashed open. Somehow, they were her eyes again. She inhabited the form of the pale, frail, millennial on the dewy lawn again—shattered and battered and bruised, yes, but alive and earthbound and heavy.

The sense of being the body she had seen from the outside, from above the Earth and beyond phenomenal existence, now replaced the feeling of disembodied being-ness, though it did not erase her realization of her oneness with all that existed. Yet, in the predawn fog and chilling dampness, tremors of bitterness and shame, deep and pitiless, took hold of her as she began to more fully associate with her body. It convulsed, and she choked on the putrid, stifling smell of men and sex and booze.

A luminous figure stood over her.

An angel?

Her heart drummed erratically, pounding, seeking a rhythm. She clenched her jaw and fists and tightened every muscle and then reached out and said, "Help me." But the luminous figure merely smiled and walked away. And she began to fade again, helpless against the forces drawing her to a calm, empty, anonymous, and ever-blissful eternal nothingness.

No, she resolved within herself. I will not go. I will finish this life. Survive.

She willed herself to sit up. She reached for her panties and her pink terrycloth shorts, but agonizing pain in her nose and the back of her head made doing so unbearable, and she collapsed onto the cool, wet grass.

Her fingers went to her eyes, ever so lightly, and with the touch, pain screamed from within and her breath left her. She could only image how the swelling, the dried blood, the gash embedded with splinters and bark that split the bridge of her nose looked.

Horror.

She'd been through a horror. And felt sure she would ever look a horror now.

A sound reached her.

Laughter?

And now voices.

The men. The ones who assaulted me. It's them, she thought. Laughing!

And now the one she knew to be the leader, the putrid-smelling one full of evil and venom, perversion and darkness, shouted from the distance, "Check it out, boys. Looks like this here Sta-sta-stranger is gonna make a swim for it."

Stranger? The luminous figure who'd stood over her?

Get up, she told herself. Get out of here while you can. Get away while he has them distracted.

But she could not stand, so she rolled onto her side and fought the dizziness and nausea, tugged up her panties and shorts, and pressed her palms into the earth.

A new bank of fog wandered in from across the lake, chilling her.

She gathered herself and crawled on hands and knees past the trunk of the nearest willow, but then the Earth violently, cruelly turned round and round as if determined to drag her deep into its depths. She stopped, retched. Her arms buckled, and she collapsed and curled into a ball again, giving in to the pounding, sickening pain in her face and her head.

Take a minute, she told herself. Breathe.

Quietly. Deeply. Just breathe.

Don't lose consciousness.

Don't die again.

Fog blanketed her. Hid her.

Shivering, she folded her arms across her chest, clenched every muscle tight, now tighter, and focused on each short, shallow breath.

Good.

Make each inhale longer. Deeper.

Yes.

Each exhale slower…yes.

She rubbed herself warm and attempted to stand again. With the movement, the blinding, painful pulses of pressure in her temples and behind her eyes returned, and she decided, breathing slowly, deliberately, one slow inhale, one measured exhale at a time, it had to be enough for now to just survive, to just lie here for a while and be still and think of something, anything, to take her mind off the pain.

She recalled the blind man. A friend she had hoped to see again, here.

When? See him when?

Is this the same morning I pictured him in the park before leaving my apartment to run?

Yes. Today. She had stood on the street and looked up at the open window of the apartment one floor below her own, hoping to see her boyfriend's face there, hoping to be called up, called back inside. But her boyfriend had not come, and she'd thought she'd better stretch before running, and while stretching she'd remembered how, a week earlier, the blind man in the park had let her see his eyes. In the quiet moments just before dawn, with the sky baby blue and pink, and the lights in the park going out in succession like a skipping stone on still waters, and the late-summer air lying flat and only hinting of car exhaust and sweaty carriage horses and half-crushed cigarettes, she had come through the arcade and seen him again: the tall, handsome black man. He'd stood beside the fountain at Bethesda Terrace, dressed, as always, in neatly pressed black slacks and a close-fitting black T-shirt and...the terrace. I live in New York. I run in the park every day. This park.

Central Park!

The blind man's German shepherd, heeled on a leash, had sat quietly beside him, here, just a week ago, right over there, on the terrace, she recalled now. She'd approached them both without saying a word, yet the blind man had sensed her presence, had known she stood close by. And after having met him here, at Bethesda Terrace, many times before, by the Angel of the Waters fountain, that particular time she'd finally mustered the courage to ask to see his eyes. When he'd nodded and she'd removed his glasses, he'd asked, "Tell me, what you see?"

"Purple marbles, in shallow puddles of milk," she'd replied.

He'd smiled and nodded and said, "Aniridia. No irises. Totally blind since birth."

"They're beautiful," she'd whispered. Then she'd asked, "Why do you come here?"

He'd shrugged one shoulder and half smiled in a way she'd intuited meant he'd rather not say because he was certain she could not understand, and even if she could, she would not believe him. And at the time, she thought, he could have lied and said, "I come because I have to walk the dog" or "because I can't sleep" or given any excuse at all, and it would have been the end of it. But he had chosen not to do so.

Why?

Now, with her stomach in spasms, blood running out of her broken nose, and her neck sticky and warm from the running gash in the back of her head, she took comfort in working on the mystery of the blind man's visits as she lay shivering, trying to stay alive on the damp lawn, the sloping bank of the fog-shrouded lake.

I am in Central Park again, beneath my favorite willows, near Bethesda Terrace, the arcade, and the Angel of the Waters fountain. I am...who?

Who am I?

No.

No idea.

She sat up. The paved path at the edge of the lawn on which she still lay stood clear in the predawn light but for the ever-thickening fog. She returned to all fours. Suddenly, she remembered she had gone running up Ninetieth Street this very morning, past Our Lady of Good Counsel Roman Catholic Church and toward the reservoir, as usual.

As usual?

Yes. And she recalled justifying her habit: Some people get up in the morning and drink coffee...but I get up and run.

These were words she'd used countless times to explain her obsessive behavior, to literally make running in the park before dawn as regular as a cup of joe.

Yes.

Running was not something she forced herself to do. There was never any question as to whether or not she would run. She didn't have a choice. It was part of who she'd become. Out of bed at a quarter of five without an alarm. Put on panties, jogging bra, shorts, and a T-shirt. A blue NYU sweatshirt after Labor Day, if it was really cold.

And today is the Sunday before Labor Day, she now knew, and it is not too cold, so no sweatshirt. Just this shirt…sliced in two and bloody now. And no bra…it's gone. They cut it off me… She knotted her T-shirt, covering herself.

I brush with Crest. Gel, not paste. Spin brush, battery operated. She recalled special running shoes. For people with low arches and excessive overpronation. The shoes were orange and white. She laced her left shoe first and then the right, always in that order, and always in the dark, so she wouldn't wake up…who? My roommate. What is her name?

No. No idea. But that is when I feel most like the blind man. In the dark.

She looked down and saw only one running shoe now.

I lost the other one.

When?

Where?

Remember…

Hair in a ponytail. Splash of cold water on the face.

Oh! We had a fight. I left early. I needed to run!

"You always run." That's what he had said, as if jealous of my relationship with fitness!

My God! What is *my* name?

A flood of pain and panic filled her, and a feeling of great weight pressed against her chest. Think!

No wallet. No ID.

No stop for a latte after my run.

I never take a key, and I never—"Who are ya-you?" The voice of her attacker, of the stuttering leader of the men who had assaulted her, boomed from the terrace and echoed through the arcade:

"Who…who…who…are… are…are…you…you…you?" And now in disjunctive, horrible flashes, the memory of what had happened flooded in.

I took a path covered by a low canopy of trees that seemed tunnel-like, and out of nowhere something came at me, at my face, and pain like being gripped by jagged claws, blinded me, and a shattering sound, like great brass cymbals, took me over. And…he…they…so many hands. No! Please, no!

But it had happened. All of it. It was real, and she remembered everything. She remembered the stammering leader, the one who had carried her to this spot—his greasy black hair, the glow of his gray eyes, his thick fingers groping her…and then she had died. Died before he could rape her, died just as someone had appeared.

The Stranger.

That same luminous figure. He had appeared out of nowhere, as if floating on air. He'd emerged out of the fog at the edge of the lake, and when he had appeared, the leader had stopped.

"You're not afraid of this here Stranger, are you, boys?" the blue-gray-eyed miscreant had said. "Why, this here is just one of them homeless head cases that wander in the park. Looks like he just es-caped a ma-ma-mental ward, wrapped up in his ba-bedsheet, come down here looking for a trash-can meal."

A bedsheet?

Yes.

It must have caught the moonlight and reflected it, making him appear bright.

She closed her eyes, shut them against the pain in her head. She swallowed back her nausea and gagged on the taste of blood. She crawled until her knees were raw and oozing, until she had made it to a paved footpath, one she now remembered as critical to finding her way to safety. This path would take her to the terrace, through the arcade, and out of the park, to people. Take her to someone who would help her, to someone who knew her name and would take her home.

Home.

The mere idea of being there brought tears. She fought them off and planted her hands and forced herself to her feet. But both knees buckled again, and her eyes rolled back.

No! She *would* stand now. She would! And she would run. And if she could not run, she would walk or crawl again. She would find a way, any way, to get out of the park. She would get back to her life, to whomever or whatever had called her soul to survive.

She clenched her teeth and stood fully erect now, feeling strong enough to take a step, and another, and hope filled her heart. Hope, for she knew her way home. Hope, for the sounds of the men had ceased. Hope, for she could walk upright, though her wounds made doing so a supreme, excruciating effort.

She came around a hedge and stepped onto the red bricks of the terrace. There, amidst the thick, low, drifting fog stood three of her four attackers. As if bewitched, they stood beside the misty Angel of the Waters fountain and stared at the lake where a great, glowing orb of light hung within an impenetrable cloud of fog.

Is there a boat? she wondered. Lights?

The leader of her attackers stood at the very edge of the terrace, barely visible in the mist, facing the light on the lake. His back to her, he shouted once more, "Who are you?"

But the light moved away like a slowly rolling, luminous ball.

One of the three men by the fountain, the one who had taken a razor to her shirt and cut off her bra, suddenly turned and bounded up the terrace stairs.

He's fleeing, she thought. As if afraid.

Why? What have they seen?

Her other two attackers turned toward her. She braced herself, but they bolted past as if in terror and did not stop or look back. They raced down the paved pathway that led to the boathouse. Now only their miscreant leader stood between her and what seemed the safest way out: across the terrace and out of the park on the west side.

She could not risk going to the east now. The two had just taken that way and might be waiting for her. She couldn't go up the stairs. The one with the razor had gone that way. She had to cross the terrace. She had to sneak behind the leader, quickly, quietly, unseen and unheard, to survive.

Off balance because she was missing one shoe, she peeled off the other and then slipped out, one bare foot at a time. Step by step, slowly, painfully, her head pounding—trying not to retch again, trying to ignore muscle spasms and the deep, dull pulses of pain in her face and head—she moved closer and closer to the leader, whose back remained to her.

The sourness of his flesh and the rottenness of his heaving breath reached her.

"You ain't got to answer," the miscreant shouted at the light. "I know you. I know who you are, and still you ain't nothing to me. You hear me? Nothing!"

He took a step backward, and then another, still fixated on the light. She could barely stand upright, could barely breathe with him so near. The light moved closer, toward her, toward them both, and as it did, the miscreant's shadow fell upon her and began to creep up her body until his darkness completely covered her. With it on top of her now, smothering her as he had, she filled with rage. A sudden inner fury at the idea of being touched again, even by the shadow of him, brought her to a new level of clarity and strength and hate and power. She would die fighting if she had to die a second time, but he would pay a price if he tried to take her again.

Small and thin and frail and broken and as near death as she surely was, she would kill him.

"You never did nothing for me," the putrid-smelling leader of the men who had attacked her shouted at the approaching light. "Nothing! You hear? You never came when I called on you! You never helped me!" He turned, and before he could realize she was standing so close, she'd clenched her fist and swung with all her might and struck him, catching him totally by surprise, totally off guard and off balance. The bridge of his nose cracked on contact with her fist, and he whirled and stumbled, tripped over his own tangled legs and fell. His head slammed the bricks and made a hollow thud, and something metallic flew from his hand. It hopped across the bricks like a wounded cricket and came to a skidding stop in the space between them.

A knife!

He rubbed the back of his head, then felt his nose. "You," he said.

The loss of blood, the dizzying thump, thump, thump of her heart, the pungent rottenness of him, and the thought of the knife and what he would do to her with it overwhelmed her, freezing her for an instant.

Then he smiled.

The knot in her shirt had come undone, exposing her breasts.

The would-be rapist leaped for his blade.

She leaped too, and they collided and bounced off one another, but she'd managed to snatch the knife off the bricks and roll over and get to her knees and clench the weapon tightly in her hand. And all at once, the blade somehow flew open and caught the ever-brightening light on the lake. It flashed, reflecting the light like a hot flare as the man sprang at her. She stuck out her arm, instinctively, defensively, and braced herself in mortal terror. The honed, pointed tip, spear-like, shot out. A shock wave traveled down her arm. The weight of his body bent her as the razor edge cut in and slid, parting flesh, severing facial muscle.

"Ahhhgggghhh!" he cried out. The point came to a jarring stop, nesting in the solid bone of the socket behind his left eye.

Like a spring compressed, she uncoiled and pushed him off and pulled out the knife.

He fell backward and curled in a ball, writhing and moaning.

"My God," she said. "My God!" She staggered to her feet and backed away from him. Her chest heaved. Her mind raced. What to do? What to do?

The knife, sticky in her hand, now glowed a muted, slick burgundy, illuminated by the strange and continuously approaching orb of bright, unfathomable light. The miscreant's blood ran down her wrist, warm and nauseating. She could not move. Could not breathe.

"My eye," he cried. "You cut out my eye!" He groaned and pitied himself in morbid, half-choked sobs. He pulled his dripping palm from his face, and stood, staring at the gel and blood and chunks in his hand.

She covered her mouth and retched.

He shuffled closer.

"Get away from me," she shouted, thrusting the bloody blade at him.

He staggered back again, bent and moaned and sobbed. He turned to the light, "Help me," he shouted.

She held her ground, arm extended, threatening more of the same if he came at her again. Though she only half believed she was capable of it. "Go," she demanded. "Now!"

But he didn't go. Instead, he shouted at the orb of light again, "Help me! I nuh-know you! I nuh-know who you are! Help me!"

Confused, she shook her head and shouted, "Just go!"

He turned to her. "I was-was just a buh-boy," he sobbed. He stretched out a hand to her. "They made me…da-do them tha-things. I didn't want to. I didn't. I was ja-just a little buh-buh-boy!"

She thrust out the knife again. "No! You go. Now! Go!"

After a moment, he nodded, turned, and took a few unsure steps. He broke into a hobbled half trot toward the arcade tunnel. As he went, hand to face, limping and shedding blood in thick, black drops, he seemed no longer human. He disappeared into the cavernous tunnel, and as he ran through the hollow space, the low thud of his footsteps echoed off the tile walls, *pop, pop, pop,* like a Hindu drum.

At her feet, all that remained of him was a trail of blood spattered on the bricks, droplets that led past Bethesda Fountain and the Angel of the Waters and into that darkness.

They're proof he's gone, she thought. It's over.

But I am dying.

I'll never make it out of here. I'll bleed to death first.

I need help.

She turned to the light on the lake, just ten yards away from the brick-paved terrace shore now. "Hello," she said, staggering forward. She stopped at the water's edge. "Please," she shouted. "If there's somebody there…please! Help me!" Her body trembled violently. Her heart could stand no more. The warmth at the back of her neck meant that her head, exploding with pain, continued to lose blood. Tears streamed. Consciousness began to fade.

She called out feebly again. "I—I need…" She fell to her knees. "Please," she prayed now in a fading voice. "Please…"

And the fog parted. And there, in the swirling mist, walking on the water, was the Stranger.

What?

How?

He paused, and stood for a moment and stared at her. A fully luminous and glorious figure now, perfectly clear to her sight. Too perfectly clear. More real than any being she had ever seen before. Flowing black hair. A fine, dark beard. Piercing blue eyes.

The fog stood off his body three feet or so, as if pushed back by his glowing halo. That halo, tinged at the edges with emerald, pink, sapphire, and golden hues, seemed itself alive, magical. A white garment indeed draped his body. But it was not a bedsheet—rather, it was a simple, light cloth, seamless and somehow elegant. A turquoise hood covered his head. It framed his softly glowing face.

He paused again, extended a hand as if to offer help. As if to welcome or receive her. And he said, "Katie. Come…"

A chill gripped Katie when she heard her name. She instantly remembered herself as Katie again. Katie: the mayor's sister. Katie: the doctoral candidate at NYU. The roommate of Dee Weiss.

"I am," she said through a flood of tears, "Katie Molinaro." And in that single instant she recalled her whole life. Every detail. The good, but also the bad. Every failing. Every shortcoming. Every sin.

Repulsed now by the knife, Katie let it slip into the lake. It sank. Disappeared into the still waters.

The Stranger took a step closer.

"No!" Katie shouted. "Please, stop," she said. She thrust out her hand as if to hold back his advance physically, as if to confess by showing the blood on it. "Don't come any closer. I—I am not good. I'm unclean. Please—"

"Child," the Stranger said, shaking his head negatively. He brought his hands together in prayer, closed his eyes, and the luminous halo emanating from him expanded and enveloped Katie. It bathed her in its warmth. Soothed her and calmed her fears. And as Katie knelt, awash in the bliss of the Stranger's growing brightness, a new kind of love blossomed in her soul. An unconditional love. And it cleansed her. Freed her. Forgave her. And somehow helped her to forgive even the stammering evil one and the others who had assaulted her.

The surface of the water lit up and glistened like starlight and formed a pathway, straight and narrow, to the very edge of the terrace, to where Katie struggled to rise to her feet.

And again the Stranger, with outstretched hand, said, "Come."

CHAPTER 3

"WAKE UP, JACK."

"Becka?" Jack squinted. The first time she had visited his bedroom, six months earlier, Becka lay beside him and nudged him awake because Jack's five-year-old daughter, Abbey, had climbed between them, as she had often climbed between Jack and his wife, Sophia, for a "family snuggle." Sophia, who was supposed to have been with Abbey in Sicily for another day and a half, came rushing into the room next, smiling, carrying a big, wrapped box topped with a bow, clearly excited to surprise her husband, the mayor, on his birthday. And surprise him she did. And Jack had felt real shame.

And his marriage had ended.

"You all right?" Becka asked him now.

"Yeah," he said. "What time is it?"

"Eight."

"Eight?" He sat up.

"I tried to call you," Becka said, her perfume light and wonderful, her hips accentuated by the close fit of a black cashmere sweater dress, her soft, doe-like brown eyes as mercilessly enchanting as ever. "You must have been dead to the world."

"Rough morning," Jack said.

"Yeah," Becka said, "the media is going crazy. UFOs. World War Three about to start. Amazing you could sleep." She righted an empty bottle of Irish whiskey that had fallen to its side on the nightstand table.

"Where were you?"

She turned away. "Holiday weekend. A day off, remember?"

"Oh, yeah. Right." He swung his legs over the bed, and a thought flashed through his mind: Is Katie okay? He wondered if she had returned home to that crackpot, Dee. He checked his phone for messages. Nothing.

"You have a visitor," Becka said.

"Who now?" he asked.

"Lieutenant governor."

"Brandt?" Jack threw his feet over the bed. "Why?"

"How should I know?"

Becka turned again, quickly this time, and her shoulder-length brown hair fanned out like a parasol spinning. The line of her hips, and the subtle, rhythmic flow of her breasts catching up with her torso as she lilted toward the door, caught and commanded Jack's full attention. Something ran into his bloodstream, some chemical or drug produced by his own too-long-deprived glands. He no longer cared about the rumors in the tabloids about Becka being his mistress. Nor did the security of the city concern him. Nor did the question of what the hell Lieutenant Governor Denny Brandt was doing in his house. He didn't even care about losing the VP spot again, if it meant he could have Becka. "Hey," he said.

"Yeah?"

"Come scratch my back?"

Jack turned on the water and waited for it to get hot.

He'd just told Becka he loved her. "We're done sneaking around," he'd said. "I'm filing for divorce. We're going to hit this head-on."

26

Stunned. It's the only way to describe her face, he thought. She'd looked truly stunned. Her eyes, glistening and suddenly too full, spoke volumes, Jack thought, smiling. Though she did not say she loved me too.

Becka had waited years before Jack had finally acknowledged his feelings for her in a physical way. She'd spent nearly a decade at his side, sacrificing her own life, her own wants, her own desires, for him. She had done so for so very long before that fateful night when he'd given in to the passion he'd long known she had for him, and they'd lost themselves in one another. She "deserved" him now. She had waited. She had earned him.

He did not mean it in an egotistical way, he told himself. It was a statement of fact.

Love is a transaction, given in exchange for a taking.

He stepped under the now warm, streaming water and thought about his wife, Sophia. She had forfeited their deal, in the countless nights of their passionless marriage.

But what of his daughter, Abbey?

The sins of the fathers are visited upon their children, as the Bible says.

The sons, and daughters.

They pay the price for our failures. Our weaknesses, he thought. And this grieved him deeply. He had destroyed the entire universe of his only child that night. A child he had once loved more deeply than life itself. His love for her was still the only nontransactional love he had ever known.

Doing what he did, regardless of the "justification," had destroyed the trust of both his wife and his voters. Hell. The fact that he could do what he did meant he couldn't even trust himself.

How is it possible we find ourselves taking action we never planned to take? How do we end up right in the middle of doing things we know are wrong, yet enjoy them?

The knowing of what's right and wrong is clearly not enough, he thought, to keep us from harming, wounding, others.

Clearly. But why?

Because, right or wrong, we want what we want, he answered himself now. And trust, like Humpty Dumpty, once broken, can never be truly put back together again.

And yet, he had acted out of truth.

In truth, he had long loved Becka.

He loved her now.

In truth, he had married Sophia for the wrong reasons. And though he had tried to honor his choice, and his commitment, in truth, she had not acted, in the marriage, as if she loved him.

A game. A drama.

It looked good to her family, and on the front pages of the papers.

Is that why we married? We were "supposed to" do so?

The princess and the soon-to-be president?

Of course, she had not cheated on him. However, her pledge of fidelity had been but one of many vows. She'd kept that one, but *had* broken most of the others. She had failed to love him in a way he needed to be loved. She had not honored him. She'd barely taken notice of him in any meaningful way.

For some reason, though, he wasn't supposed to mind her failing in the other vows.

Why? Didn't they count too?

He massaged the shampoo deeply into his scalp.

And then there was Becka.

Becka, ever beside him. Becka available to him, with eyes that stared deeply into his own. Becka who adored him. Respected him. Told him she would do anything for him. Be anything for him.

Becka, not his wife, had been true to him. Always, consistently true, though she had taken no vows.

Becka had loved him. Honored him. Served him. And just now, Becka had made love to him like this was her last day on Earth.

He felt alive again now, like a man again. A real man, thanks to her.

"Becka! You're amazing, you know that?" he shouted now, from the shower.

Good, he thought. So good…

"Brandt," Becka shouted back. "Downstairs. Remember?"

"Right," he said to himself. He made the water hotter, turned to let it flow over the back of his neck. "Thank God for Becka."

She'd be with him now too, in this coming fight with Brandt.

He'd really have to be on top of his game for this one. Brandt wasn't waiting to discuss the preparations the city had made to deal with acts of terrorism. No. Jack knew better. The visit was about politics. Hell, it was about Jack's political survival.

A former district attorney, Denny Brandt sought and deftly accumulated power for power's sake, and he employed it with un-questionably merciless skill. His only hobby: the domination of his fellow man. Republicans or not, Brandt always demanded a political death sentence for his rivals. His credo: "It is proper politics to kick a man to death when he's down. In fact, it is a personal responsibility if he is a rival." And Jack was now both: down and a rival.

After being passed over for the VP spot on the national ticket, Jack had decided he wanted to be the next governor of New York. But so did Brandt. Each saw it as their respective, rightful stepping stone, the penultimate step, in fact, before a run for the White House.

In that fight, Jack had looked like the better candidate for a number of reasons. First, his "Horatio Alger" life story: As a boy of twelve, on his way home from an early-morning fishing trip, Jack had noticed smoke pouring out of the windows of his Gerritsen Beach, Brooklyn, neighbor's home. He dropped his bamboo pole and string of snappers and raced in to find its occupant, a young woman, passed out on the living room floor. As he dragged her out, she muttered, "My baby. Please." So Jack went back in, though by then the place was engulfed in flames. He found the infant in her crib, snatched her up, and shielded her with his body. He emerged from the collapsing building with his thin red flannel shirt fully ablaze, neck scorched, third-degree burns over much of it. When he returned home after three painful weeks in the hospital, the fire chief who had witnessed his bravery made him an honorary member of Engine Company 321, and the firemen, the child's mother, and her family—in fact, the entire neighborhood—had started a college fund for "our hero, Jackie."

At school he'd worked so hard not to let them down, he'd earned a scholarship to Columbia Law. When he decided to enter politics, his hero reputation made him a shoo-in. The old neighborhood came out in force and elected him city councilman, the first GOP candidate to win the district in decades.

Brandt, on the other hand, a Westchester private-school preppie, could claim nothing more heroic than scoring the winning goal in his high school polo match. This made him the personification of everything a poor kid from Brooklyn—and working-class folks in a lot of other New York neighborhoods—despised.

Second: Jack's sex appeal. Unlike his short, pink, balding rival, Jack was tall with a thick mop of chestnut-colored hair, hazel eyes, and a bright smile. He appealed to women voters of all ages and political persuasions.

Conversely, female support eluded the rather puggish—as the *New York Post* had called him—Denny "The Dog" Brandt. The *Post* had, in fact, run a mock poll with a photo of a Dutch bulldog beside that of the lieutenant governor. The caption: *Who's uglier?*

Brandt won.

Third: Jack possessed the advantage of personifying three of the big political constituencies in New York—Irish, Italian, and

Catholic. Many voters were predisposed, by nationality or religion, to vote for him over Brandt, whose pedigree as a silver-spoon-fed mutt didn't help a bit. As for religion, Brandt didn't have one, save self-aggrandizement.

Fourth: Jack's wife, Sophia. A stunningly beautiful, bona fide Italian countess from the south of Italy, the press all but worshipped her as NYC-adopted royalty. Her net worth topped eight hundred and fifty million Euros—over a billion US dollars—making Jack's "rags to riches" story truly complete. Sophia's dowry had not only made it possible for Jack to fund his own campaign for mayor; it had cemented his relationships with the world's financial elite, men who could write million-dollar checks to any super PAC he named on the very day he said the word *president*.

Brandt's "fortune?" Mostly inherited, and reported at a paltry two million.

Finally, like Brandt, whose wheelchair-bound seven-year-old son Rikki suffered from SMA Type II, Jack and Sophia had a special-needs child, though Abbey's condition wasn't fatal, like Rikki Brandt's. Rikki's spinal muscular atrophy had progressed to the point of wasting, and the boy had only a short time left to live. Abbey had a disorder on the autism spectrum, hardly noticeable most of the time, but the label itself had made her "royal" parents very sympathetic figures. So all told, when Jack had publicly announced his desire to run for governor, seven months ago, he'd had the advantage.

Of course, things had now changed. Rumors about possible charges of corruption against Jack and other damaging gossip and innuendos had started immediately after his announcement. Brandt was behind them, of course. But a month later they began to stick like never before, because Jack had been caught cheating on his wife. Sophia walked out on him and, in a rage, very publicly spilled all the gory details of finding him in bed with another woman. Though, for reasons still unknown to Jack, Sophia had not named Becka publicly. So now Jack had to face Brandt *without* his wife's fortune and *with* his own ever-mounting baggage.

He turned off the water, grabbed a towel, and stepped out.

He found his bed empty again.

Becka: Gone.

When they first crossed the lake, she'd felt sure she was dreaming, and as in all such dreams she'd wake up once she started falling. However, Katie's foot had come down on the sparkling surface of the water and she'd found herself weightless, as if she consisted, then, of pure energy.

The self-luminous Stranger had been waiting for her, and when Katie had reached him, he had taken her hand and looked into her eyes, and her soul had been filled with love and peace and bliss and wonder the likes of which she had never before known. She had stepped out in true faith, and in so doing had unshackled herself from all earthly wants, freed herself of desires and needs, and empowered herself to love without need of love or anything else in return—not because she had lost anything, but because she'd found everything in the simple act of obeying the command of the Stranger.

Katie had gained physical strength too when the Stranger's hand had touched her, and so her steps on the lake, though physically tentative at first, had quickly become sure. She had inhaled deeply on the way across, grateful for every breath she had ever taken in her body. It had died in the park, and because it had, she had seen her true self. And in it once again—and with it somehow strengthened, though not visibly healed—it had again defied all the laws of nature by walking on the water.

Yes, she had told herself. It had. This is real.

They'd crossed the lake, walking on the water as if on solid ground, and reached a place called the Point, a narrow, rocky peninsula in Central Park, directly across from Bethesda Terrace and the Angel of the Waters fountain. On that foggy shore, as dawn broke, they'd climbed a sparsely treed little incline. There, in a clearing atop a flat plateau, a humble structure stood. Something a homeless person would construct with the help of Mother Nature. Four young trees anchored the corners of the abode and served as support for its walls. Each wall had been made from discarded cardboard boxes opened and flattened and laced to their living supports by new vines that seemed to have miraculously grown and woven themselves together for just this purpose.

Truly a shelter for one who had no place to rest his head, she'd thought.

The Stranger had gone inside, and Katie, following closely, now realized that though its outer covering was of this Earth, the thin walls of vines and leaves and cardboard merely hid the abode within: an orb of pure, glowing light-energy unlike anything ever seen on this planet.

She stood motionless inside an endless landscape of pure light, indistinguishable from an endless white sky above. She remained in full possession of her memories and in full command of all of her intellectual faculties. Though she had suddenly lost all track of time, and she could not say how long ago any of what she'd experienced in the park had happened.

A day? A year? A lifetime?

She'd wondered if she could speak, for her body, like the space, now consisted of nothing but light. Perhaps this is a third form of being, she thought. Me with body. Me without a body. And now this "me." In here with him. Yet, this new light body is very much the same in appearance as my physical body.

Like a hologram.

She decided to begin with her most pressing question and put it to the mysterious, glowing being who had saved her. She moved closer to him, faced him, reached for the comfort of his hand, and took it. She asked, "Who are you?"

The mysterious Stranger smiled, and his physical form morphed into a perfect likeness of Katie's own, as if it was a mirror image. The Stranger's face was a version of her own, but infused with a beautiful light and surrounded by a halo sparkling with tiny bursts of gold and sapphire and emerald green. "I *am* thee, and thou art one with me," he replied.

"How?" Katie asked, truly bewildered. "In what way?"

"Can one be different than one's own Source?" the Stranger answered.

"But," Katie said. "You are good, and I am not. I was filled with hatred. I nearly killed that man. I am a sinner, and you, you are—"

"You are not a sinner," the Stranger interrupted as he returned to his own form. "You have sinned, yes. However, no one 'is' the evil they have done in the world unless what they have done they so enjoyed doing—and have done for so long, with so much passion—that it finally became their essential, spiritual character."

"So, it was self-defense, right? In the park, I mean. That man. He tried to—"

"Self-defense is the Religion of the Dead," the Stranger said. "Inexcusable, but not unforgiveable. There is still time for you to be redeemed, to be born again. Focus not on what you have been. Focus on what you are becoming. Repent. Sin no more. Be saved."

"I don't understand. He would have killed me. Don't I have the right to defend—"

"I have told the world this already. It is written. Surely you are aware of it. In the garden, just before they took me to the cross, I told Peter: Put down your weapon. Those who live by the sword shall die by it. It's also recorded in the book of Matthew. Chapter 5, M-39: *Do not resist evil.* If someone strikes you on your right cheek, offer them your left. And I have said, 'Give *love* for *hate.*' What do you then not understand? Were these not simple, clear commands?"

"Yes. But others have said that the whole book must be taken into account. That murder is forbidden but not killing. Not self-defense."

"Others? Yes. They are other than mine. My command is clear, unambiguous, and though difficult, salvific. Those others are not mine. They may claim to be, but no. They are their own. For this reason, I have come again. To remind this world that mine are to turn the other cheek or *all shall perish.* As I have said: Self-defense is the Religion of the Dead, the religion of those who are already dead though still in a living body. The spiritually dead. All that's left for them is to have their bodies die, which in time will happen, and that's the end of them. You must not follow the Religion of the Dead if you are one of mine, Katie. You must put down the sword. You must not resist evil, but offer the other cheek when struck. Lest this world now perish."

"That is too much too ask. Too difficult. Please…he wanted to rape me. He would have killed me."

"Killed you or your body?"

"Yes. My body. And," she reflected aloud now, "this whole thing started when I realized I am not my body."

"You are not. Nor am I. Do not protect your mortal body at the expense of your immortal soul. *This is the point of my going to the cross without fighting, and transcending death for all the world to see.* The body can be raised again after death. Have I not shown this? Have I not promised it to mine? However, the soul, once lost, cannot be redeemed except by my blood. Would you have me go again and again and again to the cross, to redeem again and again and again those who will not put down their swords? If you live by the sword, you'll die by it. And if you live by the old law, you'll be judged by it, judged and condemned to everlasting fire, but for mercy, which is bought by my blood."

"You pay for our sins."

"Daily. And yet I have showed you all the way back from Golgotha. And yet, even today, you bring me back to do it again. Why?"

"I am so sorry."

"You cannot serve two masters, Katie: the old law and the new. Your body and your soul. Your selfish wants and my fulfilled law. You must choose between the two."

"The Religion of the Dead and…"

"The Religion of the Deathless."

"You are deathless."

"As are you. Those who practice the Religion of the Dead believe they are just their bodies, and they fear that they will disappear from existence completely at the time of their physical deaths, so they live for the sole benefit and pleasure of themselves. They protect their bodies at the expense of other people's bodies. They kill in self-defense and do so, directly and indirectly, through proxies and armies and in the name of patriotism and national security, for personal gain. They form militaries. They invade. Put up border walls. They live as if all they are is one mortal being enjoying one short, mortal lifetime. They kill. Murder. Rape. Lie. Steal. All in order to gain one more day of physical life in comfort."

"I don't live that way, do I?"

"A variation of this is to live for the benefit and pleasure of your own family, or group, or 'people,' or nation. This is a distinction without a difference. It's the same as living for one's own self alone. It is merely the way those who live for themselves ensure their own pleasure and personal safety—in numbers—and at the expense of others. But when it comes right down to it, even these will kill one another—kill so-called friends, fellow citizens, even family—if that seems the only choice, if it is them or some 'other'—their body or someone else's that must die."

"Yes," Katie confessed. "I have lived for my own little circle. My group. My family. My nation. At the expense of others. I have sinned."

"Those who truly realize they are immortal souls arisen from the One Source, risen as immortal spirits in mortal human bodies, are mine. The Lord has given these to me. Mine know that they exist not because of themselves, but because of their Source: the very Source of all. The all-pervasive, omnipotent, omnipresent, omniscient consciousness of God gone forth into the phenomenal universe as the all-enlivening Word. And what is the Word but intelligent, God-begotten vibration? Even science confirms that, at the quantum level, everything is this, essentially, vibration. God-consciousness enlivens all things. Mine have realized this. They realize they are one with the One out of which everything that appears in the phenomenal world has arisen. They know they could not think or move or act were it not for the vivifying power of God. Thus, those who truly follow me live as if they are one with the Source of All—which they are! They see that while appearances may be confusing, we are yet, literally, one, as waves are merely different forms of the same sea."

"I am one with all? Even you?"

"Does not the sea rage in some places even as it lies tranquil in others? Yet it is one sea. Can any one wave ever truly be lost or separate from the sea?"

"No."

"Thus mine live as if *all* men and women are their brothers and sisters, not just those of their own blood, or group or faith or nation. *All.* For those who know themselves as inseparable from all of their brothers and sisters, inseparable because they share the same Source, and further, as inseparable from all sentient beings and from the Earth itself because they share the same Source, can do no harm to any so-called 'other'—for no 'other' actually exists for them. For them, *all* are *one*."

"I see. To harm anyone or anything," Katie said, "is to harm one's essential self within that 'other' one or thing or being, even though, by outward appearance, we all seem to be separate. Yes. I understand. I do."

"You awaken. If your spiritual evolution continues, you will live in your body knowing that you truly are immortal. You will behave as if you owe the life of your earthly body to your timeless, essential, immortal, spiritual Source: the One Source of All. In a word, you will live according to the commandments of the Word of God and love others as you love yourself, knowing they essentially are yourself."

"But what of my sins? Must I not face punishment?"

The Stranger extended his arm pointed into the whiteness. A scene appeared. Two men, angry and wet with perspiration, dragged a woman by her hair through the dusty street of an ancient village while a crowd, stones in hand, jeered. The men released the woman at the feet of the Stranger.

"What's this?" Katie asked.

"They wished to test me," the Stranger said. "To trick me and trap me so they would have an excuse, under the law, to execute me. And her. The woman was an adulterer, and under the law, it was written that she must be stoned. But I came to fulfill the law, to make what was incomplete, complete. I came so that the old law would be made whole, for what use is the old and incomplete and hollow if the new and complete and fulfilled has come to replace it? If I'd wanted the old law obeyed, I would not have come to complete and fulfill it. Even a child can understand this. Yet grown men and women do not, or will not, for if they do, they'll have to put down their stones and swords. They'll have to put down the Religion of the Dead and be born again. Truly born again. But that requires a faith so power-ful, it holds up even in the face of bodily death. Few possess such a faith, for they love their physical bodies more than they love God."

Katie took the Stranger's hand. "You told them: 'Let he who is without sin cast the first stone.'"

"Yes."

"And they all put down their stones. And you said to her, 'There is no one left to condemn you, so neither do I condemn you…go, and sin no more.'"

"I am mercy personified, thus mercy is the Way, the Truth, and the Light. Mercy. Love. Forgiveness. These I offer you and all. Mercy in place of punishment. However, to receive that gift, you must also give it to one another."

"That's beautiful."

"It is the truth."

"And that woman that they wanted to stone, she changed. Her heart overflowed, and she became one of yours. Not out of fear of punishment, but out of love and because of mercy."

"Yes." The scene receded, and the Stranger said in a loud, clear voice, "Know this: I fulfilled the old law of punishment, of an eye for an eye and a tooth for a tooth. I made it whole, and replaced it forever with my law: the law of mercy. I came for that reason, to replace the emptiness of it, for to fulfill is to make full an emptiness, a hole, a cavity. I have said as much, and lived and died and rose again as a way of demonstrating the *truth* of it. So it must never be referred to again as 'the law,' or I came and lived and died in vain."

Katie stared in wonder at the Stranger.

"Those who follow the Religion of the Dead," the Stranger said, "demand that others be judged and punished and sent to Hell. Those who follow me are immortal. They follow the Religion of the Deathless. They know that if one is judged by any law, all must be judged by the same law, so they neither judge others nor condemn others, for to do so will mean to condemn all to death. For as none are righteous. None are without sin. And all will be punished if any must be. All will go to Hell and remain there eternally, but for mercy. And so, if only to save yourselves, you must always forgive others."

"One cannot judge another or punish another," Katie reasoned, "without forcing the punishing of one's own self or children or family or race—for if the old law applies, it applies equally to all. I understand," she said.

"Yet for millennia, after asking me to purchase for you, with my very blood, a new way, you continue to ignore that new way. It's as if you've been given a new vehicle, bought with my blood, yet you park it and continue to drive the old one. Even a child can understand that this is an even worse sin."

"We must choose, actively or by lazy, ignorant default," Katie said, "to continue to live according to the Religion of the Dead, in fear and in judgment of others, self-interested and practicing self-defense, or as immortals in mortal coils, one with God, the Source of All, knowing that your promise is this: Turn the other cheek, and if the body is killed, God will raise us up again."

"Yes. And when you yearn for retributive justice, you must forgive instead, and pray that those who hurt and offend you will see the error of their own ways and repent. Rely on the fact that God sees all, and you and he, working together, can change hearts with love and forgiveness."

"No punishment?"

"True remorse is its own punishment."

"Yes. I've never felt so punished as by my own conscience."

"The conscience brings forth mental and spiritual anguish, a cleansing pain, and finally essential spiritual growth that eradicates the self-centered ego. It acts as a catalyst for spiritual evolution, the freeing of the soul from the delusion of being a mere body. Once this delusion disappears, the soul may take charge of the bodily existence and not be a slave to the body's intense, seductive, and corrupting sense desires, of which the strongest is self-preservation. This is what is meant by being called, Katie. I call you, and all men and women, to examine their own conscience, not point to the flaws and evil actions of others. Your spiritual destiny was fulfilled when you followed my command to 'come to me' when I called you. All may do so. All may come unto me, like little children…"

"It took so much for me to reach that point."

"The realization that you need to surrender to God often only arises during or after severe trials of the soul, and it only takes hold in the hope and faith of the possibility of the Immortal Spirit, which is to say, when facing death itself. It comes when under intense pressure, when in intense pain. It comes to those fortunate enough to know they must ask to follow me, not just in life, but to the cross, humbly, while forgiving those who sent them. There, by the falling off of anger, hatred, selfishness, and sin, under the greatest pain and pressure and mortal duress, comes the opportunity for transformation and transcendence. For salvation. Unless and until each individual realizes the need to make God-within paramount, they will live in ignorance of the choice they have made—ignorant of the fact that they have even made a choice: the choice to protect their own physical bodies at the expense of their immortal souls."

"I understand."

"So, as to your sins, and as to your punishment, and as to all sin and all punishment, I shall ever pray: Father, until each soul awakens to *me* and truly comprehends the choice I offer, forgive them, for they know not what they do."

"You remain mercy personified until we repent. You do not judge us. You forgive us. You forgive me," Katie said.

"Yes, dear one. You felt rage, hate, and sought to kill the man who had harmed you. You saw him as separate and evil and worthy of punishment. Though merely out of physical reflex and the desire for self-preservation, you struck out at him and sought to harm him in order to protect your body, which you thought was your self. You could not forgive him. By the old law, your action was justified. It was legal. You were free to defend yourself and kill him. Self-defense, under the old law, is not forbidden, so those who live by it need not ask for my forgiveness. They are free to turn their backs on the fact that I came and fulfilled that old law. You see?"

"But then they will be living under the old law too. They will have to be judged by it."

"Yes."

"No. If there is no mercy, no forgiveness for others, there's none for me. Forgive me. I want to be one of yours. I want to live under your new law!"

"Even at the expense of your body?"

"I am not my body," Katie said. "I am one with the One out of which all that exists has arisen. I am Immortal Spirit. I am yours. Knowing this, I will never again do harm to any other beings. Not even in self-defense. Never, ever again. I now know that I cannot harm others without also harming my own true, essential self and causing you to suffer for my sins again and again on the cross. I pledge to you, Lord, I will give love for hate, forgiveness and kindness for offenses, and when I see one who thirsts, I will say, 'I thirst.' When I see one who hungers, I will say, 'I hunger.' I will be thine, Lord. Inseparable from thee. I will be thine. I will. I will!"

"Then, Katie, to you, I am no longer a Stranger."

CHAPTER 4

JACK HATED CIGARS, ESPECIALLY LIT ONES IN THE HANDS OF SHORT, bald bullies with thick, hairy necks, Neanderthals who put their wet, muddy shoes on his coffee table.

On the sofa in the famous patent-yellow parlor of Gracie Mansion, watching the president's press conference interrupt coverage of the mystery UFO and take over the Sunday-morning TV news, Brandt seemed amused by a reporter's revelation that Iran had publicly confirmed responsibility for the missile attacks. The Iranians were calling it a "measured retaliatory strike, just and righteous given the recent lawless violation of our borders and the murder of hundreds of innocent Iranian civilians by the United States and its puppet, the uncivilized Zionist regime."

The Iranian statement referred to Israel's missile attack against thirteen of Iran's nuclear power plants and support facilities a few days earlier, sites the Israelis had insisted had not actually fallen into the hands of ISIS, but which had willingly been turned over to them by the Iranian government. The Israelis, who had cited the George W. Bush doctrine of preemptive strikes to avoid war as the justification for their attack, had made it clear at the time that they'd acted unilaterally. The president himself had confirmed this, and now, on television, disclosed something that only his closest confidants had known: the late vice president had been dispatched to defuse the situation and demand the Israelis stand down, make reparations, and seek a diplomatic solution before this madness escalated to a world war.

Too late now.

"Unfortunately," the president said on TV, as Jack stood over the reclined and all-too-comfortable Brandt, "the murder of our people makes this our war. The Iranians will regret this action. I promise you that."

"I bet that open seat a heartbeat away from the Oval Office had you up all night, salivating, eh, Jack?" Brandt said.

"Furthest thing from my mind, Denny," Jack lied. He picked up the remote, turned off the television, and tossed the remote onto the sofa. "What are you doing here?"

"It's time to sign off on that new NYPD contract."

"What?" Jack laughed. "You're kidding me, right? You came here to ask about that? Today? With all this going on?" Jack shook his head.

"That's right, Jack."

"Really?"

"Sure," Brandt puffed his cigar bright.

"All right, Denny. I'll play along: Those bastards didn't even endorse me, so why on God's good Earth do you think I would do them the favor of—"

"Oh, you won't be doing it for them, Jack," Brandt said. He stood. "You'll be doing it"—he reached into his inside breast pocket, pulled out a fresh, plump Cuban—"as a favor to the governor." And now he stuck the cigar right up against Jack's nose.

Jack snatched it roughly. "What the hell are you talking about?"

Brandt grinned like the Cheshire cat and relaxed into the sofa again. "Tomorrow. Nine o'clock," he said, and he struck a flame with a silver lighter, parked his feet on the coffee table again, and puffed his own cigar stub bright again. "You'll be at my swearing-in."

"Swearing-in?" Outside, the rain fell like a waterfall. Nearly deafening. Jack stepped closer, stood over Brandt. "The hell, you say."

"Oh, that's right," Brandt said. "I forgot. You get all your news from the TV." He checked his watch and picked up the remote. "Well, that's where you made your mistake, Jackie-boy. Inside information is the lifeblood of politics, and if you have to learn what's going on in your own political party from the news, well, I'd say it's too late to influence the outcome." Brandt turned the set on again, switched to NY1, and turned up the volume.

The anchor came on and said, "We'll have more on the death of the vice president and the situation in the Middle East in just a moment, but first some breaking news from Albany this busy holiday weekend..." Jack suddenly felt like a dazed seaman who'd spotted a swell that might wash him over the gunnels. The anchor said, "In a surprise announcement that has rocked the state capital, Governor Michael Swanson just moments ago released a statement in which he said he is resigning as of 10:00 a.m. tomorrow, Labor Day morning, after a little more than two and a half years in office..."

Brandt had somehow forced this, Jack knew. The son of a bitch had come to Gracie Mansion merely to gloat. He was the governor now. Or would be in a day.

"Citing poor health, and the need to spend more quality time with his family, sixty-eight-year-old Governor Swanson expressed regrets for having to leave office in the middle of a crisis but said the state would, quote, 'now be in the hands of Denny Brandt,' who, according to sources, will be sworn in tomorrow morning as New York's eighty-sixth governor at a private ceremony at his home on Staten Island."

"You know, Jack," Brandt said, "you should look at the bright side." He got up and crossed the room. "Now you can retire from politics. Maybe put things back together with the wife. Move to Italy. Play with your kid." He smiled and pulled on his raincoat. "It's a once-in-a-lifetime offer, Jack: Get out now, and I'll let you go clean." He paused. "But if you make me come at you again, I swear on everything I honor, I'll bury you."

Brandt walked out the side door and onto the porch.

Jack stood in his own living room with his mouth hanging open, holding a big, fat, brown cigar. "Shit."

Remorse. The etymology of the word interested Becka: *re-* + *mordere.* Literally, it meant: to rebite, to bite again or bite back. If one was so hurt, so wounded, so bitten that one wanted to bite back, one felt remorse.

Is that what I feel? she wondered. Remorse?

Certainly, Becka did not feel remorse in the modern and commonly used sense of the word, for the only nagging misgivings she'd admit to, the only remorse she had known, came from the damage she'd done to the child, Jack's daughter, Abbey.

Becka did deeply regret that.

She adored Abbey. Everyone did. A sweet five-year-old, full of love, and as bright as a new penny, Abbey never failed to run to Becka and hug her whenever, wherever they met. She never judged, never held a grudge, and seemed biologically incapable of telling a lie.

"Go say hi to Daddy," Becka had heard Sophia say when Jack's wife and Abbey came home to Gracie Mansion in the middle of that night six months ago. Abbey had then climbed into Jack's bed and thrown her arms around Becka's neck and given her a big, dramatic, heartfelt hug.

Jack had awakened and sat up, eyes wide with surprise.

No. With terror.

There would be no time for him to adjust. Becka had taken care of that. No warning call from the guard at the gate when Sophia arrived a day and a half early. No message from his secretary that his family was coming home sooner than expected.

Emails?

Text messages on his BlackBerry?

Becka had secretly deleted them all.

There had been booze too. Lots of booze. And sex. Lots and lots of frantic, reckless, fantastic sex. The kind of sex you can only have with someone you've longed for and held back from for far too many nights, too many years.

Finally, the "surprise" of the child, and then Sophia. Wow. The look of shock and pain on Sophia's face seemed to Becka like an image of her own, years earlier, when Jack had announced he was going to propose to the then-pregnant countess.

And now, sitting on Abbey's bed, hiding in the darkness of the child's room, she tried to convince herself she'd been totally justified when she set him up for Denny Brandt. After all, she told herself, she had waited a long time, had given Jack many chances to see the error of his ways, had loved him and told him so. So, six months ago, when she caught wind of the fact that Sophia wanted her fired—had insisted Jack "terminate that bitch"—she'd cut a deal with the devil…Denny Brandt.

"Remordere," she whispered. She had certainly bitten back.

A tear ran down her cheek. She smeared it across her face.

No, she thought. She couldn't allow feelings for Jack again, not now. He had done this to himself. She had been right for taking Brandt's deal. Right for arranging for Sophia to find *her* in Jack's bed…yes. Right.

So right.

And while Jack, downstairs, now faced what was likely the beginning of the end of his storied political career, she wondered, why, since she *was* certainly right, could she not control her tears?

Surely it wasn't remorse she felt.

No.

It was pity. In politics, a little-used word of unknown origin.

By late morning, Dee Weiss had resigned herself to two facts. First, none of her so-called friends were going to help her search for Katie. Second, the rain would not cease anytime soon. So she resolved to take matters into her own hands. She dressed as quickly as she could, pulled on a shiny yellow rubber rain jacket, big black rubber galoshes with a lip of yellow around the tops, and a floppy yellow rain hat. She stuffed Katie's cell phone into her pocket and paused for a look in the mirror. Bloodshot eyes. Thin, pale lips. Wild orange hair, curling and poking out randomly from under the brim like flames escaping a sabotaged school bus.

I look like one of those lunatic crossing guards, she thought. Katie would be mortified.

Dee sighed and stepped into the hall anyway, and as she hurried down the stairs, galoshes audibly puffing, the disapproving glance thrown her way by an aging Catholic priest in full black regalia tempted her to stop and tell the priest a thing or two about God's love for everyone. No exceptions. But she had more urgent things to do. She had to focus on the fight against a persistent voice that shouted in her head, over and over, like a broken record. It said: Katie is dead. Dead. Yes, she died this morning, and it's your fault. Your fault Katie is dead. You fought with her again. You knew she had started to run in college, in order to cope with the shocking death of her parents, and had been running ever since. You knew she'd run when confronted with the fact that you had feelings for her that she didn't have for you.

"I forced this," Dee said aloud now. I did.

I did.

"Go! Run!" Dee had insisted, when the alarm clock went off in the middle of the argument. "It's what you do! You run away!"

And now she's gone. And it's my fault.

Mine.

Quiet, Dee told herself.

Your fault, came the reply.

Quiet, she insisted again, instructing her mind to settle down, refusing to let her own vicious mental chatter or Jack Molinaro's damnable incredulity on the phone a couple of hours earlier triumph.

Dee's hope, dim as it was, came from the very same source that had earlier brought her the intuitive conviction Katie needed help. It came from God.

God, she told herself now, would not abandon Katie.

Not my Katie.

Too good-hearted.

Too pure.

True, Dee intuitively "knew" Katie had died. Which is to say she had sensed it viscerally, and had realized it essentially. However, she also now knew, inexplicably, that Katie might also yet live. And so she exited the apartment building and kept moving, resolved to systematically retrace the route Katie always took from their apartment on East Ninetieth to the park, to do so in an effort to find out whether she was correct in both her hope and her fear. To see if Katie had died, and yet lived.

Katie had chosen their apartment over Dee's objections, not because of the easy access to Catholic Mass at the church next door—Katie wasn't Catholic anymore—but because it was a straight run to the park.

The park.

I'm here, Dee realized now.

She had been in her head for the entire walk and yet had arrived.

People don't realize how big it really is, she thought now, looking over the great expanse of rolling lawns and spreading trees and uneven paths paved with black asphalt. And the pitiful few who do are probably the ones who've had to comb every inch of it looking for someone they love and fear lost forever. It covers more than eight hundred acres, she recalled having read somewhere. And all eight hundred of those acres were now plagued by too many vagrant miscreants and policed by a mere half dozen cops, thanks to Jack Molinaro's most recent budgetary atavism. "Fool," she said aloud.

Dee had also read that the idea for the park came as an overreaction to an enormous jump in the urban population long, long ago. Around 1850 or so, she felt sure it was, when the city census had swelled from fifty thousand people to six hundred thousand inhabitants in just two decades.

Eight hundred acres, in the middle of Manhattan. That's what they'd set aside. And about nine *million* people live near it now, Dee thought.

And one in nine million.

That's my task.

To find that one, in the pouring rain.

She passed a park bench with a homeless woman sitting on it. The woman struck a match and lit a crumpled cigarette butt while peering out from the shade of a crippled umbrella. Tucked between pillows of black trash bags under the bench, a child tensed like a feral cat fearing a kick.

Half the shelters in the city are closed. Nowhere else for them to go. More of Jack Molinaro's handiwork.

Insane.

Doesn't he see this shit?

Dee moved on.

There are nine thousand benches in this park, she thought. Eight thousand, nine hundred, and ninety-nine more to look under.

Eight thousand, nine hundred, and ninety-nine!

She put her head down and marched. Her galoshes stomped puddles into spray; her fear rose again and increased with each soggy step.

She'd never see Katie alive again. They'd never reconcile. Never be lovers.

Okay. But if she is *not* alive, then where to look?

Not under a bench. No. Intuitively, Dee felt sure of this.

Certain.

Where, then? Where will her body be?

Perhaps in the Ramble?

Yes. The Ramble: it was a million and a half square feet of undisturbed nature directly across the lake from Bethesda Terrace. Unlike Sheep Meadow, the park's famous expanse of open lawn lined with benches, the Ramble, a forest of mature hardwoods covering uneven, rocky terrain with plenty of thick underbrush, stood as a great place in which to hide…a body.

Or bury one.

A painful shiver ran up Dee's back.

"Katie never went there," she said aloud. "And I won't go either. She's alive still. Somehow. I sense it."

But in the dark and fog, Katie could have been dragged there, beaten, taken into those woods and…Dee feared this most, had nightmares about it often. She'd had one this very morning after Katie had left, one that had prompted her to call the mayor and ask for help.

She moved on, thoughts racing, hardly seeing because of the mind chatter. She walked and walked for hours and hours, calling out, "Katie! Kaaaay-teeeee!"

She paused again and again to look at any pile of leaves or fallen branches, and, because her mind was playing tricks on her, she felt false horror after false horror, for the rain fell in sheets now, making it impossible to see clearly, and so each patch of rotting mulch seemed to conceal a body part—an arm, a leg, a half-buried hand, a twisted, bloody finger.

Dee's tears mixed with the rain as she kicked at the decaying leaves and sniffed the sweet stench of decomposing oak and maple rising from veiny leaf fragments.

Death and rot.

She combed every inch of the lower half of the park, walked every footpath, went to the west side, and then south again. It was getting late, almost dark. Her legs ached. Blisters on her feet bled.

Damn this rain!

It was why no one had come out to help her look for Katie.

Yes, she told herself now. That was why. Though she knew most of Katie's friends despised her, thought she was off her rocker, said she had cried wolf too many times about too many things, had too many drama-filled fights with the mayor's sister. So, when she called this time, no one listened.

Just like Jack Molinaro.

He thinks I cried wolf?

God.

Idiot!

He's probably home right now, glued to his hi-def flat screen, sipping cocktails, sucked into the latest "breaking news."

Another crisis.

Another goddamn war.

Hawk. Lemming!

Cold, hunger, and worry had by now brought Dee to the point of near-incoherence. She headed through the section of the park called the Mall, and then down to Bethesda Terrace by the lake. She'd nearly reached it, and after the terrace would have nothing left to do but head for home.

But Katie *is* my home, she thought. How can I go back without her?

She entered the shelter of the arcade at the edge of Bethesda Terrace, cursed the sting of blisters now slick with blood and ooze inside her soggy rubber boots. She loathed the sound of them on the arcade tiles, the echoing *ga-gush…ga-gush* off the walls. She sat, wiped her face, let her head drop. She rolled her neck and rubbed it. She wanted to just sprawl out and pass out, but the floor was filthy and spattered with…blood?

A trail of dried spots, like rust-colored paint, caused her gut to burn with fear and spurred her back onto her feet, and now sent her onward, faster and faster, her heart racing, her mind a whirlwind.

The trail of spots led outside the covered tunnel of the arcade and in the direction of the fountain: the Angel of the Waters. She stepped out. The rain fell as if hurled by the gods through the thickening fog. It pelted the red bricks of the terrace so violently, the drops bounced up like shards of broken glass. The torrent had long since washed away the blood trail out here, she thought. Erased it, leaving no trace.

Dee's fear turned to panic. She stood alone on the terrace, alone in the park with only the Angel of the Waters watching over her. Then, in a flash of psychic insight, Dee stood witness to the crime. A shock followed by an internal flash of light consumed her, tearing at her, like an animal, a creature clawing from the inside out. The pain shot up from Dee's bowels and into her throat and began gnawing toward her brain. The pain brought a picture into her awareness: a greasy, black-haired miscreant stripping off Katie's clothes.

And now, the terror in Katie's eyes as her sockets filled with her own blood.

And now…nothing.

Nothing!

"I don't believe in you," Dee shouted at the angel statue. She lifted her gaze to the heavens. "I hate you," she shouted, the rain needling her eyes.

She staggered forward, bent, doubled over in sickening pain at the thought of Katie in the clutches of the greasy, demented bastard. She cursed the heavens: "God! I hate you! Why do you allow such cruelty! Such madness!" She lost control and wept and shook, and then gave in to the impulse to run, to go, as fast as she could from this place, to race home, to find someone, anyone, and tell them about the blood, and the vision of her friend, the one woman she wanted to love, in the hands of a rapist. A murderer!

She could not find her stride in the sloppy boots, but nonetheless gathered speed. However, the relentless rain had stolen her sight, and just has she turned for the hill, she tripped and fell and tumbled across the slick, red bricks. Palms and knees skinned and stinging, she sat, soaked to the bone, and began crying softly, overcome now by hopelessness. Helplessness.

A little stream rushed down the paved path and gathered speed as it passed the three spreading willows before spilling onto the already flooded terrace where she now fell back, lay on her back, and looked skyward.

Lightning flashed.

The heavens thundered.

And now she turned her head. Beside her on the bricks, the cause of Dee's fall came into focus: a brand-new Brooks Ariel running shoe, orange and white and stained with blood, and pelted by a stone-colored rain.

"Katie…"

CHAPTER 5

SUNDAY, CRAZY WITH A VISIT TO ST. PATRICK'S CATHEDRAL FOR A "peace" Mass; press inquiries about NORAD's confirmation that some kind of craft, small but verifiable, had entered the atmosphere over Manhattan; the coming war; the political ascendancy of Denny Brandt; phone conferences and requests for political favors and deals; city council intrigue; and too many people in his house—it had finally ended around dusk.

No. It never ends, Jack knew. But at least it slows down when I kick everybody out.

He had kept only Becka and Karl Kastleman—his police commissioner and second-most-trusted political confidant—to finish up the day with a political strategy session at the mansion in the patent-yellow parlor. To talk things through, over cocktails.

After all, their careers were at stake too.

"You've got to drop out of the race, Jack," Becka said. "After Brandt's sworn in as governor tomorrow, you have to publicly say that you won't be challenging him." She poured herself a drink, filled another tumbler with Jameson on ice, and handed it to him. "He's won. He'll have the nomination when the remainder of the term is over. You're done."

"She's right," Karl said. "You can't announce you're going to run against a sitting governor from your own party. Not with the country at war and the threat of suicide bombers and maybe missiles coming into the city. This has to be your focus. One hundred percent. I mean, of course you *can* run against him, Jack. Legally, there's nothing stopping you. But, in my opinion, a primary would be political suicide against Denny Brandt on any given election day, and never more than now. No one will support us. He's won. You're done, as Becka so aptly puts it. It's over."

"You're both wrong," Jack insisted. "As long as we keep playing, the game is not over, and if it's not over, Brandt hasn't won."

"You mean 'keep playing' as in, continue to prepare to primary him?" Karl asked.

"What other choice do I have? He's got me on my back right now, Karl. No matter what I try to run for next, even reelection as mayor, he'll get someone to primary *me*. He'll cancel state contracts and pressure anyone who contributes to my campaign, including the Wall Street guys—and without them, any hope of financial contributions evaporates. He'll have his minions threaten people with investigations…me, you, all of us," Jack said. "Hell, it's the Denny Brandt playbook…no. I may be weak now, but I'll only get weaker, and he will only grow stronger if we don't take a stand. Besides"—Jack swirled his drink and took a sip—"I'm not going to sit still while that corrupt son of a bitch turns this state into his private political fiefdom."

"Okay." Karl raised his eyebrows. "I'm all ears," he said. "What's the plan?"

"Brandt expects me to hide in a corner and lick my wounds, right? Try to keep what I've got, serve out my term as mayor, and stay out of his way. But that's a political death sentence." Jack crossed the room, turned, and came back. "Instead," he said, "we're going to threaten what *he's* got. Create enough doubt that he can hold the governor's mansion that the big contributors, the unions, and Wall Street are all going to have to hedge their bets by supporting both sides in a primary."

"How are we going to do that?" Karl asked.

"Anybody who gives to him and doesn't also support us," Jack said, "we make them feel pain if they're within our reach. We call in favors, delay legislation, permits, contracts…we lock down the city and make it clear: we not only don't *mind* a war, we *welcome* one. But it's going to be a fair fight. We do that, and worst-case scenario, the pressure mounts and he has to call a truce and cut a deal."

"Mutually assured destruction," Karl said.

"Right," Jack said. "Just like the Cold War: We die, you die too. We make it clear to the rest of the party we'll tear the whole thing down if we're going down. We make them create a pathway out of here for us, and make sure I am able to take care of my people. You guys and the rest of the team. All of us. And we live to fight another day."

"A Senate run?" Karl asked.

"Maybe," Jack said. "With state party support. Maybe a cabinet appointment from RJ that Brandt won't try to block. Maybe even vice president." He refilled his glass, raised his eyebrows, and turned to face Karl and Becka.

"Vice president?" Becka asked.

"RJ called me this morning. Personal call. On my cell." Jack raised his glass. "Anyway, we get something or everybody pays a price…that's the plan."

"Okay, Jack," Karl said. "And publicly? How do we position ourselves?"

"We oppose everything Brandt does from now on. He says black, we say white. He takes a stand, we oppose it. It won't be a total shock. Everybody knows I was planning on running against him. Maybe they'll respect the fact that a war and terrorist threats change nothing for me. I just say that I still think I'm the better man for the job, and for the state, and the people. That's all I have to say, and then I disagree with him every time he opens his mouth so there's not one major news story that he's in that doesn't include me."

"Okay," Karl said. "It's your call."

Jack turned to Becka. She turned away, speechless.

Jack went to the window. Night had established itself fully. Pitch black. Rain falling in sheets. "Karl," Jack said, "do you remember when I was a summer intern, working for the Suffolk County executive, in Long Island?"

"I do," Karl said. "You were 2L at Columbia."

"Yeah, and Brandt was Suffolk County district attorney. I sat in on this meeting…the county exec had called in all the department heads. Brandt too. His budget was part of an overall county financial crisis. Everyone was going to have to make deep cuts. From Brandt's budget, the county exec wanted ten million bucks. That meant layoffs, the inability to make promised political payoffs…it was a disaster for him…"

"And?" Karl asked, standing now too and stretching.

"Brandt came in. Twelve assistants followed him, each carrying a stack of manila folders. On each folder, they'd written the names of the county exec's department heads, big, in black marker, so everyone could see."

"The names of the actual guys sitting at the table?" Karl asked.

"Yes. It's an old J. Edgar Hoover move," Jack explained, turning to Becka, hoping to get her to engage. "The folder gave the impression that each of them, county exec included, had already been investigated. They were all seasoned pols. Every one of them had crossed some line or had some secret, and even if Brandt didn't really know about it, they did."

"So?" Becka said.

"So, 'I'm accepting pleas,' Brandt said."

"Plea bargains?" Karl asked. "He said that? As district attorney?"

"Yes," Jack said. "And then he waited for a reaction. They thought he meant from them, of course, and they began to squirm and sweat. But he didn't mean them. He had made quite an impression, though, so not one of them dared speak against what he proposed next."

"Pray tell," Becka said. "What did he propose?"

Jack nodded. "He informed the county exec he would not be cutting a dime from his budget. He said what he meant was that he was going to have his ADAs accept pleas from every defendant in the system, petty thief to child molester."

"I don't get it," Becka said. "Why?"

"He let criminals cop a plea to a lesser charge if they agreed to pay a fine," Jack said. "Those who could afford it were happy to do it and stay out of jail. It saved the system a fortune in prosecutions and jail costs, *and* it brought in tons of actual cash at the same time."

"Brilliant, really," Karl said.

"But it gets better," Jack said. "Next campaign, Brandt ran on his record: a 97 percent conviction rate."

Karl laughed. "Of course. A guilty plea, even to a lesser charge, is still a conviction, technically. Truly brilliant."

"So what?" Becka asked. "You're suggesting Brandt had a file on Swanson too?"

"Exactly," Jack said.

"You think he blackmailed a sitting governor into resigning?"

"I think Swanson's wife or kid or someone close to him got in some kind of trouble. Maybe Swanson himself. There *have* been rumors. I don't know. But I am sure of one thing: There's no way he left voluntarily."

"Okay," Karl said. "And?"

"Look," Jack said. "After the stunt with the folders and the county exec, Brandt won reelection in a landslide. Record-breaking numbers. Both the Democrat and Republican party chairmen endorsed him, handed him the line on the ballot without so much as a screening," Jack said. "The Conservative Party of New York State did too. He had no opponent."

"That win was so big, it made him a statewide political figure," Karl said. "He sold himself as 'above party politics.' Endorsed by both parties. A man of the people. A man only concerned about justice. It set him up to be LG." Now Karl poured himself a drink. "Ironic," he said. "Sickening even, given the fact that he trampled everything that's supposed to be sacrosanct in our system. But beautiful, politically speaking."

"So," Becka said, crossing the room and pouring herself a refill too. "He's a political animal. We all know that. What's the point?"

"The point, my dear, is that he had files with their names on them too," Jack said. "On elected officials. Political leaders. Everyone. It's what he does. How he operates. And I'm willing to bet my political life that he did it to Swanson too."

"And?" Becka said. "If he did?"

"Karl's going to find proof."

"What?" Karl asked.

"You heard me. Start an investigation. Get someone to talk."

"With what resources?"

"NYPD still has an organized crime task force, doesn't it?"

"You're suggesting going after him on RICO?"

"I am. People start to fear they'll get indicted for racketeering if they help that son of a bitch, and maybe this becomes a fair fight. Which is where Becka comes in."

"What do you mean?" she asked.

"Don't worry. Nothing too sinister," Jack said. "You're just going to start a whisper campaign. Go to the press. Off the record. Say we've heard that some people believe Swanson was forced out. Get together with some of your friends in the city council, have them do the same. State House too. Give them the inside gossip. Get them sniffing around. If we get lucky, someone will talk. But it doesn't matter if they do or not—the idea of it becoming public will be enough to slow Brandt down, make him and his people cautious."

"Make Brandt cautious?" Becka asked. "He'll come for your throat. Publicly this time."

"Fine," Jack said, smiling. "That would play right into our strategy: My battle with him becomes the top political news story, second only to the Third World War. We stay relevant. I'm still a contender. It looks like he has something to fear or wants to stifle debate. It's a win, no matter what."

"A win? This kind of battle could damage the entire party, Jack. Statewide," Karl said.

"Or save it," Jack said. "From Brandt." He crossed the room to Becka and stood facing her. "Besides, what choice do we have?" He took her hand. "Fold? Give up? Let him drive us out?" And now Jack noticed her eyes were oddly bloodshot, as if she'd been crying.

"All right," Karl said. "I'm with you." He poured himself another drink. "Like I always say: If you're going to go down, you might as well take the other guy with you." He raised his glass in a toast and smiled. "Isn't that right, Becka? Mutually assured destruction?"

"Calm down," Officer Melinda Saragossa said, fighting the feeling she always had when she was in a patrol car at night without a partner. The feeling that butterflies had emerged from cocoons and fluttered to life inside her belly.

Idling now on East Drive and Seventy-Second, at the entrance to Central Park, she had rolled her window down to address a crazy-looking person with fiery red hair poking out from a floppy yellow rain hat. The redhead clutched an orange-and-white running shoe. She'd flagged Saragossa down with it, swinging it wildly from the laces while racing out of the park, screaming for her to stop.

"This belongs to the mayor's sister," the redhead said, gasping to catch her breath while holding up the sneaker.

"What?"

"We have to hurry. Look: that's blood!"

"Right," Saragossa said, shaking her head in disbelief and admonishing herself for being stupid enough to stop five minutes before the end of her shift. "I'll get right on that," she said, the window going up, the car starting to roll. "Now you go sleep it off."

The redhead lunged, grabbed the top of the car window and forced it down as she ran alongside, yelling, "Stop! Goddamn it, I said stop!"

Saragossa did, throwing the cruiser into park and flinging open the door. The redhead went flying, landing on her back. She lay dazed on the pavement. Saragossa leaped out, drove a knee into the redhead's back. "Hands," she shouted, fighting to stay calm as she cuffed the loon.

"What is wrong with you? Didn't you hear what I said?"

"You're under arrest." Saragossa rolled her over.

"She'll die!"

"Enough!"

"Call the mayor!"

"What's your name?"

"Please. She lives with me. She's my…fiancée," Dee lied. "And—"

"You carrying any weapons or drugs?" Saragossa patted the redhead down and found a cell phone. "Do you have any ID?"

"Please! Use it! My phone. Call him!"

"I said: Do you have any ID?"

"Her name is Katie. Katie Molinaro. She lives with me. She's missing—in the park somewhere. There's a man. A rapist. A murderer! Get the shoe. It's hers. Call him!"

Saragossa yanked the redhead to her feet and shoved her toward the car.

"*Ouch!* You idiot!" the redhead shrieked. "Look, you have to believe me."

"The mayor's sister is your fiancée?"

"His number is in there! Under *J* for Jack."

"All right. But if you're screwing with me, I swear to God, I'll—oh, right."

"What? What is it?" the redhead asked.

"It's dead."

The 8:00 p.m. curfew Sophia insisted upon had often proved a life-saver, so Jack habitually kept it, even after Sophia left. He'd dismissed Karl, feeling satisfied with the game plan. He'd sent the house staff home too and was now alone with Becka who had disappeared into one of the mayoral staff offices in the house to "tidy up some loose ends." He checked his cell. Nothing from Katie.

A horn blew. Jack went to the window and pulled back the curtain. The headlights of a black Lincoln Town Car tunneled through the darkness like a mole through fertile soil. He hurried out to greet his favorite person in the whole wide world, thankful the rain had finally stopped long enough for him to comfortably greet her.

"Daddy! Daddy! I'm so glad to see you!"

Abbey leaped for him, and he caught her and held her tightly, and they spun around in a circle. She wrapped her arms around his neck and her legs around his waist, and he kissed her and said, "My baby girl! How are you?"

"She's good," Abbey said, not quite looking him in the eye, though he didn't take his eyes off of hers, not for an instant.

"We say 'I' when talking about ourselves, honey. We say 'I am good.'" Jack nodded an unspoken thanks to the driver, who put Abbey's overnight bag and teddy bear on the porch steps.

"I'm a real girl, Daddy," Abbey said as the car pulled away.

"You sure are," he said, still holding her.

"Not a puppet made of wood."

"You've been watching that video again, haven't you?"

"Yes."

"No scripting, remember?" Jack felt embarrassed when she repeated lines from her videos over and over, especially when people who had no clue about autism were around. Their half-whispered yet fully ignorant comments—and snide use of words like "weird" and "not right"—hurt him much more than they hurt Abbey. In fact, she never even seemed to notice. Still, he felt the need to correct her as a way to protect her.

"Ooo-kay!" she said. "I won't do scripting. I promise!" She slapped her hands on his face, one on each side, a prompt to blow up his cheeks with air so she could pop them.

He complied.

She shrieked with joy and squirmed each time she patted them down and he sprayed her with spittle. "You're scruffy," she said, rubbing her hands on his five o'clock shadow and giggling wildly.

"Don't make me whisker feet you," he said on cue, and she shrieked again, so he grabbed her palm and rubbed his stubble across it roughly, saying, "Don't make me! I will!"

"That's not a whisker feet! It's a whisker palm," she squealed. "Oh...Becka!"

Jack spun around.

"Hi, Abbey," Becka said as she descended the porch stairs.

"Did you know me and Mommy and Daddy aren't going to be living together ever again?" Abbey said.

Becka kissed Abbey on the cheek. "Well, don't be too sure, honey. You never know what might happen."

"No," Jack said, surprised by Becka's response. "You're right, Abbey. Mommy and Daddy won't be living together anymore. But you'll be seeing a lot more of Becka."

"But Becka's not my real mommy," Abbey said.

"No, but maybe someday she can be your stepmommy."

Becka flushed and turned her back on them both.

"What's wrong?" Abbey asked.

Jack stepped closer to her and leaned around to look Becka in the eye while still holding Abbey in his arms. "You okay?" Jack asked.

"Don't ever do that again," Becka said.

"What? I thought you'd—"

"I'm not some…consolation prize we can offer her as a way to make up for what we've done." Becka marched back to the house.

Jack lowered Abbey to the ground. He had blurted out words without thinking things through. Yes. Still…Becka seems so emotionally erratic, he thought.

He took hold of Abbey's hand and walked her toward the edge of the mansion grounds, closer to the East River, where she liked to look up and wish upon the stars.

Scanning the vastness of space and pointing out constellations to her, he wanted to make a wish too.

But for what?

As a boy, he'd read Lincoln: "Every man is said to have his peculiar ambition. Whether it be true or not, I can say for one that I have no other so great as that of being truly esteemed of my fellow men, by rendering myself worthy of their esteem." Jack had committed it to memory because he too had wanted to be appreciated—no, loved and admired—for so rendering himself. And he had not yet failed, because the game was still afoot. Which meant he still had a chance to win.

To be a winner, he told himself, did not mean he'd have to be some kind of a saint. On the contrary, people loved effectiveness. Perhaps never more so than in Lincoln. Even if effectiveness required a bit of corruption now and then.

Lincoln had moved the entire political world in his day to get what he wanted, and he had paid off more than a few opponents to get his work done. And Jack wanted to move the world too. He'd long since settled on the idea that the personal and political philosophy of Ayn Rand best served that goal. Rand's Objectivism allowed him to pursue his desires without regard to how doing so impacted the lives of others, precisely because he could tell himself he acted in an intellectual, and so only seemingly "selfish," way to serve others by single-mindedly pursuing his own ambition. Titans of industry had done so. They'd poured themselves into great endeavors with godlike dedication to their own goals, and the whole world had benefited (at least in the long run). He'd told himself that since he meant to be a political titan, he must do so too. Some may suffer, but the progress to be had would make their pain too salutary to regret.

Standing beneath the heavens with Abbey, some nearly forgotten part of himself—perhaps his soul—protested. It demanded the death of that old, weak, "selfish" identity. Objectivism had failed him, especially on a spiritual level, and deep down inside, he knew it. That was the real difference between him and Brandt. And fresh from the embarrassment and pain of being so outmaneuvered by that political animal, and now aching with Becka's all-too-quick rejection of his marriage proposal, this self-acknowledgment shook him. He turned to the house. "We should go in now, Abbey."

"One more minute," Abbey said. "She wants to see the moon."

"Okay," he said. He smiled and didn't bother to correct her.

He thought about his most cherished desire: to have the ability to control outcomes. And he wondered about the value of having the free will to try.

A domino in a line of dominoes might possess all the free will in the world, he thought. However, absent the means, the power, to move itself or others, without the strength to resist the momentum of any other domino's movement, it would surely fall when any of its neighbors fell…just as men do when economies or nations fall.

No. One domino down the line of time cannot change the inevitable outcome produced by the first fall.

Can it?

Who, by free will, can overturn the momentum of an entire civilization?

Who can even get his family to safety if civilization itself starts to fall?

And why is it so hard for me to admit the obvious fact that the entire premise of my philosophy is fatally flawed, because for any one man or woman's "free will" to be done, the will of all the others in the entire world would have to serve it, lest they get in the way of that one person's desires? Which means only one person could even have the ability to deliver a specific outcome by hard work and good intention. Which is, of course, absurd.

Why is it hard to admit?

Because accepting that idea means we have no control, he reminded himself. It means free will guarantees nothing. Worse, any attempt to exercise it beyond choosing how to think or feel about any event is insurrection…against God! If a man could actually get what he wanted, every time he wanted it, if a man could exercise his free will and control outcomes, even God's Divine Will would have to serve the fulfillment of the dreams and desires of that one individual. The entire universe and everything in it would have to bow when one individual asserted "I am the master of my fate...the captain of my soul..."

No, Jack thought. We do not control outcomes. All we ever get to control is how we choose to feel about the circumstances life presents, whether or not we will try to live with integrity, and as God has commanded.

"There it is!" Abbey pointed.

The clouds passed the moon, and a stripe of waves on the East River brightened like liquid silver had been poured onto each crest.

"Abbey?" he said.

"Yes, Daddy?"

"I'm sorry I hurt you and your mommy. I'm sorry we're not...we don't live together anymore," he said.

"Why, Daddy?"

"Why what, baby?"

"Why can't we?"

"Sometimes grown-ups, well, we—" He stopped himself. "Abbey," he said, "the truth is, I don't really know why. I don't know why we do what we do, or why I did what I did. But I hurt your mother. And that means I hurt you too. And I am truly very sorry."

"What did you do, Daddy?"

"I made a mistake. I did something bad, something wrong. I got caught up in a story in my own head, and I—most of the time, you know, we plan things, and we promise to do things, good things, but then we find ourselves doing other things, different things, and—"

"Like Pinocchio?"

He laughed. "Yes, Abbey. Like Pinocchio."

"Don't worry, Daddy. It's okay," she said. "I've seen it lots of times. He only looks like he's dead."

"*Curious George*, *The Biggest Boy*, and *Super Fly Guy*." Abbey rattled off the titles of three books as Jack dug through the bookcase in her bedroom, upstairs, two doors down from the master suite.

"Are you sure?" he asked.

"Yes. *Curious George*, *The Biggest Boy*, and—"

"*Super Fly Guy*. The same three?" He moaned, feigning thorough disappointment. Then, fighting the emergence of a wide smile, he plopped on the bed beside her and started to tickle her. "Again? Huh? The same three books? Again and again and again!"

Abbey shrieked and laughed, and Becka came in and sat beside her on the other side of the bed.

"*Super Fly Guy?*" Becka said. "Did somebody say *Super Fly Guy?*" She stuck out a finger and curled it up and "flew" it in circles above Abbey. "Buzzzzzzzz!" The pointed finger made big, sweeping, swooping spirals. "Buzzzzzzzzzz!" Becka said again.

Jack watched and smiled widely as Becka finally plunged her finger down like a dive-bomber and joined the frenzied tickling.

"Ahhh!" Abbey laughed. "Again! Do it again, Becka!"

"Buzzzzzzzzzz…"

Jack felt grateful Sophia had let Abbey come. She could have been a bitch, could have kept Abbey from him. But, with Becka's rejection, he felt now as if he stood in the no-man's-land between two lives, two women, both just beyond his reach. He wanted an answer to his doubts. A resolution to both situations. A complete home again, for himself, and for Abbey.

"Daddy, I told you, three stories and three songs. That's what she wants!"

"Okay," he said. "Right." He cracked open the first book.

Three stories and three songs, he thought. Every night. It's still her routine.

Good.

She's okay.

We'll all get through this…

"And my teddy! Did I bring my teddy?"

"It's right here, sweetie," Becka said.

Abbey could not rest without it.

Jack read and read, and they laughed and buzzed and laughed some more, and Abbey got all her sillies out.

Later he dimmed the lights and took his classical guitar from the stand in her bedroom where it had gathered dust for months. He tuned it and sang the lullaby song, and "God Bless America," and though she'd drifted off and could no longer hear him, he decided to play the third song anyway because he'd promised he would. And he played it the way Abbey liked, for he had made it his own for her, like his mother had for him when he was a boy, with some new words. He even put on a thick Irish brogue, while singing…

"Too-ra-loo-ra-loo-ral…"

Half an hour later, Becka sat on his bed. Her black cashmere sweater dress hiked up, revealing her slender thighs. She handed Jack a teacup filled with iced Baileys and a splash of Jameson. "Busy day tomorrow," she said.

"Yeah, the entire world is going to war, and now we have—"

"No, I meant Brandt. The swearing-in ceremony…" She pawed at the wrinkles in her dress, flattening them. "I assume we'll be preparing some kind of a statement, given what we discussed this afternoon—"

He took hold of her hand. "On the lawn tonight, with Abbey, I was serious—"

"No. It's not a possibility, Jack." She stood.

"But just now, with Abbey. You're perfect. You'd be a wonderful stepmom."

"How I feel about her has nothing to do with how I feel about you. Or us."

"Of course it does."

"No. It doesn't."

"Then why did you make love to me that night? And this morning?" He stood now too.

"Because I wanted you."

"That's really screwed up."

"Only when a woman does it." She began to pace.

"I'm sorry. You're right."

"You had years, Jack. And you knew how I felt about you."

"I—"

"You made your choice. You can't change the past."

"No," he said. His cell phone buzzed. He'd turned the ringer off, for Abbey's sake, so as not to disturb her sleep. "That's not acceptable to me," he said in a tone that betrayed a seething rage that rose in him whenever he didn't get his way.

"Mind your temper, Jack."

The phone buzzed again.

"We have to talk," he said. "I can't let you go."

"That's not up to you."

She went to his phone. "It's Katie," she said, showing him the caller ID on screen. She handed it to him. "I guess she's not missing anymore."

He took it. "Katie?" He paused. "Yes, it is. That's right. Yes, the mayor. Jack Molinaro. Who is this?" Jack paused. "I see. Yes. I know Dee…well, I'm glad you did."

"What is it?" Becka asked.

"A cop. Dee has Katie's cell phone and—yes, Officer. Yes, Katie is—I mean, I haven't heard from her all day, so yes, if Dee says so, I suppose she could actually be missing."

"Get her name," Becka said.

"What?"

"The cop. Get her name," Becka said.

"Tell me your name again?" Jack asked. "Saragossa? Okay. Yes, please…take Dee home. No. I've got it. Just take her home, drop her off, and…yes. I am sure. Do not call it in or report it. I'll have the police commissioner handle everything from here. Thank you, Officer Saragossa. Thank you very much." Jack hung up.

"So? What is it? What's happened?" Becka asked.

"Dee found a shoe, a Brooks Ariel running shoe, in Central Park."

"Katie's?"

Jack nodded. "Stained with blood."

CHAPTER 6

ONLY FAITH CAN OVERCOME THE TRAUMA OF WHAT SIGMUND FREUD once likened to an unannounced train wreck: the shocking, tragic, often violent event that strikes before you even have a chance to brace yourself. The life-defining, horrible, and totally unexpected experience that you then relive over and over in your mind in an attempt to cope by knowing that this time—the second or third or fourth or hundredth time you relive it—you'll see it coming.

A simple warning can save you from this mental film loop of posttraumatic train-wreck agony, a *Groundhog Day*–like waking nightmare without escape. But without that warning, after a train wreck happens, you'll surely find yourself in a mental Hell, a place of spiritual desolation where an evisceration of the soul strips you of the ability to ever live in the moment again. You arrive in that Hell after a shocking flash of insight, an epiphany that knocks you to your knees and leaves you debilitated—you've realized that anything can happen, anyplace, at any time, and the things you said or did because you felt they might be a source of some simple comfort or lasting joy can suddenly turn out to be the cause of the deepest and most terrible kind of suffering imaginable. Even your demise.

But NY1 reporter Terry Stone knew Dee Weiss had had no such warning when the train of her life had derailed.

Stone knew that no one had told Dee to brace herself for her own personal train wreck, and because of that, she'd never be the same. He knew too that when such events happen, they make you permanently gun-shy. They leave you with PTSD. They can even turn you into one of those people who collect cats, or newspapers, or don't go out of the house. Many who suffer such shocks also find the soul-crushing, unfathomable, incomprehensible happenings are accompanied by a cruel, even sickening, irony. Like: You convince a brother to enlist in the Marines so he can get off the streets and make something of himself, serve God and country, and he does—but he goes to Iraq, and you find out he has gotten his arm and one of his legs blown off by friendly fire.

Friendly fire!

Cezar, Stone thought. My kid brother. And it was my fault.

That's my train wreck.

Like: You rush to get your six-year-old child off to school even though she has a cold. You do it even though it's against your better judgment, even though your intuition tells you not to. You do it because you're a single mom, and you have her all the time, and you just want to take a little break, put your feet up, and relax. Just once, have one cup of coffee in peace, quiet…and hell yeah, you deserve it. That's what you tell yourself. You do. And four hours later a jarring rap on the door startles you. And a cop in tears says he's so sorry but your baby girl got shot by a madman with an assault rifle at her preschool, and you have to come right away, to say goodbye, because she did not make it.

Connecticut, 2012. My aunt…

She blamed herself.

Now she's institutionalized from *her* train wreck.

Or like: You tell your roommate "to Hell with you" because you've had a fight, and she heads out the door early to go for a run, and you don't even try to stop her because some madness has entered you, a madness that you later confess through tears that had you believing you *wanted* her to be hurt, to be taught a lesson for not loving you the way you love her, to be taught you are worth far more than she knows. Far more than any man. Yes, you do it. You let her go even though you *know* from your nightmares and intuition she will never return. And when she doesn't come home, you search for her and find her bloody running shoe, and right then you know in your heart that she's never coming back…never.

And it's because of you.

Yeah. You, Stone thought.

It's your fault, Dee Weiss.

Katie is your train wreck. And not even God can help you now.

Dee had confided it all to Stone and their mutual friend, Mike. She'd done so at the apartment that Dee and Katie shared, and Stone had felt for Dee.

Now, in the park, Stone dialed the studio and tucked his cell phone safely under his hood, protecting it from the rain.

"This is Connie," Stone's producer answered on her personal line.

"They found a body," Stone said, his voice nearly drowned out by the drum of the rain on the flat tin roof of the nearby ambulance and the hum of its engine. "Yup," he shouted now, stepping away a bit. "Central Park. The Ramble. No…by the boathouse."

Dee and Mike, Stone's cameraman, had been college drinking buddies. Dee had called Mike first thing that morning and offered him a huge exclusive on how the mayor had turned his back on his own sister and left her to die in Central Park.

Mike had called the studio to tell Connie what they had: a lead worthy of coverage even with everything else that was going on.

Connie had listened and pulled Stone off the UFO story. "The mayor's sister, murdered?" she'd said. "Yeah, that's big."

He'd met Mike at Dee's apartment, and now all three of them were in the park together. The scene looked like an episode of *Blue Bloods*, but for some reason Stone had yet to figure out, it felt more like an episode of *X-Files*.

"Tell Connie I warned him," Dee said, referring to the mayor, tears streaming down her face. "I did. I warned him."

Stone nodded then turned back to his phone conversation. "Yeah," he said to Connie. "Dee says she warned the mayor. We've got some video of the scene, but…no. They won't let us near the body." Stone gestured to Mike, who stood beside him, listening. "Okay, right, we'll try."

On cue, Mike lifted the camera to his shoulder and started moving toward the gurney, looking for an angle on the body bag and the two paramedics zipping it up. The gurney sat in a small clearing in the woods, about thirty feet away, behind yellow crime-scene tape.

Stone listened for a moment and then said, "Okay. I will. Give me about an hour." He hung up and turned to Dee. "She's going to call the mayor's press secretary, see if she can get a reaction from him."

A cop came around from behind the ambulance. "What the hell is *she* doing here?" the cop asked, glaring at Dee.

"You two know each other?" Stone said. The cop's name tag read *Saragossa*.

"You could say that," Dee replied.

"Oh, no," Stone said, turning to Saragossa. "You're the one who arrested her?"

"Turn that damn camera off," Saragossa said.

"The body," Mike said. "Dee was right?"

"We found the other running shoe," Saragossa said, "and a bra, but—"

"Oh, my God." Dee covered her mouth in horror.

"Take it easy," Saragossa said.

Mike pointed the camera in Saragossa's face. "Ask her, Stone."

Stone stuck out his microphone. "Is Katie Molinaro dead because of you, Officer?"

"Turn it off," Saragossa said, shoving the camera aside and pushing past Mike.

"Give us something," Stone said, "and maybe Dee will smooth things over for you with the mayor."

Saragossa stared at Dee for a moment, looked around. "If another cop confronts us," Saragossa said, "you'll tell him who you are and that I'm following the mayor's orders. Yes or no?"

"Yes," Dee said.

"Okay." Saragossa ducked under the tape, then glared at Dee and Mike. "They stay here," she insisted.

"What?" Mike blurted.

Stone turned to Dee.

Dee nodded and said, "I don't want to see her."

Saragossa held the tape up for Stone. He went.

Mike waited a few seconds, then snuck under and followed, filming.

Saragossa noticed but didn't protest.

The three trudged over the gravel path and damp leaves to the gurney and the rubber bag and the two paramedics. "Two minutes," Saragossa said, gesturing with the toss of her head that they should get lost. The taller of the two EMT guys stared at her for a moment, then nodded, and he and his coworker walked away, wandered back by Dee, and lit and shared a cigarette.

Menthol and ammonia drifted into Stone's eyes. He squinted as Saragossa unzipped the bag. She yanked it wide open, and it began to rain.

"*Ohhh…damn!*" Stone said.

"Whoa," Mike said, camera high and rolling. "Brutal. Probably an antigay thing."

Saragossa said, "That's enough."

Stone patted Mike on the arm, and Mike lowered the camera. Stone noticed the "record" light still glowed. Mike pointed the camera at the body bag from his hip.

"What makes you think it's an antigay thing?" Stone asked, dialing his cell.

"It's the Ramble," Mike said.

"So?" Stone said. "Hold on. Connie? Yeah. No, it is not Katie Molinaro. No. Just some guy from out of town, maybe in the park for a hook up," Stone said, his hand tucked inside his hood. "Listen, his face was laid wide open. Looks like he's missing an eye. Yeah. Like someone tortured him before offing him. Uh-huh. Mike thinks it's some kind of a hate crime. Yeah. Maybe." Stone turned to Saragossa and asked, "We got a name?"

"Thomas Breckenridge III."

"Really?

Saragossa raised her eyebrows.

"Okay," Stone said to Connie. He hung up.

Rain splattered off the dead guy's face, filling the hole where his eye had been. The water formed a thin black puddle that quickly overflowed.

Saragossa shook her head. "It's not an antigay thing."

"Why not?" Stone asked.

She gestured to the woods and began walking. "Don't touch anything."

Stone followed but gestured to Mike to stay put beside the dead guy's gurney. He and Saragossa tromped into the woods. The rain, showering down, made a loud *fffffff* sound in the trees.

They stopped.

Saragossa pointed to a rope, dangling like a dead snake from the branch of a tree above them.

"They hung him?" Stone said, his voice rising in surprise.

"He hung himself," said Saragossa.

"And what? He gouged out his own eye first?" Stone asked. "Not buying it."

A movement caught Stone's attention: a boat, drifting on the lake about twenty yards from where they stood. For a moment it seemed stuck, as if it had hit up against something unseen, perhaps a submerged log or branch. Then it moved again, blown by a gust, but it slid sideways, perpendicular to the direction of the wind.

What the hell? he thought. It's like it's against some kind of wall or something.

"Two separate events," Saragossa said. "First the knife fight. Then the suicide. See this?" Saragossa pointed to the trunk of the tree. Moss had come off in chunks. She bent and picked up a piece. "We found it on his shoes," she said.

"Okay. So?"

"Look." Saragossa pointed up.

Stone had to back up to see the knot on the top of the branch.

"So, you think this guy climbed up, sat on the branch, tied off the rope, then wrapped it around his own neck and—"

"That's how I see it," Saragossa said.

"No way. He gets into a knife fight, loses an eye trying to stay alive, then kills himself? No. No way."

"It may not make sense, but that's what the evidence suggests. At least to me."

"You think he took that boat too?"

"What boat?" Saragossa said.

"There." Stone pointed to the lake.

Saragossa walked down the slope toward the shore.

Stone looked around. Definitely freaky, he thought. He took a few steps deeper into the woods. The ground cover appeared to be disturbed in a back-and-forth pattern. It looked like this Thomas III character had paced along a fence for a long time before he—but there is no fence, Stone thought. So why did Breckenridge stop?

Saragossa returned to his side.

Stone moved toward the disturbed area. The clouds broke. Directly across the lake, the Angel of the Waters fountain caught the light and began to glow. "Beautiful," he said. "Look." He took hold of her shoulders and gently turned her to face the fountain. He pointed to the Angel of the Waters across the lake. "There."

"Wow."

"Yeah."

After a moment, he turned back to the woods. "See that line in the turf? Looks to me like he was trying to get to someone or something up that ridge there," Stone said, pointing toward the Point. "But, for some reason, he couldn't, and so then he—"

"Hey, you guys," Mike called out, waving his arms frantically, signaling them.

Stone turned in time to catch a glimpse of a sudden flash of light.

"Hey! Hey!" Mike raised his camera to his shoulder. "Get over here!"

And the dead guy with one eye sat up and screamed.

"Say it," Governor Denny Brandt insisted, his fist full of Becka's hair, tugging hard, turning her to face him fully. "Say it now," he said, his breath stinking of cognac and Cuban tobacco. "You say that you love me. Now!"

"No," Becka managed through clenched teeth. "Let go!" She wished she'd never agreed to come up to this hotel suite to talk to him face-to-face, to tell him that it was over, that she'd decided to leave New York and go back home to Texas. She was done. Had given Jack her notice. Finished. "Let me go!"

"That's a laugh," Brandt said, tightening his arm and pulling her against his body. "You? Not in the mood?"

"Bastard!" she yelled, telling herself she'd get through this. "I said *no*! Jack's expecting me!"

Brandt just laughed and said, "So am I, kiddo. So am I…"

At the water's edge on Bethesda Terrace, Stone turned his back on the Point and faced the fountain. Mike stood between him and the famous Angel of the Waters bronze. A favorite of locals and tourists alike, it rose tall out of a circular fountain on the expanse of red bricks on which they all now stood: Stone and Mike and Dee.

The strange feeling he'd felt when, on the Point, the angel seemed to glow, arose again. Only stronger now. And it nagged Stone, gnawed at his gut. He turned his attention to the lake again, and now to the narrow, crested, rocky peninsula thick with trees and brush just fifty yards away: the Point.

They'd all just had quite a shock. The dead guy, Breckenridge, had sat up. Though much of what he said on his way into the ambulance seemed incoherent, his claims had deeply disturbed Terry Stone. "That Stranger," Breckenridge had screamed. "Murderer! He done this to me! He did!" The EMT guys had barely been able to restrain him. "He fell from the sky and he cut me up and he done her too!" Breckenridge shouted over and over. "The Stranger! It was him. Damn him to Hell! Damn him to Hell!"

Stranger? Stone thought. Fell from the sky?

Stone turned his attention upward, then scanned the park. The rain had finally stopped, but it had left everything glistening.

The lawns sparkled with a billion tiny droplets, each a brilliant crystal jewel seemingly alive, glowing with the light of the very same, single source: the brilliant, glowing, golden sun. The trees hissed as gust after gust rustled leaves and flipped them over and back, causing flowing cascades of darker to lighter shades of green. And now a single, bright beam fell on the angel statue's wide wings, and its bronze feathers threw a long, saw-toothed shadow across the fountain waters and the bricks.

"Give me a check," Mike said, bending to adjust the viewfinder of his camera.

Stone lifted the microphone and turned it so the NY1 news logo faced forward as he said, "Check…check." He searched his memory for another instance of the strong, strange feeling that had so suddenly overcome him.

Is it anticipation? Stone wondered.

About what?

Perhaps excitement?

Nope.

Fear?

Hell no.

This is something rare. Something I've only ever felt once before, on the Point. "Maybe I need a checkup from the neck up," he said, deeply uncomfortable and totally unsure of what to do now with his growing uneasiness. "Check. Check."

"Again," Mike said. He wiggled his headphone connection, adjusted a leg on the tripod, and bent for a closer look at the viewfinder.

"Seriously," Stone said, his voice full and assertive now, the microphone close to his lips. "This is how we spend the Labor Day holiday? World War Three on the horizon. A hanged man. A missing girl. Some murderous 'Stranger' on the loose, and a UFO that fell to Earth that nobody can find any trace of anywhere? Really?"

"Imagine how Katie feels," Dee said, sniffing and pulling her hands into the sleeves of a faded blue sweatshirt. Stone had watched Dee grab it from a pile of dirty clothes heaped on the floor of her apartment right before they'd started this painful waste of a day. Elbows worn, neck frayed, its big white NYU logo cracked and peeling, the garment screamed Goodwill.

"It's hers…and it smells like her," Dee had said, holding it to her face and inhaling. Dee had wiped away her tears with it before pulling it over her head.

"I'm sorry," Stone had said, "that you're going through this. And I know it won't do any good to say it, but you've got to stop blaming yourself." And now Dee looked even worse than the worn old rag. Her bright-green eyes were bloodshot from crying, her mascara had run and turned her face raccoon, and occasional stiff, erratic gusts had tossed her already-wild hair in all directions. Orange coils and shiny ringlets stuck out like the vipers on Medusa's head.

She wiped away a tear.

Yeah, Stone thought. Katie's disappearance is a Freudian train wreck for Dee, for sure…

"Again, please," Mike said.

"Right." Stone raised the microphone. "Check. Check."

And now a contingent of Senegalese women wearing colorful kaftans—probably UN staff or diplomatic corps, based on a badge he glimpsed hanging from the neck of one of them—wandered closer and lingered, apparently to watch him interview the grieving Dee.

Naturally, Stone thought. Interest is always piqued by the camera. And by tragedy. And tears.

Some among the Senegalese, and other tourists and passersby, moved closer and held up smartphones and nodded sympathetically as they took Dee's picture, as if they didn't need to know why she grieved but could assume it was bad, based on the presence of the news team. Then, smiling, they each snapped a few of Stone.

"He looks like Harry Belafonte," one of the Senegalese women said.

Stone smiled and wished it were so.

A pair of old women shuffled across the red bricks, hand in hand, admiring the view of the lake. They glanced at the angel statue atop the fountain, turned their Q-tip heads his way, and checked him out too. And now a power walker eyed his watch and looked up too, right at him and Mike and Dee, and then picked up the pace of his freaky march as if he couldn't care less. A stout old man with a white pug and a plastic glove stooped to pick up after his pet but missed the pile. His eyes were on Stone. Now he found the load.

Yuck.

Wish I hadn't seen you, Stone mused.

A boy on the nearby hill lost his concentration and let go of his balloon. As the child woefully watched it soar, his bent mother wagged a finger in his face and taught him how to add insult to injury.

All but one of the onlookers—a tall black man, older, strikingly handsome—had taken stock of the situation. That man actually *did* look like Harry Belafonte, and he could have passed for one of Stone's uncles. He held a big German shepherd close on a leash and coaxed the dog forward with soft kissing sounds.

No wonder he didn't check us out, Stone thought. He's blind.

"Mike?" Dee said. "Can we *please* get on with it?"

Mike shook his head but didn't even glance up from the camera.

Stone gestured for Dee to look at the young lovers who'd broken off making out just long enough to sneak a peek at them from the arcade tunnel. "We're being watched," he said.

Dee shrugged and pouted and sighed and crossed her arms.

Stone wondered why it was called that. The arcade? No games in there.

Well, no *arcade* games.

He'd talked Tabby Wilson into making it with him in there on a dark night right before he and Cezar had shipped out to Iraq, two weeks before his kid brother's near-fatal encounter with friendly fire, and his own soul-eviscerating train wreck.

Two kids, Hispanic boys on rollerblades, raced across the terrace now, flashing in and out of the shadows cast by wandering puffy white clouds, their plastic skate wheels clumping over the countless bricks. The cop at the top of the stairs to the right of the arcade shook her head and glared menacingly at them: No skating on the terrace.

It's Saragossa, out of her rain gear, Stone realized. Pretty. But odd.

The boys gave her the finger, glanced at Stone, flipped him the bird too, and then hightailed it down the blacktop-paved path to Bow Bridge.

A hot dog vendor with a new customer flicked open his stainless boiler with a long steel fork, and the smell of dogs and kraut, accompanied by a hard metallic ting, tripped a pang of hunger for Stone. He waited. The vendor, poised with a pierced dog limp on the fork, glanced up, then nestled it into a bun.

Yup. The vendor had looked too.

A couple paddled a canoe on the lake; another couple picnicked on the near shore under the three big willows between the terrace and the Loeb Boathouse; some old, others young, came and went, all having been drawn to the edge of the lake and the fountain and the appearance of sunshine, drawn to the magnificent sight of the Angel of the Waters sculpture in the heart of Central Park. And once there, not one had failed to shoot at least a quick, casual glance or make at least one small gesture that said: Check it out. A reporter from NY1.

"Try it now," Mike said. "But say something real this time."

Stone raised the microphone. "So," he turned to Dee, "when you called the mayor and told him his sister had gone missing, what did he say?"

"He blew me off," Dee said.

"Perfect!" Mike said. "All right. We're rolling…"

"Really," Stone said. "I wonder how he feels about that now?"

"Still rolling," Mike said. "From the top."

Stone raised his eyebrows and nodded his head, and Dee nodded back, an unspoken yes to the unspoken question: Ready?

Stone turned to the camera. "I'm here in Central Park where NYPD found a second running shoe today, still laced up and stained with blood, right over there, just up that hill." He pointed to the path that ran along the lake to the Loeb Boathouse. "The running shoe belongs to Mayor Jack Molinaro's younger sister, Katie, who has been missing, and is now presumed dead." A brilliant yet silent explosion on the far shore of the lake shook the ground beneath Stone's feet. "What the hell?" he said, turning away and shielding his eyes.

The onlookers shrieked and bent, and they turned away too.

Stone's military experience kicked in, and he braced himself, but there was no shock wave. It was not a bomb, he knew. But what?

Mike turned and bent and shut his eyes. "Damn," he groaned. "Too bright!"

"What is it?" Dee asked, squinting and turning too. "What's happened?"

It seemed a star had exploded on the shore of the Point, and now it burned just short of impact with the Earth. Its light faded just enough to make it possible to follow it. It moved down the slope to the shore.

Stone shifted for a better angle, still shielding his eyes and squinting.

The light pulsed, and the surface of the water glowed and sparkled in a glistening path leading from the far shore to the brick-lined terrace where Stone and Dee and Mike cowered.

It came halfway across and stopped in the very center of the lake, between the two shores. A mist formed, like steam or fog all around it, and the cloud grew, a halo of gold and sapphire and emerald and pink expanding from its core. And now in the midst of the light emerged a being of light, ghostlike at first, but then the being stood in the form of a young man, beautiful, dark skinned, with full, flowing, silky brown hair and a neatly cropped beard. A turquoise veil covered his head like a hood and framed his shining face, and even from this distance, Stone felt he had the most captivating eyes he had ever seen.

The eyes of the Son of Heaven…

"My God," Dee said.

"The Stranger," Stone said.

Mike scrambled to adjust his camera. "Stone," he shouted. "I'm getting it!"

Now the light pulsed and a hot gust blew, and from nowhere a young woman became visible beside the glowing being, and she too stood on the water—alive, flesh and blood, barefoot, wearing pink shorts and a stained and spotted white T-shirt knotted just below her breasts. Her face battered and bruised. Her hair matted with blood. Her complexion the lifeless hue of sun-bleached sand. She nearly collapsed under her own weight, but then she leaned on the glowing Stranger to gather herself.

"Katie!" Dee shouted. "Yes! Yes!" Dee fell to her knees and gasped and covered her mouth.

And now Stone fell to his knees too, suddenly unable to speak another word. And Mike fell to his knees. And Saragossa, at the top of the stairs, overlooking it all, suddenly knelt. And the Senegalese women knelt. And the kid who'd been reprimanded by his mom, and his mom, and the man with the white pug, and the vendor—they all got on their knees now too. The couple in the canoe stopped paddling. They sat still and drifted closer to the two walking on the water and stared at them, eyes wide, mouths open. Then, like the stray craft Stone had seen hours earlier in the rain, their canoe hit something and slid sideways.

An invisible wall, Stone realized, set out there by the Stranger.

Stone leaned toward the water. He reached out his hand, and it came into contact with something solid. He pushed, and the wall lit up, as if charged with light.

Clear. Impenetrable.

How?

Dee strained and tried to stand, but could not, so she tried to crawl into the lake. The wall stopped her too. She pounded on the invisible barrier with a closed fist. Her mouth opened, but no sound escaped.

The two, walking arm in arm on the water, continued to approach. Stone thought, either this is real or I am totally crazy.

But it seemed *not* real to Stone, more like a scene from a Hollywood movie or some wild special effects sequence in a TV commercial or a stunt for some high-end PR event.

Katie and the strange being of light stopped. His halo of gold and sapphire and emerald and pink spread in all directions, wide and high and bright and beautiful. He turned to Katie and held Katie's broken, swollen, bloody face and caressed it lovingly in his hands. He smiled.

He's saying goodbye, Stone thought. He's letting Katie go…

And now Stone realized Katie held something.

A scroll?

Katie smiled and nodded a silent goodbye; she let go of the Stranger and walked on her own, tentatively, unsteady, shaking violently, but in small, careful steps, inching forward on the glistening surface of the lake, coming straight toward the terrace, straight toward Stone and Mike and Dee.

The Stranger adjusted his soft blue veil, fully covered the crown of his head, and pulled the long, blue cloth so it draped across his chest. He closed his captivating cobalt-blue eyes, raised his hands to his heart, and pressed his palms together in prayer, and something deep and powerful, something wonderful, came over Stone. By some heavenly grace he suddenly felt a long-forgotten inner knowing, an unshakable peace, given by the power of only God knew what. He had to stay on his knees in the presence of the one who looked like a child of the sun itself. He could not rise and did not want to do so. He could not speak and had no use for words now anyway. He could not look away.

Tears streamed down Dee's cheeks.

Everyone had fallen eerily silent. Some on one knee now, some on two. Though all were, like Stone, awestruck, reverential, and unwilling or unable to move from their spots. All of them witnessed the Stranger praying and Katie coming toward the terrace. Everyone could turn their bodies and their heads, continue to use their hands, cameras, and cell phones. All were able to take pictures and capture video, even as many wept in awe and wonder—overcome, Stone concluded, by the same overwhelming sense of love and joy and hope that had overtaken him.

And Katie kept approaching, one slow step at a time, closer and closer.

She's so badly hurt, Stone thought. She can barely walk. And yet she's so determined.

Katie struggled but managed to step onto the terrace, just a few feet from Stone. Mike followed her every move with the camera as she passed through the invisible wall. It lit up and streamed light as she passed through. She paused to look into Dee's eyes, to touch

Dee's cheek gently and brush away her tears. "I'm all right," she said to Dee. "Don't worry." She smiled, and even with her face so mercilessly shattered and bloody, even with her body so visibly weak and in danger of giving out, Stone felt her confidence, her faith, would sustain her.

Katie continued across the terrace, trembling, stepping awkwardly, as if in physical agony, crossing to the man Stone had noticed a few moments earlier. The blind man. He's not kneeling, Stone realized. He can stand while all the rest of us cannot. Who is he?

The blind man's big German shepherd began to bark. Then, like an ox pulling a plow, it lurched forward, dragging the blind man toward Katie, as if the two were old friends. The dog stopped beside her and sat and licked her hand.

"Is it you?" the blind man asked. "Is it Katie?"

"Yes," Katie said. "It's me." She patted the dog on the head. The dog whined and barked, louder and louder now, and tried to pull the blind man toward the edge of the terrace.

"What is it," the blind man asked, pulling the dog back, coaxing him to sit. "What's happening?"

"He's here," Katie said. "Like a Stranger in a strange land. He's come back."

"Yes."

"Standing on the surface of our little lake. Walking on the water…he's really here."

Stone turned to the lake. His face flushed. The Stranger glowed with an effervescent light; a halo of gold and silver and sapphire and pink light encircled him.

A chill rushed up Stone's spine as he recalled a passage from the Book of John. After the crucifixion and death of Jesus, the disciples had gathered beside a fire to eat with the Stranger who had, moments before, commanded them to cast their nets once more on the Sea of Galilee. On retrieving those nets, they had miraculously hauled in a great catch. Then none of the disciples dared ask the Stranger, who are you? For they knew with whom they held company. It could only be their master, in a new body. A new form. Stone now knew too with whom he now held company in New York's Central Park. He realized the Stranger's true identity, and he had to fight a sudden rush of emotion in order to stay calm and focused.

And now a new light had begun to gather. It formed atop the head of the Angel of the Waters statue in the terrace fountain, and suddenly it spread out wide around the wings of the bronze angel and kept on growing and spreading. Lightning flashed in a clear sky, and thunder cracked and rumbled high above. And the light around the statue grew brighter and brighter. And the blind man nodded and said, "Now you know why I been coming."

"Yes, Jeremiah," Katie said. "He told me about you, about how long you've been waiting for this day." She removed the man's sunglasses. Katie turned to the lake and smiled. "He said to tell you the voice you heard was real. It *was* him."

Katie touched Jeremiah's hand, then took the leash and unclipped the dog.

The shepherd ran past Stone and Dee and Mike and leaped through the invisible shield and onto the magically lit surface of the lake. It went straight to the feet of the Stranger, where the dog was greeted and now sat, panting on the surface of the lake.

The glowing light of the Angel of the Waters statue grew even brighter, as if a million tiny stars had exploded and were swirling around it. And the light at the head of the statue silently spread out in waves that infused the flowing waters of the fountain with a brilliant luminescence. The waters now boiled with effervescent hues of gold and sapphire and emerald and pink. Unguided, Jeremiah stepped toward the light, toward the flowing, glowing waters of the fountain. He reached them, knelt, pressed his thighs against the base of the circular pool, and bent over the wall. He stretched and reached his hand out to find the waters, and then slowly, blindly, bent more deeply and plunged both hands in the light-infused waters. He raised them to his face and bathed his eyes in the water.

Lightning flashed and arced, and, as Stone looked on in wonder, Jeremiah lifted his face and turned to the lake, to the source of his miracle, to the glowing Stranger in white.

He can see, Stone thought. The Stranger has cured him. He can see!

Jeremiah lifted his gaze to the heavens and stood and began to turn around and around in a long, slow, glorious circle, his eyes alive and new, his face surrounded by a golden light, infused with sapphire and silver and emerald and pink. He leaned back and stretched his arms to the heavens, and all who had gathered raised their faces too, taking their cue from him. And Stone did too. Clouds quickly blew in, and the sun now lit a fire inside them, turning them bright orange and red and purple at the edges, even as they floated across a powder-blue sky. And the deep-green, late-summer leaves, tinged with hints of orange and red, stirred in the swirling wind. Brown sparrows and red-breasted robins and bright-red cardinals darted about on fluttering wings, and a single dove descended and perched on the wing of the Angel of the Waters as all the other birds called out in a joyful chorus, chirping, singing to the presence of God. God in the faces of strangers. God in the blades of grass. God in the leaves of the trees. God in the very bricks of Bethesda Terrace. God, embodied and alive in our world, in the form of a glorious and beautiful Stranger in white, walking on the water of the lake in Central Park!

And tears flowed from Jeremiah's eyes. And Stone wept too, tears of joy, of liberation from fear, of release from doubt and guilt and angst. Tears that somehow cleared the wreckage of past sins from his heart.

Katie stepped toward Dee but swooned and faltered, and Jeremiah rushed to catch her but arrived too late. She had collapsed and lay now in a heap on the bricks, and the scroll rolled from her hand and stopped at the feet of Terry Stone. He picked it up, and the moment he touched it, a feeling of peace overcame him.

A sudden calm.

Joy.

It was…papyrus? Ancient. Sealed with red wax. It bore a single letter and numbers. Stone read them aloud: "M-39."

Dee rose and raced to Katie's side.

Stone stood, turned, and caught one last glimpse of the one with the eyes of Heaven. Then the Stranger disappeared.

CHAPTER 7

"What day is it, Daddy?"

"Monday, honey."

"But there's no school today, right?"

"Right. It's Labor Day."

"What time is it?"

"About noon, I guess," Jack said, going to the window, looking for Abbey's ride.

Damn it, Jack thought. Her driver should be here by now. I need to get back to work.

And Becka. Where is she?

After calling Karl and ordering the NYPD to launch a search for Katie—and checking in with everyone he could think to call to see if they'd heard from his sister—he and Becka had talked things through. Becka had said she would go to Brandt's ceremony as a sort of spy for him, but she intended to resign, as soon as practical, and move back to Texas, to get away from New York, take a break, regroup. She then tried to convince Jack to reconcile with his wife, to quit politics and focus on his family. He'd said no and told her she wasn't making sense. Not after what they'd just done, and shared.

How godlike he'd felt when she'd stared into his eyes this morning while making love. How powerful and fulfilled. So he'd promised to make things up to her. He'd promised to get a divorce. But she'd refused him and said again and again through tears that it was over.

Over...

"Daddy? What time is it?"

"I just told you, Abbey," he said. "Is there something on TV you want to watch, sweetie? I'm going to have to have someone sit with you for a while until your ride gets here so I can get back to wor—"

"But it's not noon, Daddy," Abbey said. "It's 12:12 p.m., and she's home now."

"What? Who is home?"

Abbey didn't reply.

"Abbey, I told you, I don't want you scripting."

"She's not scripting, but she doesn't feel very well."

"Are you sick, honey?"

"No. It's Aunt Katie, of course. She's in the park. She's very sick, Daddy. She needs help."

"Abbey, why would you say such things?" Jack crossed the room. His footsteps shook the floor, and her tower of wooden blocks suddenly tumbled.

Abbey leaped to her feet and raced toward the foyer and out the door, shouting, "Mommy! Mommy!"

He ran after her. "Abbey. Wait!"

The door flew open. Jack followed. "Abrianna!" he yelled. "Stop!"

A Rolls-Royce Silver Cloud III hit the brakes just inside the gate, and Sophia did not wait for the chauffeur to open her door. She stepped out from the back seat, absolutely stunning in a floral-print dress that draped her voluptuous figure in wild tropical orchids, accentuating curves that rippled and shimmered yellow and bright pink and orange and purple on hand-dyed silk. The midday sun suddenly lit upon her flowing golden hair, and it sparkled in her green eyes. She looked so alluring, so wounded, so thoroughly enchanting, Jack could hardly swallow or breathe or blink. Sophia caught Abbey in the air and spun her around once, hugging their child and humming with the unique expression of her love as vibration, as sound.

"Abbey, sweetheart, you can't run off like that." Jack came up to them both and posed a stern look. "We stick together, remember?"

"We stick together?" Sophia said. "Really?" Her eyes shot darts at him as she set Abbey on her feet.

"Come on," Jack said, "back me up on this. It's not safe."

"I'm sorry, Daddy," Abbey said.

Sophia looked at her. "How's my girl?"

"She's good."

"She had bad dreams," Jack said. "And she said something about Katie, just now. What did you say, sweetheart?"

"Not bad dreams, Daddy. I have sweet dreams, remember?"

"Look, Sophia," Jack said, "Katie's missing, and just now Abbey said—"

"Missing? What do you mean? Why didn't you call me?"

"Call you?" Jack said. "What…what are you doing here? I mean, I'm surprised you came and didn't just send the driver aga—"

"Momma. Can we go to the angel fountain in the park and see her? Pleeeease?"

"Not today," Sophia said.

"What fountain?" Jack asked.

"I can see him from my bedroom window if I stand on a chair."

"See who?" Jack asked. "You mean Aunt Katie?"

"No, silly Daddy. Him!"

"What are you saying, baby?" Sophia asked. "You don't make any sense."

"Mommy says I should not do it, but he says it's all right," Abbey said.

"Do what? Who—" Jack shook his head. "I don't know what's real and what's not anymore."

"Abbey." Sophia set her down. "Get in the car, honey. Mommy and Daddy have to talk."

Abbey did. Sophia closed the door. She stood in the sunlight beside the car and took hold of Jack's hand. His heart raced at her touch.

"You should know better by now," Sophia said. "She can't cope with all this. None of us can."

These words stunned Jack. Not the content of them, but the fact that it was Sophia saying them, and how she was saying them, with tenderness. Love. And she was right, this was too much for Abbey, and Jack blamed himself for all of it. Whenever Abbey experienced too much stress, she became incoherent. And what could be more stressful than having your entire universe torn apart?

"Why are you here?" he asked, looking her up and down again, trying to sound neutral, trying not to want her.

"For her."

"Meaning?"

"For Abbey. Why don't we take her to the park, like she asks?"

"We? I don't understand."

"Yes," Sophia said, "you do."

Their eyes met. "I can't," he said.

"Yes, you can. If I can, you most certainly can," she said. "Please"—she drew herself to him—"for our baby." Her lips reached his, and she kissed him.

He let her.

When she pulled back, she said, "I know I haven't always been there for you, Jack. I know you have needs and I haven't—"

"No," he said. "Please. Don't. I'm the one who—" She held up her index finger and pressed it against his lips. "Shhhh. For once, Jack, just don't say anything." And now, with her eyes closed, she leaned in and kissed him again, and he let her again, and he let himself kiss her too, and the foyer door of Gracie Mansion exploded open.

"Jack!" Becka shouted, holding his cell phone out, waving it as if to offer proof of what she announced next. "They found Katie and—" The sight of them kissing seemed to catch Becka like a garrote. She stiffened with the look of a woman sick with the realization that she should have known better, and dropped his phone. It crashed against the deck, tumbled down the steps and cracked. Tiny shards of glass flew like ice crystals onto the steps.

Becka bolted into the house.

Sophia pulled back, and Jack had to let go…

After Joel, the fill-in producer, had watched about twenty seconds of the footage and said, "Yeah, right. You're a funny guy, Terry," all Stone could think of was *Mary, Queen of Scots*. Not the monarch, the film: *The Execution of Mary, Queen of Scots*, a short from the year 1895. It contained the first special-effects sequence in cinema history. When the ax fell, Mary's severed head rolled right off the block. The executioner retrieved it, palmed it like a basketball, and held it up for all to see. Even in that grainy black-and-white footage, you would swear the actual severed head of the queen had fallen. The magic of cinema.

The Vanishing Lady followed a year later. One minute the woman was there, the next she was gone, then poof: back again!

Ooooooh.

Ahhhhh.

A hundred years go by, and it's all old hat. We've seen avatars and mutants, lightning thieves and *space* aliens, T. rex, and the kraken.

We've got it all 24/7 on hi-def, 3D, RealD, Blu-ray, and video games. We can even watch it on our cell phones. Hell, we can make it on our cell phones. So news footage of the Stranger walking on water? No big deal.

"Come on, Joel," Stone had said. "Think about it. The world is on the brink of nuclear war. If God was going to com—"

"Who?"

"Look, I was there, okay? And I know what this must seem like, but—"

"Enough," Joel had said. He'd ejected the tape and tossed it in the trash. "Next time, see if you can get the chroma-key right. Your 'God' looks all fuzzy around the edges."

So, yeah. *Mary, Queen of Scots*. Stone decided he would go bold. He'd call Connie again and tell her she had to come back into the studio or he was taking the tape to Fox News. The networks had to have received some of the footage and photos taken by the tourists in the park. Many had already been posted online. He had no choice—he had to get his footage on air now or risk the biggest story of his life getting scooped. The phone rang. "Connie," Stone said. "Look, you just have to come back in and see it for yourself. I swear, it's real!"

Connie finally agreed, and by 5:00 p.m. she sauntered into the studio and watched the tape. Then she checked out the videos and pics posted online. But even after all that, she didn't buy it. Not totally. So she made some calls and reached her friend Becka in the mayor's office.

"Wow," Connie said. "Really?"

"What?" Stone said.

"NSA satellites picked up the flash when you say your 'Stranger' appeared."

"Wow."

"The DOD has repositioned satellites, pointed them at New York. They're recording some kind of energy field or something over the Point in Central Park. FBI is all over it. Homeland Security says it may be their UFO. So whatever it is, it's real."

"That's what I've been trying to tell you!"

"The White House will be issuing a statement in an hour. The rest of the press will have loads of questions, but we have confirmation. We need to be first on air with this. Write it up. You're on air live, at six."

"Good evening. I'm Terry Stone," he said from the NY1 anchor's chair. "Tonight, we ask: What if a messenger from Heaven itself suddenly appeared, right here in our city? What if he possessed superhuman power—could walk on water and make a blind man see? What if he performed these miracles in front of scores of eyewitnesses *and* a television news team? Would you believe your own eyes?" Stone took a breath. "Would you believe in him?

"Well tonight, we're not only asking these questions—we're bringing you exclusive videotape *and* an eyewitness. That's right. I personally witnessed one of the most wonderful and moving experiences the human mind can conceive of: an actual miracle. While interviewing Dee Weiss, roommate of Katie Molinaro, sister of New York City's Mayor Jack Molinaro, in Central Park today, I saw, and my film crew captured, what we are about to share with you. As you may know, Katie Molinaro had been missing since yesterday morning, and police were on the scene conducting a search for her. I'll have a lot more to say about all this in a moment, but first, I want you to see it for yourself, uncut, unedited, and, in every sense of the word, the real footage of the mystery man many are calling the Stranger."

They aired the entire video from the opening with Dee through the walking on the water and the miracle with Jeremiah.

When it was over, Stone explained why he felt these events had happened in New York City, why the Stranger might have chosen Central Park. "Bethesda Terrace," he said, "was named for a biblical place of miracles where, each day, the first person to bathe in the fountain waters after the appearance of an angel received a divine healing. We do have an angel here, only ours is a statue called the Angel of the Waters," he said. "And, as you just saw, it came alive with light right before the miracle of Jeremiah's restored sight. So it seems that the light of the Stranger, when it engulfs the fountain, carries the power to heal."

Stone next told how NYPD officer Melinda Saragossa had seen the whole thing and called for an ambulance for Katie when she'd collapsed. He described how they had taken Katie, unconscious and near death, to the same hospital to which a one-eyed man named Thomas Breckenridge III had been taken just hours earlier, after being found hanging from a tree outside what authorities now knew to be an invisible barrier of some kind that still surrounded the Point. Breckenridge, like Katie Molinaro, was now reportedly in a coma. Unresponsive. The White House had, Stone also said, now issued a statement: They had found no source for the silent pulse of light, and they had no idea who or what sustained the invisible barrier. They could not rule out the possibility that this was some sort of extraterrestrial being or event. No scientific or even earthly explanation had yet been found. But since America was on the brink of war, the president had dispatched FBI and National Security teams to the city to work in cooperation with local authorities. They would get to the bottom of this, President R. J. Santorro had promised, 'as soon as humanly possible.'"

Then Stone produced the scroll. He showed the red wax seal, which bore the stamp that read *M-39*. And he read the contents of the scroll aloud:

I have commanded: Resist not evil, but turn the other cheek.

The commandment of God to Moses too is: Thou shalt not murder.

But I have made that teaching whole. I have fulfilled it. I have taught: Love thy enemy.

Love him! Do not resist him. Do not fight or kill him. Love him.

Thus, there are no exceptions to M-39.

Have ye not heard: Those who live by the sword will die by it?

Trust ye not the Way of the Lord?

Was not my death on the cross too salutary to regret?

Did I not conquer bodily death?

I did.

So what do you fear?

Put away your swords! You are about to impale your own immortal souls upon them!

Remember: I have promised to raise you in a new, heavenly body if you follow me.

Do you doubt me?

Can you not see that I am in you, and you in me?

I am the Light of the world. I am in each of you. I am the Light in the body of thy brother and thy sister. Thus, their bodies are my temples, as is yours. Cherish them, and treat all with love and respect. And if you see that one of them is hungry, say to yourself, "He is hungry." And if you see that one of them thirsts, say, "He thirsts."

Feed my sheep. Feed my lambs.

And woe unto those who lead you or your sons or daughters unto the slaughter in the name of self-defense, for I have prohibited it!

Resist not evil.

Thou shalt not kill, even in self-defense.

Love your enemy, and bless them that curse you.

Do good to them that hate you.

Pray for them that despitefully use you, and persecute you, that you may be the children of your Father, and be my brother or my sister...

Believe not those who call themselves by my name while defiling my bodily example by telling you God condones taking up arms. It is a deadly lie.

Were it so, why would I—who could have called upon a thousand legions of angels—I, who was innocent of sin, have allowed them to whip the flesh from my bones, to pierce me, crucify me, and kill my body?

Would I have allowed the men of the world to kill my martyrs if, by defending themselves against evil, my martyrs could reach Heaven?

No.

I allowed my own bodily death for righteousness's sake, for this very message: Thou shalt not resist evil, not even at the cost of your body.

Turn the other cheek!

M-39.

My dear children, it is time for a new gathering.

Will you come unto me?

Will you take up my cross, love your enemies, and follow me?

Lay down your arms. Please.

Do it now. Turn your swords to plowshares.

Love.

Serve.

Forgive, and pray for your oppressors, and on your day of bodily death, you shall not die, but be raised again, and stand beside me in the everlasting light of Heaven...

Connie posted the entire video and the full text of the scroll on the station's website. It broke all records for hits before crashing the site. The NY1 phone lines jammed. People gathered outside the building, and security had to lock the doors. Stone's video had bumped the war as the lead story on all of the networks, worldwide.

The Stranger had arrived.

At five minutes to six p.m. on Labor Day, Jack Molinaro exited the intensive care ward of the hospital. Katie had only spoken a few words to him before being sedated and rushed into surgery. "Promise me," she'd said, "you'll let the people stay."

"I don't understand," he'd said.

"In Central Park. Bethesda Terrace. No matter what happens… when they come to see him, you make sure everyone can stay. Promise me…"

He'd heard some crazy story about how she had been escorted across the lake by some being of light or something, but he didn't believe it. Still, he'd promised. So he'd instructed Karl to get down to Bethesda Terrace personally and find out what the hell had really happened, but to keep the park open, using any and all of the city's resources if necessary. And to find out who had done such terrible harm to his sister.

Her last words to him came over and over again into his head: "Truth," she had said. "He told me: It is the most powerful weapon in the universe, Jack."

Jack entered the elevator.

"Find it, Jack," she'd said. "Read the scroll."

Everything is moving so fast, he thought, trying hard now to dismiss his sister's strange plea and attend to the matters at hand.

He'd gone back inside Gracie Mansion after Sophia had left, hoping to explain and to get Becka to come to the hospital with him. But she'd already left.

He now knew in his heart she wouldn't come back to him again, even if he actually did file for divorce. He stood now a man between worlds, a man without a true friend, in the midst of a world gone mad.

And how could he have contemplated doing that to Abbey, anyway? Divorce? Was he not a noble man? More noble than one who would put himself and his needs ahead of a child's? Could he not have tolerated being invisible to his wife for Abbey's sake?

And yet he knew it had been as if he'd had no choice at the time. Only hindsight and guilt, and personal suffering, had brought him to these questions. At the time, all he knew was his own pain, needs, fears.

I felt unhappy then, Jack recalled.

Am I happy now?

And what about Sophia? What had happened to her to make her so willing to forgive him? Was it really all for Abbey, or did she want him back now too, because she really did love him? Did he dare believe that?

Could she forgive him?

"Truth. Find it, Jack." Katie's words echoed in his mind.

The elevator reached the lobby. A flash caught Jack's eye, and he stepped closer to a muted waiting-room television set that hung from the ceiling. Just as he did, the first Israeli Merkava Mk IV tank to cross the border into Syria exploded in a fireball that washed out the night vision view of the live-action video in an eerie white-blue flash.

"Find me a remote," he barked to one of the two NYPD officers assigned as his bodyguards. "Now!"

The anchor's mouth moved again, and they cut to video of another tank exploding. And now they cut, live, to a reporter on a rooftop in downtown Beirut. The reporter's face turned upward as a formation of American Lockheed Martin F-35 Lightning IIs streaked through the heavens on their way to Iran.

Nearby, a nurse attended to an Asian boy with a crushed hand as the child's mother yacked on and on in Mandarin, and an old man coughed, and someone's cell phone ringer played Roger Daltry belting out, "Who are you? Who? Who? Who? Who?"

The cop he'd sent had disappeared.

"Where's the remote?" he shouted across the room at the nurse.

She nodded and scurried off, leaving the Asian boy to bleed.

And now, on the TV, they cut to Russia. MiGs and Blackjack intercontinental bombers scrambled to get airborne for "exercises." And then they cut to a new Chinese aircraft carrier, a catamaran-like vessel that carried a nuclear submarine between its hulls, on a collision course with the American fleet in the Sea of Japan.

It's escalating…

Insanity!

"Mr. Mayor," the doctor said, suddenly beside him again, "I understand you've been asking to see me again, and I am very sorry to keep you waiting, but—"

Jack held up his hand to stop the sentence short. "Please. I just want to say thank you, and to ask you not to let my sister die." He pushed a tear from the corner of his eye and smeared it into oblivion. "Please."

Israeli tanks exploded, MiG engines flared, and Patriot missiles launched, turning the television screen into a flashing strobe of fire and light.

"That's not up to me, sir," the doctor said.

Jack's head pounded with each flashing white pulse, and he swallowed hard and searched for words to convey, with all the power of his office, that this doctor *must* keep Katie alive. But all he could do was look the man in the eye, through tears.

"I'm sorry, sir," the doctor said. "I have to go. We'll do our best."

The television flashed again, and again, and bomb after bomb exploded, and wave after wave of fighter aircraft took off from Israel. And now mobile missile launchers rolled, and tanks and ships lined up, and soldiers and sailors and marines and airmen rushed to war, and Jack wondered if anyone would survive what looked to be coming next.

The nurse returned, remote in hand, and hit the wrong button. "Oh, sorry," she said. She'd changed the channel by accident. A voice rose over the waiting room chatter.

Jack recognized it: Terry Stone. NY1. He sat in the anchor's chair and said, "Ladies and gentlemen, I give you the man we're calling the Stranger." Another light exploded on screen and then slowly faded and parted, and a luminous being emerged, wearing what looked to be white robes. A halo of gold and sapphire and emerald and pink emanated from him as if he were the source of light itself.

The little Asian boy's mouth dropped open.

So did Jack's.

Everyone in the waiting room gathered around the set and watched in silence.

And now Katie came onscreen…and they were both…walking on the water?

Jack took a step back, and a small, warm hand slipped into his. "Daddy!"

"Abbey." He smiled, bent, and scooped her up and held her. "Sweetheart!" He kissed her face.

She turned to the television, and said, "That's him! See. I told you he had come."

CHAPTER 8

DENNY BRANDT CONSULTED NO AUGURS, NO POLLSTERS OR STAFFERS. He kept his own counsel and liked his own advice best. In fact, he always took it. What most in his line would consider isolationist paranoia, he considered good political practice. He never shared his process, so he never had to worry about leaks or up-and-coming rivals using inside information against him. And he never had to worry about dissension once a decision had been made.

After the swearing-in ceremony—and after recovering from the pain inflicted by Becka's knee—the new governor had a driver take him to his predecessor's office on Central Park West, alone. He wanted time to recover, yes, but he had a decision to make now too. A big one. He had one more card to play, one more move to make in his bid to capture the White House. The only question was, when?

He had planned on waiting until RJ announced his reelection campaign. He'd planned on using his file to move up from governor of New York to the number-two spot on the national ticket when the sitting VP "retired" at the end of his first term. But now that option was gone. And that particular spot would not, could not, stay empty for very long.

So what to do?

He took a call from the White House deputy national security advisor, one of his guys inside the administration.

"Syria and Russia have lined up with the Iranians."

Expected.

"North Korea, as opportunistic as ever and hoping to capitalize on the situation, has moved a million troops south toward the border."

Bastards.

"China has made it clear that if we attack Syria, they're ready to protect their interests in the region."

Right.

"We're calling up every reservist, and every unit of the New York State National Guard is going on standby, under the president's command."

"No," he said. "Under my command."

"I'll advise the White House."

"Thanks for the call," Brandt said.

In the conference room, at a long, wide oak table, the state commissioner of Homeland Security and the director of Emergency Services waited. Denny bluntly told him, "Bring everyone in. Immediately. I'll be damned if we're not ready for any contingency. Understood?"

The commissioner nodded, and said, "Yes, sir."

Brandt went upstairs, settled in behind his new desk, and got on a conference call with the outgoing governor's top staff. He received face-to-face briefings on everything from the possibility of Wall Street being ordered closed by the president the next day to the status of ongoing budget negotiations in Albany. Then he told his staff to demand resignations from about fifty of his forerunner's closest people, and he began plans to officially install his own. He ordered the furniture and files and personal possessions of the former governor moved out of his space, and he asked for a cup of black coffee, over which he glanced at dozens of notes of congratulations. Then he flipped through a pile of requests for callbacks from political benefactors and "friends," and perused the résumés sent in by county chairmen from all over the state calling in favors and asking for immediate consideration for their picks for the newly empty seat of lieutenant governor. Finally, he called and checked on his son, Rikki.

"All good?"

"Great."

"Love ya, boy."

"You too, Dad."

At 6:25 p.m., his chief of staff came in, pale and shaking.

"What the hell, Will?" Brandt asked. "What's happened?"

"NY1 just broke a story."

"And?"

"A man—they're calling him the Stranger—he walked on water. And he healed a man and delivered some kind of message about peace—"

"Walked on water?" Brandt said.

"Yes," Will said. "Katie Molinaro was with him. She'd been attacked. She was missing and—"

"Molinaro? How come I'm finding out about this now?"

"It just happened!"

"I want to see it. Get it on a computer."

An hour after he'd viewed the footage from Central Park, the press awaited Brandt downstairs, loaded up and ready to fire questions, armor-piercing rounds, in rapid succession. No way he'd have the luxury of saying, "I just got here. Give me a chance. Let's wait and see..."

No, Brandt thought. No way.

In a situation like this, the public expected their elected officials to take a stand, to lead. In fact, they expected elected officials to tell them what to think. To define events.

They demanded it.

And the press, knowing this, was ready to pounce. To test his mettle.

More importantly, once he took a stand, he'd be stuck with it. A successful politician never flip-flopped, or second-guessed himself, or even ruminated publicly about wishing he'd considered other possibilities, or he got crucified.

No. He had to instantly assess the vagaries of the situation, see all the angles, identify all the potential pitfalls, and then argue the public into agreeing with his conclusion.

Precisely why being a great lawyer was the best preparation for this job, Brandt thought.

Any mediocre lawyer must possess the skills to argue a case and win. But a great lawyer argued both sides, quietly, to himself, well before a case ever came to court. He anticipated weaknesses in his opponent's arguments, overcame objections before they were raised, and figured out how to win before the actual trial even began. And Brandt considered himself a great lawyer, called by destiny, at a critical time in world history, to lead. Called to use all his many well-honed skills and training to judge quickly, and to issue a verdict immediately, and by so doing, to define the situation for all the pedestrians. And so now, on the pressing question of the Stranger, with the masses waiting to be led, with the press demanding that the nation's leaders take an instant stand, Brandt secluded himself for the few moments he had left before stepping in front of the cameras.

He'd seen the video now. He'd read the contents of the scroll on the NY1 website. He'd learned the facts. Now he would mentally argue both sides of this case himself, as he stood alone in his new office, looking down on the rapidly filling park.

Yes. Argue it myself, before I argue with the world.

First, for the defense: The Stranger has healed a man, given him back his sight. He has done so, we may assume, as proof that he's brought a message from God. We now have to heed that message. It says: Self-defense is wrong. God says so. Has said so through his prophets, through Moses, and most certainly through Jesus. Resist not evil. Love your enemies. No exceptions. Turn the other cheek. As simple as that.

So now it is time for America, a God-fearing nation, to be like Switzerland. Neutral. Swords to plowshares. If you want to ensure peace, share your wealth. Feed the world. End your quest for world domination by force, and win it by helping people, curing poverty and disease. All this is on the website, and in the scroll. Its author claims to have the authority of Christ himself. Pundits, already posting comments and parsing the text, say that doing so will cost less than half the money spent on war machines. Let the corporations fend for themselves, defend their own oil fields and shipping lanes and profits, they say. We can't kill for them. It's against God's law, they say, and the government cannot force people to disobey God. That's not rendering unto Caesar what is Caesar's. It is rendering unto Caesar what is God's, by forcing man to act in ways that condemn his very soul to Hell eternal.

So there it is. If we agree with this Stranger, we must heed the words of his scroll. We must foreswear all violence, even in cases of self-defense, even as punishment for the most heinous of crimes.

It's pacifism from here on out. Turn the other cheek, even if it means following Christ to the cross. Period.

Yes.

And so I rest my case for the Stranger.

"And now, for the prosecution," Brandt said aloud, though still alone. And in his head, he carried on: I ask you: What do we really know? Only that this "Stranger" was certainly present when a man, purportedly blind beforehand, regained his sight. But do we even know that? Was he blind in the first place? If not, he was not really healed, and this is at best a hoax! At worst, it is something far more sinister.

The "blind man" has disappeared. So we have no way to verify the facts. We don't know anything. Not for sure.

One would assume, however, if the miracle had been real, the first thing he would do would be to establish it as such, beyond any shadow of a doubt. Go to a hospital, produce records of his former blindness, remove any question.

Did this "Jeremiah" do that?

No. He did the opposite. He's hiding.

We don't even know his last name!

Meanwhile, a woman, Katie Molinaro, whom we do know to have been physically healthy before her contact with this "Stranger" lies in a hospital bed near death, the victim of an assault, possibly at the hands of this foreigner or maybe even an extraterrestrial alien who has taken up residence as a squatter in Central Park. We don't know what really happened to Katie Molinaro, do we? She's in a coma. We cannot question her.

We cannot question her. We cannot question Jeremiah. We cannot question the Stranger!

He doesn't even speak directly to us. Not directly.

We do not know the source of his power—the energy field or whatever it is—that keeps us at bay.

We have to ask: Why would a messenger of God need such a defense if he were here to proclaim peace?

No. We don't have answers to any of our questions.

However, we may safely assume two things. First: A being from Heaven, a man who can actually heal a blind man would not, or at least should not, have left Katie Molinaro in her present near-death condition. Nor the man Breckenridge, for that matter. Think of him and his condition. His face laid open. His eye gouged out!

Who did it to him?

Why?

I will find out. Believe me I will.

Second: A truly holy being would not or at least should not have to hide from us. We are a God-fearing people. God-loving people. So, again, we have to ask: Who or what is he, if he must hide from God's chosen people: Americans?

Finally, we must consider the Stranger's appearance, and his message, in context: We are at war! Our vice president has been killed, assassinated by cowards who hurled a missile at civilians. Meanwhile, there's a Stranger among us, dressed in the garb of our enemies, espousing a radical doctrine he claims came from Jesus Christ himself! A message that is no less than a call for surrender!

That call is by any standard treason in time of war!

And yet, if the call had come from Jesus himself, we would have to consider it. But this Stranger has not said he is the Christ. So, is he, really? There are no marks on his hands or feet. We can see no wound in his side. He claims nothing! He just offers some dubious scroll. A scroll we cannot even examine!

Oh, NY1 claims to have it. But they refuse to turn it over to authorities.

Like the blind man, it's nowhere to be found.

So we can verify nothing.

And we cannot just trust these people: Jeremiah. Stone. The Stranger. Not on such slim evidence. Not unless we are willing to risk our very nation for the promise of some unseen Heaven.

So that's it.

That's the question. Trust? Or protect?

And the answer is: Beware America! If we take the Stranger and the scroll and its message as true and righteous and from God, we must be prepared to acknowledge that they bring an indictment—not only of our system of government—but of every organized religious institution in the Judeo-Christian world. Have they not all condoned self-defense?

We're going to have to reconcile the fact that spiritual and religious experts tell us, and have told us for centuries, the doctrine espoused in that scroll is wrong and false. They've assured us that turning the other cheek is not to be taken literally. Jesus did not mean what he said. Not that simply.

No!

Self-defense is our birthright, legitimate, and approved by God as just, even if M-39 says it is not!

But again, that's the question we face.

Do you see what happens if we trust the scroll and the Stranger?

Do you?

Ask yourself: Have our armies sinned by fighting against Hitler and Al Qaeda? Against Communism and Fascism? Or have they done God's work?

Have we been wrong to execute criminals who have victimized and molested children before tearing them to bloody pieces and consuming their very flesh? Or have we done God's work by capturing them, putting them on trial, and executing them?

Have we been deceived for centuries by our religious leaders, our Bible scholars, and ourselves?

If you say yes, you are with this so-called Stranger.

If you say yes, you are an enemy of your nation's history, religious and secular.

But if you say no, and if you say we have done good work, and do good work now, by fighting against the enemies of freedom, then the solution is very simple. And here it is: The so-called Stranger and his minions must be stopped, no matter what the cost, for he and they are the real enemies of civilization as we know it.

No other conclusion is possible.

Agreed?

I rest my case with this: We cannot embrace this Stranger or his strange doctrine unless we're prepared to change the very fabric of our nation forever.

Are we, Americans, on whom God has shed his grace, to become sniveling pacifists? Or are we off to war?

I say *war*!

Stone surveyed the scene: Nineteen million people lived in the New York metropolitan area, and it seemed all nineteen million of them were trying to get to Bethesda Terrace. People streamed into the park from all sides. Cars clogged every entrance, and the park's transverse roads were bumper to bumper. The Mall, the main pedestrian thoroughfare that cut across the park and ran straight into Bethesda Terrace, was packed with people on foot and on bicycles, skateboards, and rollerblades. Some pushed wheelchairs. Some wore hospital gowns like they'd just walked out of the ICU and into the park. Some limped along on crutches.

"We're going to need another miracle," Connie said, "just to get you back down there."

Stone was headed to the park with her, Patrick, and Mike. Patrick drove the big satellite truck reserved for the top stories. Connie—well-known as one of the best field producers in the business before she'd been kicked upstairs—had come along to make sure they got what they needed. She'd coordinate everything with the studio and do whatever it took to get him into position, including trading favorable political coverage for access and positioning. Mike had never left the terrace, so he would be there, waiting.

If we ever get there, Stone thought.

They'd sat in the shadow of the Dakota, at West Seventy-Second Street and Central Park West, and had not moved an inch in an hour.

"This sucks," said Patrick.

Stone threw open the door. "Let's just grab what we can and go."

Connie nodded her approval, took a battery pack and an extra camera light for Mike, and jumped out too. "I'll call you on your cell," she promised Patrick. "See if I can get you down there."

They waded into a sea of people packed so tightly on the paved path they had to shuffle their feet. "Who can you call?" Stone asked. "Somebody must owe you a favor."

"Yeah," she said. "I'm on it." Connie dialed her cell phone. After a little back-and-forth with her connection, she updated Stone. "Seems Jack Molinaro promised his sister everyone would have unfettered access," Connie said. "Press is getting red-carpet treatment."

"Who is that?" Stone asked, gesturing to Connie's cell phone.

"Becka again. She's hooking some of the network teams up with a police escort. Ours is on its way. On horseback."

"Horseback?" Stone said. "No way."

"Hey. That's what they use for big crowds."

Within minutes, they made their way out of the crowd and found "the Mounties," four horses, in a flying wedge formation. Even with their help, though, they didn't reach the terrace until around midnight. When they did finally arrive, they stopped at the top of the stairs that flanked the arcade. Nowhere left to go. No room to advance.

Wall-to-wall people.

Between the police floodlights, the TV crews with their hand-held cameras and battery-powered lights, hovering choppers with searchlights, and the light of thousands of cell phone screens and lit candles, Bethesda Terrace glowed as bright as day. There wasn't an inch of room on any of the paths, stairs, lawns, or hills surrounding the expanse of red bricks. Frantic seekers tried to get to the Angel of the Waters fountain, crowding around the circular pool at its base, packing in, pushing forward so forcefully that some had started screaming for help.

My fault, Stone thought. I kinda promised them another miracle when I told them about the biblical terrace and the Angel of the Waters.

On the paved footpaths, some in the crowd had signs: *The End Is Near!* or *Jesus Is Lord* or *Save Me, Mother of God!* Some were *in* the lake, trying to swim across, but about halfway, they'd come against the invisible barrier. They treaded water, struggled, and were trying to climb on top of one another to get to the Stranger's little house of light on the hill.

Mayhem.

Pandemonium, Stone thought.

Across the lake, on the other side of the park, a ring of human bodies encircled the Point.

And now from above, the whir and rhythmic battering of helicopter blades rolled louder and louder as chopper after chopper swooped down for a closer look. They couldn't get near the Point either, not even from above. The invisible barrier kept everyone away.

"What the hell is it?" Connie shouted to the lead cop.

"We don't know," he said. "Right out of a sci-fi flick though, huh?" The cop gestured to the stairs. "Force your way through. Those guys will take you down."

Five more cops pushed toward them, hugging the railing, shouting, "Coming through! Stand aside. NYPD. Coming through!"

Stone and Connie followed.

At the base of the terrace stairs, someone in the crowd spotted Stone. "It's him! It's Terry Stone!"

Others—people who had obviously seen the broadcast—started shoving toward him. Reporters held out microphones while yelling: "Who is he?" "What is he doing here?" "Where did he come from?" "Stone! Is it true he's from outer space?" "Is he a foreigner? Does he have a passport?" "Did you get to meet him?" "How do you know he's a stranger? Is that what he calls himself?" "Is he an illegal alien?" "An angel?" "A terrorist?" "The Antichrist?" "Is this for real?" "What about that blind guy?" "Was the blind guy really blind?" "How do you know?" "Did the police arrest anybody?" "Was Katie Molinaro raped?" "Where did the dog go?" "Is the Stranger still here, still on the Point?" "Did his spaceship take off?" "Who has the shoe, and what's the connection to the woman who threw a shoe at the mayor?"

What?

Someone threw a shoe at the mayor?

"Is the Stranger coming out again, Stone?"

"I don't know."

"Why is he here?"

He shook his head. "Maybe because of the war?"

"Is it the end of the world?"

Someone grabbed at him as if touching him might help or heal them, as if what the Stranger had and could do was contagious and Stone had caught it.

"I'm nobody," he said. "I'm nothing."

The cops circled him, pushed everyone back. One of them got a message into his Bluetooth and said, "Stay close! They're going to clear the area!"

"How?" Stone asked.

Just then, what seemed like an unending line of mounted officers in riot gear came down the hill and forced its way into the sea of people. Somewhat roughly, the cops guided their horses to the edge of the lake, shoving a few onlookers into the water as they went. When they'd secured a narrow corridor along the shore, they turned their horses and nudged forward, announcing over a bullhorn: "Clear the terrace! Move back!"

Fifty, maybe sixty, maybe a hundred horses now, side by side, pushed steadily, until there was enough room for the next wave of cops, on foot, in riot gear, and carrying barricades. They fell in behind the Mounties, their backs to the lake, and as the horses forced forward, they set up a perimeter of blue wooden barricades. They pushed the crowd back onto the grassy hills and into the arcade until they had cleared the entire terrace around the fountain.

Stone, with Connie beside him, still safely tucked behind the cops on the stairs, now possessed a clear view. He moved to step out.

"Hold on," the cop with the Bluetooth earpiece shouted. "That was Phase One."

For Phase Two, the cops employed the same method to open up the paved paths on either side of the terrace, clearing them of pedestrians and creating a thoroughfare wide enough to allow emergency vehicle and squad car access. Official city and state vehicles, including a mobile response team with scuba divers, now pulled in.

Connie tried Patrick on her cell. She got him. "Yeah, I know," she said. "They're doing the road now. I've got five uniformed city cops on their way to get you down here…we'll need all the portable stuff you can carry. Okay. Good. Just look for us. They'll probably create a press pit of some kind. Yeah…as soon as you can."

It didn't take long after Phase Two was completed before they had it all sorted out. The cops allowed press access to part of the newly cleared open area of the terrace and set up a perimeter for it with the blue barricades; Connie had aptly named it "the press pit." It sat at the lowest point of the terrace, right at the edge of the lake. Stone and Connie were in almost the same spot where Mike had filmed the Stranger and Katie coming across the lake.

Perfect...

Select news crews from all over the world got into position. They rolled in mini generators, pulled cables, and fired up floodlights. Hum and exhaust filled the air.

"See if you can find out where the mayor is," Stone said to Connie, who dutifully nodded and made another call. "And the new governor. Brandt. And what the White House has to say about all this..." Stone just realized the power in the relationship had definitely shifted. He'd become the lead, the star. Connie took orders from *him* now. He turned around in a big circle to survey the situation, to take it all in one more time. It was a new world—for him, for everyone in Central Park, for everyone everywhere.

And now cigar smoke stung Stone's nostrils and choked off his breath, and he lost his balance a little, and backed into someone accidentally, and said, "Pardon me. I'm sorr—"

"Where is he, Stone?" the someone with the smelly cigar asked.

"What?" Stone turned. "Who?"

"Your buddy, that fraud Jeremiah," Brandt said.

"How should I know?"

"Don't give me that bullshit. You're in on this left-wing, peacenik bullshit."

"With all due respect, sir, I don't think—"

"I know you don't. Thinking is *my* job." Brandt puffed. "So here's the deal: you get this Jeremiah, and your 'Stranger' friend, to turn themselves in to me, you understand? To me and no one else, or you're going to find your sorry ass in jail..."

CHAPTER 9

AT 11:00 P.M. SHARP ON MONDAY NIGHT, OFFICER MELINDA Saragossa stood in uniform at the threshold of the patent-yellow parlor in Gracie Mansion and tried her best to calm her butterflies. Flanked by fellow officers in riot gear, she'd been escorted through a crowd at the gate. The sick and dying had descended on Gracie Mansion, and they were screaming demands. They wanted a special area on the terrace, beside the fountain, in case one of them was chosen as the recipient of the next miraculous healing.

An aide escorted Saragossa to the entrance of the room and introduced her to Mayor Jack Molinaro, then left. Now, Saragossa set down the brown paper bag she'd brought along and stepped in.

Looking almost catatonic, the mayor sat quietly on the sofa, a small brown teddy bear beside him. He gently strummed a vintage guitar, holding it as tenderly as a lover.

"Sorry I'm late, sir," Saragossa said. "It's pretty crazy out there."

"I'm giving them what they've asked for, Miss Zzzzaragoza," he said, plucking a guitar string for emphasis. "Buses are on the way to take them to the park."

"Oh?" She slipped the envelope she'd brought along into her pocket. She'd been surprised by a knock on her apartment door just before leaving to come here, and even more so by what the visitor who'd come had asked her to do. She'd agreed because she hoped it would somehow influence the outcome of this meeting. She expected a dressing-down for having arrested Dee Weiss. Hell, she expected to be kicked off the force.

"Habitational name, isn't it? Zaragoza? Capital of Aragon?" the mayor said.

He's making small talk?

She spied an empty bottle of Jameson.

"Ever been?" he asked.

"Oh, yes, sir. I mean, no, sir. My father was born there. But I've never been."

The television news flashed footage of Governor Brandt's press conference, but the sound was off.

"Well, it's beautiful," the mayor said. "Saint James, the brother of John the Apostle, had a vision of the Virgin Mary there in the first century...according to the legend, anyway."

"Yes, I'm familiar," Saragossa said.

"Interesting, don't you think, that someone named Saragossa stood watch at Bethesda Terrace today and saw the Divine Messenger? Or do you call him the Stranger?"

"I don't know what to call him, sir."

"Neither do I. They say Saint James brought true Christianity to the whole of Europe. The Holy Mother appeared, standing on a pillar, and they built a beautiful basilica in Zaragoza to commemorate it."

"Nuestra Señora del Pilar."

"That's right."

"When I was a girl, every Columbus Day my father would talk about it. Both holidays are on the same day," she said.

"October twelfth," he said.

"Yes. My father celebrated Las Fiestas del Pilar and El Día de la Hispanidad with the parade and the Ofrenda de Flores to the Virgin, and he told us stories about Zaragoza…"

"And yet he hasn't taken you? Shame on him."

"He's dead, sir."

"Oh. I'm sorry," he said.

Her face flushed.

"How old are you, Saragossa?"

"Twenty-six, sir."

"You're very pretty. Does it get in the way?"

"Sir?"

"On the job. Do your looks get in the way?"

"I—um…honestly. Yes. Sometimes. Not in the way, but—"

"I get it. Come. Please," he said, and his eyes went to the sofa, to the empty space on his right, beside the teddy bear, and he began to play his classical guitar again.

"'Adios Nonino'?" she asked.

"You know it?"

She nodded. "It's a tango, written by Astor Piazzolla for the composer's own father, a few days after his death. My dad used to play it whenever he missed his dad."

"Does it disturb you?"

"Pardon?"

"The song?"

"No. It's okay," she said. "I mean, well, it does remind me of him. And it is kind of intense. It's been a long time since I've heard it played." She tried to quiet her mind, to contain her emotions.

He leaned closer to her now, and the heat of his body mixed with her own, and his scent, strong from a long day, bright with whiskey and tinged with another woman's perfume, roused her sexually. She blushed, a little ashamed.

"It's never okay to lose someone you love. No matter how much time passes. Is it?"

"No, sir."

"Jack," he said. "Please. Call me Jack."

The pace of his strumming quickened, and he plucked the strings with fury as the melody crested, and the sound of desolation rose and filled the room, pulling at her heart, tearing her soul. A tear rolled off her cheek, and she knew he'd noticed.

"She's in a coma," he said. "My sister. Katie. They say she's not even alive. Not really."

"I'm sorry," Saragossa said. An image of herself, at age nine, standing over her father, came to her. He, lying in a pool of his own blood on that worst of days, flashed into her mind.

"Don't worry," he said. "I don't blame you. Dee Weiss, I mean. She is crazy, you know."

"Thank you. I mean, I had no way of knowing she was your sister's…lover…or fiancée…when she—"

"She isn't," he said. But he didn't look at Saragossa now. "It's a lie. My sister has a boyfriend. Had one, anyway." He just kept playing, softly. "Tell me about what happened in the park today. I mean, how do you feel about this…Stranger?"

"Oh. Well…his eyes…his light…overwhelming."

He nodded. "I'm reassigning you," he said.

"Sir?"

"To my daughter. Abbey."

"I don't understand, sir—NYPD's Municipal Security Section has a team of specially trained officers for such—"

"I want someone I pick. Someone with no ties to anyone else around here. Besides, you were the one Dee encountered in the park. You were present when my sister came across the lake with the

Stranger, and you witnessed the miracle. That's too many coincidences. Clearly, you have some kind of role to play."

"Sir?"

"Jack. You'll be extraordinarily vigilant. Won't you? You've lost a loved one. You know I can't have anything happen to my daughter."

"Yes, sir." Now Saragossa realized he knew everything about her. "I know."

"We're at war. On high terror alert. There's a suicide bomber in the city. Even if it means putting yourself in harm's way, you'll do whatever it takes to protect my child?"

"Yes. Of course, but—"

"Good. Report only to me. Understood?"

"Yes."

"And you'll do as I ask, no matter what? I need your word."

"Yes," she said, finally. "I will. I'm honored. Really. I don't understand, but—"

"Chalk it up to politics, Saragossa. It's something very few people understand. If you're me, you can't trust anyone." He held out the bear. "Be sure to give this to Abbey," he said. "She won't sleep without it."

Saragossa took it.

"There's a car waiting. Get over to the Dakota as fast as you can. No stops." He tugged the bear's paw. "She's waiting."

"Yes, sir." Saragossa stood and made her way to the door.

"Oh, and Saragossa," he said. "Tell Sophia that I love her."

"I'm sorry?"

"My wife. Sophia. And tell her how much it meant to me, her coming to the hospital today, and bringing Abrianna…"

"Yes, sir." Saragossa's heart fluttered and a burning sensation rose in her gut. Then she remembered the note. "Oh. Sir?" she said. "I brought you something."

"Say again?"

"Jeremiah…the blind man. Well, he's not blind anymore. You know? He brought this to my apartment just before I left to come here." She held out the note.

"Jeremiah? Why?"

"I don't know, sir."

"But how did he find you? And how did he know you'd be coming here—"

"I don't know. But, the note…it says it's from your sister, Katie…and there's this." She pulled out the M-39 scroll from the bag she'd brought along. "Stone gave it to him, and he said to give it to you."

The unmarked police sedan stopped at One West Seventy-Second, at the corner of Central Park West, and Saragossa thought about how life can change in an instant. Like when John Lennon paused to sign an autograph for Mark David Chapman. Like three hours later when Lennon came home from the recording studio and Chapman, now wanting more than just black ink, emerged from the shadows of the Dakota and fired five hollow-point rounds from a Charter Arms .38 Special revolver.

The first round went high and wide.

The other four did not.

Imagine…

Teddy in hand, buds in her ears, eyes wide, she crossed the street and entered a throng of pedestrians crowding into the park, all of them no doubt trying to get close to the terrace, hoping to see the Stranger. The usual thirty-second walk took ten minutes because of the throng, but finally she stood at Strawberry Fields. She stopped at the *Imagine* mosaic and let the others stream around her. They filed past by the hundreds, the thousands. She stared at the Dakota through the rustling leaves of the trees. The checkerboard of lit windows set against a black, starless sky made the Renaissance-style building seem a beast's castle from a fairy tale. And she felt like a naive child in a coming-of-age story. The uniform and weapon and cuffs she wore had fooled many into believing she was strong and tough, someone to be taken seriously, and while wearing them and staying "in character," she did pull it off. But she knew better.

The butterflies always came to life inside her whenever she felt pressure.

Fear…

I can't go in, she thought.

Not yet.

I still have not come to grips with this.

The mayor of New York City has given his child to me to protect.

Me!

How could this happen?

How, and why?

Maybe he's right.

Maybe it is just part of God's plan and I do have a special role to play.

Okay.

Yes.

If that's it, then I have to do it.

I'll do whatever he asks.

She blessed herself.

I swear to God, I will.

Suddenly she recalled something she'd often overheard her father say to her in times of celebration: What seems great today can end up tragic tomorrow. And what at first seems bad sometimes turns out great. So always remember, the present moment is not defined by what led up to it. The present moment is defined by the future. We never know what anything really means, not until later. Sometimes much later…so, Lindy: Temperance. Self-control. Never show fear in the moment. Never.

She turned her attention to the mosaic. "The present moment is never defined by the past," she said aloud now. And you can never know which of the thousands of seemingly meaningless moments in your life might turn out to be meaningful in ways you've never imagined.

You can't know until later, like maybe three hours later when you hear the shots and feel the bullets tearing through your back and understand life flows in crimson and can come streaming out of you, like it did for John Lennon.

Like it came out of my dad that morning he climbed the stairs and entered the foyer, his arms full with Christmas presents…I will protect her, she thought. This child. Abbey Molinaro. She's in my charge now, and I will. No matter what.

If her mother will let me…

She walked against the streaming crowd, hurried out of the park and across the street toward the big wrought-iron gates. She could not feel her legs, but they moved anyway. She waved, feigning confidence, to the guard on duty. He leaned over as she passed, squinted to check the name on her uniform, nodded, and smiled.

She went into a place not just anybody could enter.

She tried not to clench her jaw too much or smile too broadly or let her self-satisfaction show.

Temperance, Lindy.

And now she stood inside, dwarfed by what seemed a canyon of stone stretching toward Heaven. She paused. Beyond the shadows, a fountain hissed like a hundred rich people, each with a single finger pressed against the lips, demanding *shhhhh!*

And now she realized that the giant itself, the Dakota, encircled her, looked down on her and saw her at its feet.

Does it want me in its belly?

It stared at her through a hundred windows, some glowing, others ghastly black, like eyes rimmed with ominous shadows—eyes that measured her, and judged her.

Am I worthy or not? she wondered. Stars and even billionaires are routinely refused entry here.

I've been sent.

I *am* worthy.

I am.

"Enter," the building seemed to say.

Each of its four interior walls housed its own lobby on the ground floor, and each lobby had its own separate elevator. Sophia's family owned the whole northeast corner of the seventh floor, facing the park. Saragossa went past another guard and crossed the lobby. Elevator doors slid open. It was a slow ride accompanied by a tenant, a silent, gray-haired man in a stiff gray Armani suit. He glanced at her, but when he saw the uniform, he nodded.

Respect.

The costume worked.

Like magic, it hid all her fears, made the butterflies impossible to see.

She thought about Dee Weiss. She had overreacted when Dee grabbed the window of the police cruiser.

I didn't really listen to what Dee was saying.

I reacted out of fear.

I responded not to what was happening but to what I feared was the case, what I feared would happen: that I'd let my guard down and get hurt.

Like my father did…

Yet somehow that failure to see, to distinguish between what was real and what was merely imagined, had brought her here.

Somehow?

By God's grace, that's how, her inner voice said now.

Yes. It had to be part of the plan.

God's plan.

The elevator stopped. The gray man got out. The doors closed again. Her heart found no rhythm. She closed her eyes and clenched her fists.

Fear.

Fear of Mrs. Molinaro rejecting her for this assignment.

The mayor had tipped her off. He'd said she was pretty. He'd asked if it got in the way. Maybe he was hinting that she should not be too pretty, not in this role. Maybe his wife would be jealous.

Saragossa's mind raced over the events again and again, and she came to a conclusion, told herself a story, the story of how her looks had almost cost her this opportunity. Jack Molinaro felt concern, was self-conscious that his wife might judge her as one of his playthings, not a serious choice. Not a real bodyguard.

Not even a real cop.

Don't look too pretty, she told herself now. Don't.

Yes. Mrs. Molinaro might be the jealous type. Insecure. After all, the mayor had cheated on her. Recently. It was front-page news when it happened, daily fodder for the tabloids for nearly a week. And now he'd sent her?

Okay. So: Don't be pretty.

Be all business.

The elevator doors slid open, and she saw herself in a gilded mirror. She stepped out and grew larger and larger, crowding out the reflected doors closing behind her. A firm, curvaceous body approached, a doppelgänger playing chicken.

That's me, she thought.

Me.

The uniform could not fully conceal the shape of her body, nor hide the soft curve of her neck. It could not hide her mother's full lips, or her paternal grandmother's high cheekbones, or the china white of her skin.

All this she saw while staring into her father's bloodshot hazel eyes, which is to say her own eyes, so like his.

Daddy…

She missed him too much. And decided again, as she had a thousand times before, that she wouldn't change anything about her looks, even if she could. Not even they cost her this job.

"7-A. I'm here." She paused before knocking.

I'll be a friend to both of them. A real friend to the mayor and his wife. It will change my life.

It will.

It's God's will.

She inhaled deeply, knocked, and immediately thought: Hide the bear!

The door opened. White leggings inside black patent leather shoes on a salmon-colored marble tile floor inlaid with sterling silver fleur-de-lis.

Enchanting. Like a fairy tale castle.

"Hello," a sweet voice chimed, and a spell was cast. The mayor's daughter, a princess in a red velour dress and white cotton blouse, with a red ribbon in her silky, golden hair, then said, "I'm Abrianna."

"Oh," Saragossa managed, squatting to look Abrianna in the eye.

"Sar…ra…go…sah…" Abbey reached out and touched her name tag. "Did I say it correctly?"

"Perfectly."

"I'm so glad to see you again, Miss Lindy," Abbey said.

"How—" A chill climbed her spine. Only her father had ever called her by that name.

"Mommy. Lindy's here!" Abbey reached for Saragossa's hand and pulled her inside. "Well, did you bring it for me? Did you, Lindy?"

The child's words, and her beaming smile, disarmed Saragossa. And Abbey's hair, a playful blend of curls and shimmering yellow waves, and her sweet, dimpled smile—held in place as if she knew and could never forget the great, magical, true secret meaning of life—made it impossible for Saragossa to even start a sentence, much less complete one. Saragossa did, however, manage to dramatically pull the bear out from behind her back now.

"Teddy!" Abbey shrieked and tugged the bear from Saragossa's hand. "Oh, yay!" She hugged it close and rocked it in her arms, and she seemed so small and fine boned, she might just blow away like an untethered kite should the slightest breeze ever catch her. She leaped up and down in joy. "Thank you! Thank you! Momma! Momma! Miss Lindy brought my teddy!"

Saragossa wanted to hug Abbey, to hold her and look into her eyes, as bright a cobalt blue as she'd ever seen, and so wide and pure and innocent, they made it impossible not to love the child instantly.

"Thank God. Now we can finally get some sleep," Mrs. Molinaro said, entering with a flourish. She too was stunning, in a floral-print dress that shimmered like silk yet seemed dull compared to her own flowing, golden hair. Her voluptuous figure jumped out in bold tropical-colored curves that danced green and pink and orange against the sepia-blue wall behind her. "Say thank you, Abrianna," Mrs. Molinaro demanded.

"I did, Momma. I did say thank you."

Who are these people? Saragossa wondered. They look like steel on television, like giants or gods. But in person they're petite, fragile, like fine crystal, glittering and wonderful. Yet it's clear the instant you see them in person that they have to be treated with great care, with delicate caution, or they might break, shatter in your very hands. And if that happens, you know you'll be the one left bleeding.

"Do you want to play Piano Wonders with me?" Abbey said.

"Is it a board game?" Saragossa smiled.

"No, silly."

"Abrianna," Mrs. Molinaro said, "this officer is not here to play with you, honey. I am sure she is very tired. It's late. I'm sure she wants to go home now." Her light and melodic voice, her slight Italian accent, made even the dismissal sound lovely.

"Oh. Um…he didn't tell you?" Saragossa asked. "I'm supposed to stay."

"Stay?"

"I mean, if that's all right with you—"

"Oh, yay! Can she, Momma? Pleeeeease!"

"Quiet, Abrianna," Mrs. Molinaro said. "Explain, please."

"With everything going on…the war…the Stranger…the crowds in the city…I've been assigned to protect you. To protect Abbey."

"Is there something I should know?"

"Ma'am?"

"Some situation? A specific danger?"

"Uh, no, ma'am. I'm sorry. It's just a precaution is all. I understand you don't usually allow bodyguards or personal protection, but the mayor, he—"

"I see. And how, exactly, do you know my husband?"

"I don't, ma'am. I just met him tonight."

"Tonight?"

Saragossa nodded. "I was assigned just an hour ago. Because of my work in the park, with his sister, I think. But he did ask me to pass on a message."

"Oh?"

"He said to tell you he loves you."

Mrs. Molinaro blushed. Now she took a step closer, extended a hand, and said, "How rude of me…come in. Please. I'm Sophia…"

Saragossa extended her hand. "Melinda Saragossa. But, please, call me Lindy."

Be still, Saragossa thought, as the butterflies fluttered inside.

CHAPTER 10

The night has gone cold, Stone thought. Some in the crowd had started slowly for home, having realized they had no chance of getting close to the Stranger or the healing fountain. The invisible barrier had receded to the shore of the Point, and on the Ramble side, it remained in place all the way to the tree where Breckenridge had hung himself. And NYPD barricades now kept everyone at a distance from the Angel of the Waters, so, yeah, nothing to see here. Generators shut down. Lights out. Show's over.

Even Governor Brandt had disappeared into the shadows of the arcade with his cadre of personal bodyguards: state troopers. Before he'd left, though, he'd gone on and on, saying he'd watched the "phony film" and asserted Jeremiah and Stone and the Stranger "were in this together." He'd promised Stone there'd be "hell to pay" for withholding information regarding the whereabouts of "that blind faker."

Brandt had seemed surprised by the public's huge reaction to the story, and by its instant embrace of the Stranger. He's miscalculated, Stone thought. And now he's on the wrong side of the biggest story to come along in maybe two thousand years.

Stone assumed Brandt was pissed too, by the mayor's refusal to turn the park over to him. Jack Molinaro had taken a "wait and see" attitude toward the Stranger, in spite of Brandt's press conference as- sertion that anyone who was not with America in this war was against us, including this "bedsheet-draped, charlatan foreigner everyone's comparing to Jesus."

The mayor and Brandt. Those two are in a political war, Stone thought. And now the world is in a military war, and all the world's people are in a spiritual one too.

And things had gotten even more complicated for the new gov- ernor, personally, as well. His son, Rikki, had come to the park. And Rikki had demanded to stay. Even he believed in the power of the Stranger. So rather than make a scene and give the media any hint of the dissension within his own family, Brandt had quietly patted the slumping shoulder of his ailing, wheelchair-bound son, kissed him on the top of his head, and left him in the care of a private nurse and two uniformed state troopers. "See what you've done," Brandt had whispered into Stone's ear. "Even my boy insists," he'd explained in angry whispers to Stone, "there's a possibility of being healed. That's the worst of it, you see? What you and your Stranger have done. Raising false hopes." Brandt had then crushed his soggy cigar stub on the bricks and stomped off.

Now young Rikki Brandt sat in the front row of a crowd of hun- dreds of the sick and dying—young boys and girls, middle-aged men and women, and the aged and decrepit—bused in and accorded a special area, set up at Mayor Jack Molinaro's direction, especially for them. Some sat in wheelchairs; others swayed on crutches or lay in gurney beds or simply sprawled on blankets on the damp lawn or in tents behind the barricades. Many strained to see across the lake, and obviously hoped for the reemergence of the Stranger.

At 2:00 a.m., the news teams started taking naps in shifts. Connie was the first from Stone's team to take a break. At 4:00, Stone went next. He curled up on a soft patch of turf—just off the terrace, but close beside the press pit area—folded his arm under his head for a pillow, and yawned.

He recalled two events: The first one, when the light on the wings of the bronze angel had transfixed him and Saragossa while they stood on the Point. And the second, when the Stranger had appeared and everyone present had knelt and gone quiet and still. Now Stone silently tried to relive every nuance of what he'd felt and experienced so he could recognize it coming again—if it ever did come again. The reporter in him needed to do so. It could give him an edge. One he would need now that the story was out and every reporter on the planet had come crowding into *his* park to cover it.

He thought about the scroll and wondered what Jeremiah had done with it after translating it and positing its contents to the Internet.

Stone faded off and lost himself in a dream of walking on the water of the lake.

"Aaah-maaay...zi-ing grace...how sweet the sound..."

Stone, awakened by the song, slowly got to his feet, stretched off the stiffness, and shook off a chill. He had no watch but knew his two hours were long since up. He searched the crowd for the source of the voice. The melody of his favorite devotional lifted his spirits. Sung with such heartfelt emotion. Lovely. Otherworldly. Ah, there...a skinny old black woman with silver hair wearing a full-length black wool jacket.

He turned to the press pit. "Mike?" He stepped over the perimeter wall and walked toward the press pit. "Mike," he shouted.

Mike waved. Stone pointed. Mike nodded and raised his camera to get a shot of the old woman. She now pressed herself against the barricade behind the fountain, not far from Rikki Brandt, and really belted out the lyrics with homegrown Harlem soul.

"…that saved a wretch like me…"

That crazy old lady looks just like my granny, Stone thought. But that voice. My God. It's the voice of an angel.

Stone stood beside Connie and Mike now, and he turned to face east, toward the Point. Dawn broke. He checked his cell phone: 5:56 a.m.

The Stranger's humble shelter had remained softly visible throughout the night. It would have been impossible to see were it not glowing with some source of light from within. Tucked neatly behind the few saplings in a clearing on a ridge that lay just paces from the water's edge, it shone like a lamp, lighting up the world with hope, though its glow was now softer than before.

Stone smiled as some of the folks who had decided the time had come to get ready for their jobs—it was Tuesday morning—turned around and returned to the terrace on hearing the song. In fact, now many others had joined in.

"Amazing grace…" The sweet chorus of thousands rose.

People on the surrounding hills held up cigarette lighters, raised candles high, and swayed with flashlights and cell phones as if at a concert. Many of the sick and bandaged and bleeding, the kids hooked up to IV tubes, those wheeled in, or rolled in on gurney beds, and many among the old and infirm and dying now sang along too. Even the cops began to move to the sound of the old lady's song, and soon nearly everyone assembled started swaying as if filled with pure love, as if all were one. And in voice, they surely were. And when the old lady smiled a big smile and started again, taking it from the top, even Stone joined in.

"I once was lost…but now am found. Was blind…but now I see…"

And the Stranger's cardboard enclosure suddenly flashed, and a hush came over the crowd.

"Mike?" Stone asked, surprised by the internal sensations taking over his body.

"Yeah," Mike said, scrambling to get into position. "I feel it too."

"We've only got a minute, and we won't be able to stand."

"What?" Connie asked.

"One minute!" Stone told her.

"I'm on it!" Mike said.

The other news teams took their cue from Stone's team and scrambled for their equipment. Generator engines started again. Lights hummed to life. Police helicopters swooped in and hovered closer now, but they had to stand off, for the invisible barrier was expanding. Connie called the studio and alerted them to be ready. She handed Stone a microphone and an earpiece and said, "We got the satellite truck in position while you were asleep." Then she gestured to Mike, who raised the camera. Stone said, "Check. Check." Mike gave a thumbs-up. They had audio—a good level—and they had a live feed.

Connie said, "We're on in five…four…three…" cueing Stone with one hand, counting down with her fingers. And now a low mist came rolling down from the woods behind the Point; it grew and spread and drifted onto the still, dark waters of the lake, even as a heavy band of clouds darkened the rising sun.

"What the hell?" Connie said.

"We still have our feed," Mike said. "And the camera still works."

A collective "ahhhhhh!" arose from the crowd, the voices of thousands in unison, all of whom—on the grass and the hills and in the woods and behind the barricades—had waited all night for this moment. Thousands now strained on tiptoes, hoping to catch a glimpse of the Stranger.

Another flash, and a sudden, silent pulse of energy greeted everyone. It bathed the terrace and the fog-shrouded lake in a soft, magical glow. And now, from the center of the brilliance, the Stranger emerged, in flowing white robes. He stepped onto the surface of the water across the lake on the Point. He glowed, enveloped in a halo of gold and sapphire and emerald and pink.

Another gasp arose, as if all the onlookers possessed a single consciousness. The Stranger's brilliance gently softened. The German shepherd came to his side, also walking on the water. And now the sun broke through the clouds on the eastern horizon, as if to greet him; he lifted his gaze and smiled, and he raised his arms as if to give praise to God for a new day. Now his halo suffused the wispy, wandering fog, and the fog became a rainbow of red and orange and yellow and emerald and purple and gold, and the colors spread onto the surface of the lake and sparkled as if paving a solid path of light on the waters at his feet as he approached the terrace.

"Stone?" Connie said. "Say something. You're li—" But it was too late. Stone had gone silent. Everyone had: the police officers, the reporters and cameramen, the thousands crowded on and around the terrace. And now everyone knelt. Mike kept filming, as he had on the first day, and the other crews did too. But none could move from their places, nor utter a single audible word.

The Stranger paused between the two shores and stood, with the German shepherd at his side. His hands hung at his waist now, and he turned them out, facing forward, as Stone had seen depicted in painted marble icons of Christ in countless churches. And now the Stranger raised his hands to his heart and pressed them together in prayer and closed his eyes.

Stone expected the fountain to glow again, as it had for Jeremiah. He expected another miracle. But no light came. Only sound. A voice. *That* voice. The one that had so moved him, and had moved thousands to sing as if in one voice, one prayer.

"I come to say thank you. That's all," said the old woman in the long wool coat who had led them to this moment by so beautifully singing "Amazing Grace." She alone could speak. She alone could stand.

She walked around the barricade that encircled the sick and dying, came toward the edge of the terrace, toward Stone, and kept repeating, "I come to say thank you. I love you, Lord. Thank you. Thank you, dear God. I love you. Thank you…"

Beside Stone, at the edge of the lake, the old woman stopped. The step down…it's too much for her, Stone thought.

The Stranger opened his eyes, held out his hand, and smiled. He said, "Come."

And now the Stranger's eye fell on Terry Stone.

No, he thought. Not me.

No. No. No. Not me! He's not inviting me!

In spite of himself, Stone stood. Microphone in hand, he went to the old woman and took her arm.

"Thank you, son," the old granny said sweetly, giving him a gentle pat on the arm.

"What is your name?" he asked, fighting the fear inside, a fear that wanted to paralyze him, force him to his knees, and render him silent once more. But the look of love cast his way by the Stranger gave him faith and helped him overcome the fear.

"Ruthie," she said.

"Thank you, Ruthie," he said. "It was your song. You brought him back to us."

Ruthie smiled and nodded. "Maybe," she said. "Or maybe it was your faith." Her eyes sparkled, and she stepped down, taking Stone with her. He'd helped her to step onto the sparkling surface of the water, and his own feet had also found the lake. He stood on the water, and it was solid.

"My God," he said. "No. I'm not worthy. I can't." He released her and retreated back to the terrace bricks. He stood, bewildered and shaking, as Ruthie shuffled slowly forward, even while glancing back at him and gesturing for him to join her.

Stone wanted to go. The eyes of the Stranger seemed so loving, so inviting. The way was clear, open to him. But he could not.

Ruthie turned toward the Stranger again, and as she crossed the little distance to him, the thickening fog fully enveloped them both. Then, in a flash, it disappeared, and Ruthie and the Stranger were gone.

People rose from their knees and began to shout and whistle and applaud.

"Did we get it?" Connie couldn't contain herself. "Did we?"

"Oh, yeah," Mike said. "We got it all!"

"The light," Stone said. "It's on again, inside." Stone gestured to the Point. A tear ran down his cheek, and he fell to his knees and covered his face and cried.

CHAPTER 11

THOMAS C. BRECKENRIDGE III HAD DESCENDED INTO SOME DEEP level of Hell where, as punishment, he'd been sentenced to tell what he and his "boys" had done in the park. Tell it *and* see it *and* relive it too, all at the same time, over and over and over again, endlessly.

Over and over and over again.

Tell it and see it and do it.

Tell it and see it and do it, over and over and over again!

He had relived the entire event what seemed a million, maybe a billion times already, over and over again, so now he just wanted to break out. To run. To die in Hell even, in order to avoid hearing or seeing it ever again. But it was too late—the hearing and seeing and reliving had looped back to the beginning again, and the telling of the tale in his own a voice had started once more:

The night was all full up with an unseasonable fog, thick enough to muffle any screams and deep enough to dull down the light of the full moon by half or more. But as far as ole Tommy was concerned, it had been wasted. Not till just before dawn did the little blonde jogger finally come along, and by then the mist had thinned, and Tommy's patience with it. Such was reflected in the ferocity of the blow he dealt. A fat, seasoned branch with its flaking bark whooshed like a whiffle ball bat that—"surprise, surprise"—came alive with the sweet sound of a genuine Louisville slugger on contact: *Crack!* She went down with a thud, flat on her back, feet together, arms stretched out to the sides, like a lady Christ ready for the nails.

"Home run!" Ole Tommy-boy held out his stick as if pointing proudly at the fences. Rye and Tivo and Sister Sioux scampered out from their hiding spots in the woods, their hands in the air waving triumph, and then they all pranced around her on tiptoes and circled her like her four limbs were bases and Tommy had grand slammed in the bottom of the ninth, game seven.

"Wooo-whooo!" Tivo whooped. "We got us a *hot* one!"

"Sure do," said Sister Sioux, standing over her. "Sure enough do."

Rye gave her a poke in the ribs with his bum foot, the way he'd once done to a belly-shot doe in the west Tennessee woods. "Gotta watch 'em," he explained with all due seriousness to Sister. "Sometimes they look done for, but they's just waiting till you let your guard down. Then they give you a good kick." He smirked in satisfaction, his mouth showing a gleam of gold, and then he nudged her again, pinned the back of his right Reebok with the toe of his left, peeled off the shoe, and commenced a little foot fondle, making a small circle on her breast as if he were testing its viscosity or something.

But she was out. Didn't so much as twitch.

Her eyes were tearing badly, and a little blood wandered out of that split-in-two freckled button nose of hers. Tommy bent for a closer look, and he figured most likely the better part of the flow was unseen and going down her throat because of her position. So when a little voice inside his head said he should roll her over, he did. He shoved Rye back, grabbed her arm, and tugged her onto her side so she wouldn't die of gagging.

She retched and convulsed and coughed out a spattering of crimson, but then her breathing settled down to a nice, regular pace, and that's when Tommy told himself he'd done a good deed by turning her.

Yup. A good deed, indeed.

And now he bent real close, and, with the help of a soft spot in the fog that let through the light of the full moon, he made a more thorough inspection. A whole lot of blood had flowed out the back of her head from when she'd hit the pavement, and that fine yellow hair of hers looked dark at the roots now, like she was maybe a bottle blonde, and this idea aroused a suspicion she might not be a natural, and if she was or she wasn't, Tommy grew more and more eager to find out. "Um-hmm," he said at the time, and he went moving on. "A tight little piece too, for sure. Probably would have been a fighter, had I given her the chance."

And yet she had a softness, a sweetness about her that made him a little sorry for having taken such a big swing.

"Too pretty to be running around the park all alone before dawn, little one," he said, getting down on all fours and bending close to her ear to say it. He ran the back of two fingers up and down her bare arm, slowly, raising goose bumps and making her full lips part enough to show a little hint of her tongue poking out between them nice, white front teeth of hers. Tommy began to swell with excitement. "Sugar, sugar," he said and smiled, wetting his own lips with a lick. "Sa-sa-sweet."

"Would have been a lot sa-sa-sweeter if you hadn't gone and crushed her goddamn face, Ta-Tom-Tom," Rye now dared to say.

"I'll cut your tongue out, you mock me!" Tommy shouted and leaped to his feet. Ta-Tom-Tom was a childhood nickname, a way to demean Tommy for his stutter, and on hearing it, the sting of all the lashings he took on account of that stammer came rushing right into him. "Take it back," he shouted. The lashings were because the people of the Breckenridge clan were people of the Book. And people of the Book believe: You spare the rod, you spoil the child. And not sparing it had worked on Tommy too. Any damn fool could see that. Even as big a damn fool as Rye.

Tommy drew out and flicked open a Rush knife in one quick move and took a thrust at his cousin's face with the point of the blade, forcing Rye to stumble back.

"Holy Christmas, Tommy-boy," Rye said. "Calm down!"

"Oh, I'm calm, all right," said Tommy as he sliced through the air again, waving the blade and barely missing his cousin's top lip.

Rye lurched back once more and fell to his butt, and he went scrambling backward like a boy playing crab soccer in a middle school gymnasium. But Tommy stepped on one of Rye's feet and halted the retreat. All Rye could do was hold up both hands and stretch his fingers wide to show he had no weapon and wanted no quarrel.

But it didn't matter. Tommy wanted revenge for the mocking.

"I was wrong," Rye pleaded. "I crossed the line saying it. I did, Tom. I'm sorry. Truly I am. Real, really sorry!"

Tommy bent down to look Rye square in the eye, then turned over his knife hand and the blade with it, showing how he was going to fillet Rye and smile while doing it. Then he pulled the blade up high and changed his grip, ready to strike his cousin in the neck.

"I *said* I was sorry!"

"Ah, he's just as dumb as an ole stump fool," Sister said, shoving Tommy away. "He don't mean nothing by it, little brother. Let him be."

Tommy glared at Sister and then sighed. "All right, then," he said. "I guess there's better things to do." And the better thing, well, she was getting cold, and cold didn't work for Tommy, no way, no how.

No, sir. Cold didn't work at all. So he folded the blade and slid it into the back pocket of his jeans and went back to the more interesting tussle. As he did, Tommy had to concede—only to himself, of course—Rye's disappointment was kind of understandable, seeing as how Rye was the one among them who had a thing for pretty faces.

Yeah, he liked to do the foot fondle and all, and he always started his rendezvous in the "ta-ta" terrain, but it was the face of a woman that stirred up and sustained ole Rye's passions.

Some like some parts. Others, others. That's what Tommy's own pa always said on nights such as these, like he and the boys were just divvying up a bucket of deep-fried chicken.

Rye bent down for one more look at the jogger's face. "Damn," he said.

Tommy shot him a disapproving look.

"I'm just saying!"

But Rye had projected that displeased tone he'd learned from their aunt May. A pathetic and sorry tone it was too, and it told Tommy that Rye must be deeply and genuinely disappointed. So now, feeling like he might have overreacted a bit, Tommy decided to concede the point. "Yeah," he said. "I guess you're right. She is a bit of a mess."

Admitting it was a way of making amends. True too. With the swelling setting in fast, her face turning colors, one eye all but closed up, and blood clotting in her split-open nose, the little gal's good looks, face-wise at least, were getting harder and harder to appreciate. "But see here," said Tommy, feeling the need for a defense, "with the fog going thin like it had, I couldn't take no chances on her letting go a yelp or putting up a fight. I had to hand it to her once, but good."

"You sure did, oh boy, oh boy," said Rye, kicking at some loose leaves on the paved path. "You sure did."

Sister Sioux made matters worse by going over to Rye and laying a hand on his back and saying, "I'll take your share, son. No worries." Then, for emphasis, she roughed up ole Rye's hair like he was a pup. Then Sister proceeded to bend herself over the bride-to-be. That's what they'd call them when joking around beforehand—the bride-to-be. "Just gonna take a quick gander at that tight little bottom," she said.

But Tommy knew better. Sister liked to take her time, grabbing a squeeze here and sliding a hand down and in there, and before you knew it she had opened a razor and sliced the little blonde's shirt and bra off, and was tugging on them pink shorts and little flesh-colored undies, pulling them all the way down and clean off one leg.

"Step aside," Tommy finally said. "I'm the one who swung for the fences, which means I get the first visit to the dugout." He flung the jogger right over his shoulder, like a fresh sack of steel-cut oats, and headed downhill.

She sure feels good up there, folded over and warm against me.

It made him aware of his own size too, and he had a sudden rush of pride in his manly strength. He carried her toward the lake without so much as breaking a sweat.

I might not be as tall as some, but I'm still twice as fearless as most.

Yes, sir. I'm a man's man.

And the shade of his eyes—though more gray than his favorite color, deep blue—had enough specks of blue in them to charm even himself when he looked in the mirror. Framed by thick, black hair that fell long on each side, and set deep into dark, long-lashed sockets, Tommy's eyes were his biggest source of pride.

So bright, they seemed to be lit from behind.

Hell, my eyes are downright magical!

Not many men could look at them without blinking, and all but a few women ever failed to be charmed by them.

All but a very few.

Tommy found that fact quite pleasing about now, because the blonde had begun to stir, and soon they'd be face-to-face and he'd make her look right into them. So all in all, he felt sure he was right to be satisfied with the hand he'd been dealt in life. And except for them lashings, he wouldn't change a thing.

Not a one...

He approached Bethesda Terrace with his prize flung over his shoulder and turned toward the three willows by the shore of the lake, heading for a nice spot he'd picked out earlier in the evening for just such a purpose, when a shooting star fell to Earth and caught his eye, streaming through the moonlit fog. 'Course, he didn't think nothing of it at the time.

Anyway, he and the boys had been up on the hill, about ready to give up for the night and catch a subway back to Brooklyn, when this pretty little filly with the bouncy ponytail had come along and changed their minds. Come up from Munford, Tennessee, they had, about six months earlier. It's not what you'd call a town, more a collection of shacks and trailers, a couple miles north of the Memphis city limits. They'd come on account of some work they'd gotten through "the friend of a friend." Kept them good and busy too, the work had, for a nose hair shy of a year. But that was a full month ago now, a month of spending and not earning. So they'd decided they'd had enough of the Big Apple and were packing their bags for the bus ride home. But before they hopped aboard, a thought had occurred to Tommy: With the Labor Day weekend upon them and all, why not "do 'er up good" one last time before heading back? Party like you can only party when you ain't in a town where the folks all know you.

So they did. They started by slamming before they left Brooklyn, needles under the tongue, hardly left a mark. It didn't break any of their pa's rules either: they never used while working, and never worked while using, and since they weren't working, they *were* using, and they were justified too. "Hell," Tommy had said, "we earned us a little recreation."

So, high as kites without tethers, they got on the F and right away started talking up how they was "gonna head up to Central Park and end this here 'adios New York, hasta la vista' fiesta with a bang."

All they needed was a pretty bride-to-be.

That's all.

Just one.

About an hour before midnight, they had climbed the stairs at the Fifty-Seventh Street stop, walked into the park, and made their way down to the Loeb Boathouse, having heard you could always find a whole herd of lonely city women down there. In Tommy's experience, wherever a man found a herd of lonely women, he always found a stray. And picking off a stray was easy. But once there, he saw straight away there were too many lights, and one or two cops too many to make it even a 50/50 proposition of getting what they'd come for without getting caught. "Oh, well," Tommy had told the boys. "That's how it is on Friday nights. Friday nights, they stretch on into Saturday mornings before anybody notices, on account of the fact folks ain't in no mood to go on home, at least not until they get what they come for." Tommy and the boys weren't any different. Since they had not yet gotten what they'd come for, they took a nice long stroll, looking for a solitary traveler, a stray from the herd, a bride-to-be, and kept it fun by passing a flask of Jack and climbing on the big rocks and howling at the moon.

After a while of walking the foggy footpaths of the park, though, they'd ended up pretty close to where they'd started, back by the bricks of Bethesda Terrace, a stone's throw from Loeb Boathouse, but still far enough away to be out of sight of the cops, especially with the help of the fog.

Sometimes, Tommy had told the boys, you could get lucky and come upon a pair of lovers in there, catch them in the middle of you-know-what in the shadows, and it was always an easy score, for sure. So they'd gone down to the terrace and hung out a while, sitting on the old stone benches, lighting a pipe and passing it, using up the last of their rock, admiring the birds carved into the staircase railing walls and hoping for a bride-to-be. Then, feeling all warm and charged up again, and too juiced to be sitting and waiting, Tommy had decided he'd make good use of the time. He'd gone on a recon and picked out a soft spot by the lake in case a bride-to-be did come, and he found another spot off the beaten path, in case they got a fighter and had to take things to the woods. But after too long a wait and no bride-to-be—and the booze running out and the meth all gone—they were getting tired and cold and a little mean. So up the path they went, heading away from the terrace, resigned to giving up the hunt. That's when the little blonde had come ambling along with a nice rhythm, prancing like a Shetland pony; small but strong, fit and supple, looking to Tommy like the type of a ride that was secretly eager to get back to the paddock and the care of the stable boys.

Yes, sir, when Tommy saw her, it was like a lit match fell on dry hay: *boom*. He was as hot as a barn-burning flame. So he took himself that big swing and *crack!* And now she lay over his shoulder, and he was walking on the very same patch of soft lawn in the little clearing right close to Bethesda Terrace and the fountain, the one he'd picked out while scouting during those cold and lonely hours a bit earlier—picked out because the soft, thick sod would be nice and easy on the knees. And because the lake was right there too, so when they were done with her, they had a place to dump her. Roll her right into the lake with only the weeping willows watching.

With the fog going thin here and there and the full moon bright as a prison searchlight, he could see even better now. He thought, this is a good spot indeed. Plenty of cover on the down slope of the hill. Cover all around. Yeah, save on the one side. But that side is all water, nothing but lake, and the boats down there by the boathouse are all tied in their slips until 9:00 or 10:00 a.m., so all four sides are safe and sound, at least for a little while, which is all this here little one is going to take.

And he especially liked the weeping willows by this particular shore—though he couldn't say why they were called weeping. And while he wondered, the hanging branches of the middle tree, the one he stood under, shed some of their long leaves. They fell on him and her like butterflies dying in midair that came spinning down to the earth. And now his feet sank into the soft, cool turf, and his heart sank too. His little bride-to-be felt kinda cold.

Maybe I took too big a swing after all, he thought.

He set her down in the silky grass, supporting her like a grand-mama supports the head of a newborn. "There, there," he said. "You hang in. I won't be but a minute…" And he began his preparations. And when he was ready, Tommy directed the boys to form a little half circle, a "man fence," between him and the terrace. He knew Bethesda was a popular place, so he figured it was good to have the boys stand between him and it, as a kind of insurance, to give a little extra cover in case some early-morning tourist or another break-of-day jogger came along. Seeing the three men standing on the lawn looking to-ward the lake, they'd likely keep on going if they did come, Tommy figured. And he'd be flat down on top of the bride-to-be, unseen. And the fog still hung pretty low, thick on the water and along the shore too, so it seemed unlikely he'd be spotted anyway. And even if somebody did spy all of them on the little patch of damp green, Tommy told himself that with the bride-to-be being so quiet and all, and not giving off no fuss, any passerby would likely figure it was just a good time being had by all, and they'd keep on their merry way.

"People do like to mind their own business, you know," he'd al-ways told the boys. "You can count on it. And nobody of no character likes to intrude, uninvited, on another man's good time. No, sir."

And as for the boys, well, they *liked* to watch. And Tommy didn't much mind having them doing it. Nope. He didn't much mind if they stood by and looked on.

However, he was in no mood for no stranger to have a look. Nope.

That was a surefire way to spoil the whole thing as far as Tommy was concerned. And just as he had gotten ready to get to it, a premonition crossed his mind, big and bold: some strange somebody *is* coming.

Upset his mood too, it did. So Tommy looked around one last time, to make double sure they were not being watched by no stranger passing by, only he paid more attention now, and he probed the shadows and fog. And yup! Sure as crow shit falling from a cornfield sky and splattering on a freshly washed pickup windshield, out of the fog by the lake rose a strange, dark-skinned man in glowing white robes, looking like a wisp of the wind and floating up from beyond the bank like a ghost.

"What the hell!" Tommy jumped up and shouted.

When he got to the bride-to-be, the strange, glowing stranger in white suddenly stopped, like the now-gone-cold little one on the turf was a layin' right in the middle of his migratory path or something. Like somebody had put up a roadblock. Like…like… "Ba-boys!" Tommy said. "Hey, boys! Take him down, now. Go on, ga-ga-get him!"

But the boys didn't move, nor blink, nor make a bird's chirp. Nope.

They were dumbstruck. Hypnotized. So Tommy had his first clue this here strange dark-skinned, glowing stranger was not *just* what you'd call any ordinary stranger nor passerby. Nope. Not *just* a stranger at all. And yet he was surely as strange a stranger as Tommy had ever seen!

"Damn it," he barked. "Tivo! Sister! Hey, wake up!" But speechless they were and speechless they remained, and stone still too, all three of them, their mouths open and their eyes fixed wide, stunned by the mere sight of this…whatever you call it—Stranger!

Tommy pulled up his drawers and zipped up and marched over and gave Rye a wake-up shove to the chest. Then he insisted again, in a loud, commanding voice, "Snap out of it, damn it. We got us four against one!"

But the boys started backing up, retreating real slow, like they'd seen something they'd never seen before and didn't ever again want any part of, nope, not ever again. And they surely were not willing to hang out there with him anymore. No, not there, not now, nor at any other place nor time ever in all time. They backed up and kept backing up all the way to the paved footpath, and even then they still kept going until they stood on the red bricks of Bethesda Terrace by the Angel of the Waters fountain. And all the while, their eyes stayed glued on the eyes of the glowing Stranger.

"Boys," Tommy called out as they went, standing his ground. "Ah, hell. Boys! Where y'all going?"

Nothing.

He turned and marched back to face the Stranger, and the Stranger smiled at Tommy. Just a smile. Nothing more. And the bride-to-be was still as a stone, almost completely naked and spread out on the lawn between them. And Tommy thought: What in the name of all things holy is this? I mean: What kind of New York Yankee bullshit is going on here, in the middle of my new favorite spot in New York City, on about the perfect night for a hoedown?

"Boys!" He tried once more. "We didn't haul our asses all the way over here on a subway train to see the trip end like this, did we? Boys? Awwww, come on!"

Still nothing.

"Shit!"

Tommy glanced at the Stranger and shouted to them once more, "Why, you boys ain't afraid of this one here, are ya? Why, this one here is just another piece of homeless, New York City trash—" Right then, Tommy's eyes found the Stranger's eyes, and Tommy instantly felt what he figured it must feel like being drunk *and* shot through the throat with a broad-head arrow. Both. Drunk and shot through the throat. At the same time.

A gripping feeling of shock and terror came over him, and with it a loss of breath, like when you're in so much pain, you think you're going to die if you have to take another lash, another blow from a wide, hard, leather strap that keeps coming, cutting into the flesh of your back and buttocks because of your stammer. Like when you have to "take it, one more, for a good purpose: to rid you of your weakness." Only now, Tommy felt like he would maybe die and slide right into the judgment seat this here time, looking into these here eyes, and, worst of all, he knew himself to be, no way, no how, nowhere near ready to meet his maker. "Na-no way."

But he couldn't break off the stare.

Tommy's skin drew back tight on his face, and his lips went thin, and his mouth went desert dry. His legs were like cement bags, and his gut burned with the urgent impulse to run like a hunted fox. But he couldn't so much as lift a foot. He couldn't laugh or cry or even blink. And he felt completely confused. No *man* had ever looked in Tommy's eyes without blinking, no man and certainly no homeless Stranger wrapped up in a white bedsheet!

I don't even know if this *is* a man, he thought.

Maybe this here really is one of them apparitions or a demon or maybe even an angel come to drag me to the Last Judgment.

And the longer he stared at the Stranger, the worse the feeling got, and the more it took him over, until it had so completely filled his head, it felt like he might explode right then and there and fly off in a million itty-bitty pieces because he was starting to believe he was looking into the eyes of God.

Jesus himself!

Ah, hell no!

Then the Stranger reached across and touched his face, real soft, right on the cheek. He put his long, cool, tan-as-the-bottom-of-the-barrel fingers on Tommy's face and smiled.

A pure bolt-of-lightning-too-close-to-the-roof-of-the-outhouse terror rose up inside of him, right alongside a desperate longing to feel something he had never felt before, never in his entire life, and didn't even know he wanted: love.

Love?

Shit! Finally, the Stranger broke it off, and Tommy blinked a few times and gathered his senses, and then he gave the Stranger a good going-over, looked him up and down.

The sheet, cotton maybe, was wrapped around him like a Hindu outfit Tommy had seen in a *National Geographic*. Covered his feet, it did too, hung over them like a wedding dress, only not fancy or frilly. Which explained it, the look of floating. And wherever his skin was not covered, the Stranger shimmered like the silvery backwaters of a Mississippi bayou when the sun is low. Not black-black, more a deep purple, like one of those fancy special-mix shades you paint on a hot rod—with little flecks of silver that make even the darkest paint glisten bright. Only, when you looked at him, you got the feeling you get when you shake your head too hard after throwing back a double shot of Jack: whoa!

Now, as challenging as this was for ole Tommy to comprehend, the Stranger's wide, bright eyes had him even more dumbfounded. When Tommy looked again into his cobalt-blue saucers, that dizzy, head's-a-spinnin', going-to-die-and-meet-the-maker feeling kept building and building inside him again. But he had no choice about it: he *had* to look right into 'em. It was like his own were cold steel balls and the Stranger had magnets in those sockets of his!

But he didn't want to look no more. No, sir. He didn't like it. So now he had no choice except to close them—his own eyes, that is. He mustered all the power he could out of a strong desire to get the upper hand, and he blurted out the only thing he could think of: "*What* the *hell* do you think you're doing?"

But the Stranger still didn't say a word. Not a word. He lifted his chin and looked over his shoulder in a gesture Tommy took to mean he should look over there too. And across the misty waters, where the fog still hung thick, a little peninsula stuck out like a finger into the lake. Tommy knew it as the Ramble, the part of the park where the homosexuals went to play.

"You're kidding me, right?"

The Stranger made no reply. Instead, he gestured again, and Tommy turned again, and this time there was some kind of shelter on the far shore there, not more than fifty yards of fog-covered lake water away. Best Tommy could tell, even squinting to see, the Stranger had made himself a house out of cardboard or something over there, covered it with leaves and vines. Hard to say how big, though, tucked between the trees and thick bushes and all. Hell, if not for the light glowing inside it, and the Stranger showing where to look, Tommy would never even have seen the sorry thing.

No one would have.

Taking all this into account, and feeling deeply uneasy about those eyes—and the strange glow of the Stranger's skin, and his strange smile—Tommy started to have second thoughts. If this here Stranger stood here doing nothing about Tommy preparing to take the bride-to-be, and if he had made his self a neat little cardboard lighthouse in the Ramble, the Sodom and Gomorrah of Central Park, well then...who could he be?

Not the Lord of lords, nor the King of kings, right?

Tommy scratched his head and looked down to avoid them strange eyes, wondering if maybe the Stranger had started tweaking, because he kept on smiling and staring at him like a lovestruck…or maybe deaf and dumb…or even a mentally touched—hey! That was it.

Yeah. This here Stranger is touched!

Now Tommy had clearly been brought up better than to be cruel to folks not born with all their faculties and facilities, but still, it was possible maybe he really was, you know, one of them head cases. And that *would* explain it.

Them people did make him nervous. Just like this one made him nervous.

He couldn't look *them* people in the eye either.

Sure! Tommy told himself he'd been wrong about who this here Stranger was—who he *really* was might just be one of them touched-in-the-head folks. "Uh-huh," he said aloud, confirming his conclusion to himself, nodding to reassure himself, and thinking the touched Stranger might be pretty easy to get rid of if this was the case. So Tommy put on a real loud voice, conjured up as much authority of tone as he could, and laid it on thick too, mostly for the sake of the boys, who still stood as frozen as an ice pop on the far edge of the terrace but well within earshot. Yup. Tommy would show them how a leader deals with the likes of such a one as this. He took in a big breath and shouted, "All right, you," but he turned his head and so as to project his shout toward the boys. "If that's where you're going," he said, looking and pointing toward the boathouse and the way to the Ramble, to the left and down the path, "then you *git* going!"

Well now. Wonder of wonders! When he said it firm and strong, and he stood aside and gestured the way out, the Stranger gave him one last smile and stepped right over the no-longer-breathing and surely now stone-cold-dead bride-to-be.

Thing is, something else happened too: in the instant that the Stranger stepped over the bride-to-be, a flash of light stunned Tommy and took his sight for a moment, and he shut his lids as tight as he could. No. Tighter. He said, "Damn my soul…" And when Tommy opened his eyes and shook off the blindness, he realized to his delight that the bride-to-be had come back to life!

Sure enough, she'd curled onto her side and started coughing!

Eyes still a bit blurry, he rubbed them and thought about the Stranger. "What the hell are you?" Tommy muttered.

Next he eyed the bride-to-be, and she looked good. Real good. And he thought: Maybe this here night is gonna be salvaged after all. Maybe.

Tommy turned to make sure the Stranger was still going on his way, but…damn. He'd turned right, not left, and gone to the terrace! And now he pushed between Rye and Tivo and brushed by Sister like she was no more than a limp hanging branch on a well-trod trail.

Arrogant. Lacking in respect. Disobeying my command!

Damn you!

Tommy had no choice. He had to do something. Leaders lead. And he was fed up with this strange Stranger—touched or not—so Tommy resolved to put an end to his strangeness. He reached into his back pocket, took out his Rush knife, and headed away from the willow and the groaning bride-to-be and toward the boys and the Stranger and the terrace. He had a good grip and was ready to flick the switchblade open, ready to do what needed doing. And with excitement building, he hurried his pace, keeping an eye on the Stranger as he came alongside the boys. Then he stopped.

He realized something and, well, it definitely changed his mood. The Stranger *was* now walking in a straight line toward his little cardboard lighthouse across the lake—but was apparently unaware that a body of water lay between him and it!

Well, that cinched it. Now he knew *for sure* he was touched. "Check it out, boys!" Tommy laughed and shouted out loud. "It looks like our strange glowing friend wants to make a swim for it."

Yeah, the mood had changed, so Tommy figured, why not make the best of it? "This ought to be fun, huh, Tivo?" he said, giving his cousin an elbow. "I wonder how deep it is."

Tivo did not reply.

"Sis?"

She blinked a few times but said not a word.

"What do *you* think, Rye?" Tommy asked. "Laying any odds on him making it across?"

No reply.

"What the hell, boys?"

Rye just started backing up. And now tears flowed from Sister's eyes, something Tommy had never seen before.

The Stranger paused, just a step or two from the edge of the water, half gone from sight in the white, moonlit fog. He raised a blue veil, covered his head.

Tommy's belly began to burn, burn and churn as the Stranger turned toward him again. The Stranger looked into his eyes again and smiled again. "Da-damn you!" Tommy said. He slid his hand into his pocket and found his blade. He stepped forward, hurried to make up the distance.

The Stranger turned to the lake, back to Tommy, and stretched out his arms. Then he held them down at an angle to his sides with his palms turned toward the lake.

He's talking, Tommy thought.

No, not talking.

Praying.

Praying in some kind of language Tommy didn't speak, yet he knew it was a prayer. Something sharp gnawed at Tommy's insides.

It felt like a team of rats was scratching, trying to get out. He tightened his white-knuckle hold on the knife, but for the first time ever, it gave him no comfort.

Then the moon broke through the clouds and reflected off the lake and onto the Stranger's white robes, and suddenly he had a halo of gold and blue and pink that got brighter and brighter, so it about burned out Tommy's eyes!

"Ma-my God," he said. "You really ain't no Stranger! Ya-ya-you're—"

And fog swirled all around the Stranger, and it came up and around Tommy too. Tommy took a step closer and—finding it hard to breathe again, and feeling sure his head would explode if he didn't figure out what the hell was going on, figure out what the hell he was dealing with, and whom—he wandered a little closer, took another little step, and another. But the Stranger, he started walking again too, straight away from Tommy.

But ole Tommy, he could follow no more.

He had run clean out of brick.

He's walking on the water! Goddamn! He's walking on the water! Tommy stuck a foot in and tried, but sank in and came out wet. Dear God, he thought. Lord, Lord! "I know," Tommy shouted, "I know who you are!" He shouted it again and again, and he felt an anguish he'd never known before, like his soul had been ripped right out of him and all his guts with it.

He turned to run. He wanted to get so far away, he'd forget he'd ever even been to this here city, but then his head lit up, and a crashing sound rang out inside it, and a shocking blow sent his head spinning, and he felt himself falling. He hit the bricks hard, and the ringing came into his head again.

And now the loop started again.

The loop that played over and over in the eternal Hell of his mind.

And he heard his own voice again, and he saw it all over again, and again, and again and again: The night was all full up with an unseasonable fog, thick enough to muffle any screams and deep enough to dull down the light of the full moon by half or more. But as far as Thomas C. Breckenridge III was concerned, it had been wasted... *no!*

And now a fiery sensation clawed its way up his forearm, up the hollow tunnels of his veins. It burned the muscles in his shoulder before tearing around the back of his neck and finding a home in the dark cavities behind his nose and breaking him out of the hellish loop.

The source of the burning sensation inside him flowed through a clear plastic tube attached to a needle sunk deeply in the bruised flesh of his left arm.

He turned his head in a jerk.

A nurse flinched and her eyes went wide, even as she continued to push a plunger to the bottom of a syringe.

I'm not in Hell anymore. It was a dream. "I da-dream-ing. Babad da-ream!"

"You just calm yourself, son," the nurse said. "You're going to be okay."

Now the burning got worse, and his eyes filled with tears. Both of them.

Both?

His free hand found his bandaged face.

No. Not both.

She took one... "She ma-my eye," he said.

In a flash, he remembered the rest: His blade. His knife. His eye, like a chopped grape in his hand. His retreat. Later, his return to the lake. The little blonde had walked on the water with the Stranger in white. He'd seen it!

He'd taken one of the rental boats kept tied up on the shore there for tourists and tried to follow them by water. He'd hit some kind of invisible barrier. He'd gotten out and tried to get to the Stranger's house of light from the Ramble side. To demand help from the miraculous Stranger. The glowing man in white who could walk on water. To get healed. But he could not. And finally, exhausted and covered in his own blood, he'd leaned against a tree and passed out, and it felt as if he'd descended into some deep level of Hell, and as some sort of punishment, he'd been sentenced to tell what he'd done, and see it, and do it too, all at the same time, and over and over and over again, endlessly.

Over and over again!

And when he woke and found himself leaning against that tree again, he couldn't take it anymore. He'd gone mad. And then the rope. He got the rope from the boat and climbed the tree.

The tree…

To Hell with you!

I was just a boy! Ju-just a ba-boy!

To Hell with everything!

Blackness…sweet and endless. But then that damn light again! It wasn't finished with him. It had flashed for him like it had for the bride-to-be, and he had sat up and lied and blamed the Stranger for what had happened, and the EMTs had wheeled him away.

"It's ma-making me sick," he said aloud now. His voice, coarse and raspy, seemed not his own.

"Doctor's orders," the nurse said, pressing the liquid from a second syringe into his IV. Her accent was distinctly Southern. "But I can sneak you some crackers if you like, honey." Her peacefulness, and the color of her skin, brown like an oak tree root, reminded him of the Stranger.

The nurse finished and leaned over to set a plastic basin on his lap. "Just in case," she said. Sickeningly sweet perfume, laid on heavy, as if she'd spilled a full bottle on herself, nearly choked him. He swallowed hard, forcing back the vomit surging into his throat.

She turned for the door.

"Wa-where?"

She wandered back slowly. "What?"

"Wa-where?"

"Where are you?"

He nodded.

"New York-Presbyterian. And lucky to be here too, you ask me."

He rubbed his throat and found a bandage.

"I'm Velma," she said. "If you need anything, you can ask for me. Okay?"

Tommy nodded.

"What do you like being called, son?" she asked. "Is it Thomas?"

He shook his head emphatically, no. "Ta-ta—ta-tom…Tom. Me…" he said.

"Oh. Well, okay," Velma said. "Do you know what happened to you, Tom-Tom?"

"No," he groaned, jaw clenching, fist closing tightly around the sheet. "Not Ta-tom-ta-tom!" He tried to sit up. "Just…Ta-tom…Tom. Me!"

"Okay. Calm down, now, son." The nurse pushed a button and a long, loud tone sounded.

A voice came over the intercom. "Yes?"

"He's conscious," the nurse said, "and a little antsy. Better get somebody in here."

"All right. I'll let them know," the voice said.

"Who?" Tommy asked. "Who…coming?"

"Oh, just some folks, is all. You relax. Okay?" Velma touched his clenched fist. "You're safe here."

He released the sheet. "How…long?"

"How long you been here?"

"Yes."

"Just a day now, give or take."

A day. "The…ma-man," he said. "Stranger?"

"Ahhhh, you remember! Well, he is quite the one, ain't he? They're calling him that: the Stranger. I mean, did you get to meet him and all? That's what everybody wants to know from you, son. Everybody in the whole wide world, I'd say."

"You…sa-saw him?"

"It's all everybody's talking about. All over the TV. All over everywhere. They're not sure if maybe he's from outer space or what. Sci-fi force fields. Walking on water. Healing the sick. Some say he's God's messenger. Others, you know, they're just saying he's Jesus. Sort of looks like him, don't you think?"

Tommy retched and vomited bile into the basin.

Velma handed Tommy a soft paper cup and started mopping him off with a towel. "There, there…take a little sip of water now…"

Tommy choked, and coughed blood. He turned his face toward the sun and looked into it, hoping the golden rays would burn right through his one eye and into his brain and end it all, once and for all. Forever and ever…

"Of course, the governor, you should know, he says the Stranger is 'seditious,' calling for peace and telling folks to turn the other cheek and surrender and all, in time of war," Velma continued. "Says he's responsible for what happened to both of you too."

"Both?" The sun slid between two buildings, and light streamed onto Tommy's face. "No," he said. He raised his hand to shield his eye.

"Okay," Velma said, and she came back beside the bed and touched his arm. "I'll close 'em back up." The nurse moved to close the blinds. "They'll be in to see you now, I assume."

"Who?"

"The governor. The police commissioner. Even Oprah wants to, from what I hear, for God's sake!" Velma laughed. "Everybody. You name it. The whole planet wants to talk to you."

"Wa-why?" He struggled to sit upright, wondered if he had the strength to leave. His head pounded. He felt nauseous again, and he slumped.

"Why, 'cause of what happened to you and Katie. Or do you mean, why the new governor himself? Because he is who he is and he don't leave nothing to nobody but himself. The mayor's going to come too, I bet. Katie was his kid sister, so, you know, it's natural he'd want to know what happened to her. Poor thing. Face all bashed in and all. They brought her in here right after you."

"Ka-katie?"

"Like I said: the mayor's sister."

"His...sister?" Tommy's heart sank. The little blonde was the mayor's sister. He was a dead man walking. Dead man walking. "She's was the ma-mayor's—"

"Sister. Yes."

"The Stranger—it was him. He—he da-did it. He musta—"

"Well, that's pretty unlikely, but that's what they want to find out, 'cause when that little girl came back from that Stranger, she did come back a mess. She's in a coma now. But clinically—" Velma looked around and then leaned close and whispered, "She's dead." The nurse paused, then said, "Mayor wept like a child when he saw her too. This very morning. Just two doors down the hall."

"No," Tommy said. "No..."

"Yes, sir," she said. "True as the gospels. 'Little Katie girl.' That's what he called her. But now, you, you're different. Doctors say you're gonna be right as rain, 'cept for losing that eye, and a painful hoarseness from that rope. And they say your voice will heal up just fine, and in no time at all. Real live miracle you are, don't you think, Mr. Tom-Tom? A real live miracle indeed."

"Da-don't call me Ta-Tom—"

"Is that right?" asked a thick, bald man in a suit as he stepped into the room.

Velma smiled, gestured to the bald man, and half whispered, "That's the new governor I told you about…Denny Brandt." And then she sheepishly left the room.

"Are you? Really?" Brandt asked, and he laughed as he approached. "A miracle—Tom-Tom, is it?"

Tommy clenched his fist, and the pain of all them lashings he'd took on account of that stammer filled him right up with hatred for this fat little man, governor or not, and did so right away quick. "Da-don't…ca-ca-ca—"

"Tom-Tom, huh?" And now another man came in too, and he and the governor crossed the room, smiling like they had a hot tip at the race track, and they stood beside Tommy's bed. "Like a drum?"

"Go ahead, Karl," the governor said.

And now the one called Karl said he was the New York City police commissioner, and he said he had a statement from two EMTs. They said Tommy had told them the Stranger was the one that did this to him, and to Katie Molinaro. And this Karl, he said that was good. Very good. Then he pulled out a plastic evidence bag with a Rush knife in it, dropped it on Tommy's chest, and said, "I think this belongs to you."

CHAPTER 12

"You get a boat in the water, and you get me over there right now," a brash young woman shouted as she pushed her way toward the front of the press pit at the edge of the lake. "If it was your grandma over there," she said, "you wouldn't be standing here in no suit, smiling for the cameras…" She stopped at the barricade, just feet from the platform and the mayor's podium. "You'd be paddling your skinny ass over there right now to get her back!"

Stone moved closer.

Twenty-something. Light skinned. A pink Juicy T-shirt covered by a puffy black down vest. Shiny black boots. Calvins. Smells like…lilacs?

"Hey! Mayor! I'm talking to you!" she shouted.

A real firebrand, Stone thought.

The mayor turned to his press secretary, who a moment earlier had introduced the "Who's Who" of Jack Molinaro's administration, including herself, saying, "As you'll all see in our written statement, this will be my last day…I'm heading home to Texas for a well-deserved break." Now Stone had a face to put with the name of Connie's NYU buddy: Becka. A name and more. Tall, fit, perhaps thirty, with a creamy complexion and big, brown, doe-like eyes,

Becka Ramirez presented quite the counterpoint to the demanding young African-American princess beside Stone. He wondered why on earth this lovely press secretary—and, if rumors were to be trusted, more—would leave Jack Molinaro now.

As Becka mentioned, the throng of world media assembled on Bethesda Terrace for the Tuesday afternoon press conference had yet to receive the mayor's statement, but Stone expected the usual printed press release that invariably included pull quotes from the mayor's as-yet-undelivered official verbal remarks.

Boring.

Why bother coming if all you're going to do is read what you're handing out?

So the cameras can capture it, of course.

Stone hoped for something more. Some truly heart-wrenching words from the mayor about his now hopelessly comatose sister. Some wise words about the now-world-famous website TryChristianity.com, started by the "New Gathering" called for in the scroll itself. The rumor was, Jeremiah was part of it, though Stone had not seen him since he'd given the miracle man the scroll for safe keeping. As expected, Brandt had manipulated a judge to issue a court order demanding it be produced. Stone had told the truth: "I don't have it and do not know where it is."

Now Stone hoped to ask: Did Jack Molinaro agree with the pundits who'd commented on the contents of the scroll posted on the site? Was this the authentic message of Jesus Christ or a perversion of it? And what about Brandt's question: Why didn't the Stranger heal Jack's sister? Did Jack Molinaro want an answer to that question too? And did he agree with Brandt's assessment that the scroll was seditious? Or that the Stranger was "worse than Hanoi Jane?" Were the "New Gathering" members "treasonous traitors and America haters?"

Now, he feared, instead of answers to these questions, they'd be dealing with the firebrand screaming about her grandma.

As Becka returned to the microphone, two mallards swooped in, really low, and Stone and the firebrand flinched. Now the birds spread their wings and splashed feet first onto the lake behind them.

"I give you the mayor of New York City, Jack Molinaro," Becka said. And Stone turned to the podium again.

"No! You have to do something now!" the firebrand shouted, interrupting again.

"You're not press, are you, miss?" Karl Kastleman, the police commissioner, asked, stepping beside the mayor and gesturing to two uniformed officers to get her.

"Hold on, Karl," the mayor said, and then he leaned into the microphone and asked, "What's your name, miss?"

The firebrand hesitated.

"If you're not for real," Stone said softly, "you'd better back off."

"You're pretty easily impressed," she said.

"What?" Stone said.

"With yourself." Her eyes ran up and down his body. "Like you did something last night."

"You pick a fight with everybody you meet?"

"You had any guts, you'd have gone with her."

"Excuse me," the mayor said. "I asked you a question, miss."

"Ruthie Eversbee," she shouted at the podium now. "That's my grandma. And she's old and sick and off her meds, and she needs them now!" The firebrand held up three bottles of prescription drugs like Lady Liberty's torch.

"And you?" the mayor asked again.

"My name's Jessie," she said. "Whatcha say yours was?"

Everybody laughed.

The mallards quacked noisily. Stone turned and came up on tip-toes, and the ducks paddled past the floating yellow buoys the NYPD had set out to mark the edge of the invisible barrier. A safety warning, Stone assumed, for their own patrol boats that floated nearby. And now the ducks had made it all the way to the far shore, like the barrier wasn't even there.

"Mr. Mayor," Stone shouted, suddenly possessed by an idea. "Why not give it a try? Like she said. A boat, I mean. The ducks seem to be able to get through."

The mayor stretched to see over the crowd. His expression changed. Stone eyed him closely. His political gears were obviously turning. This could turn out way better for him than giving a speech, Stone thought. Talk about imagery. Jack Molinaro, the hero kid from Brooklyn, once again comes to the rescue...

Becka bent to whisper something in the mayor's ear.

"You're not afraid, are you?" Jessie shouted.

Ohhhh...Stone thought. Checkmate.

The mayor smiled. "And you," he said, looking right at Stone. "Terry Stone, right? You broke this story?"

"Yes, sir," Stone said smartly.

"Well, good," said the mayor. "Now that we're all on a first-name basis, let's the three of us get in a boat—as you suggested, Mr. Stone—and go over there and see what we can see. We'll pick this up in a few minutes, folks," the mayor said to the rest of the press and the crowd, "after I get a closer look."

Becka left the stage and disappeared from view. The reporters in the press pit began to shift and mill about, turning toward the lake, jockeying for a new position. The crowd, released for the moment to its own devices, stirred. As in a stadium at the seventh inning, many rose and stretched and began to chatter; a little break in the action, then the show would go on.

The mayor motioned to the police commissioner, Karl Kastleman. A few words into a police radio followed. The ducks climbed the shore of the Point, quacked, rustled their feathers, and settled in, soaking up the late-morning sun. The Stranger's makeshift house still glowed, visible in bits and pieces through the trees.

No sign of Ruthie, though, Stone thought. Or the Stranger.

Out of nowhere, SWAT team officers trotted toward the terrace with an eighteen-foot inflatable craft held high above their heads.

The mayor peeled off his jacket and rolled up his sleeves, unknotted his tie, unbuttoned the top button of his shirt, and ran his hands through his famous mop of thick, brown Kennedy hair.

Handsome dude. Stone felt sure he knew it too. And he knew how to stand still while the photographers got their shots.

Connie, back in sight now, beside Mike in the press pit, gave Stone a reassuring nod: they were rolling tape.

As a crowd of tens of thousands packed the terrace and surrounding hills and watched, the SWAT team splashed the craft, and one of the cops boarded. "No. No. No," said the mayor smartly. "This isn't *Band of Brothers*, guys. No guns. No cops."

A cheer rose from the crowd.

"And Mr. Stone will run the boat. He's an ex-Marine. Isn't that right, son?"

"Uh…no, sir," Stone said. "There's no such thing as an ex-Marine."

The mayor laughed and said, "Everybody's a comedian today. Great." He slapped Stone on the back, then gestured to the inflatable and said, "But you do know how to drive one of these things?"

"Yes, sir. Sure do."

The mayor stepped in and parked himself in the bow. Jessie sat in the middle, facing the stern. Stone took the aft bench seat, facing Jessie. "Mr. Mayor, I advise we approach slowly, sir." He handed a paddle forward and took another for himself. Jessie passed the paddle, then absentmindedly fidgeted with her vest zipper, suddenly at a loss for words.

The mayor said, "Okay. Let's do it."

Stone suddenly felt a much deeper appreciation for elected officials, for what they did—had to do, day in and day out—in public, regardless of what they suffered in private. Here's the mayor, Stone thought. His city is the most prime terrorist target in the world—a world on the brink of war—his family's in pieces, his sister's in a coma, his closest political advisor's bailing on him, and he's rowing an inflatable boat across a lake, trying to help some smart-assed college girl who clearly has no respect for him, and with the whole world watching! And most folks are probably hoping for some kind of wreck, like at an Indy 500 race.

Stone pushed off.

The mayor too started to paddle.

The crowd erupted in applause.

Jessie grabbed onto the sides like she was in a failing airplane.

"Can't swim, can you?" Stone said.

She didn't respond.

"Never thought he might ask you along, did you?"

Still no reply.

Stone laughed. "Me either…"

She just ignored him.

Two more mallards swooped low and landed on the water beside them. Sparrows flew about too, able to go back and forth all the way to the Point. And on the Ramble side, squirrels rummaged through the leaves and bounded to and fro as if there were no barrier at all. Yet Stone caught occasional glimpses of the crowd at the far side of the Point by the boathouse, lining the shore all the way around to the terrace. Some looked like mimes, restrained by a force field or whatever it was, as they tried to get closer to the Stranger. His makeshift house stood in view now, though still heavily obscured by trees and brush, about ten feet long by perhaps eight feet wide, made of unfolded boxes patched together and held up by branches. Shafts of light, rays of gold and white and sapphire, shot out in all directions, streaming from the cracks and overlaps as if the cardboard structure housed the sun itself.

The mayor looked over his shoulder and said to Stone, "The barrier…those yellow buoys, right?"

Stone shouted forward, "Yes, sir. Maybe a foot or two inside them, I'd guess is where we'll hit. Or not, if it's down."

"Okay."

"Sir, can I ask you a question?"

"Sure, if it's off the record. And if so, call me Jack."

"Okay. Thanks, sir. I will."

"So what's your question?"

"How has it changed you? The presence of the Stranger, I mean."

They slid past the floating yellow ball.

"I don't know yet," Jack said. "Maybe if I see him with my own eyes, I'll believe. But, again, that's off the record."

"Yes, sir. I mean…Jack."

The rubber boat went *bump* and glanced off to the side. Jessie stiffened and gasped.

"It's still up, but check it out," Stone said. The ducks just kept on going like they had a weekend pass for shore leave.

"Yeah…it's crazy," Jack said. "How?"

"I have no idea. It seems to know if it's people or nature."

"We have to get over there," Jessie said, her voice full of desperation, her eyes tearing. "You have to do something."

"I don't think there's any way to get past the—"

Jessie stood up and almost tipped the boat.

"Hey! Sit down," Stone shouted.

Jessie crouched and crept forward using her hands and knees and feet to brace against the sides.

"Get us closer," Jack said. "I want to try something."

Stone paddled. Jack reached out a hand for Jessie and helped her forward. The boat rocked violently, and she fell into his arms, and the two of them fell into the soft, pillowed bow. A loud, collective "*ahhhhh!*" rose from the shore.

Jack came to his knees, looked back, and waved. People cheered and applauded.

Stone paddled them gently toward the barrier again.

Jack stretched out his arm and reached for the invisible wall. They were about to hit again. "Pull us up against it," he said. His hand lit up with light on contact.

"It's not possible," Stone said. "We can't get through."

"Keep us as close as you can," Jack said.

Stone did. Jack ran his hand up and down, and a charge, like blue-white static electricity, was visible whenever he made contact. He dipped his hand into the lake now to see if the barrier extended below the surface, and when he touched it, it glowed even there.

Jessie pushed alongside him, grabbed him for balance, and stood up again. "Grandma! Are you in there? Granny! Are you all right?"

"Sit down," Stone shouted. "Before you fall in."

She peeled off her down vest and tossed it onto the deck.

"Hey! No. She can't swim," Stone said.

Jack grabbed her wrist and looked at her for confirmation. She tried to bluff, but he wasn't buying. "You'd better sit," Jack said gently. "Like your friend over there says."

"Hey, no," Stone said defensively. "I don't know this crazy chick."

Jessie sat. "Thanks a lot."

"Hold this," Jack said to Jessie, peeling off his watch. Then he took off his shirt and shoes and socks, gave Jessie his wallet and keys, and carefully, but ceremoniously, stood. He paused for a moment, posing, waiting for the press to get their shots, and then, as Stone saw it, New York City's mayor began his comeback: Jack Molinaro dove over the side.

Nicely done…

And the longer Jack stayed under, the more the world press and the thousands of onlookers stirred, waiting for him to resurface.

The people packed on every inch of turf and footpath and brick—and all along the shore, the arcade, and the staircases on either side, and pressed against the barricades behind the fountain, and climbing the trees for a better look—all were fully captivated, breathless.

Great theater.

Man can really hold his breath…

Stone searched the water for a sign, some bubbles, something.

Nothing.

Damn…

The petite young brunette leaped to her feet as he entered the office reception area. "Welcome to the Church of Babylon, *Governor* Brandt." She tilted her head and accentuated the title as if it were some big secret and she was in on it, even though the story of his swearing-in had been all over the news for a day and a half.

I remember this one. Not too bright, Brandt thought. Good.

And now she tossed her shoulder-length hair, flattened her short skirt, and pranced over on tiptoes, jiggling in her plunging red V-neck sweater.

Such enthusiasm. Like a groupie.

"Deacon Hoff will be out momentarily."

She offered her hand. He took it. "Call me Denny," he said.

She pursed her lips and batted her eyelashes, and he took the gestures to be a promise that she would be demonstrably grateful for being on a first-name basis, if given the opportunity.

"In the meantime," she said, "if there's anything I can do. *Anything* at all."

A groupie, indeed… "As a matter of fact," he said. He pulled her close and whispered a filthy suggestion in her ear. Her fingers, still pressed into his palm, twitched at the words, and her cheek warmed against his.

"*Oooooh*," she said. "I'd like that." She giggled.

He released her, and she took her time making her way back to her desk. He noticed that on her way, she checked over her shoulder twice to make sure his eyes were still on her ass.

They were.

In the next room, behind hollow doors, two clearly overeducated men argued. One, with an Irish accent, asseverated firmly: "No religious institution founded on traditions it claims are divinely inspired can accommodate significant changes of doctrine without weakening the very foundations upon which rests its entire future."

"With all due respect, sir, that's not an answer," the other voice said, in an Indian accent.

Blah…blah…blah…Brandt turned the knob, pushed open the door a crack, and pulled out a cigar and clipped an end, letting the stub fall to the floor.

"Let me put it this way, Doctor," the Irishman on the other side of the paper-thin door said firmly. "It is impossible, and in my opinion will remain so for all eternity, for the Catholic Church or any other Christian church to entertain the idea that God's messengers come and go on this planet like they have some kind of a cosmic bus pass, bringing new additions to the Bible. We are his representatives here, and that's that. Clear enough?"

"Yes. Clear," said the Indian. "In your view, Satan, the dark angel, can ride the so-called bus, but not God's messengers, yes?"

Brandt opened the door some more, with his foot. "Did somebody say 'Satan'?" he said through a half cough, half laugh.

"Governor!" Deacon Hoff rushed to greet him. "I'm so sorry. We didn't realize you'd arrived."

"Been too long," Brandt said. He shook the aging deacon's hand with feigned enthusiasm as he surveyed the room. "Place looks as charming as ever…" Dull furniture. Dull lighting. Dull paneling on the walls where there hung the all-too-familiar dull posters: "If you love someone, set them free…" and "That's when I carried you…" with one set of footprints in the sand. Oh, and of course, "Be the change you want to see in the world…" complete with a picture of an emaciated, toothless Gandhi. The kind of junk you find marked down to four dollars in strip-mall card stores and lava-lamp novelty shops the day after Christmas.

Charming indeed.

This particular collection, enshrined in faux-wood frames—as if framing could somehow elevate the dull to profundity—had been dusted perhaps once in the three years since he'd last been here. He'd "saved" the place back then, and saved its deacon too, and Hoff's ten other, larger, but no less rumor-plagued and financially questionable operations. Enough cash had miraculously shown up to pay the late mortgages and the hospital bill for the difficult birth of the premature child of the uninsured and then decidedly underage brunette out front. She had discreetly put her baby, sired by Deacon Hoff, up for adoption immediately, of course. She'd never said a word. The father's name on the birth certificate was left blank. Doctors were hushed. Scandal averted.

Yes. Very discreet.

She could be useful to me, Brandt thought. Very useful indeed.

He smiled. "Sounds like you've started without me," he said, shoving his cigar between his teeth and reaching into his trousers for a light.

The two men whose voices he had heard while waiting outside were now on their feet, awaiting an introduction, along with Hoff and a fourth man. Brandt assessed each, and he immediately intuited the red-faced, gray-haired man was the Irish Catholic priest, his black clothes and white collar making it less of an assumption and more a statement of the obvious.

Man's a goddamn cliché, Brandt thought.

Brandt immediately wondered too about the usefulness of the other two men—one a slightly built, brown-skinned man with frail hands, obviously the source of the Indian accent, and the other, thus far silent, a sloppy Jew, given away by his yarmulke. He wore tan khakis, a wrinkled white shirt, and brown leather boat shoes out of which bulged small, fat feet in thick white socks, bunched at the tongue.

Not promising, Brandt thought. And he needed help. Especially now, given the evidence that "Tom-Tom" had been Katie's assailant. Though he'd already taken care of that, and he was safe as long as Katie didn't wake up from her coma. But the second "miracle," the old woman walking on the water, *that* was far more problematic, and it had left Brandt feeling he needed a little divine intervention himself.

When the story first broke, he'd immediately, emphatically—and, he felt, irrevocably—gone way out on a limb politically and defined the Stranger as someone to be regarded as dangerous. Then he'd called his doctrine and the message of the M-39 scroll seditious. Treasonous. He knew if he changed his tune now, he'd look like a fool.

Worse. Spineless.

So he had no choice, really, if he didn't want to be a laughing stock and give up on his plan to ascend to the White House.

And he didn't.

Besides, the Stranger's message *was* dangerous. He still believed that. So, he reminded himself now, when Karl Kastleman, his now favorite mole inside Jack Molinaro's camp, came to him with news of Tom-Tom's criminal history, and the physical evidence of the knife, he'd simply done what he had to do in the interests of the nation. He'd focused on the select facts and arguments that suited his version of the truth. He'd done that a thousand times before. Every good lawyer had, though seldom as effectively. But he also knew it would not be enough. Tom-Tom was an ace in the hole, but he needed to build a stronger hand before pulling out his trump. He needed to continue to raise doubts about the so-called Stranger if the Tom-Tom story was going to sell. Better yet, he needed others to raise doubts about the Stranger. Help from men who knew how to herd the lowest and dimmest of democracy's sheep. That's the ticket, he thought. Men with flocks and flocks of them, like these hypocrites.

So here he'd come, to start the stampede with Deacon Hoff and his congregations.

He could count on the deacon. Hoff owed him, big time. But what about these others? Hoff's friends? Brandt still had to determine whether or not they could be of any use in creating a 'spontaneous, grassroots movement' against the Stranger in Central Park.

"Well?" Brandt said, gesturing to the deacon, indicating he should make the introductions.

"Oh, yes. Certainly," Deacon Hoff said, "Father Malachi Martinson, Society of Jesus, please say hello to Governor Dennis Brandt."

"Pleasure to meet you, sir," Father Malachi said, his accent thinner now, his voice calmer but still distinctly Irish. He leaned over to shake the governor's hand.

"And this is Rabbi David Salzmann," Deacon Hoff said.

"Pleasure," the rabbi said.

Brandt nodded.

The Indian stepped closer to Brandt.

"Uh, this is Dr. Chandra Bhumi," Deacon Hoff said.

"Doctor of what?" Brandt asked.

"He holds two doctorates," Deacon Hoff said proudly. "One in linguistics and another in comparative religion. Both from Columbia. And he's an MD."

"Another imported overachiever, huh?" Brandt said. "You know the Molinaro family?"

"No, sir." Dr. Bhumi said.

Brandt lit his cigar. "Good."

Bhumi reached into a pink paper gift bag that sat on the floor beside one of the four metal folding chairs arranged in a small circle around a low coffee table. "I've brought you this, sir," he said. "If I may?" He handed the governor a bronze statue, about ten inches high. "A gift. It's Ganesh. Hindu Lord of Wisdom. Remover of obstacles."

"Ganesh?" Brandt puffed the tip of the Cuban red, filling the air with swirling white smoke. "An elephant head on the body of a man with four arms. Okay…"

"Mind the rat," Malachi said.

The governor raised his eyebrows.

"Down at the bottom," Malachi said.

Bhumi laughed nervously. "Mooshika. He symbolizes desire. Ganesh rides on his back. Mooshika can get in anywhere, but must be kept under control—tamed, if you will—"

"No," Brandt said, shaking his head negatively as he set the statue on the table. "I don't think so."

"I'm sorry?" Bhumi said.

"Against the rules. You know: No gifts," Brandt said.

"I see," said Bhumi.

"I appreciate it, though. Everyone, please sit." Brandt motioned to the chairs and then parked himself in one. "Let's get down to business, shall we?"

Hoff nodded.

"First of all," Brandt said, "we're at war. As you all know, the vice president has been assassinated. Our closest ally, Israel, faces an existential threat, and now, out of nowhere, a couple of very suspicious, very dark characters show up and start telling our troops to put down their weapons and refuse to fight. This so-called Stranger, he and Stone and Jeremiah, they're obviously in it together. Yes?"

"Obviously," Deacon Hoff said.

"And of course the liberal media loves the drama. Meanwhile, a young woman is brain-dead. Mayor Jack Molinaro's own sister, in fact. And another innocent citizen has suffered a brutal knife attack, at the hands of this so-called Stranger and his minions. It's true, you know—there may be more of them over there. We have no idea."

"Is it true?" Hoff asked. "He had him lynched, you know, hung from a tree…cut his eye out too."

"You're blaming the Stranger?" the rabbi asked.

"He did it," Brandt said. "According to the victim himself."

"Really?"

"Name's Breckenridge. Thomas C. Breckenridge III. He gave a sworn statement that Katie Molinaro was alive and well when she went over to the Point with this so-called Stranger. And more importantly, he says three of the Stranger's followers, men with beards and head coverings like the Stranger—"

"It's a hood," Bhumi interjected.

"—attacked him in the Ramble, gouged out his eye, and hung him while the Stranger watched. The New York City police commissioner himself just released copies of the guy's statement to the press."

"Karl Kastleman? Wow," said the deacon. "That certainly helps our cause."

"But the mayor is on the other side of every argument you make, Governor," Hoff said. "That has to be disappointing. What's happened to party discipline?"

"Good question," Brandt said.

"Well," Hoff said. "If you ask me, Jack Molinaro is way too far off the reservation, and he should be punished."

"He will be," Brandt said.

"What sort of person is he, this Thomas C. Breckenridge?" the rabbi asked.

"A solid citizen," Brandt said, puffing smoke. "An innocent victim who just happened to be in the wrong place at the wrong time. But you asked me here, so I assume you men want to tell me something?"

"Yes, of course," said Hoff. "Well, Father Malachi, if you don't mind…"

"Certainly. I believe," Malachi said, "first and foremost, we need to make sure the people understand the ability to perform miracles is not necessarily a sign of holiness."

"What?" Brandt said. "Explain."

"Yes," said Malachi.

"Yes, please, for the governor, for all of us, and share your unique qualifications in these matters," Deacon Hoff asked.

"Well, sir, before my retirement—"

"Retirement," Bhumi interjected. "Was it voluntary?"

"My job," Malachi pocketed the insult and continued, "was to report on such events as have happened in the park. So-called miracles. To determine whether they were authentic, and if they were, whether they were acts of God or of Satan."

"Miracles can be acts of Satan?" Brandt said. "Is this what you two were discussing?" He gestured to Bhumi.

"Yes," Bhumi said. "But—"

"Hold on," Brandt said. "I want to hear what the priest has to say."

"Thank you. For over thirty years," Malachi said, "I investigated the miracles attributed to candidates for beatification when what we Catholics call 'the Cause' of a Servant of God reached the stage where the pontiff was considering declaring a new saint."

"And?" Brandt asked.

"Well, miracles are *never* part of the criteria for judging whether or not a person is holy, which is to say, of God."

"Never?" Brandt asked.

"No. Take the case of Padre Pio. He was a Franciscan from the south of Italy. A man who lived and died in our time. A modern miracle worker. All documented, mind you. A *true* saint, unlike this 'Stranger' or whatever he thinks he is. Anyway, we laid Padre Pio to rest in 1968. I attended. It was—"

"How is this relevant?"

"Padre Pio was canonized, made a Catholic saint, *in spite of the fact* that he was a great mystic who conversed with Jesus and the angels, bore the stigmata—the wounds of Christ in his wrists and feet and side—and possessed the divine gift of miraculous healing. And in spite of the fact that he could levitate, walk on water, and even bilocate," Father Malachi said.

"Bullshit," Brandt said. "You're not serious."

"Of course I am. Men of science, independent men have witnessed and verified these things."

Brandt stood, puffed his cigar. "What did you mean when you said: in spite of?"

"Because," Deacon Hoff interjected, "not one of the things the Stranger did is considered proof of holiness—certainly, miracles are not. And even when Padre Pio had been found to be a holy man, the

Church still had to determine whether or not the miracles themselves, separate things, were actually of God."

"Yes," Malachi said. "That *is* the point. You see, those in charge of investigating such things in the Catholic Church know that miracles may be performed by men and women of God *or* by those doing the bidding of the Adversary."

"You mean Satan?" Brandt said, staring into the Irishman's eyes. Brandt liked saying it. *Satan.* It amused him.

"Yes. So while the fact of miracles associated with a candidate is important, we discount them completely when deciding on a candidate's holiness, and that's the question we must answer first. You see?"

"Yes, I do." Brandt asked, "Rabbi? Comments from your perspective?"

"I concur," the rabbi said. "Miracles alone are no sign of holiness in our tradition either."

"So you men believe there's a good chance this Stranger is a fraud?" Brandt asked.

"Worse. We believe he is, at the least, an agent of the devil," Father Malachi said.

Brandt smiled. "Really?"

"Governor," Father Malachi said, "according to that Jeremiah's new website, the scroll has a lot more to say. In fact, it says, 'Satan masquerades as an angel of light.'"

"So?"

"It's a quote from the New Testament. Second Corinthians," Father Malachi said. "I believe it could be the preemptive use of the one scripture that we would have used against the Stranger if he is in fact an agent of radical Muslim terrorists, or—"

"Or of evil, of Satan himself…" Deacon Hoff interjected. "There was a star, seen falling from the heavens the night of his arrival. Luke 10:18 says: 'I saw Satan, falling like lightning from Heaven.'"

"Your point?"

"He and his followers may be undermining the credibility of their critics by calling us what *they* are," Malachi now finished his sentence. "Frauds, and agents of darkness."

"It's an effective technique. Politically, I've seen it used to great effect," Hoff said.

"Yes," Brandt chuckled. "It is textbook…accuse your political opponent of whatever evil you've done so he can't bring it up without having to answer whether he's guilty of the same thing! Complete fabrication or not, it clouds the issue and pretty much gets you off the hook. All but neutralizes the issue in the press too because they have to report both sides, both accusations. Beautiful tactic."

"Governor, I will be issuing a statement and telling the press, every chance I get, that if the Stranger won't turn himself in and submit to questioning, to an examination, the government *must* conclude he is an agent of evil sent against us, against America in this war, and against the Christian religion in general," Malachi said.

"Good. And you'll be calling for his arrest, I presume? I mean, how else can we question him, officially, about the violent, heinous crimes Breckenridge accuses him of committing?" Brandt asked.

"Yes…yes," Hoff said. "Of course we will."

Malachi nodded. "He has taken sides against the Jews who have been attacked in the Holy Land itself, and he has sinned against all Christian nations. He deserves no less."

"How has he sinned?" Bhumi asked.

"By telling them not to defend themselves," Hoff said.

"Right. And so," Malachi said, "if he performs any more miracles, we simply must say they are of Satan, not of God."

"And that means," Hoff said, "that we are not just at war with Iran, or even the whole Muslim world. This is the war Saint John foretold in Revelation."

"You're going to sell this as the end of times? The Apocalypse?" Brandt asked.

"And the Stranger as the Antichrist," Malachi said. "Who else would do what he's done?"

"God?" Bhumi said. "There are dangers along this path, sir. Dangers and obstacles. In my tradition, there are many forms of the Divine Incarnate. The people want peace. You see? And war has never given it to them. So, maybe you have made a mistake—"

"Me?" Brandt barked.

"Yes, sir," Bhumi said. "Many have embraced the Stranger. Maybe you should too."

"Really?" Brandt asked, impressed by the man's courage. He even enjoyed hearing both sides. "So you think the Stranger may actually be the 'Divine Incarnate.' Thus, you sense dangers and obstacles for me, because I oppose him?"

"Yes," Bhumi said.

"And that's why you brought the fat little elephant guy and his friend the mouse?" Brandt stood and lifted the Ganesh statue off the coffee table. "Right?"

"Yes," Bhumi said, and he stood too.

"All right. I'll take this with me after all, then. Might come in handy," Brandt said. "Though not in the way you intended."

The others stood now as well.

"Do you approve of our course of action, Governor?" Hoff asked.

"Who am I to argue with the true men of God?" Brandt asked. "Do what you must, gentlemen. But do it quickly." He shook their hands and nodded his goodbyes. And now Brandt walked out, carrying the Hindu Lord of Wisdom.

Rules be damned.

"Mike!"

The voice sounded familiar, and upset, and so Mike took his eye off the shot and scanned the terrace for its source. No luck. He turned back to film Stone and the mayor and the cute black chick in the vest on the water in the inflatable. That's when the voice called him again.

"Mike!"

He turned just in time to see Dee Weiss, waving to him from the general mass of people across the terrace and held back by a cop. She wasn't getting any nearer to the press pit. She'd been lighting up his cell phone with calls and texts and emails ranting and raving about some kind of wild psychic experience she'd had in which she "saw the whole thing."

"Dee! What's up?" he shouted.

"That son of a bitch! He did it. He's the one who hurt her!"

Mike took a deep breath. "Who?"

"I saw it. The whole thing! I had a vision. Tell them to let me through! I want to talk to the press!"

Connie, beside him, turned so she was even less visible. "Is she insane?" Connie said.

"Uh, yeah," Mike said. He turned to Dee. "I'm sorry," he shouted. "But I have to get this shot. But I'll tell Connie. My producer. See what we can do. Call me!" Mike winked at Connie, turned to the lake, and raised his camera.

Jack, about six feet under water, swam in the direction of the barrier. The anchored buoy rope brushed his arm as he passed it. He pulled another breaststroke and then reached out. A light flashed where he made contact. This is incredible, he thought. How on earth? He went deeper, worked his way along the wall of light, lighting up the barrier time and again as he moved toward the Point. He kicked. He reached out again.

Sophia brought Abbey to the hospital, he thought. God, I love my baby so much. I just want Abbey to be happy. At least Abbey. Wait. Go back. Here. No light? No resistance?

He needed to inhale.

Not yet.

He reached again.

Yes. Not wide. But it's here. Right here. A way in!

When he broke the surface, he gasped for air. Everyone on the shore shrieked and cheered him. Then, on the Point, the German shepherd came bounding to the water's edge, teeth bared and growling, barking and pacing and charging toward him.

"Did you find something?" Jessie asked, leaning over the side and shouting over the noise of the dog. "Did you?"

"No," he said, his political instincts kicking in automatically. No way I'm going over there now, he thought. Not with that dog there. This story is fine just as it is. He shook his head and said, "I'm sorry. No way in. Just like Stone said." He took a mental note of where the gateway was: two buoys from shore.

Not going in. Not until I absolutely need to use this. And even then, not until I can get past that animal without being ripped to shreds.

And the crowd on the shore started chanting, "Jack-eee... Jack-eee!"

CHAPTER 13

TOMMY CHECKED THE BACK POCKET OF HIS TORN, SOILED JEANS. HE found some comfort in the presence of his old razor-edged friend, but only because he'd forgotten for a moment the Rush knife had been turned against him in the hand of the bride-to-be. "Katie," he said aloud.

"What's that?" the driver asked.

"Na-nothing," Tommy said, and he slowly, painfully exited the car and stood in the afternoon drizzle. He closed the door and caught a glimpse of his reflection in the tinted glass, his one good eye.

Less than intimidating.

I look pathetic.

The Karl guy, police commissioner, had dropped the Rush knife, tucked into a clear plastic bag, on Tommy's chest in the hospital room. Tommy had looked down at it but hadn't said a word. He had not dared reach for it, either. Though he wanted to do so every time Brandt taunted him. Every time the governor called him 'Tom-Tom.'

Son of a bitch.

"Divers retrieved it last night," the commissioner had said. "At the edge of Bethesda Terrace. It's yours. Got your fingerprints all over it. And your blood. And some of Katie's too, from your hands.

But, don't worry. We're not going to ask you to explain how that's possible. At least not for now."

The governor had then dismissed the commissioner, to talk privately. "We're gonna be close, so you can call me Denny," the governor had said. "And I'm going to call you Tom-Tom." The man was mocking him now, Tommy knew, because he had the power, and because he'd noted how the named irked him.

"Not Ta-Tom-Tom," he'd said, giving away the fact of his vulnerability. "Tommy."

And Brandt had laughed and said, "Hell no. Tom-Tom makes a much better story for the papers."

Tommy had wanted to flick open that knife and gut the bastard right then and there.

"Get dressed," Brandt had said, and he'd read him some words from a typed sheet of paper and told Tommy to say the words were his own. A sworn deposition.

"Wa-why?" Tommy had said.

"Never ask me for an explanation again. You understand?" Brandt had said.

Tommy had turned his face to the sun again and prayed for death. But not even death wanted any part of him.

Now, as the car drove off and Tommy walked toward his apartment, his legs rubbery and trembling, he wondered if this was why he'd been spared, brought back to life, to be a pawn in a king's game.

Brandt had asked what Tommy had done to Katie, and what she'd done to him in return. But, even when he'd heard it all, the governor didn't react. This Denny Brandt, he was cold, for sure. And Tommy didn't like cold, no way, no how.

He went upstairs to the two-bedroom shithole he'd so recently planned on leaving behind forever. It sat above an out-of-business convenience store, smelled like mildew, and had all three of its cracked windows nailed shut and painted over.

Oh, he had mustered some "demands," as best he could with a half-crushed larynx. "Immunity?"

Brandt had smiled and said, "You're innocent, remember? You don't need it."

His apartment? "Lease is up," he'd said.

"Taken care of…"

Now Tommy unlocked the door, went inside, and searched for his secret stash of meth.

Gone.

Most of his other stuff was still there, though, packed in boxes, ready for the move. A Yankees hat sat on top of the lamp in the living room. A can of beer, open.

Warm.

Flat.

Some moldy doughnuts.

A drawer full of junk in the kitchen. Scissors. Some duct tape. A couple of ballpoint pens. Small change. Yeah. Most of his stuff. And boxes of stuff that'd belonged to his boys.

Rye and Tivo and Sister? he'd asked Brandt.

"Will be on a one-way bus trip back to the sticks as soon as we find them."

And then Brandt had said that the police commissioner would personally tell the mayor that he, Thomas C. Breckenridge III, was a victim, not a suspect. Not even a person of interest. "An honest, upstanding citizen, a victim who doesn't want to talk to anyone, and who just needs some quiet time to recuperate from his ordeal until the Stranger can be brought into custody. Then you'll be going to court, taking the stand, and testifying against him."

Tommy had nodded, and, with hatred rising for this old bald

bastard who'd mocked his stutter too many times, he'd scribbled his signature on the statement. The mark made the paper a legal document, Brandt had explained, meaning to recant was perjury, and in no uncertain terms, doing so would mean Tom-Tom would "rot in prison" for a decade.

"Later today, when my driver takes you home," he'd said, "you'll find a cell phone on your kitchen table, and some cash. But don't go out. Don't even buy a cup of coffee until tomorrow. Understand? Just rest. And don't even think about taking anything but the painkillers and sleeping pills that I have arranged for you. No meth. No crack. Nothing."

"I understand," Tommy had managed.

"Good."

Now Tommy spied the phone and the cash on the kitchen counter. He emptied his pocket of the pills, opened one plastic bottle, and popped two painkillers. Then he set the bottle on the counter beside the other, the one with the sleeping pills.

"Wa-what…na-na-next?" he'd asked before "you can call me Denny" had left the hospital room.

"Wait for my instructions. I'm the only one with the cell phone number. And don't you talk to anyone but me, you understand, Tom-Tom?"

Bastard.

Tommy lifted the prepaid cell phone and checked it.

Charged. Good signal. He thought, maybe I'll just leave it here and run…but there was no escaping Brandt. He could see that. And suicides don't go nowhere but Hell. Plus, he'd been there already, and he did not like it, no way no how. Besides, hanging hadn't worked anyway. So I'd better just do what I'm told, Tommy realized.

A knock on the apartment door startled him. He crept across the room and peered through the peephole, expecting Brandt. But a bulging blue eye lined with red veins stared back at him, and under it a big, rosy-red, freckled nose tilted to show a gaping nostril. Now a cracked and twisted pair of red lips showed up in the little glass peephole.

A woman's lips.

They parted, and a pink tongue licked 'em.

Tommy liked that.

And all of a sudden, all of that got topped by a flash of wild, orange hair.

What the hell?

"Hey!" the crazy carnival freak-show face said, pounding the door with a closed fist. "Open up! I know what you did! You son of a bitch! I know what you did to my Katie!"

The Rush knife flicked open in Tommy's hand as he unbolted the door and turned the knob. And now the barrel of a 12-gauge shotgun came at him, right through the crack.

Stone had returned Jessie to the shore, and the SWAT team had trotted off with the inflatable, and Connie and Mike and the local and national and international press, still behind the barricade in the press pit, had begun to shout questions, eager to get the scoop on the invisible barrier and anything else Jack or Stone or the firebrand had to say.

"Give us a minute, folks," Jack said, patting himself dry.

"She'll die without her meds," Jessie said.

"Try to be patient," Jack said. "We're doing everything we can."

"Patient?" Jessie pointed across the terrace to the legions of sick and dying. "Like them? Like your sister?"

"That was cold," Stone said.

"But true," Jessie said.

"Let's talk about this later," Becka said. "It's time."

"For what?" Stone asked the mayor.

"Well, if I'd been allowed to conduct my press conference, this wouldn't have been such a big surprise, Mr. Stone." Jack turned to Becka. "Did you let the other press teams know?" he asked.

"Yes." She turned to Stone. "Don't worry. Connie's been briefed too."

"About?" Stone asked.

"That," Jack said, gesturing to the paved path that led past Bow Bridge and to the terrace. A long line of men and women in full military dress uniform approached.

"What the hell?" Stone said.

"Terry!" one of the Marines now crossing toward the fountain shouted.

"Cezar?" Stone said. He turned to Jack. "That one in front...he's my kid brother. I can't believe he didn't tell me about this!"

"M-39!" Cezar began a chant, and others joined in. "M-39! M-39!"

The press clamored for position, camera shutters fired, and the crowd stirred and pointed.

"M-39! M-39!"

"He's a Marine too, eh, Stone?" Jack asked.

"Staff Sergeant Cezar J. Stone, sir. Yes, sir," Stone said. "God love him."

And Terry Stone watched as his own kid brother headed up what appeared to be an unending line of soldiers with an incredible assortment of weapons, all of them headed for the terrace.

"M-39! M-39!"

They crossed the expanse of red bricks and approached the fountain and Stone and Jessie and Becka and Jack: Marine blue, Navy white, Air Force gray, and Army green, many limping along on at least one artificial limb. Some had horrible, visible wounds: burns, missing body parts, empty eye sockets, faces torn beyond recognition…

"Firing pins are out, sir," Cezar said to the mayor. He looked over his shoulder. "As promised. All of them…just like you said." He wore his Purple Heart. He had given his right leg and half of his right arm for it.

Jack just stared at him. "Good. Thank you for your service, son."

Jessie leaned close to Terry as a young female US Army hero, a corporal bedecked with medals and escorted by a man who looked to be her father, came forward. The sight of her—badly burned about the neck and face, and missing part of the left side of her skull—brought Stone back to the horrors he'd seen, and participated in, at war. A knot formed in his gut. Bile reached his throat. The corporal laid down her weapon at the base of the fountain. The other troops began to file past and do the same.

Behind the uniformed men and women came a motley crew of gangbangers wearing drooping jeans and carrying handguns and shotguns, and a bunch of guys Stone knew from a story he'd done on the turf battles between the Irish and Italian mobs fell in too with meat cleavers and switchblades and ceramic pistols, and cases full of all sorts of weapons. A crew of black-leather-clad bikers with wallet chains and face tattoos came next. And now came scores of men and women in camo, with hunting rifles and shotguns. Assault rifles. Machetes. A grenade launcher.

Crazy, Stone thought.

"How'd you do this?" Stone asked Jack. "How did you keep it a secret?"

"I didn't do it, Stone. Your friend Jeremiah called and asked if I would instruct NYPD to allow some folks to come down here and surrender their weapons in support of the Stranger's call for peace."

"And you agreed?"

Jack nodded. "Promised my sister," he said. "Besides, I knew it would piss off Denny Brandt."

"Wow," Stone said. "It's surely going to do that."

"Well, to tell you the truth," Jack said. "I had no idea it would be this big."

And the line kept coming, and the pile grew and grew. Jessie moved to Stone's side and threaded an arm through his, startling him, and sending his heart racing, though he did not fully realize why. He hardly knew this girl. Yet...he had feelings for her, strong feelings.

"Please." Cezar offered the mayor a weapon. "Take it, sir. It would mean a lot to all of us if you set it down. Symbolic, you know? Swords to plowshares," he said.

Jack took the weapon. "These others..." He gestured to the gangbangers and bikers. "You all know one another?" he asked Cezar.

"Yes, sir," Cezar said. "More or less, I mean. We're all related or friends, or friends of friends. You either go the way Terry and I went, or you go their way. What other choices do we have, coming from where we come from? We enlist to get to college or go the way of the streets."

"How many do you think are here?"

"Hundreds, sir," Cezar said.

"Hundreds?"

"Yes, sir. And it's just the beginning. Word's spreading to other cities. It's on Jeremiah's blog, TryChristianity.com. Starting a new gathering, a new kind of war. He says we're the new soldiers, you know, and if we disavow violence in all cases, like Jesus—and the scroll says it too—then we might make it tip back the other way."

"Tip it?" Jack asked.

"Like that book...by Malcolm Gladwell. All the gun killings," Cezar said. "You know, Columbine, that theater in Colorado, the kids in that Connecticut kindergarten, the murder-suicides, the mall shootings, Gabby Giffords, the Boston Marathon bombing, Trayvon. Congressman Scalise. It's tipped, just like Gladwell talks about in the book. Violence is now the norm. One million, eight hundred thousand Americans dead since 1968 by civilian guns and nothing changes, can't even get a bill through Congress. Not even when Congress's men and women are being shot by crazy people. But something has to change now. It has to…right?" Cezar turned and shouted to the men and women who'd surrendered their weapons. "It has to stop now! Right?"

"M-39! M-39!" the men and women, and now the entire crowd, began to chant. "M-39!"

"Hell yeah," one of the men said, stepping forward and tossing his .38 Special at the mayor's feet. "Time for a new gathering…like the Stranger says."

"Damn right." Another nodded, laid down a gun case, popped it open, and showed off his chromed prize. "I'm giving it up for Jesus, and for my kids."

Another man came forward. "You should take them away from cops too, Mr. Mayor. Like they do in England," a young woman said. "And these too," she added, laying down her pepper-spray canister. "Turn the other cheek. Love your enemies. Invest in jobs, not prisons!"

"I can find a new hobby too," said one of the guys who went to his knees in his camo overalls, as if beside a grave, and laid down a Bushmaster .223 assault rifle with a thirty-shot clip. "M-39," he said, "because my niece got shot with one of these. Shot by her little cousin. Nine years old. An accident that couldn't have happened if the damn thing wasn't in the house, if we hadn't made it so kids think it's cool to shoot and kill, to want one of these weapons like the grown-ups."

"Thank you," the mayor said. And as he laid down Cezar's weapon. The crowd applauded and cheered.

"Jackie! Jack-eee!" Cezar began to chant. Others joined in. "Jack-eee! Jack-eee!"

An hour later, when the last of the weapons had been surrendered—and the pile of them beside the fountain stood seven feet tall and spread out wide on the bricks—Jack said, "Let's take a moment of silence, and all pray now, for peace at home and abroad..."

And ten thousand people in Central Park bowed their heads and closed their eyes and moved their lips in prayer.

Stone turned to Jessie. She'd closed her eyes too and begun to whisper. "Please, God. Please. My grandma. Take care of my grandma." And in that moment, the German shepherd began barking loudly again on the shore of the Point, and everyone turned.

"Uh-oh," Stone said, having a now-familiar sensation.

"Uh-oh, what?" Becka asked.

"Try to move," Stone said, staring at her feet.

Jessie shouted, "Look!" and pointed, and a collective "ahhh!" rose from the crowd as, across the lake, at the shore of the Point, an African-American woman wearing a long wool coat came alongside the barking German shepherd, patted his head and quieted him, and raised her gaze. And, as a bright beam of sunlight fell on her face, she waved.

"Is that Ruthie?" Becka asked.

"Yes. Yes!" Jessie burst into tears, and she tried to walk toward the Point and the far shore but found herself stuck in place.

"Stay calm," Stone said. "It's just what happens."

"Grandma! Over here!" Jessie shouted and waved.

The mayor, looking bewildered, suddenly dropped to his knees. So did Becka. And so now did Stone and Jessie too, and Connie and Mike and everyone in the press pit. Everyone everywhere, over the hills and on the stairs and in the arcade, knelt and fell silent. And now the old woman with the sweet voice, the one who had sung to God with all her heart the night before, began to glow. She stepped forward, then paused, as if considering something very important. For a moment, she turned back to the Stranger's cardboard house of light, and then she turned toward the terrace again. Suddenly, the surface of the lake came alive with light for her, just as it had for the Stranger, and Ruthie stepped onto it as if she had done it a thousand times before and walked on it as if on solid ground. As she came closer, Stone couldn't even tell for sure if she was the same old granny.

She's...younger. Maybe twenty or thirty years younger, Stone thought.

How?

Jessie, eyes wide, had obviously realized this too, and she seemed captivated and elated by the sight of this new Ruthie. Jessie and everyone watched in silence as this now magically young grandma, on magically youthful legs, kept coming across the magically glistening water, the dog at her side until about halfway. Then the dog stopped and sat in the middle of the lake, right where they'd just rowed into the invisible barrier, as if sitting on dry land. And Ruthie continued toward them, coming the last few yards to the edge of the terrace alone and then stepping onto the terrace and crossing to Jessie and the others. Ruthie stood for a long moment, admiring the face of her granddaughter, smiling tenderly, lovingly.

Tears streamed down Jessie's face.

Ruthie dipped her head and said in a soft voice, "I saw your momma in there, girl..."

Jessie trembled, cried, shook her head and bit her lip.

Ruthie continued, "She loves you *soooo* much…and she says to tell you she's sorry, but she had to go. It was her time."

Jessie nodded and tried again to speak but could not.

"And now she wants you to *please* stop being so angry," Ruthie said, and she stared deeply into Jessie's eyes for a few seconds, then raised her right hand in a fist and when she loosened her grip, a small gold crucifix fell and dangled from a gold necklace. "She asked me," Ruthie said, "to give you this…"

Jessie heaved and sobbed and lost all control at the sight of it.

Ruthie put the necklace around Jessie's neck. "She said to tell you to remember, child: It won't do you no good if you don't pray on it."

Jessie raised her face, coaxed by Ruthie's tender touch, and the two women smiled at one another. And now Stone watched as Ruthie walked briskly across the terrace to the barricades on the far side of the fountain, to hundreds of the sick and dying with whom she'd stood the night before.

But where's the Stranger?

There's no light.

Ruthie pulled back the barricade, moving as if she knew exactly which one to choose. She picked her way through the crowd of kneeling nurses and parents and sentinels behind their charges in the front-row wheelchairs, until she came alongside young Rikki Brandt, the governor's seven-year-old son.

Poor boy. So sick and weak, Stone thought. Most of his life in a wheelchair…yes. Please, God. Heal him…maybe that would do it. Maybe that would change Denny Brandt.

Ruthie leaned in, placed a hand on Rikki's shoulder, and whispered something to him.

He smiled and labored to shake his head. "No," he said.

He can talk.

He is the one! Chosen, like Jeremiah. Like Ruthie!

But there is no light…no Stranger.

The Angel of the Waters statue…it's not glowing.

Ruthie patted Rikki on the shoulder, nodded assurance to the nurse and bodyguard troopers beside the boy, and then she reached for the handles of his chair, but he struggled to catch the runners and stopped her. "No," he managed again.

Ruthie bent down to him again. He labored to breathe, slouched and tilted to one side. He smiled and touched Ruthie's hand, and their eyes met and held one another for a long time, and then he nodded, and when Ruthie did too, he lifted a trembling hand and pointed to the child beside him, also in a wheelchair, and said in a loud voice, "Help him."

The boy Rikki had chosen appeared so helplessly twisted, so small and emaciated and gnarled, he barely resembled a human boy. Perhaps seven or eight years old, he shook violently with tremors, and he jerked and twitched more and more desperately as Ruthie turned his way.

Ruthie looked to the lake—then, after a moment of reflection, she stepped behind him, as Rikki had asked.

Stone's heart broke as this other boy, obviously in terror, struggled to control his muscles, fought his own body to turn and look back to a woman Stone felt sure was that boy's mother, even as Ruthie pushed him toward the flowing waters of the fountain.

Stone started to panic: No. This isn't right. There is no light!

Please, God…don't let her do this!

The woman Stone took to be the boy's mother attempted to follow on her knees, and, amazingly, overpowered whatever held everyone else still, though only barely. She clawed her way along, an inch at a time.

Ruthie turned again to the lake and the Stranger's cardboard lighthouse, and now she too began to tremble.

Jessie shook her head frantically, her eyes wide and filling with tears.

Ruthie has disregarded the Stranger's instructions, Stone thought. She's taken the wrong child. There's no light!

The wheelchair hit the curb that ran around the circular pool at the base of the Angel of the Waters fountain. The boy jerked forward, slumping, twitching, trembling with his eyes wide, his mouth open. He expelled a pained groan.

Don't do it! Not without the Stranger. Not without the light!

After what seemed an eternal moment, as if to comply with what Stone felt she must have considered a Divine Command to save somebody, Ruthie lifted the boy out of his chair and pulled him toward the fountain. He fell heavily against the low wall of its circular pool and groaned in pain. He struggled to move, clearly dumbfounded and panicking, eyes bulging with terror, shaking and trying to escape his fate.

His mother clawed her way closer, inch by inch. "No," she managed from the depths of her soul. "Please! No!"

But Ruthie heaved the boy up and slid him over the side. He splashed in and sank. Bubbles rose.

Ruthie walked away.

The child's mother collapsed in despair.

Ruthie came toward Stone, and Jessie and the mayor. "There's no need for no more swimming now, you understand, Mr. Mayor?" she said to Jack. "No matter what happens here, you stay off of that lake."

Jack's eyes went wide.

Stone tensed every muscle and tried to rise. He could not, but by straining his neck, he could see the drowning boy. Like a dark, still shadow, he lay motionless at the bottom of the pool. The bubbles had ceased to rise.

Someone help him! Lord, God! Help him!

"Terry," Ruthie said to Stone. "You take care of my Jessie. You hear?" And she touched her granddaughter's cheek gently. "You two

have a history. A long, spiritual history together. I've seen it, inside."
She gestured to the cardboard lighthouse.

Stone stared at her in disbelief as she walked away. What about
the boy! he thought. But Ruthie merely stepped on the glittering surface of the water and headed across the lake toward the wagging dog.

What seemed an eternity passed in silence, broken only by the
sobs of the drowned child's mother.

Finally, Ruthie climbed the hill of the Point and disappeared into
a new bank of low, wandering fog.

Everyone remained still. Stuck. Silent.

Somewhere, a bird finally chirped.

Now two ducks, paddling for the far shore, shook their tails and
quacked.

The crippled boy's mother on the red bricks crawled forward and
lay prostrate at the very edge of the fountain, chest heaving, sobbing.

Everyone but Stone and Jessie had closed their eyes and brought
their hands together. The crowd did the only thing they apparently
thought they could do to help the child: they prayed.

On the East Side, a siren rose and wailed…it's a jeremiad, Stone
thought. Yes. I see it now. This whole thing is a warning.

A new feeling rose within the heart of Terry Stone, a feeling of
worship. Of love. He began to pray now too, and as he did, movement caught his eye, and there in the middle of the lake stood the
Stranger, eyes closed, hands at his sides, palms out, facing forward.
And now, an aura of light exploded around him and spread across
the waters to the terrace, and at the edges of the aura, the colors of
sun-infused emeralds and sapphires and rubies sparkled. And the
water of the fountain pool began to boil and sparkle too, like it had
when Jeremiah had washed his face in it. Golden light emanated from
the Stranger's dark yet luminous face and filled the entire terrace with
a blazing glow that shone brighter than the noonday sun.

"Do what the scroll commands," the Stranger said in a loud clear voice that carried across the waters and filled the terrace. "And death shall have no hold on you. Look! See the power of the Lord!"

And he stretched out his hand, and the crippled, drowned child exploded out of the water. He rose to his feet, stood tall and straight and strong, and, raising his arms in triumph, shouted in a voice like a trumpet, "Mother! Oh, Mother! I'm alive! I am alive!"

And the boy's mother leaped into the fountain and pulled him into her arms and held him. And the crowd exploded. Thousands of onlookers stood and shouted and applauded and laughed and cheered.

Yet, somewhere, Stone felt, something had gone wrong.

Terribly wrong.

And now a panicked voice, a cry among the joyous chorus, a plea filled with terror and horror and disbelief, rose to his ears: "He's dead!" someone shouted. "Please, God. No!"

"What's happened?" Jessie asked, rising to her feet, straining to locate the source of the horror-filled voice, even as she wiped at her own tears of joy.

"Help me! Oh my God. Please. Help me," the voice cried out. And Rikki Brandt's nurse broke through the crowd, screaming, "Please! Somebody!" She raced the slumping child in his wheelchair through the hysterical mass of people pressing toward the holy fountain, through and past them all, past Stone and Jessie and Jack Molinaro, and past Becka, who'd stayed on her knees and continued to weep, bitterly.

And now the nurse stood at the very edge of the lake and cried out, "Please. Wait!" She fell to her knees. "I beg of you. Please! Not Rikki. Not this little boy!"

CHAPTER 14

GOVERNOR DENNY BRANDT LEFT THE PERKY BRUNETTE CURLED ON her side and went to the desk at the foot of his hotel room bed. Naked and hungry, he scratched himself. He lit his stub and lifted the elephant man with four arms off of the burgundy attaché case that sat on the hotel dresser. "Ganesh," he said. He opened the case and pulled out the thick manila file folder and opened it. He took a moment to gloat over its contents again, and over what it had just enabled him to put into play. Of all the files he'd ever collected, this one was his most valuable.

Years in the making…

Its contents traced the career of the man he now held in the palm of his hand. A man who, at the age of twenty-two, got a night job to help with the bills as he made his way through law school, a job pumping gas at a mob-owned station that held an exclusive contract to fill the fuel tanks of the Town of Brookhaven Highway Department's fleet of trucks with bootleg diesel and gasoline. After hours, when no one came around, the kid also filled the Suffolk County Republican party chairman's Town Car, and the cars and trucks of his friends, and on occasion, he shared a smoke with the chairman, known to the locals as Uncle T—a big, lovable, gregarious fellow with deep ties to the boys in Brooklyn and the big organization across the river in the Garden State. Uncle T had taken a liking to the kid, had seen him as an up-and-comer and, after his graduation, had promoted him to a cushy, high-paying job in Highway, where he could really make hay.

Years went by. The relationship strengthened, and the kid organized the place and its political patronage employees into one of the most powerful Republican clubs in the county. They raised money and put up signs for Republican candidates and made sure challengers knew the score. In short, they did the things that won elections, no holds barred.

And they did something else: they received heavy equipment from all over the East Coast—asphalt finishers, milling machines, chip spreaders, road wideners, vibratory compactors, and rubber-tired rollers, in whole or in parts. All of them stolen from other municipalities. All of them "cleaned up" and given new serial numbers, and "bought" with taxpayers' money, funds that went directly into the pockets of the mob bosses. The best part was that neither the cops nor the feds ever pulled over a town-owned truck, never even thought of looking for stolen vehicles or equipment in the municipal yard. After all, Brookhaven was a thousand miles away from where the stuff had been lifted.

It was a beautiful thing, and it could be duplicated over and over, in any state, county, or township. And it was. Within a decade, the kid had risen through the ranks, made his fortune, moved to New Jersey, and been elected to his first statewide political office.

That's when Brandt, then DA of Suffolk County, first got wind of the scheme and picked up the trail of the kid, quite by accident. One of his assistants uncovered a purchase order initialed by the kid himself for a brand-new road paver that had mysteriously vanished from inventory. Stolen or sold, the department did not know, and no one on staff remembered or would offer a guess. And though the PO had been issued, the equipment had been purchased, and the invoice paid to a company called Pegasus Paving of Newark, no record of the paver's use had ever been documented by the town.

"Boss," one of his assistants had said, "the Highway guys still have it listed as inventory, but it's nowhere to be found."

Brandt, smelling dirt, had pulled on a rubber glove and begun to poke around. He'd found the multimillion-dollar chop shop and hot-equipment operation that spanned five states. He'd held the card close to his vest. Worth perhaps a high-profile trial and a month or two of great press at the time, now it was worth the leadership of the free world.

"RJ," he said aloud and smiled. The kid's initials. He had penned them on the top right-hand corner of the file with a black Magic Marker years ago.

My ticket to the top.

He should be receiving his copy right about now.

Brandt had dispatched Will, his chief of staff, to the White House with the file. Will, who had no idea what he was delivering, also unwittingly tendered an urgent correspondence for the president's eyes only, and an absolute demand: He, Denny Brandt, would head up the search committee for the new vice president.

It went without saying that Denny Brandt would end up recommending himself.

The brunette said, "More…"

"Oh, there is more," Brandt said. He smiled.

More indeed…

All he had to do now was to make sure he placed his little insurance policy in the hands of someone RJ would never suspect would have it.

"This is it, sweetheart," Brandt said, lifting the folder and holding it up for the brunette to see. With the file safe, there was no way

RJ would even entertain the idea of having Brandt disappear, or be killed. "Now, you remember what I told you," Brandt said, confident that her nominal intelligence, lack of any known connection to him, ability to keep secrets, and boundless desire to please, made her the perfect person for the job.

"Yes," she said. "If anything happens to you, I'm supposed to bring that file to somebody in the press. Somebody…big. No. Reputable."

"That's right," he said. "Reputable." He laughed. Soon, the once-unstoppable rising star of the GOP, the handsome wunderkind Jack Molinaro—old, slow-to-catch-on Jack—would learn how badly he'd been outdone. "Get dressed," Brandt said to the brunette. "Time for you to run along."

"But you promised," she said, and she rolled onto her belly and raised her feet into the air. "I want more…"

But now, Brandt's cell phone rang. He checked it. "Rikki's nurse?" he said, and he answered. And when she spoke, a pain, like one might feel if shot by a gun, bent him in two.

Rikki Brandt lay in the cold metal drawer there, in the basement morgue. Now, after having had Rikki's body moved to a funeral home on Staten Island, his mourning father, Denny, sat alone, head in his hands, beside the drawer that held his child's body. And he sobbed as he thought of Rikki entering a cremation furnace.

He'd sought and received reports from Rikki's bodyguards about what had happened in the park. He'd learned his son had refused to be the one taken to the pool. He'd learned another boy had been healed in Rikki's place, at Rikki's insistence.

His son was a hero.

Selfless.

A saint.

And yet all the priests and rabbis had already come out publicly and said this latest miracle was part of a Satanic plot, an act of the devil, and the story of Rikki's sacrifice had been lost in that noise. Not even Brandt could set the record straight without saying the Stranger was God, which he would not, could not, do.

In the morning too, he knew the headlines in all the right-leaning papers and the lead on all the right-wing networks would be the same: *Stranger: Angel or Agent of Evil?*

Messenger of God or the Devil?

And he, Governor Denny Brandt, had engineered it all.

A thought came to him: What if I have rendered the wrong verdict? What if the Stranger really does have some kind of divine connection to God?

What if he *is* the messenger of the Lord?

Jesus.

No.

A Divine Messenger would have seen Rikki's sacrifice, after a life of suffering, and healed him too. For God's sake, a mere human would have that much heart, that much compassion. Would not God? So, no, he concluded. Only an evil force would let one boy die so another might live. Only an enemy would tempt a God-fearing society to a life of passive victimization by offering the relief of the suffering of just one or two at the expense of all the others.

All or none. That's my way. My test.

All or none.

So I was correct, Brandt concluded. If the Stranger had anything to do with God, he would have saved my son, and Katie Molinaro too. And killed that piece of shit, Breckenridge.

Hoff and his friends are correct too, Brandt convinced himself: Miracles are no proof of God. They can just as easily be performed by Satan to lead people astray.

And Brandt assured himself again that the Stranger's message revealed his true character. And his message represented an attack, a potentially fatal chop at the very roots of the tree of American liberty.

M-39?

It's a bunch of pacifist crap!

Yes, he told himself. And the Stranger's scroll, its demand for what amounted to surrender, did represent a clear and present danger to the entire American way of life. And as governor, Brandt had just taken an oath to uphold the Constitution of the United States and the Constitution of the State of New York. He had to oppose him. Had to…hell, the Stranger had called for Americans to be passive, and to surrender! He hadn't done so himself, though. He hid out behind some kind of alien, space-age force field from the future. Shit. Hypocrite! Extra-terrestrial demon! Coward who will not come out from behind his "shield" and face the people, face me, Brandt thought.

This can't go on, he told himself.

I can't!

But to stop the Stranger, he would have to take him into custody. And to do that, he'd have to find a way to get to him, to get past that damn shield.

Yes, take him. Dead or alive. That's the ticket.

But how?

He did not know.

However, he did know this: He would cremate the body of his son tonight.

But he would not mourn for too long.

He'd turn his pain and desolation into anger instead, and use it to get to the Stranger, to seek revenge.

No. Not revenge.

Justice.

For my Rikki. My boy.

He gave the funeral director instructions and signed the paperwork.

Now he said goodbye to Rikki forever.

He wept again as he pictured the door of the cremation oven closing and the pine box inside on the conveyor belt moving inexorably toward the flames. In his mind, the inferno whooshed and roared and consumed the only real love in his life. He cursed God and held his head in his hands again and choked on his pain.

If my child has to burn, he thought, then so does the Stranger. And with this thought came a sudden epiphany, for the way to get to the Stranger had come to him, come roaring into his mind like the crematory inferno.

Of course, he thought.

Brilliant.

"Hello, Rikki," Katie said, recognizing at once his bright presence, and she admired the tall, strong body he had chosen. Same age as on Earth, she thought. About eight years old. Same sandy-brown colored hair. Same freckled cheeks and bright smile.

Even though they'd met only once in earthly life, at her brother's swearing-in as mayor, Katie had felt an instant kinship with Rikki Brandt. Each of them had endured difficult, though very different, personal and family challenges. Now, here, on a verdant world orbited by five tiny, glowing orange suns, each of which shed ribbons of warm pink and sapphire light, she felt they were both totally at ease and unfettered. "You were very lucky to know the moment of your transition had come upon you, and you should be proud of yourself for your intention to save the other boy. It's why you remained conscious as you crossed over. That selflessness…it was beautiful, and spiritually transformational."

"You saw?"

"Yes."

"So you can go back and forth?" he asked.

"Yes," Katie said. And now she noticed her own hands appeared much more translucent than his. She had left her physical body again and taken on this light-energy body as she had in the Stranger's house of light. How long ago in Earth time, she could not say. At least this time, she thought, her physical body lay in the care of physicians in a hospital, safe, though it was all but lifeless.

"Why?" Rikki asked.

"Because I'm only visiting."

"Oh. So you have not left your Earth life yet?"

"I am on a sort of cusp, awaiting a resolution of family karma."

"What's karma?"

Katie laughed. "It means action, and every consequence that follows."

"But you'll stay with me here for a little while at least?"

"For a little while, yes. But don't worry. There are others waiting very patiently, and they are very excited to see you again."

"Like who?" he said.

"Well, that's up to you."

"Really?"

"Yes."

"Wow…that's so cool," he said, his face brightening.

Katie smiled and led him out of a broad circle thrown by a great shaft rising from the Stranger's house of light in the park into the vastness of space. The beam, invisible to those on Earth, curved toward one of the small suns overhead in the black and starry sky, the sea of a vast cosmic Heaven on which floated the other four sun-like orbs of orange. And then the shaft of light led on to other, more distant, perhaps higher, realms.

"This is an astral world," Katie said. "A sort of Heaven. From here we can see the denser worlds, but not the finer ones. For instance, we can see Earth, but the people there cannot see us, because here our bodies are made of light. Likewise, we cannot yet see the higher, causal worlds."

"Is my dad still there?" Rikki asked. "On Earth?"

"Yes," Katie said. "But I don't think you'll be seeing him for a while."

"Will he come here when he dies?"

"Not everyone does. It depends on how we live our lives, what we do…"

"I understand," Rikki said. "He's not a bad man. He just doesn't know…doesn't understand."

Katie smiled and nodded. "Never stop loving him," she said.

A hill of green, made of denser light waves, beckoned them. Atop the hill stood a spreading, wild-looking, gnarled old tree with a dozen thick "branches" of bronze-colored light, and a hundred smaller, progressively finer ones laden with little "fruit"—different colored self-luminous lights, hanging ripe and ready for the picking. They walked up a worn, mossy path, through a field of impatiens of every pink and purple hue, and approached the great tree. It greeted them with warm, sweet fragrances and a continuously hummed melody.

"Is there food here? I mean…that we can we actually eat?" Rikki asked.

"Simply think of any fruit, and this or any other tree here will produce it for you in abundance—and yes, you may eat it."

"Wow! And what if I'm thirsty?"

Katie pointed to the valley below. "When we go, we'll head that way, to the village there. We'll cross a little river of light, and you will taste its waters, and they will enliven you and fill you with the power of dreams. After drinking from it, you'll never thirst again."

"Really? What kind of power is the power of dreams?" Rikki asked.

"Well, do you recall, in sleep, being able to swim underwater without the need to breathe? Or being able to float into the air and fly?"

"I do," Rikki said. "It was such fun! And I could materialize whatever I wanted, like a magician. Only it wasn't a trick. It was real, and all I had to do was think of it and it would show up!"

"That wasn't a just a dream, Rikki. It was a real experience recalled in a level of consciousness we simply call dreams. A memory. You had those powers here, in this Heaven, before you were born on Earth. And you will have them again, very soon."

"Are you kidding me?"

"No," she laughed. "I swear."

"Is that why it felt so real?"

"Yes. Because it was real here, in as much as all experiences are real."

Rikki turned his gaze to the surrounding mountains. Katie did too, to the far-off peaks, capped with white, luminous snow, and to the grassy hills downslope from them, and to the spreading pink and white clouds above, and to the songs that came from each object in the astral consciousness into which they had arisen, melodies sweet and soft and inspirational, and everywhere, everything made of light.

"It's so beautiful," he said. "What's it called, this world?"

"Gaia: The union of the Divine Male energy force, Uranus, with the Divine Mother aspect of God. In our world, Uranus was the mythical personification of the heavenly skies, and Mother Earth, beneath him, held him in her orbit, entranced. This is your home now, Rikki."

"Will I die here too? I mean, you know…someday."

"Here you can live and play and work at whatever you like. You can eat and sleep and love and, yes, even 'die,' though, as you now know, the process is more like a graduation to a higher level of consciousness than a finality."

"The astral world? Right?"

"Yes."

"Anything I think of will be there, just like in my dreams?"

"Yes."

"Anything and anyone?"

"Anyone who can come, will come—but not everyone can come, Rikki."

"I understand," he said, biting his lip. "But *if* they can, they'll meet me wherever I want, right? If I think of them."

"Yes. That's right."

"How do you know these things?" Rikki asked.

"The Stranger told me."

"Will he teach me too?"

"I don't know," Katie said. "Perhaps." She gestured to the valley. "Shall we walk a little farther?" she asked.

Rikki paused and suddenly stood very still and closed his eyes.

"What is it? What's wrong?"

"Nothing," he said. "I'm thinking of seeing my mom again."

Katie looked to the valley and smiled. "She'll like that."

"She's here!" Rikki's voice rose to a high pitch. "I feel it!"

Katie nodded, and Rikki took her hand and tugged her, and they headed down the hill. He said in a loud and happy voice, "She's going to meet us at the river of dreams!"

"Yes," Katie said. "Wonderful." And now Katie slowed, and Rikki released her and ran ahead, and Katie paused and held her ground. She felt the presence of someone. Someone Divine. And his voice came into her consciousness before he arrived within sight. And the voice said: "Katie, if you truly wish to be my follower, you must take up my cross and engage in my war, in the battle of light against darkness."

"Yes, Lord," Katie said aloud, turning around to locate the source. "I do. I will take up your cross. I will follow you."

"And if you would come after me, you must deny your very self and take up your own cross, and the wounds thereof."

"Yes, Lord," Katie said. "I will. I promise. I will."

"By what power do you answer thusly?"

"By the power of faith, Lord," Katie said.

"Then this I promise: You shall be as an apprentice unto me, and with your faith, verily, nothing shall be impossible for you. Should you command a tree to be uprooted and planted in the sea, it shall be uprooted and planted in the sea. Should you say unto the mountains, 'Move there!' they shall be moved. Such is the power you shall command. And if you should ever call for me, I shall come."

On hearing these words, Katie fell to her knees and touched the pierced feet of the Word of God.

Darkness had fallen, and Stone had caught a chill. Hours had passed since the miracle with Ruthie and the healing of the crippled boy and the sudden death of Rikki Brandt. The mayor had provided a car and driver for Stone and Jessie, transportation to a private dinner at Gracie Mansion at Jack's invitation. Jessie had insisted on stopping at her East Side apartment for a change of clothes, and Stone, warming himself in the vehicle, waited for her to come back down. After the hours of drama, joy, mourning, and mayhem in the park, he needed a break.

Stone had watched as Becka wept bitterly after seeing the Stranger. She had stayed on her knees long after the miracle, and when the mayor had come beside her, she'd clung to his leg, saying over and over, "I'm sorry. I am so sorry." She'd cried and cried, even as Rikki's nurse cried, and the rest of the crow rejoiced. But she'd refused to say for what. Jack had pulled Becka to her feet, held her close, and kissed her on the forehead, like she was a child. It had become clear then, even to clueless bystanders, that Becka was indeed Jack Molinaro's lover. And she loved him. Any fool could see it. But no one said it. Not even Jack's worst enemies in the press pit.

Jessie came down from her apartment and got into the car, clutching a small bag. She hadn't changed. She'd just grabbed some fresh clothes. "Hey, you all right?" she asked Stone.

"Yeah," he said. "Just thinking." She had warmed to him even more since the incident on the terrace with Cezar, probably because of what Ruthie had said. His heart had skipped a beat when she'd threaded her arm through his on the terrace. It felt like she belonged with him now, and always had, like somehow they'd known and loved each other before, perhaps in another life or another world, as Ruthie had intimated.

The mayor had closed the city to cars. Only cops, emergency vehicles, cabs, and buses could navigate the streets. Stone now tapped the driver on the shoulder, signaling they were ready, and they rolled through the streets again, slowly, silently, the tan sedan like a sun-bleached tumbleweed at the bottom of a dark canyon, veering side to side to avoid double-parked trucks, idling cabs, and clueless pedestrians crossing while texting.

Thinking back to the park and the miracle, Stone felt Jack had seemed deeply conflicted. After comforting Becka, he'd come over to Stone and Jessie and Rikki's nurse, and when he'd calmed the nurse enough for her to call Brandt, they'd all stepped away and talked about what had happened.

"Why do you think the Stranger heals some," Jessie had asked, "and leaves others to die?"

"What is a human body to one who creates the very universe?" Jack had replied, quoting the TryChristianity.com website.

"So you have read it?" Stone had said.

"Yes. And now I have seen him with my own eyes."

"And…" Stone asked, "is he the messenger of God?"

"If he is, frankly, I'm pretty disappointed," Jack had said. Then he'd gestured to the throng of sick and hopeless, the same people who'd surrounded Gracie Mansion demanding access to the terrace and who were no better off than when they'd arrived. "I have a hard time saying this, but I agree with Brandt, and with what Jessie said earlier: If he can heal one, why doesn't he heal them all? Why didn't he heal Katie?"

"It's true," Stone said. "It's baffling. But then again, maybe that's not what he's here to do. Maybe he's trying to get us to understand that we are not our bodies. They're important, but what really matters to him is how we use them. At least that's how I read the scroll."

"I wish I had such faith," Jack Molinaro had said. "I just don't."

The car pulled through the gates at Gracie Mansion.

"Been here before?" Becka asked, greeting them as they exited the vehicle.

"Never," Stone said, turning to admire the view of the East River, and the waning moon over the water, and the lights in the thousands of windows on the far shore in the countless Queens high-rises. "But I've Googled it."

"Mind if I go in and change?" Jessie asked, looking to the house.

Becka said, "Sure," and with a tilt of her head gestured for Jessie to go up the stairs. "Bathroom is—"

"I'll find it."

"Okay," Becka said. "She's a pip."

"Yup." Stone smiled.

"Kind of instant connection, huh?"

"Yes."

"Been there, done that," she said. "So what did it say?"

"What did what say?"

"Google?"

"Oh. Well, I'm sure you know more about it than they do," he said.

"Impress me," Becka insisted.

"Well, it was once an ice cream parlor."

"Gracie Mansion? Really? Wow. What else?"

"Ah, there you are…" Jack called out from the back porch. "Good. We can get started. We have a surprise for you, Stone. A special guest."

Jessie returned to the patent-yellow parlor and said, "How do I look?"

Her voice spun Stone around.

Out of her jeans and now in a short, silvery, silk chiffon sequined sheath, she looked "stunning," Stone said. The dress followed her every curve, and Jessie flowed on her feet like oil on water. Effortlessly slick. She stood taller now too in new, skin-tight glove-leather gray boots.

"Well, I suppose it is Fashion Week." Jack smiled. "Even if the world is upside down."

The gold crucifix around her neck, the one given her by Ruthie, glistened, and Jessie's fingers kept going to it, as if to confirm it still hung there, as if she still couldn't believe it did.

"Yeah," Stone said. "I've covered it. Last year, in fact. At Javits."

"NY1 sent a combat Marine to cover a fashion show?" Becka asked. "I have to talk to Connie."

Stone laughed. "Hey, those catfights down there can get pretty intense, you know."

Becka managed a smile.

"So, you're a model?" Jack asked Jessie.

"Sometimes," she said. "But tonight I just wanted to—"

"I'm sorry, I didn't realize everyone had arrived," Jeremiah said, entering now from the other side of the room, nestling a teacup in the palm of one hand.

"So you're our mystery guest?" Stone said.

"Cool. I was hoping to actually meet you, you know, face-to-face," Jessie said.

"A great pleasure," Jeremiah said. He held out his hand, and Stone took it. Then Jeremiah turned to Jessie and said, "She told me you'd be sassy."

"I'm sorry. What?"

Jeremiah ignored Jessie's question for the moment and said, "Hello, Becka." He nodded to her and then sat in one of two high-back greenish-yellow chairs near the fireplace, just a few feet from the coffee table that separated the chairs from the sofa.

Jessie took the empty chair beside Jeremiah and stared at him. "What did you just say?" she asked.

Jeremiah merely smiled.

Stone pulled over a Chippendale chair with a green-and-yellow-striped seat, and he sat too. With Becka and Jack now parked on the sofa, he completed the circle of five.

"So, what is it you've come to talk about?" Jack asked.

"Wait," Jessie said. "Nobody's asking anything else until I get an answer: Who said I'd be what?"

"Your mother," Jeremiah said. "She told me you would be sassy."

"You talked to my mother? How? When?"

"This afternoon," Jeremiah said. "Katie was there too."

"What the hell are you talking about?" Jack said. "My sister is in an ICU unit at—"

"Yet she wrote you a note, and saw your swim in the lake, and she witnessed Ruthie's miracle, and the passing of the Brandt boy. Katie is with him right now, in fact."

"Seriously?" Stone said.

"That's what I've been asked to come here and explain."

"Asked to come here?" Jack moved to the edge of the sofa. "By whom?"

"By the author of the M-39 scroll."

"You mean the Stranger?" Stone said. "If so, why not just say so plainly?"

"Because once you know him, you can't call him that, as you shall see."

"I'm already confused," Stone said.

"You're all going to have to wait your turn," Jessie said. "I want to hear about my mom."

Jeremiah gestured to Jessie's crucifix. "Do you want me to tell everyone where that came from and why it's so special?"

"You know?

Jeremiah nodded.

"She told you?"

"Yes."

Jessie took a moment and then said, "No." She held the crucifix between two fingers and shook her head. "It's private," she said.

"Well," Stone said, "then do tell us more about the author of the scroll. Please. I for one am fascinated by it and the message it contains."

"I have it," Jack said.

"You?" Stone asked. "But, I gave it to—"

"I sent it to him," Jeremiah said. "For the translation of the other messages on it, and for safekeeping from Brandt."

"Other messages? Okay…and?" Stone said.

"It's…impossible," Jack said.

"Meaning?"

"Some friends, experts up at Columbia, tested it. Carbon-dated the pigments in the ink on the scroll to around 9000 BC.

"What?" Stone asked.

"That's right: It was written nine thousand years *before* Christ, and yet it quotes Jesus, word for word, from the book of Matthew—"

"Chapter five?"

"Verse thirty-nine…" Jack said. "M-39. 'Resist not evil, but turn the other cheek.' The experts at Columbia said it's either the best fake ever made, or it's real and time is simply the Stranger's plaything."

"That was the point," Jeremiah said. "To establish himself as the author of time."

"And the note?" Stone asked. "Was it really from your sister?"

"In her handwriting, citing an event she, or it, says will happen soon. But that's all, Stone. I'm not going to say any more about the note," Jack said. "Except that I have no idea when it was really written or by whom, and there's no way to tell."

"Fair enough," Stone said.

"Now I have a question for Jeremiah," Jack said. "Why didn't the Stranger heal my sister?"

"I asked that too," Jeremiah replied. "He said I had to be the first one healed. Katie has a different destiny."

"That's not very comforting," Jack said.

"And when you say you were 'with' my mom?" Jessie asked now. "Can you prove it?"

"Sa-weena," Jeremiah said.

Jessie's eyes went wide.

"What?" Stone asked.

"It's her name," Jessie said. "I'm the only one who ever called her that. As a baby, I couldn't pronounce Sabrina, so I called her—"

"Sa-weena. Wow."

"Why were Katie's wounds so fresh," Jack asked, "after a whole day and night with the Stranger? And how could Ruthie come back younger?"

"Good questions. And since I've now presumably passed the test, and you all at least allow for the possibility that I am telling the truth"—Jeremiah's tone had become firm—"let's get down to it. I have been sent to explain some things. Three things, in fact. First, I am to tell you about the Stranger's house of light. Second, I am to tell you about the true nature of all your experiences in what we call time. Finally, I will clarify some things about Jesus. Okay?"

Everyone nodded agreement.

"First: The Stranger's house of light," Jeremiah said. "Time does not exist in there. A lifetime in the world can be a minute in the light, and a minute in the world, a lifetime when merged."

"Wait. The Stranger took you in there?" Jessie asked. "Into that house of light? And that's where you met my mother?"

"Yes. But there is no 'there' there. No time. No actual, physical place," Jeremiah explained. "That's the point. It's a sort of portal to other worlds, and to the many Heavens."

"Many Heavens?" Stone asked.

"Yes. Jesus referred to these when he said, 'In my Father's house, there are many mansions.' God's house is the phenomenal universe, and it's much bigger than the one we see. It exists on many planes. The worlds he refers to are spiritual abodes, the mansions."

"Okay, so Ruthie is not physically inside that little house on the Point right now?" Stone asked.

"No. This is actually the most important thing for you all to understand about those who go into the house of light with the Stranger: When you enter, you leave this plane of existence and become a purely spiritual being. When you return, you become physical again and are mortal and vulnerable. Understood?"

Again, everyone nodded.

"Now, the second thing I must convey…"

"Wait," Stone said. "Just to be clear, for Jessie's sake—while Ruthie is in the light, she does not need her meds?"

"That's correct," Jeremiah said. He turned to Jessie. "She's fine. She's with your mother, and others, and you must be prepared for the possibility that she may want to stay where she is now."

Jessie bit her lip again. Tears welled up in her eyes, and her gaze drifted.

"Well, she certainly looked great," Stone said. "And happy. But that begs the question that's already been asked: How could she have come back younger and so much stronger and healthier?"

"This is the second thing I am to tell you. Time is merely a construct, one that is necessary for the experience of separateness."

"Separateness? From what?"

"From that out of which the experience of 'I' has arisen, like a wave."

"What?" Jack shook his head.

"Think of your whole life like a reel of film, a long one," Jeremiah said. "You 'live' it, you experience it as a flow of experience, though it really passes one frame at a time, one captured moment of 'now' at a time. But the whole thing has already been shot and developed. The entire experience is now."

"Okay," Stone said. "That doesn't help at all. And?"

"It will. Think on it. In the light of God-awareness, of your true being-ness, and when given Divine Permission, you may control the projector, the enlivening energy that shines through the frames, bringing the film of your life in a particular body into apparent existence, or what we call personal experience. From there, you can unroll the whole film if you like, and pick any moment, and return to any frame, simply by consciously willing the light to shine through at a particular frame. It's not exactly like that, but it is in a way. And that's what Ruthie did. She came back to now, from a sort of heavenly then."

"Give me a break," Jack said. "I mean, really." He stood and began to pace. He went to the bar and poured himself a drink.

"Becka," Jeremiah said, ignoring Jack's emotional outburst and sudden rudeness. "I saw you crying at the park today. I felt your longing for God, and for forgiveness. I know, even now, the source of your shame at what you have done, for I went back in time to then and saw it all, to help me prepare for now."

"What are you talking about?" Jack asked.

"It's all part of the Akashic record. The book of life. Forward and back. It's why prophets know the future, and why Katie could write what she wrote you, Jack."

Jack turned to Jeremiah but did not reply. "What she wrote is impossible now."

"Like walking on water. Healing the sick? Raising the dead? That kind of impossible?"

Becka went to the bar now too and, with her hands visibly shaking, she started to pour herself a drink. Jack took the decanter from her and filled her glass. He handed it to her, eyes intensely focused on hers. "What is he saying?" Jack asked Becka. "What have you done?"

"What have you done?" She glared at him. "What have we all done?" She surveyed the room, and Stone recalled a Bible verse: *There is none righteous, no not one.*

"Like you, Jack, she has sinned," Jeremiah said. "We all have. Yet Becka doesn't really want to believe in any of this now because she feels she can't. If she does, she fears she'll have to pay. Isn't that right, Becka? It's torturous to know what we've done, and have to face it, to face God and judgment."

Becka stared at him but did not respond.

"If you do believe, you fear you'll face the old, stern, ruthless Father in Heaven. But please, do not fear that, Becka. The Son of God says, 'Judge not and ye shall not be judged.'"

"Not judged?" Jack asked. "For what?"

"No. No one will be. You'll just carry your karma with you as part of your energetic body, a kind of soul-based blueprint of your phenomenal existence and human being-ness, until you realize your true nature, your essential oneness with the One out of whom all arise. When you do, you'll be free of karma, because you'll have realized your unity with the Source, with God. In the meantime, please, try to sin no more. For the sake of those whom you love, those whom your sins will harm, and in order to help cultivate and sustain your own peace." Jeremiah turned to Becka again and said, "Please. Confess. Make amends. Be contrite and ask for God's mercy."

"I want to go," Jessie stood up and said. "Right now. Take me into the light."

"The only way in is to be called," Jeremiah said.

"Then I want to be called."

Jeremiah stood now too and took her hand, and stared at her like a caring father. "What do you know about God, Jessie?"

"Nothing. I have no idea," Jessie said.

"What about Jesus?"

"He's deaf," Jessie said, and she pulled away and sat again, arms crossed. "As far as I can tell."

"And your grandmother?" Jeremiah asked, sitting again too. "How does she feel about him?"

"What is this? A shrink session?" Jessie asked.

"Shall I tell you how your grandmother feels about Jesus?" Jeremiah asked.

"She loves Jesus. Never misses Mass, all right? Communion every single day. Right?"

"Why?" Jeremiah asked. "Ask yourself why she loves Jesus. But, to answer, I promise, you'll have to understand his essence. Do you know the passage about Jesus being the Word of God?"

"Yes," Jessie said.

"It describes, perhaps more aptly than any other passage, the essential Jesus, the Son aspect of God: God incarnate, in a physical form, a body. For what is a 'word' if not intelligent vibration, intelligent energy going forth from God with materializing power?" Jeremiah asked.

"Okay," Jessie said. "So what? Jesus was not a man?"

"He said as much. His body was not him. You are *not* your body. He realized his oneness with all creation and therefore could never act against anyone, because he saw himself in everyone. Can you claim that?"

"No," Jessie said.

"Yet you must. We all must. He said we are one with him, and he is one with the Source, our Father. If you conceive of the Messiah as Saint John does, Jesus the carpenter, the physical body, is merely the suit of clothes worn by the Divine Word within it, the Divine Animating Force within *all of us* being the only begotten 'offspring' or Son of God, for God is not confined by time or space or physicality but is the omnipresent, omnipotent, and omniscient Source of All that appears as the universe. You see? And God's 'children' cannot be essentially different from that out of which they have arisen. We are one with him, with God—thus we cannot strike one another without striking the very Lord. And this is the final message for you, Jack. To you, I came to bring a warning: Accept the Stranger's authority, see him as God's messenger, as the Word incarnate, and submit to the Lord's instructions, even when all seems lost, even when you know yourself to be in mortal danger."

"What does that mean, exactly?" Jack asked. "Am I facing death?"

"It means God has long whispered to your soul, Jack, and tried to reach you. There is so much good in you, but you are still so stubborn. You want what you want and cannot say, 'Thy will be done,' as Jesus did. Your shortsighted hatred for Brandt clouds your vision and keeps you from seeing the Divine Hand in all that happens. You reject the command to trust the Lord. You actively resist evil with evil even though you have been commanded not to do so. You take matters into your own hands and justify your sin because you tell yourself you are fighting an even greater sin. Don't you see? Like Peter, you take up the sword and become what you loathe in your enemy! You must learn that though you are entitled to work, you are not entitled to the fruits of your labor or any particular outcome. Nor are you entitled to try to force the world to give you what God withholds. Just as fruits are not produced by a tree, but through it, by the grace of God, and the power of the sun and the earth and the rain, all that is produced through you belongs to God. Alone, you produce nothing. So here again I give my final warning: Put down your sword or you will impale your soul on it. Submit to the teachings of God, for they are clear and need no interpreter. Love thy enemy and trust God to bring about good things. Say, 'Thy will be done,' when faced with even the most terrible fate, and trust God to bring forth goodness from it, even if it seems like the end, like death to you or those you love. Do this and you will live forever. Ignore it, and you and yours and indeed all of mankind will surely perish in the coming war the world has prepared for its own end. The death of every man, woman, and child looms. Heed M-39."

CHAPTER 15

DEE WEISS STRUGGLED AGAINST THE SILVER DUCT TAPE, BUT IT DID not give. She flexed her legs. The chair creaked, but it did not give either.

Impetuous. Reckless. Hardheaded. Willful. These were surely her worst traits. But loyalty, and the desire to protect those she loved, and the drive to demand and deliver justice, to get it even if by force, these were attributes worth a life. Worth her own life. What would her life be now anyway, without her Katie?

"You her sa-sister?" Thomas Breckenridge asked.

She shook her head and stared at the shiny blade, and then at her raincoat, heaped on the floor with her clothing, and now at her silly floppy hat on the one-eyed man's head. Her father's 12-gauge shotgun sat on the kitchen counter, and beside it a canister of pills, prescription drugs, stood like a round of ammunition. Her head throbbed. Blood, a dry, red river delta of it, spread across her naked breasts from, she assumed, the stinging wounds he'd punched into her face after he'd taken away the gun.

"He knows what I am," he said now. "The one they're calling the Sa-stranger. He knows, and still he didn't let me die." Tommy went to the counter, picked up the shotgun, pulled up a chair and faced her. "What were you tha-thinking, coming here with this? Huh?"

In her mind, Dee screamed: My mouth is taped shut, you idiot!

"Your eyes say you're more angry than scared," he said. "That's ga-gonna change."

He slid a finger up the wound on his own face. He'd peeled off the bandages an hour earlier. His finger bumped over each tightly knotted, black stitch. He picked at his eye socket, winced.

Blood.

He showed her.

"She done this to me." He laughed a hoarse laugh. "Your Katie," he managed. "I seen the light too, that na-night on the lake. When she ca-cut me, I thought: eye for an eye. Justice done. Repaid in ka-kind." And now he touched the bloody tip of his finger to Dee's forehead. "Thinking about a sa-sin is the same as doing it, the Bible says." He ran the finger down her face, dragged it under pressure, over her left eye. "So sa-since you ca-ca-ca-come here thinking of da-doing me harm, it's the same as if you'd da-done the harm, so maybe you owe me one. Ma-maybe," he pushed harder on her eye.

"Muuuhhh!" Dee turned away sharply and squirmed. Her heart pounded.

"There ya ga-go," he said. "That's what I'm ta-talking about. Fa-fear, when you look in my eye. You see it?" He stood again and began to pace, shotgun in hand, voice returning. "I figure he's wrong. That Da-denny. You know…the governor. But then again I figure he's just like me: He is who he is and can't help it. He knows it, that Stranger man, yet he lets a man like that Denny run around and do what he does. Maybe even run the whole world into Hell."

Dee thought, if I get the chance, I swear I'm going to—

"Yeah," he said. "You wa-want to ka-kill me. I can sa-see it. Seen it a lot. Makes it easier, 'cause it means you're ja-just like ma-me."

Dee turned away, closed her eyes.

"But here's what, and you listen up, you hear?" He touched her.

Her eyes flashed, and she squirmed wildly.

"There's a good ga-girl," he said. "I'll da-do you a good deed. I will. I'll give you some of them sleeping pills I seen you eyeing over there on the counter, so you won't have to, you know, ba-be here for the fun."

She shook her head wildly: *No!*

"But first you're going to tell who na-knows you come over…" He reached for her again. "To pay ole Ta-tom-tommy a va-visit." He took hold of the edge of the duct tape covering her lips and started to peel it back.

Dee sat perfectly still.

"Mind now," he said with a smile, "you whisper in my ear, nice and soft, 'cause if you ra-raise your voice, they're gonna need a sa-sewing ka-kit to stitch you back together when I'm done cutting you…"

Almost immediately after Jeremiah left Gracie Mansion, an aide summoned Jack to the phone. The White House was on the line.

Stone sat with Becka and Jessie, and they awaited Jack's return. No one spoke. Stone, his mind still far too active with all that Jeremiah had said, tried to put things into context. A story he'd heard once, while stationed in Iraq, came to mind. A Hindu relief worker had told him the intriguing tale late one night after Stone had complained aloud about being unable to sleep because of having too many thoughts racing through his mind. The Hindu had asked Stone if he could hold on to any two of the many thoughts at the same time. "Go ahead and try," he'd said. But Stone couldn't do it. Then the Hindu said that Lord Krishna, a kind of Hindu Christ—an aspect of the Divine personified and embodied, in Jeremiah's terms—had come to Earth in part because so many people were suffering from the very same problem. No one in the Lord's kingdom, it seemed, ever thought of God anymore because their minds were always preoccupied with other thoughts. And being also unable to hold two thoughts at once, they'd all chosen, if only by default, against being with God.

The Lord decided to take on bodily form to remind people of his Divine Presence. Yet soon after Lord Krishna had been born into the world, this problem returned. Even with God in their physical midst, people had returned to their daily routines, to their wants and needs, to their thoughts of past and future, and they'd forgotten the Lord again. "Yes, Mr. Stone," the Hindu had said, "Lord Krishna, a beautiful child at that time, a prince among them, had only been with them a few years. Yet they quickly became so used to his presence that they began to ignore him, to take his Divine Presence for granted."

Frustrated, Stone recalled, the young Lord Krishna had next decided to take a radical step: He would go from house to house in the middle of the night and steal the people's favorite delicacy, their precious cheese curds. Soon word spread of the thievery. It was all anyone could talk about: How much they'd lost! And when the kingdom learned that the Lord himself had stolen the food, everyone ran about searching for the child, shouting his name: "Krishna! Krishna!"

Stone had laughed, but the Hindu was somber.

"Don't let it be so with you, Terry Stone," the Hindu had said. "Don't ignore God so much that he must take from you that which is most precious, just so he can hear you call his name again."

Now Stone thought of Cezar. What had happened to his kid brother had driven him to question all his beliefs, especially about God, but also about guns, war, even self-defense. He had fallen to his knees and prayed to God for forgiveness when Cezar lay near death, an act he never would have considered but for his pain and loss. He knew he had failed often, since then, to keep thoughts of

God in his mind and in his heart. His ego, his pride, his desire for glory had pushed God out.

Denny Brandt…

Stone could see the man's face in his mind's eye. He wondered: Had the death of Rikki caused Brandt to reassess his life? Or had it merely further alienated him from all things divine?

Had he called out for God, even if only in anger?

And Katie Molinaro? What of her? Was she really in Heaven with Brandt's son?

And will Jack heed Jeremiah's words?

What *would* Jack have to have taken from him in order to get him to think of God first? To trust and put himself in God's hands?

And now Jack returned to the patent-yellow parlor with a broad smile on his face, and said, "Sorry about dinner, but he's sent *Air Force Two*."

"What? Why?" Becka asked.

"*Air Force Two*," Stone said, surprised by Becka's question. "Why else?" He stood. "Congratulations, Mr. Vice President."

"I don't get it," Jessie said.

"*Air Force Two*," Stone said. "It means—"

"Oh," Jessie said. "So, like, you're going to be the next—"

"Vice president." Stone shook Jack's hand.

"It doesn't make sense," Becka said.

"What do you mean?" Jack asked.

"Did he specifically ask you? Did he say that was why he was going to fly you down there?"

"No, but—"

"It's not right, Jack. There've been no screenings, no—"

"I've already been screened," Jack said. "Look, I have to change and go." And he bounded up the stairs.

Avizheh Ali Beheshti watched CNN. On the television screen, smoke rose from the city of his birth like a dark genie fleeing a broken lamp. Bomb after bomb exploded. Missile after missile lit up the night sky. The Americans and their allies were reducing the Iranian capital of Tehran to rubble.

Seven hundred and fourteen miles to the southwest, on the border with Iraq, Iranian troops streamed across the Shatt al-Arab River and raced toward the Basra International Airport. American transport planes were landing, charged with the job of reestablishing Camp Bravo, abandoned since the US withdrawal in 2011.

"And now comes word that the city that served as home port for Sinbad in the tales of *The Arabian Nights*," the CNN anchor said, "is the site of what sources have called the first American M-39 casualty. Here is the next chapter of a story that in many ways is stranger than fiction…" An unsteady phone camera zoomed in on a lone young American army lieutenant, moving as if in slow motion across a dusty expanse of red earth littered with twisted steel and concrete and puddles of black crude oil. As fighter jets screamed overhead, the unarmed American in combat fatigues raised his hands in surrender to Avizheh's former countrymen. The Iranian troops fired anyway. The soldier's helmet flew from his shattered face and tumbled to the dirt. The *M-39* emblazoned on his helmet in white paint hit the ground first. His limp body followed, kicking up a puff of red clay dust on impact.

The news network cut to Central Park and showed thousands laying down arms at Bethesda Terrace: US military veterans first, then petty criminals, organized-crime thugs, drug dealers, hunters, ex-cops…M16s, AK-47s, rifles, pistols, grenades, rocket launchers, machine guns, and machetes formed a huge pile at the feet of the Angel of the Waters statue.

And now the screen showed a list of conflicts and places in which conflicts had cost American lives: the Korean War, Formosa,

Vietnam, Egypt, Lebanon, Thailand, Cuba, Laos, the Congo, Dominican Republic, the USS *Liberty* in Israel, Zaire, Cambodia, Cyprus, Operation Eagle Claw in Iran, Operation Bright Star in Egypt, El Salvador, Libya, Sinai, Granada, Honduras, Chad, Libya again, Bolivia, the USS *Stark* and the Iran–Iraq war—military action after military action, undeclared war after war after war. "M-39!" they shouted. "Enough killing! No more war!" And the gathered crowd sang John Lennon's classic: "All we are saying…is give peace a chance…" Over and over they repeated the lyric, while hundreds of NYPD police officers stood by in riot gear, watching without making a single arrest, by order of the mayor, who had "defied the governor and allowed this to continue," according to the newscaster on the scene.

Avizheh flipped through the channels. The same thing was happening all over America, in towns and cities everywhere. People were putting down their guns "for the sake of the children."

His mother came into the room. "It's beautiful," she said.

"You've read it?"

She nodded. "Thank you for telling me. Allah be praised."

"You'll have to show him," Avizheh said. "He won't listen to me, and I can't let him do this. This is my home now, mother. We can't let him—"

"Yes," she said. "I will. Now go and tell him good night. Tomorrow is for school, and you must be up early."

"But—"

"Please. I promise you, my son. Everything will be all right."

Avizheh rose from the sofa and quietly descended the stairs of his family's Brooklyn brownstone to the dimly lit basement. Two steps from the bottom, he paused to watch as his father, Arash, pulled a dusty tarp off of a large brushed aluminum suitcase that sat on a workbench. Arash opened the case to reveal an electronic death machine with twisted, wiry guts and canisters of lethal doom.

Avizheh took another step down. The stair creaked.

His father spun to face him, eyes wide and body tense.

"You cannot do this," Avizheh said. "Please, Father."

Arash Beheshti exhaled audibly and turned and pushed a button. A timer lit up, and numbers began to count down. "Allahu Akbar," he said. He closed the lid, latched the case, lifted it by the handle, and crossed the floor. He slid past Avizheh and climbed the stairs.

The door at the top opened. But when Avizheh turned, he realized that his mother stood in the light at the top, blocking his father's path.

"No, Daddy! No! Help me! No!" Abbey shrieked and sat up in bed, weeping and waving her arms and slapping and hitting and screaming, "No! No! No!"

"Oh my God," Saragossa said. "What do we do? She won't wake up."

"Last night too," Sophia said. "Okay, baby." She stroked Abbey's hair. "Okay..."

Abbey finally settled down and drifted back to what appeared to be a peaceful sleep.

"Have you eaten?" Sophia asked her.

Saragossa shook her head: no.

"Come," Sophia said.

Saragossa followed her to the dining room.

"William," Sophia shouted toward a door that led to the kitchen. "Wine, please. Bring one for Miss Lindy too. She's off duty."

"No, really. I couldn't."

"And some feta and olives and oil and some fruit and bread," Sophia added. "And warm pita." Sophia turned to Saragossa. "Please...sit. You are Greek, yes?"

"On my mother's side...and Catalan."

JAMES PATRICK DILLON

"Of course: Saragossa. Beautiful city. Jack and I have been many times. He loves it there."

After a few moments, William entered with the food and wine. "Thank you," Saragossa said as he set down the tray and placed everything neatly before her. He then slipped away silently.

"You didn't say anything." Sophia took a sip of her wine and stared with eyebrows raised. "Earlier…after the bad dreams."

"You mean about you and the mayor?"

Sophia nodded. "And how it's affecting Abbey."

"He's my boss. And he's the mayor. And I hardly—"

"So what? Truth is truth, no?" Sophia said.

"I suppose. But what do I know about marriage?" Saragossa took another sip of wine and then sneaked a peek at the bottle. "I'm just two years out of college, and I've never even been in a serious relationship."

"Well, I've told him I don't want a divorce."

"Really?"

Sophia nodded. "Anyway, you will stay here tonight. You have to sleep sometime, and it's so late already, and you'd have to come back early, I think?"

"I do, but I don't know…" Saragossa said.

"You stayed up all night last night, so that's it. Consider it an order. I'll lend you some clothes and…why not?"

Saragossa felt exhausted. She washed down the pita with another gulp of what she concluded must be the best wine she had ever tasted, and said, "Yes. Thank you."

Sophia nodded and smiled again. She raised her glass.

Saragossa held up hers too. "This is amazing."

"Tormaresca Castel del Monte Rosso Bocca di Lupo, Puglia. Two thousand."

"Dollars?" Saragossa's eyes bulged.

241

Sophia nearly spit her wine out, she laughed so hard. "You are so cute!" She shook her head and regained her composure. "The year two thousand."

"Oh my God!"

"It's thirty dollars per bottle!"

"No!" Saragossa laughed too and took another big gulp. "Then I'd like some more!"

Sophia laughed again. "William. More wine!"

"You think it's really possible?" Jessie asked, standing on the back lawn under the stars, pausing for a moment to look into the heavens and take in the clear, cool night air.

"Do I think what's possible?"

"That he's a messenger from God?"

"I don't know. Feels like it when I see him."

Tears filled Jessie's eyes, and spilled. She touched her crucifix.

"Can you tell me about it?" Stone asked softly.

"It was a gift from my mother, when I made my first Holy Communion."

"It's beautiful," Stone said.

Jessie bit her lip. A tear tumbled out of her eye and rolled like a tiny glass bead down her cheek. "But it's not possible." She shook her head.

"What's not possible?" Stone asked softly, taking hold of her hand. "After all we've seen?"

"I gave it to her when she was in the hospital. I gave it to her and she…" Jessie began to sob, her face in her hands. "She was buried with it!"

Stone stood speechless.

"Do you understand?" Jessie asked. "I mean how do you explain that?"

242

"I—I can't," Stone said. "But I'm thinking that a lot of people wish they could have proof of the existence of God, and here we are, and we seem to have it. We've seen miracles, and Ruthie getting young, and now this—and yeah, me too. I'm like: How? But at some point, maybe you're just going to have to believe that we really are never far from God. We're not our bodies, and our lives are meant to be something more than a rat race for money and power and—"

"I'd really like to see her again," Jessie said.

"You will. I'm sure of it."

"You really think so?"

Stone nodded. He looked deeply into her eyes and leaned in to kiss her.

"Ah, there you are." Becka came out of the house and spotted them.

"Hi," Stone said. "Uh, maybe give us a minute?"

"Sorry. We don't have one. Follow me." Becka led the way.

"What's it all about?" Stone asked.

"You'll see," Becka said.

Tucked into the very end of the driveway and mostly hidden by the clump of trees, a trailer hummed with activity. A couple of uniformed cops moved about in the shadows along the perimeter walls. Others, in sport coats and wearing earpieces, rushed about so quickly that Stone couldn't count them. "Where the hell did all these people come from?" he asked.

"Been here for two days. A Special Mobile Counterterrorism Unit," Becka said, pausing at the three-step metal staircase that led to the trailer door. She banged twice with a closed fist, pushed open the door, and with a wave of her hand, invited Stone and Jessie in.

Inside, she made the introductions. "This is Joe Black," Becka said, "and these guys are part of his team." She gestured to the three techs in the trailer, each at a different workstation.

"Joe Black, huh? No way," Stone said.

"What?" Becka said.

"Never mind," Stone said. "I'm just a movie buff."

"Brad Pitt played Death, the title character in a movie by that name," Agent Black said. "You know, *Meet Joe Black?*"

"Oh, yeah. I've seen it," Becka said. "Funny. I never put two and two together before."

He held out his hand to Stone. "Call me Joe."

Stone shook his hand.

"Joe is an old friend and Jack's man at the FBI. He runs this field operation."

"By Jack's man, you mean?" Stone said.

"College buddies," Joe said. "He pulled some strings, got me posted to the city."

"This is Jessie," Stone said.

"Hi," Jessie said.

"Okay," Stone said. "So, what are we looking at?"

"We have live video feeds from all over the city." Joe pointed over the shoulder of one of the techs sitting behind a desk with a wall of monitors in front of him. "And we have links to the Situation Room at the White House, DOD, Homeland Security…"

"Cool," Stone said. He counted the monitors: a dozen, each with different images. One flashed views from different cameras and angles, up and down Wall Street. Others monitored the Statue of Liberty and the George Washington Bridge. Two—live and in color—captured Bethesda Terrace in Central Park.

"We've also positioned some highly sensitive scanning equipment at a number of these critical locations. We have them all over the country. All the major cities."

"Scanning for what?" Jessie asked.

"Explosives. Chemical agents. Poison gas. Radioactive materials…"

"Has there been a threat?" Stone asked.

"Ten a day," Joe said. "But that's not what you're here to talk about."

"No?" Stone said. "Then what?"

"You hear anything about people surrendering their weapons in other cities?"

"No. But I half expected it," Stone said.

"Well, it's getting worse. Happening all over."

"What do you mean, worse?" Stone said.

"Yeah, why worse?" Jessie asked. "Why not great!"

"Because it's a coordinated effort…"

"Which means?" Stone said.

"Someone in power might consider it a conspiracy to undermine the morale of our military."

"Someone?"

"Put it this way: the governor's men are all over the TV networks, including your station, Mr. Stone, giving interviews, kicking Jack to pieces. The entire New York State congressional delegation wants him investigated for treason for allowing this gun amnesty in support of the Stranger's M-39 initiative."

"M-39 initiative—wow. So now the words of Jesus Christ are treasonous?"

"Not my call, but I can tell you this: Brandt has gone on record as saying he intends to arrest what he calls 'this foreigner, the so-called Stranger,' by force, if necessary, and have him questioned. And anyone who stands in his way will be charged with aiding and abetting an enemy of the United States of America during a time of war."

"You're kidding?" Stone said. "What makes him think he has that kind of authority?"

"Exactly," Becka said. "That's the point. He's slipped up. Tipped his hand."

"I'm not following," Stone said.

"Let's step outside," Becka said.

They did. As they walked toward the river, Becka said, "Brandt never says anything he can't back up. He's too disciplined for that."

"Meaning?" Stone asked.

"Meaning he's gotten to the president somehow. He has the authority, federal authority, to act against anyone he feels is engaging in treason during a time of war."

"No one but the president has tha—ahhh. I see what you mean. Have you told Jack?"

"Yes. Just now."

"And?"

"He doesn't believe it. He's known RJ for years. They're friends, and Jack wants to believe he's the number two in the administration, RJ's choice."

"I don't understand," Jessie said. "What does all this have to do with me?"

"I've recommended you both to stay here tonight," Becka said.

"What?" Jessie asked.

"Jack has agreed," Becka said.

"Wait. You mean he wants us to sleep here?" Jessie asked. "What the hell?"

"I believe Brandt has made some kind of move, and the president has summoned Jack to the White House to talk to him because there are some things no one, not even he, can say on the telephone."

"You mean you think Brandt is going to be coming after us?" Stone asked.

"Yes," Becka said. "Both of you. And me, if I stick around."

"What did I do?" Jessie asked.

"Your grandmother is with the Stranger. You were in the boat with Stone and the mayor. Brandt's going to want to question you, and I assure you it won't be pleasant."

"So what makes you think we're safe here?" Stone asked.

"If I'm right, you might not be. But I think it's worth waiting until Jack gets to DC and finds out what the hell is really going on. Look, Joe Black in there tells me that Brandt has taken control of the National Guard and has started looking for Jeremiah. You think you two won't be next?"

Stone took a moment and then said, "Where would we sleep?"

"In the private family quarters. Upstairs," Becka said. "There's a guest suite, and one of you can use Abbey's room."

"And the mayor's okay with that?"

"His idea."

"What do you think?" Stone asked Jessie.

"I mean…okay, I guess," Jessie said. "This is insane."

"Great," Becka said. "Jack's dismissing the staff. You'll have the house to yourselves until he returns. There are cops at the gate. You'll be safe." She started for the gate. "Good luck."

"Wait," Stone said. "You're leaving?"

"I told you, he'll be coming for me too if I stick around."

"But what about Jack?"

"Believe me, if what I think is happening actually does happen, Jack's not going to be missing me."

"Try these," Sophia said, holding a bright-red silk pajama top up to Saragossa's blue uniform. "It's your color, don't you think?"

"Yes," Saragossa said nervously, her head still light with too much wine. "I love it…"

"You're a four? Like me?"

"Um-hmmm. But you're bigger on top," Saragossa said.

Sophia smiled and pulled out the bottoms from a built-in dresser, then tossed them on the foot of the king bed. The red pants contrasted starkly with the baby-blue down comforter and soft white pillows Abbey had tossed about. The pillows looked like clouds now, reflected on a quiet Bahamian sea.

Saragossa unconsciously began disrobing, but then she caught herself. "I…um…can I use the restroom?" she asked.

"Ah…yes." Sophia gestured with a toss of her head and led Saragossa to a white door with a gold knob about twenty feet away, across a bright, hand-waxed bamboo floor.

The master bath, the size of her entire apartment, was bright, with a white marble floor and lots of glass and mirrors, and had a huge whirlpool bathtub tiled into one corner.

"Wow," Saragossa said. "This is amazing."

"So take a bath."

"No."

"All the others have only showers," she said. "So you don't really have a choice."

"I couldn't."

"Of course you could. Anyway, you'll sleep in this bed tonight."

"What?"

"You have to sleep somewhere. Really." Sophia said. "I'll go in by Abrianna. Just in case she's having those dreams. Now go ahead. Take your bath…"

Thirty minutes later, Saragossa came out to find Sophia beside the bed again. She'd set black lace panties beside a blue Prada wool-and-silk pleated turtleneck and a pair of black Chris Benz silk pants. "Holy shit," Saragossa gushed. She raised two fingers to her lips. "Oh my God. I'm sorry. I—"

"It's okay," Sophia smiled. "I've heard 'shit' before."

"It's just…these clothes…"

"You'll wear them tomorrow," Sophia said. "And from now on, no uniform. Something about it scares Abbey. The gun, I think."

"Oh? I had no idea. I'm sorry."

"Don't be silly. How could you know?"

Saragossa blushed. "You're so nice to me."

"Abbey adores you already," she said. "And I think you need her too. It's true?"

"Yes," Saragossa said. "It's true. I'd do anything for her."

"Jack said so. He knows people, right away. A politician's gift, and he trusts you. I do too."

CHAPTER 16

AN HOUR BEFORE DAWN ON WEDNESDAY MORNING, JACK STOOD OUT-side the Oval Office for the second time in his life. On his first time there, as a kid from Brooklyn, after the fire and his heroics, he'd been the guest of his dad's friend, a longtime political heavyweight nicknamed Uncle T. Uncle T had brought him along to meet the newly elected president, Ronald Reagan. On that day, in this same famous (and to Jack, hallowed) place, he had also met "the Kid"—Raneri Jacaruso "RJ" Santorro, one of Uncle T's rising political stars. "A real killer. The future of the party," Uncle T had said. "My political protégé."

RJ, a Long Island transplant who'd made it big in the heavy equipment business, had just won election to his first term in the Garden State legislature. Within two years, he sought a US Senate seat and, with the help of Uncle T and Reagan, and political con-servatives from all over the country, he had won in a landslide. Now Reagan was long gone, and RJ himself occupied the most powerful office in the world.

Jack stepped in.

RJ spread his arms wide and offered a bear hug. "Thanks for coming," he said as he grabbed Jack and gave him a series of solid slaps on the back. "Good flight?"

"Yes. Good," Jack said. "Thank you. But I'm already getting calls. The press knows I was on that plane tonight, and it seems a little insensitive to…I mean, unless…"

"Yes," RJ said. "I'm sorry about that. But we've issued a statement and made it clear we needed you here for an emergency meeting. It has nothing to do with the VP spot."

"I see," Jack said.

"Let us handle the press, Jack. No comment. That's all I want you to say."

"Right."

RJ crossed the room and poured them each a double. "Twenty-one-year-old Aberfeldy single malt. I know you won't turn it down. Neat, isn't it?"

Jack hesitated. It's five o'clock in the morning, for God's sake, he thought. But he took the drink.

RJ gestured for Jack to take a seat on the sofa as he downed his double in a gulp. "Sometimes," RJ said, "the thing we think is going to be the source of our salvation ends up being the cause of our demise, eh, Jack?"

"I suppose," Jack said, thinking the comment came out of left field. He took a sip and let the scotch melt down his throat.

Lincoln, in a photograph taken by Alexander Gardner just ten weeks before the esteemed president's assassination, stared at Jack from across the room. The great man's eyes, hauntingly sullen and deeply melancholy, seemed alive in an otherworldly way.

"So, tell me: What's going on, RJ? Why the emergency ride in the middle of the night if you don't want me on the team?"

"Cards face up on the table. No bullshit. That's my Jack," RJ said, and he began to wander around the Oval Office. He paused on the big, round presidential seal on the floor and spoke while gazing down at it. "This…Stranger. The whole thing with the scroll and the things on that website. I understand your impulse in the park. But you broke ranks with the party, Jack. And that means you broke ranks with me."

"You're serious?"

"Come on, Jack. You played right into their hands." RJ came back to the sofa and sat beside him now, uncomfortably close, and held his drink in two hands. He hung his head. "You have to know that."

"Whose hands?"

"You supported the opposition. Your own state delegation wants you skinned alive."

"This sounds like some kind of a prepared speech, RJ," Jack said. He stood.

"An army officer at Camp Bravo tried to surrender to the Iranians today," RJ said. "He refused to fight, and you know what he got for it? A bullet in the face." He raised his glass as if to toast. "And you know what he had, Jack? He had *M-39* painted on his helmet." Now RJ stood. He began to pace again. "We're at war. And if people start questioning whether or not fighting back is a Christian thing to do…well, we might as well take the red and blue off the flag, leave just the white, and change the national anthem to 'Kumbaya'…"

"Are you drunk?" Jack asked.

"Hell yeah." RJ stood again, face-to-face with Jack. "But that doesn't change the fact that you're on the wrong side of this. And if you want to avoid being in a whole world of shit too, you'd better get back on the right side of it, right now."

"Okay," Jack said, moving close enough to smell RJ's breath. "I'll play along, Mr. President. Please. Go ahead. With all due respect: Tell me: How? How do I get on the 'right side' of it?"

"You get the Stranger to surrender."

"Surrender?" Jack laughed and turned his back on the president. "So, he's what? The enemy now?"

"Damn right he is."

"Okay. He's the enemy. What do you want me to do?"

"Use your contacts. That reporter—"

"Stone?"

"Get that black girl to use her grandmother if you have to."

"Black girl?" Jack shook his head. "Jesus. Have you been paying any attention to what's been going on down there?"

"Have you?" RJ asked.

"Right," Jack said. "I'll go home and march across the lake and arrest her. Thanks for the plane ride, old friend. Goddamn waste of time."

"If you can't, someone else will."

"Someone else?" Jack said. "Really? Who?"

"You know who," RJ said, suddenly sounding rather sober.

"Is that what this is about? Did Denny Brandt put you up to this? To calling me in here and trying to get me to fold? Well, I'm not going to fold, RJ."

"I told him as much," RJ said. "But he said I had to try." He rubbed his face.

"He said you had to—what are you saying? You take your orders from Denny Brandt now? Come on!"

"Ah, screw it, Jack, the truth is: He wanted you out of town. He's making his move, right now. He had me send for you."

"Making his mo—what?"

"Now I can wash my hands of the whole mess," RJ said. "I'm sorry, Jack."

"Sorry? Really? Washing your hands?" Jack turned toward the door. "For God's sake." He turned back and paused. "What the hell is happening?"

"He warned you, Jack. He said he did."

"You know what? Becka told me not to come here. She said you—"

"Becka?" RJ laughed. "Of course she did."

"What's that supposed to mean?" Jack came back toward RJ.

"Poor, poor Jack." RJ held up a manila file like a trial lawyer with the final, damning evidence. "Here. You need to see this." He held out the file for Jack to take now. "Go on," he said. "But I warn you. It's going to sting."

The file had the name R. Ramirez penned on it in black marker.

Rebecka Ramirez.

Becka.

"Take it," RJ shouted.

Jack opened it, heart pounding. He came to some photographs. His knees suddenly turned to jelly. He stopped breathing.

Becka…naked. In bed with me. In bed with… "Brandt?" Jack said aloud. "No." He closed the folder and dropped it on RJ's desk. His guts twisted in a knot, and his eyes stung and began to tear. He closed them, rubbed them, and squeezed them so tightly he saw pins of light. "Where did you get this?" he asked.

RJ laughed again. "Where do you think?"

"It's not possible," Jack said. "She wouldn't, couldn't—"

"Couldn't she? What makes her any different than the rest of us? God only knows what he's got on her or what he promised her, but he set you up, Jack. He put her up to it that night when Sophia was out of town. He had Becka get you good and drunk and—"

"No. I don't believe it."

"He said he gave you an out a couple of days ago, but you didn't take it."

"He can go to Hell," Jack said. But he knew better. It wasn't Brandt who was going to Hell. No. Jack was. He was already in it.

And now Jack realized Brandt had a file on RJ too.

Of course.

And in no time at all the music would stop, and Denny Brandt's ass would be the one in the now-empty chair of the vice president of the United States.

And President R. J. Santorro would continue doing exactly as he'd been told…like a puppet on a set of invisible strings, until he had to resign because of "health concerns."

After a night he'd never forget, Terry Stone awakened in the guest room of Gracie Mansion at noon to a wonderful dream, and to the voice of an angel. An hour later they'd dressed, Jessie in her street clothes and vest, Stone in a borrowed pair of Jack's tan khakis and a freshly pressed white cotton shirt. Then they'd gone downstairs.

Still no mayor.

Stone had called Connie and shared Becka's concerns about Brandt with her, but Connie had told him to come back to the park anyway. "No way Brandt would have that kind of clout," Connie had said—and even if he did, she'd gone on to add, he wouldn't mess with a reporter of Stone's newfound prominence. "No great hurry, though. It's been pretty quiet down here."

When he told Jessie about the call to his producer, Jessie had agreed with Connie—it was time to go back, she'd said. So they decided to take a long walk, hand in hand, back to the park to Bethesda Terrace.

And the governor can go to Hell, Stone told himself.

Troglodyte…

On arriving, Stone had noticed the makeup of the crowd had changed a little. A small counter-gathering had taken over a section of lawn, but far from the terrace, on Sheep Meadow. And, overall, far fewer people shouted angrily as looked on with hope and love. But the Stranger did now have some vocal enemies.

Yet, believers continued to steadily feed the pile of surrendered arms, so Stone felt good about that. Swords to plowshares…

Now, back behind the press pit barricades, Jessie turned to him and said, "You think Ruthie is over there? I mean, now?"

"I think she's probably in the light, like Jeremiah said, and if you really want her back, you have to ask."

"Ask?"

"I mean, you know," Stone said. "Pray."

"I can't." She turned away.

"It worked last time you tried it," he said.

"No. That was everyone. Not just me."

Stone understood why she didn't trust her own prayers. The night before, he'd learned that, as a child, she'd prayed for her mother in the hospital. She'd prayed as she'd been told, believed she had to trust God—but either her prayers had failed or she had failed, and her mother had died, and what did that leave a little girl but emptiness and pain, doubts and anger?

She'd either had to blame God for her mother's death or blame herself for being unworthy or a sinner, someone to whom God had turned a deaf ear.

Stone reached for her hand. "I'm sorry," he said. "I don't know what else to say."

Across the lake, the little cardboard lighthouse on the Point softly glowed. "Hey," Stone said, "maybe you should just do what she taught you to do. Maybe you should sing, like Ruthie."

Jessie shook her head no.

About to protest, to try to convince her, he stopped himself. She wouldn't respond to that approach, and he didn't want to risk pushing her.

If you want to bring someone closer, don't push—pull.

Pull…

Like last night.

The best night of my life.

After Jack had driven off to LaGuardia to get on *Air Force Two*, and after Becka had left Gracie Mansion, Stone and Jessie had decided to explore the mayor's residence. Jessie had found Sophia's famous wine cellar. But *he* had found Jack's vintage 1961 Gibson C-O guitar. It felt perfect in his arms. He had taken another big slug of wine and tried his best to make Eddie Vedder proud, singing "Hard Sun."

"From the top," he'd shouted, banging out chords from his cross-legged position on the floor in the guest bedroom. "Come on. At least sing the chorus with me."

Jessie had stood over him in her fancy clothes and belted it out too, and they had sung and drunk and laughed for nearly an hour before she'd finally kissed him—but once she did, the dam burst. The kisses had then flowed, one into another, down their faces and necks and chests, and on and on until there was no place they had not explored one another.

Later, just before dawn, she had stared at the ceiling and said, "If you want to understand what we *really* value in this society, all you have to do is look at—"

"School buses and armored cars." He had completed her sentence.

"How'd you know?" she'd asked.

"You said it already," Stone had replied.

She's an adorable drunk, he'd thought.

He'd started kissing her again. They'd made love again, and showered together, and she'd pulled on a pair of Jack's white monogrammed boxers she'd pilfered from his bedroom bureau. Stone, wrapped in a white towel, had found her in there, and she'd shoved him and run away and said, "Race ya!" and they'd darted for their bedroom.

He'd lost the towel running but got around her and dove under the sheets first. "I win!"

"No way! Cheater!"

They'd rolled and laughed and squirmed and panted, trying to catch their breath.

"Your feet are freezing," he'd said.

"Yeah, and you're an out-of-shape jarhead. I beat you!"

"Not even close."

They'd kissed again, and again, and when they'd exhausted themselves on one another, Jessie had stretched for the nightstand and tried to drink from an empty glass. She'd given it a surprised look, like it was responsible for disappointing her, got up, poured their third bottle dry, gargled with the last of it, and then said, "Do you know what you have to go through to get a job driving one of those things?"

"What?"

"A background check. All kinds of credit history checks. A psychiatric evaluation. And you have to be in tiptop shape, you know, physically, to protect the money. Which would leave you out." She'd poked him in the belly.

"Ouch…"

She'd climbed over him and rolled onto her back, and now lay naked in the moonlight. "You have to know how to Taser a bad guy, and do the death grip…"

"Death grip?"

"Then they put all the money inside, safe and sound, and they strap it in, just in case of a rollover or an accident or a heist…God forbid we dump out a bag of nickels, you know?"

"Did you say heist?"

"You know, a robbery."

"Yeah, I know what a heist is."

"The tires are bulletproof," Jessie had said. "So are the windows. The walls are like an inch thick, solid steel."

"Uh-huh." He'd begun to run his fingertips along the length of her dark, slender body, from her thigh up to her neck, her lips, across her cheek to her earlobe…

"And there are *two* drivers, not just one."

"Two."

"And real guns. Real bullets too."

"Real."

"Why?" she'd asked.

"I don't know," Stone said. "But I'll bet you're going to tell me." And he'd slid over and pressed even closer.

"Because they've got something that's really important in there. You know? They've got *money* in there! But they let a goddamn pigeon drive the school bus."

"Uh," he'd said. "I think that's just a kid's book."

"What?"

"Never mind. It's just…hey, isn't this the coolest house in New York? I think I'm going to live here someday."

"No," she'd said. She'd rolled onto her stomach and lifted her heels up and started rubbing her feet against each other. "Politics is for crooks and egomaniacs."

"That's turn-on number one for me, right there. You know that, right?" he'd said.

"What? Oh, you mean this?"

"Yeah. That."

"Rub my…oh. Yeah…right there…"

Okay, so it makes no sense 'cause I just met her, but I love this woman, he'd thought. I do. And now, in the park, standing with her hand in his in the press pit, she turned to face him, and he felt it again.

"What?" she asked.

"I think I love you."

"Yeah?" Now she turned and smiled. "After one night?"

"Yeah…" He waited. She didn't say it back to him, and so he filled the awkward, somewhat painful silence. "But before we go any further with this, I gotta know: Do you always get so worked up, about armored cars and school buses and pigeons and such…when you've had too much to drink?"

"Pigeons? I said something about pigeons?"

"You did."

"And you don't like pigeons?"

"Uh…well, I mean, they're a really dirty bird, you know."

"Yeah. They are. But I kinda like that in a bird…" She kissed him.

"Seriously." He looked across the lake to the Point again. "None of that talk, you know, last night…the science, the philosophy, none of it matters. You hear? I'm an engineer by education and a reporter by trade. I grew up poor and struggled for everything I've ever had. I've done good. And I've done bad. I've killed men in battle and seen men killed…"

"Is there some point to all this?" she said. She touched her fingers to his bottom lip and pulled it down playfully, looking deeply into his eyes again.

"Yes," he said. "You have to do it. I feel it in my heart."

"No."

"Okay, I wasn't going to tell you this, but I had a dream."

"Yeah?"

"So I know what I'm supposed to do now. And I know what you're supposed to do too."

"And I said no. I am not going to pray again, not all by myself. And that ain't you dreaming me saying it. So let it go."

"Do you want to see Ruthie again or not? Do you want to see your mother?"

"You know I do."

"And you won't do as I ask?"

She shook her head. "It wasn't because of me praying that she came out last time. It was because of all of them." Jessie gestured to the crowd.

"Okay. Then," Stone said, "you leave me no choice." He let go of her and stepped out of the press pit and walked boldly across the terrace and shouted to the crowd: "Everyone! Hey! Everybody! Please pray! Pray for Ruthie! Pray for her to return to us, to that woman right over there. Her name is Jessie, and Ruthie is her grandma, and I love her. Please! Can you do it? Can you help her?"

The crowd hooted and applauded. Someone shouted, "Go Stone!"

A cop came alongside him and grabbed his arm. "Okay, big shot," the officer said. "Back behind the barricade."

The crowd began to cheer: "Ter-ree! Ter-ree!"

News teams perked up. Cameramen raised their gear.

"Ter-ree! Ter-ree!"

"Ruthie has been in there too long, and Jessie is very worried about her!" Stone shouted. "Please, help us! Please, just...*pray*!"

The cop escorted him back.

Jessie crossed her arms and threw him a look.

"All right. I'm done. I promise, I won't even say another word—"

Jessie softened. "Look," she said, her eyes widening.

One by one, people started to kneel and move their lips in silent prayer. And all across the terrace, and on the lawns and hills on both sides of it, people began to pass on the message, and some pointed to Stone and Jessie, and now hundreds of people had folded their hands and bowed their heads and begun to pray.

"That's what I'm talking about. Collapse-the-wave potential."

"What?"

Stone reached out and touched her crucifix and said, "Remember what Ruthie said: It won't work if you don't pray on it." And he closed his eyes too and folded his hands and got on his knees and prayed: Lord…Stranger…Mother of God or Jesus Christ…Divine Light or whoever or whatever you are up there causing all this to happen, please help me…please, help Jessie…let her know it's safe to love again…safe to trust…

He opened his eyes. Jessie had gone to the edge of the lake and stood, her back to him, staring across the water, and now her voice slowly, softly rose over the din of the crowd, and grew louder and stronger, and became clear and bright as she sang "Ave Maria." An amazing, sorrowful, mournful plea! Stone felt his own heart bursting with a longing for God.

And as the setting sun streamed through dark, gathering clouds over the terrace, Jessie poured forth verse after pleading verse. Thunder suddenly boomed. And lightning flashed. Stone felt Heaven itself was applauding the purity of Jessie's plea to the Madonna of the Ages, for mercy, for grace, and, as she knelt, raising her arms to those heavens, crying, weeping, pleading with all of her broken soul, a sudden, silent light exploded on the lake, and the earth shook…and now came the Stranger, and with him, two beautiful young women…

"Ruthie," Stone said. "And, is that—"

"Oh my God!" Jessie gasped, covering her mouth with her hand. "It's my momma!"

Called forth by that irresistible force, by the prayers of thousands and the song of one lost child, by a broken and contrite heart, and by faith, and hope, and love, the Stranger led the women forward on the glistening waters of the lake. Their radiant bodies were not flesh-and-blood forms, but somehow translucent.

Bodies of light.

And they reached the middle distance between the two shores and stood, waiting. Jessie turned to Stone and smiled, and she cried and laughed and said, "It's her! It's my momma!"

"Go!" he said, and he stood, even as everyone else on the terrace and surrounding hills knelt. Jessie ran to him and threw herself into his arms and held him. Then she took his hand and pulled him toward the lake. "No," he said. "I'm not—I can't—"

"What? You have to!"

"I told you: The dream. You'll come back to me. I've seen it. I know. But you have to go alone for now. Go!"

Jessie looked to the lake, then turned back to Stone and kissed him. She pulled a small envelope from her vest. "This is the letter," she said. "From Katie to Jack. I found it in his dresser when I was looking for something to wear last night. If I don't come back, promise me you'll read it before you give it back to him?"

"You will," he said. "You'll come back."

"If I don't." She looked at the crowd on the hills and the terrace. "Read it. I know it was wrong to take it, to even look at it, but I felt I had to do it. And help him if I could. Help all of us believe. If what it says is true, he's going to get the chance to save a lot of people."

Stone tucked the note into the pocket of his borrowed khaki pants and wiped away his tears. He pulled her close and kissed her hard and said, "Okay. Go…"

And she said, "I do love you too, Terry Stone. Even after only one night…" And she backed away, saying, "I do. I really, really do." She stepped onto the glittering surface of the waters and sprinted across the lake and into the open arms of her mother.

Jack had spent five hours traveling back to New York in a limo, calling Becka every thirty seconds at first, then every ten minutes. He had to confront her. Had to hear it from her. Hear it for himself.

No answer.

Anger.

Pain.

Loneliness.

Bitch!

I'm an idiot, he'd told himself. I've ruined my own life for her?

On the way, he'd remembered the warmth of RJ's scotch, remembered it fondly. Wanted more. So he'd decided to buy a bottle and take a detour and drink himself into oblivion in the parking lot at Jones Beach, windows open, gulls barking.

At 4:00 p.m., he'd pushed past a team of reporters at the hospital and sat down in a critical-care room beside his unconscious sister, Katie, and talked to her in whispers.

"What is truth?" he asked.

She did not reply.

After a while—or a long time, he really wasn't sure which—he'd passed out in the chair beside her bed.

Now, at 9:00 p.m., he'd awakened again and felt sober enough, and angry enough, to go home and plot revenge.

Brandt. Becka. They would pay.

Jack recalled the conversation in the patent-yellow parlor, how she'd played along, and how Karl…wait, he thought. Then it hit him, the things Karl had said too. That traitor! Son of a bitch! He's in on it too.

No doubt.

Bastards!

He checked his phone. Joe had called him five times. So, first thing on arriving on the grounds of Gracie Mansion, he headed for the ops trailer.

Yeah. See Joe, he thought. He's a true friend. He'll help me.

I'll take control.

I will…

"Oh God. I'm glad you're here," Joe said. "We have the bomb, Jack."

"What?" It took a moment for the words to register. "Where?"

"There," Joe said. He reached over the shoulder of his technician and moved the remote camera to the pile of surrendered weapons on the red bricks of Bethesda Terrace in the long shadow of the Angel of the Waters, a shadow cast by NYPD floodlights. "Sons of bitches hid it right out in the open," Joe said. "The one place we'd never think to look."

"I don't see anything," Jack said.

"That big aluminum suitcase, left side of the pile…it's the source of some low-level radiation readings. Probably biological agents too. Based on the intel reports we have, maybe sarin. We're tracing the drop-off back in time on the video now. Hopefully we didn't miss it. Some crazy lightning storm knocked out all the equipment this afternoon, and our agents say there was another miracle."

"Why haven't you cleared the park?" Jack asked.

"You said not to! Remember? No matter what! But Brandt's moved in troops, Jack. National Guard. He's cleared out the whole east side at least."

"He told them?"

"Hell no. Not even Brandt's that stupid. The panic would probably kill more people than the device."

"Right. Well, let's get the bomb squad down there and get it out of there," Jack said.

"They're rolling right now. But it could go off if they move it, so we're in a no-win, unless we can defuse it—"

"Wait. Tell the bomb squad to hold off until I get there."

"Are you crazy, Jack? You're not going down there. We have to get you out of the city. If that thing goes off—"

"The crowd sees them in those blast suits and they'll panic for sure, just like you said. No. I have to go. They see me, they'll assume it's safe."

"I told you, we can't move it, Jack. There's no way I'm going to let you—"

"Sir," one of the techs said, "we've got it. About an hour before the lightning storm. There. That's him." He froze a frame on the monitor. "That's the suitcase."

"Get a tight shot of his face," Joe said, "and match it up with the data files at Langley."

"Already working it," the tech said.

"We get the bastard, and maybe we can make him turn the damn thing off," Joe said.

Jack nodded and leaned closer to the computer monitor. Photos flittered like a deck of shuffled cards, thousands of them, in what seemed seconds. Then they stopped.

"Arash Ali Beheshti," the tech said. "Iranian national. Under surveillance. It's a bomb, all right. Guy's an expert, trained in Yemen."

"Well, you guys did a hell of a job, then," Jack said. "Son of a bitch!"

"Last known whereabouts: Brooklyn."

"NYPD has a counterterrorism team on standby at Coney Island," Joe said. "Tell them to pick him up. Now!"

"Yes, sir," the tech said.

"Karl Kastleman's with Brandt," Jack said. "That means we'll have no control."

"Well, we don't have a choice," Joe said. "He's got the manpower. I can't do this without NYPD."

"I know. Let's go," Jack said.

Joe nodded, strapped on his weapon, and threw on a sport coat. Jack turned for the door.

"Sir…Mr. Mayor," another tech said. "Wait!"

"What is it?" Jack said.

"Look…there. I just switched back to live and—"

The tech reached up and touched his monitor screen. He zoomed in. "That's the bridge…by Bethesda Terrace. That child, there, with the teddy bear…"

"Abbey!"

Terry Stone sat cross-legged at the edge of the terrace and read aloud, pulling various passages from a Bible that one of the women in the crowd had handed him after the miracle with Jessie and her mom and Ruthie. "'Now, in Jerusalem,'" he said in a whisper, "'by the Sheep Gate, there is a pool called Bethesda which has five porticoes. In these lay many invalids—blind, lame, paralyzed. For an angel went down at certain seasons into that pool and troubled the waters: whosoever then first after the troubling of the waters stepped in was made whole and healed of disease forever.'"

Stone turned to the next page, marked with a ribbon. A letter from the Apostle Paul, First Corinthians. "'There are moreover heavenly bodies and earthly bodies, and the splendor of heavenly bodies is one thing, and the splendor of earthly bodies another. And brothers, this I assure you: Flesh and blood cannot have any inheritance in God's reign. That is the secret thing I am telling. We all may not die. Some may be altered at a stroke, at an eye-blink, at a trumpet blast. Then will disintegration be clothed in everlasting integrity and death forever clothed in deathlessness.'

"I see it all clearly now," he said. "Flesh and blood cannot have any inheritance in God's reign. He's not the body. Nor is Jessie. I really have not lost her. I can trust."

Trust.

The night had grown cool. The leaves of the late-summer trees had begun to change. A thick blanket of clouds floated over the city and turned the sky the color of steel. The incandescent lights had been on for hours, and the park smelled of the exhaust of too many generators. A continuous flow of people—more sick and dying, more lost and crippled souls—had poured in. When the moon broke through, the surface of the lake became a dark watercolor, dappled with green and red and yellow and orange, and the white-barked trees shed tear-shaped leaves that seemed to Stone to spiral down to meet their own reflections on the surface, as if heading toward a reunion with their souls in a mirror.

Okay, he thought. So I've begun to wax poetic. But I miss her already.

Connie approached.

Stone closed the Bible. "So, what's the word?" he asked. "Did we get it on tape?"

"No," she said. "That big pulse of light when they disappeared, it knocked out all the equipment."

"The other networks?"

"Same."

"So nobody else saw it?"

"Nobody that wasn't here. And CNN just broke the news that Denny Brandt is heading up the VP search committee right after he secures the park with the National Guard and arrests the Stranger."

"How's he going to get past the shield?"

"Has a plan. So he says."

"So Becka was right," Stone said. "He has already taken control of the federal government. Damn."

"Seems so. Oh, hey." Connie pointed. "The mayor."

"Yeah. That's the FBI guy I told you about," Stone said. "Joe Black. Wonder what they're doing here?"

"Oh, no. They brought the bomb squad," Connie said.

"Did you secure the perimeter?" Brandt asked, standing outside his new command headquarters: Loeb Boathouse on the shore of the lake in Central Park.

"Yes, sir," the full bird colonel in command of the 69th Infantry Regiment of the US National Guard—the "Fighting Irish"—said. "Done."

"Good. Let's have a look," Brandt said.

The eleven hundred troops at the colonel's command had moved into position at dusk. Four companies of men had cleared the Ramble all the way up to the invisible shield and then set up a perimeter that kept onlookers well back from the scene. Two additional companies stood ready to commence Operation Phoenix and take control of the Point.

Brandt and the colonel now walked up a wooded hill toward the barrier.

"What about you, Colonel? Catholic. Eight kids. Don't bullshit me, now."

"Governor?"

"I hear there was quite a light show earlier today. Mass hysteria. Maybe you think he's for real?"

"If you want to know how I look at this, sir, I can offer this: during the Civil War, President Lincoln once rather astutely remarked that both the North and the South used the same Bible and prayed to the same God."

"Go on," Brandt said.

"Well, sir, Lincoln also pointed out that both sides believed their cause to be right, and just, and he said each had called on God to deliver victory, which was of course impossible. Not even God could deliver a battlefield win to both sides."

"And you think this situation is similar somehow?" Brandt asked.

"I think Lincoln concluded that one thing, and one thing alone, determines whose side God was on."

270

"What's that, Colonel?"

"Winning."

Brandt laughed.

"I wasn't being flip, Governor. With all due respect, sir, I do my best every day. I fight for what I believe is right, and I go to bed every night and lay my head on my pillow and say, 'If it happened today, it was God's will.' Win or lose. Life or death. Because if it actually happened, it couldn't be anything but God's will. End of story."

"So you're a God-fearing man, eh, Colonel?"

"Yes, sir."

"Then tell me—all this 'turn the other cheek' and 'swords to plowshares' talk. You buy it, or you think it's all a load of crap?"

"As you know, sir, there are a lot of bad people in the world. Evil people. It's my duty to stop them."

"Your duty? You don't trust God to do it?"

"As far as I know, sir, God never said he would. Jesus didn't either, not even to save his own life. His kingdom was not of this world. Mine is. I got kids to protect."

They came upon a platoon of guardsmen suiting up for special duty at the perimeter of the invisible barrier on the Point and preparing tear-gas rounds, hot and cold canisters.

"But," Brandt said, "Jesus *did* imply that if we turn the other cheek, the hearts of the evildoers will change, and eventually they'll put down their weapons. Didn't he?"

"If I had that kind of faith, I wouldn't be standing here, sir."

"Good," Brandt said. "I admire your honesty, and your integrity, Colonel."

"Besides, sir, this Stranger—he's a bit young, don't you think? And he doesn't look like Jesus to me. No wounds. You know: stigmata. He doesn't have a scratch on him."

"Yet," Brandt said.

Karl Kastleman came up the hill, flanked by two uniformed NYPD officers and said, "We got them. The terrorists. I've interrogated them, and it's just as you suspected."

"All right," Brandt said. "Then we have no choice. Bring them here. And put the boats in the water. I understand there may be as many as three women over there now, plus the Stranger."

"It's hard to say—we have conflicting reports," the colonel said. "Some say the three women were, and I'm quoting, 'taken up to Heaven in a flash of light.'"

"Bullshit," Brandt said. "They're in there." He checked his watch. "Colonel. It's up to you now. Smoke 'em out."

"Yes, sir."

Brandt made his way down the ridge. About halfway, he peeled off the trail and climbed to the top of a huge, smooth rock on the shore by the boathouse. He lit his cigar and puffed away, and the breeze carried the smoke across the lake to the Point.

Wind's at my back, he thought.

Perfect.

He raised his gaze to the stars. "Rikki," he said, fighting back his emotions. He had so wanted his boy with him in the White House, so wanted to make him proud. "I hope you can see me, son. I love you."

Focus on the task at hand, he told himself.

It's a brilliant plan.

Bound to work.

The tear gas would drive the Stranger out. If not, the flames would. The invisible barrier would not stop fire. Every bird and squirrel had gone right through. Anything natural would. Anything but man.

This was Brandt's epiphany.

And the tear gas would be their cover. It had been known to start fires before.

Like at the Branch Davidian compound in Waco, Texas. Another phony prophet up in flames. And now fire will take this one too.

Oh, he might fight back if he really has some kind of extraterrestrial power. Or he might not. He might actually live by his creed and turn the other cheek. Either way, a quick surrender or a provoked confrontation, I win because if this so-called Stranger defends himself, I'll have shown the world the whole M-39 thing is a farce.

A hypocrite's scam.

Brandt came down from the rock and walked around the boathouse and onto the path that led to the terrace. On his right, the NYPD SWAT teams had splashed an inflatable. And now all three members of the Arash Ali Beheshti family appeared out of the darkness, escorted by Karl Kastleman and six more SWAT team cops.

Brandt approached. "Take off their hoods," he said.

Pop! The sound echoed in the woods of the Ramble, and Beheshti's wife flinched.

Brandt smiled.

A second *pop* careened percussively off the water, and the bright flash of the hot tear-gas canister igniting illuminated the bloody, beaten faces of the three confessed terrorists.

And now on the Point, a German shepherd began to bark, wildly, and the terrorists dropped to their knees…

CHAPTER 17

"Abbey's run off!"

Saragossa had advised Sophia against coming to the park. She'd warned her there were too many people here. Too much going on. But Abbey had insisted, and Sophia had been gone all day and had wanted to please the child, and to spend time with her outdoors.

Saragossa scanned the surrounding area and paused at the top of the stairs overlooking the terrace.

"There!" she said, pointing the child out to Sophia. "By those Red Cross tents on the hill. No. No! Down there!" Saragossa shouted.

Sophia's eyes went wide. "Abbey!" she shouted. "Abrianna!"

Pop! A sound came from across the lake, and a flash lit up the woods by the Point as Abbey picked her way through the crowd and made her way toward the terrace.

Another *pop* and a flash startled Saragossa.

Now, across the lake, the German shepherd began to bark. And the woods, deep in the Ramble, began to glow...

Smoke. Flames...

"There's a fire!" Saragossa shouted. "A fi—" And she fell to her knees.

An NYPD bomb squad truck came down the hill on the paved footpath and stopped beside the terrace. Five men in heavy gear poured out. "Clear! Clear! Clear!" the bomb squad team leader shouted.

Now the crowd took notice. Many stood and pointed. A murmur rose. People began to scramble. Jack spoke slowly and calmly over a bullhorn, "Please, everyone, stay calm. This is the mayor. Please…this is just a precaution. If you want to move out of the area, please do so slowly. The situation is serious, but we have it under control…"

A bomb squad team leader pushed past the mayor and said, "Step back, please, sir." He squatted beside a pile of surrendered weapons and carefully cleared the brushed aluminum suitcase the FBI team had identified from the trailer at Gracie Mansion.

On the Point, the dog came to the edge of the lake and barked. The bomb squad team leader opened the suitcase. "Whoa…" he said.

Red letters glowed: Ten minutes. *9:58, 9:57…*

A *pop!* went off in the woods in the Ramble. Jack flinched.

A second *pop!* echoed off the water, and a bright flash caught Jack's eye.

Brandt, Jack thought. He smelled smoke. No. Tear gas.

Shit.

"Fire!" someone behind Jack shouted. "There's a fire!"

Jack turned. Sophia at the top of the stairs? No. Saragossa? In Sophia's clothes? What the hell? Why isn't Abbey with them? he wondered. Where is she?

And now, on the Point, a bright orange light.

No. Not light. Flames.

And smoke…

And now all the generators just quit, and all the lights on the terrace went out. In a flash, a ball of white light silently lit up the Point.

The crowd stirred.

"Stay calm," Jack said over the bullhorn. "Please, everyone—"

"What is happ—" The bomb squad team leader's voice stopped, and he struggled and tried to stand, but couldn't. The FBI agents and the other bomb squad cops and everyone in the press pit and on the terrace, and everyone standing on the surrounding hills, now dropped to their knees.

The light, brilliant and spreading, infused with gold and sapphire and emerald and pink, floated closer and closer on the water.

Jack shielded his eyes and fought the feeling, but he could not stand and could no longer speak.

The Stranger emerged from a spreading halo of light in the middle of the lake and held his hands at his heart in prayer.

The clock on the suitcase bomb continued to run down: *8:59. 8:58...*

Abbey? Jack had spotted her. She was coming onto the terrace. He wanted to call out to her but couldn't.

She can still walk. How? Why?

A pathway lit up, glistening on the lake.

Abbey walked slowly, steadily, toward it, teddy bear in hand.

No! Jack struggled to stand.

The Stranger stretched out his hand.

No! Jack screamed inside.

The flames on the Point reached the treetops and roared.

Jack's eyes went wide. He had to stop this, had to get to Abbey, but he could not move.

Abbey stepped onto the lake and walked on the water.

Abrianna! No!

The flames leaped from tree to tree.

Abbey took the hand of the Stranger, and they turned and walked to the far shore, where they disappeared into the light. The smoke and the flames raced toward them.

And the timer on the bomb read *6:59...6:58...6:57...*

Katie sat beside the river of dreams, and Rikki Brandt bent and took a drink.

A man, still a little distance away, paused and waved. "Jeremiah!" Katie stood and saw that now beside her once-blind friend from Central Park was the one she recognized as her Teacher. "Jesus," Katie said aloud.

Jeremiah raised his gaze and waved back to Katie, as if to say good-bye, then he departed and disappeared over the crest of an astral ridge.

Now Jesus approached her and Rikki.

Katie had felt the Lord's presence on the great, green hill of dense light earlier, when walking with Rikki.

And now, having taken a drink from the river, Rikki rose into the air and floated higher and higher, propelled by his own growing inner joy.

"I can fly! Just like you said! I can! Do you see me?"

"Yes! Yes, we see you," Katie said glancing at Jesus, who stood beside her now.

"There she is!" Rikki said. "My momma! She's coming, just like you promised!"

"Yes," Katie replied, unable now to take her eyes off the man she knew to be the embodied Messiah.

"I'm going to go to her. I'll come back. I promise!" Rikki shouted.

"Yes," Katie said. "Enjoy!"

"He's so innocent and full of love," Jesus said.

"And you are the source of his brightness, Lord. And the source of mine," Katie said, and she fell to her knees.

"Please. I have often told you, as my apprentice, you must stand beside me."

"I am compelled, Master," she said, refusing his gentle coaxing and finding it difficult now to look directly at his bright face as she continued, "by the love I feel for your true God-nature, to kneel. I've learned so much with you here, from our talks and travels and lessons, and I understand now that you are the embodiment of my Source. In truth, you are my very essence."

"Then it is right and fitting that we both bow to our Source, and give thanks and praise to the One God, our Father, for bestowing his grace upon you that you might be a worker of light." And Jesus bowed too.

After a moment they stood.

Far off, in the verdant hills, a rapturous sound arose: the sound of a loving reunion. Rikki had found his mother, and she had shrieked, filled with joy at seeing her beloved son. "It's such a gift," Katie said, "to be in this light body, to help him, to learn from you and be in your presence."

"The gift of faith," Jesus said. "You had it when you came to me on the lake, and you kept it here, through many trials. Even now you see the rising and receding of life and yet hold firm to the unchanging oneness that is your essence. Your apprenticeship is thus complete."

"Thank you," Katie said, daring to take hold of his hand. He held hers softly yet firmly and led her to an outcropping of crystal rock, a glassy stone garden hewn by astral nature into a perfect place to sit beside the flowing light-infused waters of the river of dreams.

His hand feels like the hand of my brother, she thought.

"I *am* your brother," he said.

"You are too kind. Please, tell me, why have you come to me today?" she asked.

"Your Teacher offers you a final lesson today," he replied.

"Yes, Lord," Katie said, sadness coming over her.

"This end is a beginning, like all ends. Be of good cheer."

Katie smiled. "Yes, Lord."

"Good. Now, you have been wondering at the constant state of war on Earth, have you not?"

"In spite of many great and unambiguous spiritual teachings to the contrary, human beings still take up arms, kill and murder one another, and wage war. Why don't we learn?"

"Desire," Jesus said, "arises and invariably leads to anxiety as the object desired grows in appeal. When what people want appears beyond their reach, they grow aggressive. On a small scale, rivalries result."

"And on a larger scale, wars?"

"Yes. Desire is nothing less than a demand for control over outcomes. Desire for any thing, any object, any possession, whether gold or even, ironically, peace, is born of the fear of people not getting what they want. People say, 'We want what we want and we want it now,' yes? Yet as that which is desired seems to recede from their reach, when it seems God may not provide what they want and feel they need, they grow desperate with the fear they may never possess what they want. Then they get aggressive and try to force their desired outcome."

"Yes," Katie said. "But why can't we see the futility of acting from fear? History provides so many lessons."

"Because when, as is the case on occasion, it is suitable and in accord with God's plan for the totality of the functioning of all phenomenal worlds and the object of our desire is delivered, people feel joy. This complicates the situation, because the reward of joy when desires are fulfilled increases the desire for the next object. People think if they get what they want again, they'll feel joy again, so they ever more aggressively seek the objects of their desire."

"But when God does not deliver the object of our desire, because it is not part of the natural unfolding of the totality, we rebel?"

"Yes. Many think they can force God's hand and simply take the outcome they want. They say: 'My will be done.' They act this way because of the incredibly strong feeling they experienced after one of their desires was fulfilled. The feeling of joy and peace."

"Yes," Katie said. "I understand."

"And now, here is a secret teaching: The joy we experience after desires are fulfilled comes not from the fulfillment of the desire. The joy is a result of that single instant of peace that results when any one desire is fulfilled. In that instant, before a new desire arises, the mind has gone still. We know God in that stillness."

"In the gap between desires, there is stillness. Yes?" Katie asked.

"Be still and know 'I am,' sayeth the Lord," Jesus said. "That stillness pervades in the rare and precious moments when all our appetites are sated, when we've eaten our fill, when we've loved to exhaustion, when we want no other thing."

"When we lack any desire," Katie said.

"And as you rightly say, 'In the gap between desires, we know God.' Thus, if we but trust God to supply what we need and desire no more than God gives, we can live in joy always, content with what comes. Resting in God's hands, with no desire, we can work as God has commanded, leave outcomes in his hands, and never suffer again."

"Who can suffer who truly knows God within?"

"If this teaching is accepted, never again shall aggressiveness arise. Nor jealousy nor rivalry nor anger."

"I know that you and I are one, and that all of us are, essentially. But will you please explain, one last time, how?"

Jesus cupped his hands into the shape of a bowl. "See this shape as a vessel," he said. "Imagine it as clay, and think for a moment: What is inside the bowl, and what is outside it and separate from what is inside..."

"Okay," Katie said. "I am ready. Please go on."

"Now," Jesus said, "the vessel shatters." Jesus pulled his hands apart and with a flick of his fingers, he threw the shards of the imaginary bowl away. "Tell me, what is inside now, and what is separate and outside?"

"They are one," Katie said.

"And always were, before and after the shattering of the walls of the vessel. And thus, we are and always were one, though it seems impossible when we are in the vessels of these bodies."

"What is separated by the walls of the vessel?" Katie asked.

"God-consciousness itself. But to be clear, the apparent separation occurs when that which enlivens the body—the 'soul,' or individuated God-consciousness—accepts the idea that it *is* the body, the individuated object or form or container with a name occupying space and existing in time. But the apparent separation does not change what actually is, any more than having a vessel, a cup or a bowl, changes the air in or around it. Air is always air. Consciousness is always consciousness. Call it Spirit if you prefer. Spirit is always Spirit, indivisible, even when associated with name and form. Love is always love. Thus, we are always essentially one, and I can no more be separate from you than I can be from myself."

"That is beautiful."

"Yes. Each of us appears as one form or wave in and on one vast sea of God-consciousness. Each may realize the Source of his or her own true self."

"Yes, Lord. I know this now, in my heart, my very essence." Katie looked to Jesus. He nodded. "I know what I must do," she said. "I will do it. But before I return, please, tell me what to say when they ask, 'What is the point of human life?' Many will ask."

Jesus answered: "The spiritual world and the phenomenal world are not two. The phenomenal world is the way the one who is common to all enjoys the experience of his many children, in whom he resides. This does not make the world or anyone's part in it inconsequential. On the contrary, it makes it and each sentient being supremely important. Life itself is an expression of God's love. The ultimate Source and only true reality, projected in the passing, transient phenomenal world of time and space, is our essence. So life is precious and sanctified. We who realize this truth must spread the news of our universal brotherhood and sisterhood. It is our dharma, our duty and our reason for incarnating, to be the lights of the world." Jesus added, "The question those on Earth must now grapple with is this: Does the fact of realizing your ultimate nature, and the ultimate nature of the universe, create in you apathy and resignation, or does it rouse an even stronger desire to act as if everything that you undertake, you undertake as the instrument of God?"

"I believe," Katie said, "truly realizing my nature has made it impossible for me to act in any way but the way you act, Lord. I now see that it is because I realize you in me that I must point to our oneness and help others awaken to theirs with one another. I must remind them to love one another as they love themselves, especially their so-called enemies, because all 'others' are really embodied God-consciousness, animated by our common Source. My life will now be devoted to helping them to realize they are God's love in human bodies too. Just like you."

"Yes, child. Yes."

"What to answer," Katie asked, "as your emissary, when asked, 'No violence? Not ever? Not even in self-defense, to protect our own lives?'"

"Tell them their lives belong to he who gave them to them. And ask them, 'Did he protect his life?'"

"No, Lord. You accepted death and asked that God forgive those who murdered your human form. Then you rose again."

"Tell them that to do so *is* the work of a Christian, and though you possess great faith, a faith without this depth of commitment can yield you nothing but life after life of separateness."

"Only by giving one's self over to thee, oh Lord, can we be said to believe."

"Yes."

"War is never justifiable."

"Never."

"They will ask, 'Should we not have stood armed against even the likes of Hitler?'"

"It is an age-old, yet false, question. Hitler was made by a culture that embraced hatred, formed by a society that cultivated a violent, martial response to internal and external challenges, like the culture that crucified me. Eradicate Hitler's cause, and the question of resisting him by force does not arise. Eradicate the fear, the retributive justice, the selfishness, and the hatred that fed his darkness and grew him into a monster, and you are left with a harmless painter. Eradicate the cause of every malefactor, every so-called criminal, and every bully by loving and caring for and educating all who are in need from the very first day of their lives to their last breath, and then tell me: Who will offend thee? Feed the world, and then tell me: Who will not love your nation? See every malady, whether mental or physical, as a cry for love and help. Refuse to punish. Give love instead. For I have commanded you to love your enemies, unconditionally, and you are the members of my body on Earth. Refuse to take up arms. Be an honest, faithful servant, a workman of love, and a laborer for peace. Then and only then may you call yourself mine," Jesus said. "Then and only then are you worthy of the name *Christian*."

"And love will conquer all?"

"Many may have to lay down their lives or go to prison if they heed my call. Many true saints already have. Yet to such as these, even this fate seems bliss. For they know more innocents will suffer and die in endless wars if they do not take a stand, and if they do take a stand, they will live forever."

"They may say you ask too much, Lord."

"More than I have myself given?"

"Yet they may say, 'We are not you. You are God.'"

"Then say, 'As are you. You *are* his body now. Certainly, you are among its earthly members. Thus, you are his arms and hands, his legs and feet, his eyes and ears, his voice and his pierced heart.' If they deny this, then I no longer exist on Earth…"

"I will tell them, Lord," Katie said.

"Yes. I know you will. Now, take my hands."

Katie did. She placed her palms on his, and a fierce light pierced her wrists, her feet, and her side. She swooned.

"I give you my wounds," said Jesus. "And with them, my power. Go now, child. And may the grace of Almighty God be with you."

CHAPTER 18

"Abbey!" Jack shouted as soon as he had regained his voice and the ability to stand. But she had long since disappeared.

"Three minutes!" the bomb squad team leader shouted.

"Well, disarm it," Joe Black shouted at him. "Now!"

"I don't know how! I might set it off!"

Denny Brandt appeared out of the shadows and marched toward the fountain with a cadre of men at his side: National Guardsmen, a half dozen uniformed cops, and some others Jack could not quite make out yet.

"Get your men back," Brandt said. "Before you set the damn thing off!"

"What have you done, Denny?" Jack shouted. "My daughter is over there!"

Sophia pushed through the crowd. "Jack! The fire!"

"Karl," Brandt said, gesturing to Jack and Sophia. "Get them out of here."

"Wait," Joe Black shouted. "Is that Beheshti?" he asked. "Jack. He's got the bomber."

"Yes," Brandt said. "I've got him. Now get back." He pulled a cigar from his suit jacket pocket and stuck it between his teeth. "Colonel…"

The colonel and two guardsmen grabbed Beheshti's wife. Two more took hold of his son. The guardsmen dragged them beside the pile of surrendered weapons and the suitcase bomb and pushed them to their knees.

Two cops now flanked Jack too. And Karl came closer. "Let's see if we can get through this calmly, Jack. Okay?" he said. "Then we'll take care of getting Abbey out of there. I promise you."

"You Judas. You traitor!"

The colonel shoved Beheshti to his knees. "Disarm it," he said, drawing out his sidearm and pressing it to the head of Beheshti's son. "Or he dies, right now."

"Allahu Akbar," the boy said. "Papa! Allahu Akbar."

"Shut up!" The colonel reached back and slammed the sidearm into the boy's face.

The boy's mother shrieked and wept, and the boy bent and groaned.

The timer read *1:45…1:44…1:43…*

"No. No," Beheshti said. "Please! I do it. You see?" He knelt beside the suitcase and turned to his son. "Avizheh, tell him, I do it. I do it!"

"Father," the boy said, his eyes wide. "Please!"

"Now!" the colonel shouted, and he pistol-whipped the boy again. "Shut it down. Now, or I will shoot him!"

The tangle of exposed wires and valves and canisters seemed an incomprehensible mess to Jack. But the timer made sense. Clear, unambiguous sense. One minute ten seconds… *1:09…1:08…*

"You heard him. Disarm it now," Brandt said. "Or the boy dies."

"Hail Mary," Terry Stone, somewhere on the terrace, began to pray. Jack recognized the voice. "Full of grace. The Lord is with you." The voices in the crowd came together as one. "Blessed art thou among women…"

"Make him shut it down," the bomb squad team leader said. "There's C-4 in there. And those canisters…that's sarin. We'll all die!"

"And blessed is the fruit of thy womb, Jesus…"

"Colonel?" Brandt said.

The colonel unlocked the safety on his weapon and pressed the barrel of the gun hard against Beheshti's son's head.

"No! No!" Beheshti said. "Avizheh! You see? I do it. Tell him! For you! I do it for you!"

"The timer is still ticking," Karl Kastleman shouted. "Do it! Now!"

"Shut it down," the colonel yelled. "Or I swear to God, I'm going to blow your son's brains all over your wife's face."

"Holy Mary…"

"We're out of time, Colonel!" Brandt said.

"No. No," Beheshti said, eyes wide and looking to Jack. "Please! You see? I told him: I already do it! I already do it!"

"Mother of God…"

"Please!" the boy said. "Papa?"

"Colonel!" Brandt shouted.

"Pray for our sinners…now, and at the hour of our—"

Bang! The colonel fired. The boy's head flew apart, and he fell into his screaming mother's arms.

"No! No! No!" Beheshti screamed.

0:20…0:19…0:18…

"Now!" the colonel said. "Disarm it now, Beheshti! Shut it down!" He pressed the weapon against the head of Beheshti's wife now.

"I already do it! I told him! I told him!" Beheshti pointed at Brandt. "M-39!" Beheshti grabbed hold of his swooning wife, even as she held the lifeless body of their son and rocked him in her arms and sobbed. "I do it! I do it! M-39! You see?" He gestured to the bomb. "Like the Stranger say! I do it…I do it…" He wept.

"M…" The colonel said, and he blinked and lowered his weapon. "Thirty-nine?"

"Why? Why?" Beheshti's wife, tears streaming, hands bloody,

feebly tried to put the shattered pieces of her son's head back in place. "He already do it. Why?"

"M-39." Beheshti wept and took his son in his arms. "I surrender the bomb. For my boy…for my boy…why do you kill my boy?"

"My God," Jack said. "What have you done?"

0:03. 0:02. 0:01…

Beeeeeeeeeep.

0:00…0:00…0:00…

Be-beep…be-beep…be-beep…

Nothing.

No blast.

"You son of a bitch!" Jack leaped at Brandt. "You knew!"

Joe grabbed him, peeled him off.

"What the hell is wrong with you?" Brandt shouted, composing himself.

"You executed that boy!"

"We're at war!" Brandt said.

Jack tried to pull free, but Joe wouldn't let him go. "He was innocent!" Jack shouted.

"His father armed the goddamn thing in the first place! Why would I believe him?"

"You're a murderer," Jack said. He turned to the colonel. "Both of you. Bloody murderers!"

"Arrest him, Colonel," Brandt said.

"No, wait," Joe said, stepping between Jack and the colonel. "Everybody calm down."

The NYPD's SWAT team's inflatable pulled to the edge of the terrace now. Two cops exited the craft and trotted up the terrace.

"Sir," one of the two shouted on his way up to Karl Kastleman, "the fire. It's out of control. We can't—"

"Jack!" Sophia cried out. "Do something! Our baby's in there!"

"Colonel, I said, arrest the mayor," Brandt shouted. "And his wife. Then we'll attend to the others."

"Yes, sir," the colonel said, and he stepped toward Jack.

Joe moved to block the colonel's way again, and Jack grabbed him and pulled Joe close. As he did, he reached into Joe's jacket and grabbed Joe's weapon and pulled it out of its holster, and in one move, he raised the gun to Denny Brandt's face and shouted, "Stop!"

"Whoa!" Karl said. "You do not want to do that, Jack."

"Don't I?" Jack slid behind Brandt and pressed the barrel of Joe's gun against Brandt's head.

The colonel gestured to his men. They trained their weapons on Jack. "He's right," the colonel said. "Put the weapon down."

"I'm going to get my daughter," Jack said in Brandt's ear. "And you're going with me."

"Like hell," Brandt said. "Shoot the bastard!"

Mike crashed on his bed and checked his phone. Another text from his old college buddy Dee. Great…

What the heck did she want now?

He read it. Then read it again.

The text said if she hadn't left a voice message for him by…he checked the time…by right about now, it meant she was in trouble, and he should send the police to an address in Brooklyn.

Shit.

He checked his phone again.

No call. No voice message.

Mike sighed.

What am I thinking? This is Dee Weiss we're talking about. Queen of drama.

He found himself on his feet.

Ah, hell no!

I am not getting dragged into another one of her dramas. Not tonight.

He fell onto the bed and closed his eyes.

I'll call her in the morning.

Right now, I just need to sleep.

The German shepherd barked wildly again and raced back and forth along the flame-engulfed shoreline. The fire on the ridge of the Point had climbed trunks and, with the help of the wind, leaped from branch to branch, treetop to treetop, even as a low, smoldering blaze crawled like a red serpent along the dry leaf bed and toward the Stranger's structure.

Jack dragged Brandt toward the lake and the SWAT team's inflatable. "And if anything happens to Abbey," he said to Brandt, "I swear to God—"

"Jack!"

"Stone…Terry Stone? Is that you?"

"Mr. Mayor," Stone said.

"Stone. The boat. I need you to help me."

"No. I don't want you to do this. Please. Not like this!"

"My child," Jack shouted, "is going to die."

"You don't know that!"

"I can get to her."

"What?"

"That day on the lake. I know a way in!"

"You lied?"

"Never mind that now. Just—I found it. There's a way in!"

"Please, sir. I know how you must feel, but not like this."

"Why? Because of that scroll? Because if we just surrender our weapons, we'll all be safe? Look at that pile, Stone. And that fire! Is my daughter any safer? Is that boy that Brandt just had murdered any safer?" he said, gesturing to Beheshti's son. "Is he?"

"I—no. But," Stone said, "but—"

"God doesn't give a shit, Stone. All right? I'm not going to let Abbey die!"

"Jack," Sophia said, pushing her way past Stone and the guardsman. "We'll go together."

"No," Saragossa said, stepping forward now too. "Let me. It's my fault she ran away. I lost her. It's all my fault." She turned to Sophia. "I promised when I took this job I'd do anything to protect her. Anything. Take me. Please. You have to take me!"

Jack looked to Sophia. "She can handle a weapon. I need her."

Sophia nodded. "Yes."

"Are you all crazy?" Karl shouted. "He'll come out now, Jack. They all will. He'll surrender and Abbey will be all right. Now let the governor go!"

"Saragossa," Jack said, "come!" He dragged Brandt toward the boat. "Get in," he said to Brandt. "Up front. Now you, Saragossa, in the middle, and keep this on Brandt. Here," he said to Saragossa, handing her Joe Black's gun. "Take it! Point it at him, and if anyone so much as blinks—"

"Yes," Saragossa said. Her hand shook visibly. "Okay."

Jack pulled out a paddle and pushed off, even as the colonel's men kept the laser sights of their rifles trained on his head. He paddled out slowly toward the Point and the smoke and the flames. Generators suddenly roared back to life. Spotlights lit up again and hummed. Sirens wailed from all sides of the park. People crowded to the shore for a better look, knocking down barriers, ignoring the police and the troops. A helicopter beat like a drum overhead, fanning the flames.

It took only seconds for Jack to reach the buoys. The boat made glancing contact with the invisible shield, and it lit up. The German shepherd barked wildly and paced and splashed into the water at the shore.

"You're going down for this, Jack," Brandt said. "You've made it easy for me now. You're going to jail. You hear me?" he said.

"This is where you get out," Jack said.

"What?" Brandt said.

"You heard me. Swim for it." Jack gestured to the terrace.

"What are we doing?" Saragossa asked.

"Letting him go," Jack said. "Now, Denny. Out!"

Brandt glared at Jack for a moment. "This doesn't change anything, Jack."

"Get out!"

Brandt glared at him, then slid over the side and started swimming for shore.

Jack paddled the boat forward again. They drifted and bumped against the invisible barrier, and it lit up on contact again.

The dog came bounding out of the shadows, barking and growling.

Jack searched the woods for the structure, for signs of life, signs of Abbey.

By the Loeb Boathouse, firemen sprayed hoses and tried to keep the building from going up in flames. The blaze had spread out of control. Jack's eyes burned and stung. It felt like fistfuls of hot sand had blown into them.

"It's tear gas," Saragossa said, rubbing her own face. "Try to stay low." She crouched.

Jack's throat began to close. "And diesel. Those bastards!" he said. "I can taste it."

"What are we going to do?" Saragossa asked.

Jack peeled off his shoes. "You are going to go back," he said, looking to the terrace. "Turn yourself in for helping me." He slipped over the side and into the cool, black, glistening water.

The German shepherd went absolutely wild. Its mouth foamed, mad with rage.

"No way," Saragossa said. "You need me to get past that dog."

"Move it!" Brandt's voice echoed off the water. He'd reached the shore by the terrace. And now another SWAT team prepared a second inflatable by the boathouse; its outboard engine roared to life.

Jack thought for less than a second, then nodded his approval. He swam past the first buoy, the one he'd taken note of days earlier. The barrier lit up each time his hand made contact. And then, by the second one, it didn't: he'd found the narrow passageway again. He turned sideways and swam through.

The crazed dog paced and snarled and barked.

"Oh my God," Saragossa said, "you did it!' She'd already slipped over the side too, and now she swam toward Jack, holding her weapon high, keeping it dry.

His feet touched bottom. He could stand.

Saragossa could too.

A searchlight shot into the clouds of billowing smoke, bounced off the lake, and careened wildly into the sky. Now it found a target, and it turned Saragossa's face a ghostly white. A second light, from the helicopter, found the crazed, barking animal, its gaping jaw frothing, teeth bared. Now the searchlight found Jack, and it lit up the shore as bright as day, blinding him for a moment.

The crowd on the terrace gasped and then roared with approval, and people applauded and cheered. A voice on shore began a chant: "Jack-eee! Jack-eee!"

Now Denny Brandt shouted over a bullhorn, "They got in! The barrier is down. Go! Go!"

"No!" Saragossa tried to wave them off. "It's not down. It's not—"

And a third inflatable with another armed SWAT team aboard roared to life fifty yards away, on the other side of the lake, near the bridge.

"Abbey!" Jack shouted. "Baby! It's Daddy! Come out! Come to me right now!" He scrambled up the hill, through the smoke. He winced and rubbed his eyes as the fumes began to choke him. He tripped and stumbled to his knees and found himself face-to-face with the dog, and Jack saw himself twice, once in each eye of the beast. He slowly, carefully stood, and the animal crept closer, frothing and snarling. "Saragossa," he shouted. "Shoot it. Now, goddamn it! Shoot!"

The chopper swooped, and the smoke swirled, and the noise became deafening.

"Drop your weapon." A voice from above came over a bullhorn. "There are firefighters in the woods. I repeat: Do not discharge your weapon!"

"Abbey's going to die, for God's sake!" Jack said. "Shoot it!" And the dog crouched as if prepared to leap at him. "Now!"

"Daddy, no!" Abbey shouted, but as Jack turned toward the flaming shelter, the source of her voice, the animal did leap at him, and *bang!* Saragossa fired.

The dog slammed into Jack's chest and knocked him to the ground, and they rolled. Then the German shepherd bolted into the woods, yelping, and finally disappeared into the smoke and flames.

The outboard engine of the SWAT team's inflatable boat screamed as the boat hit the invisible barrier at full speed and went airborne. It tumbled, end over end, and rolled, side over side, scattering bodies, dumping the entire team into the lake.

"Shots fired! Men down," the voice from the chopper boomed. "Men down!"

Jack got to his feet. "Saragossa?"

"I'm all right," she said. She'd slipped and fallen too, after taking the shot. "Go! Get her out of there!"

Jack scrambled up the hill. "Abbey!" He shielded his face from the heat and flames and the swirling, ember-glowing soot. An unfathomable shaft of light caught his eye. It came streaming like a laser from a perfect, small circle in the flimsy wall of the Stranger's structure, and it nearly blinded him. And now every crack and seam of the cardboard house flashed and brightened from the inside. "Abbey!" he shouted again. The flames seared his face. He could get no closer. He fell to his knees, wanting to die, to become nothing if he could not save her. But now the structure glowed with such an intense fury, it overtook and obscured the light of the flames engulfing it. And the fury grew and erased every line and shadow, bleaching everything white. It was as if the sun itself had fallen, so bright, so hot, Jack had to turn, to crawl away or die.

Saragossa fell to her knees and crawled to the shoreline.

On the terrace, the crowd, stunned into silence, seemed a montage of faceless, hollow forms. Jack couldn't face them, couldn't face himself or life without his child. He had to go back, to dive into the fire, the flames, the light, and find her. He had to!

He inched forward, one slow, painful step at a time, bent over, one hand on the ground, half crawling his way back up the slope. But now a high-pitched, piercing sound, a squeal that cut through the sounds of the chopper and the sirens and the crowd, grew in intensity with the still-growing, furious brightness of the house, and it stopped Jack in his tracks. He turned his face away. The light and the sound reached those on the terrace and on the hills and in the arcade, and the bystanders and troops and cops and the firefighters by the boathouse all turned away from it and bent and covered their ears.

A third SWAT team inflatable had arrived at the edge of the barrier, and the men on it had begun fishing the cops out of the lake, but they all now curled and bent and collapsed from the sound.

The ground beneath Jack's feet quaked. It felt like all the energy from the very core of the planet had been pulled to the surface to wreak havoc on the world, and the volume of the deafening noise rose even higher. Jack shouted, "Give me my daughter. Goddamn you! Give her to me!"

And all of a sudden, it all stopped.

No more blinding light.

No more deafening sound.

Like someone had thrown a switch.

Jack stood upright and took a single step, and now everything moved as if in slow motion, as if he'd been transported inside a silent film shot in black and white and glowing orange. Every light in the city went out. Every window in the skyline went dark, and every light on the terrace disappeared. Flames engulfed Jack as he walked forward, and the flames should have burned him but did not. Stinging, blinding smoke should have choked him too, made it impossible for him to see, to breathe. But it did not. And now came a single tone, long, whining, followed by a chest-shattering pulse, like a silent nuclear blast, and the flaming structure exploded, but then it immediately collapsed into itself as a single point of blue-white light, like a black hole swallowing itself, and then *bam!* A shock wave hurled Jack through the air, and did the same to Saragossa, and the SWAT team, and their boats.

Bodies skipped like flat stones across the surface of the lake.

Jack hit and splashed.

Everything went black for what seemed an eternity.

He began to sink…but now a surge from the depths lifted him, and a wave brought him to the surface. It stormed toward the shore and crested and broke and sent Jack rolling onto the lawn beside the weeping willows.

The wave washed onto the terrace too, knocking the crowd and the cops and guardsmen and reporters off their feet, washing them back through the arcade, spreading people and cameras and weapons everywhere.

Jack gagged and coughed and—deaf, mute, and nearly blind—choked and gasped and spit out mouthfuls of water. He rolled onto his side and felt himself fading into the shallow numbness of unconsciousness, but he fought it and gathered his strength and sat up. He leaned against the trunk of a willow. He focused on the flaming Point. The entire peninsula now roared, consumed by a hellish inferno.

And now, out of the smoke and towering flames, floating like a wingless angel over the agitated black waters of the lake, came the Stranger. He reached the shore and came up the bank and stopped and stood at Jack's feet.

And a small, broken puppet, not a real girl, hung limp and lifeless in his arms.

"Abrianna…"

CHAPTER 19

J EREMIAH HAD BEEN AFFORDED THE GIFT OF SIGHT, AND NOW HE prayed he'd lose it again, forever. For what he saw was death, everywhere.

Battlefields strewn with lifeless bodies. Souls rising into the Heavens by the thousands. Inexplicable, deadly terror in schools and malls and movie theaters and office buildings and even on baseball fields. Meat-cleaver hackings, finish-line bombings, beheadings in the name of God, and murder.

And now a child lies dead in the arms of God's own son.

The little, innocent lamb, Abbey Molinaro. Lifeless.

He sat cross-legged on the floor of his apartment.

He cleared his mind, turned his awareness on itself…but thoughts arose, and he could not stop them. Long ago, God had come in human form and preached a gospel of peace and universal brotherhood. He'd been crucified for the "crime." But he had risen again, proving that love overcomes death. Hundreds of millions had taken his name: *Christian*. However, few had taken up his cross. Few would lay down their lives for him. They could not turn the other cheek, despite the promise of Heaven, and the proof of resurrection, despite the fact that an eye for an eye was leaving everyone blind. They could not love their enemies and leave the outcome to God. And now, even in our time, when God's love had come again, in the form of a Divine Stranger, and the Stranger had delivered the words again, too few had listened. Yes, for a moment it had appeared things might be different. Tens of thousands had come to the park. Millions had heard the call. The realization had dawned, even on some in the military, that taking human life, even in self-defense, and putting nationalism on a pedestal and placing God at its feet, screamed sin.

Yes—called again, reminded of Christ's true teachings by the M-39 scroll, some had put down their swords. But others had picked them up and used them to slice off ears and arms and legs and heads.

Again.

So what will happen now?

What could happen?

Would this war of good versus evil rage on forever?

Would God's messenger face trial again?

Would men once again attempt to execute the Immortal Divine?

And what would we do this time?

Would we stand mutely at the feet of this cross too?

Will we? Now?

Again?

The morning after his "victory" in the park, Denny Brandt knew the press was waiting to pounce. We're at war, he'd say. Beheshti and his whole damn family are enemy combatants on American soil. Thousands of lives were on the line. Maybe millions. The colonel is a hero!

But the bomb had already been defused, they'd said.

Hindsight! Next question, he'd say.

What about the fire? How did it start? they'd ask.

An accident, I'm sure. The tear gas…

The death of the mayor's child: How?

Ask the Stranger, he'd reply. Ask: If he is such a miracle worker, why didn't he save Abbey Molinaro and my little boy, Rikki?

Then he thought, I'm still playing defense. I need a card. An ace in the hole.

Breckenridge!

Yes!

All he needed to drive his point home now was a good visual aid. A prop, like they use in the movies. And he'd planned that too. He was on a first-name basis with a prop named Tommy. He laughed. "Tom-Tom." Almost forgot about the bastard. Head bandaged, face still black and blue and swollen, an eye torn out…the perfect prop to pull out when reminding the dazzled public that while some had been healed, others had been injured, and while some had lived, others had died.

Just look at what happened to this man's face, he'd say. Stranger? Christ-like? Really?

Yes…Thomas C. Breckenridge III. My indispensable prop!

Brandt called the cell phone he'd left for Tommy. It rang and rang and went unanswered, and suddenly a pang of nearly forgotten sharpness pinched his guts. And when he recognized it as the fear that had occasionally come over him when he'd felt, as a younger man, things were not quite yet under his control, he had to remind himself to stay cool.

Detach, as you would on any case, he told himself. Be the lawyer for Denny Brandt, not the witness on the stand. You can make a jury doubt anything, even what they've seen firsthand, if you stay cool. Nothing is personal. Nothing's at stake, not for you. You've got this under control. Not a worry in the world.

Now is not the time for Americans to fight with one another, he'd say.

Yes, but: What about the missing women? Their bodies still have not been found. Surely they weren't the enemy?

We have no explanation for their disappearance.

Then they're dead too? Burned to ashes? Couldn't you have just waited? Or are you saying you didn't know they were over there when you ordered the tear gas? If you did know, why did you do it? And if you didn't know, you should have known, right? You were in charge, weren't you?

And for an instant, Denny Brandt drew a blank, and the pain in his gut returned, and he thought perhaps it had come back again because his goddamn prop wasn't answering the goddamn phone, and that meant he had lost control of the situation, and when you lose control of a situation, anything can happen.

Anything.

He began to pace. He thought to himself, ready or not, they are outside right now, on the sidewalk, with lights and cameras and microphones, and every word I say will be caught on film, and talk-show pundits will parse my answers for days, and they'll become part of the public record, and the Democrats on the Hill will use my words against me in hearings. Oh, yes, they will subpoena me now. They will, if they sense any weakness at all, if I can't turn this story my way. They'll create a long, drawn-out media circus and make it impossible for RJ to appoint me. Impossible to appoint myself.

He dialed again.

It rang again, and again, and again.

The press is like a hungry beast. You must feed the beast, give them a story or become the story, the next meal.

He's the key. Tom-Tom. He's their next meal.

Still no answer…

Shit.

No answer means no control.

So take control. Go and get him. Go down to the goddamn basement and through the laundry room and up the back stairs to the street. Go out the goddamn back door. Now. Have a car waiting. Go to Brooklyn and come back with the one-eyed bastard. And then go out and meet the press with your prop at your side.

Right. That's it. Do this, then go to Washington and take what's yours.

He smiled and shoved his phone in his pocket.

It's a good name. Tom-Tom. Makes him sound like an innocent child. And he doesn't have to say a word. Stupid son of a bitch. All he has to do is stand beside me and bleed through his bandages.

Mike had no idea what time it was when he woke up, and he didn't much care. He needed coffee, and he didn't have any in the house, and the coffee shop around the corner had plenty.

Funny, he thought. No matter what the hell happens in my life—or in the world, for that matter—the first thing I think about when I get up is coffee.

And he deserved it.

What a week.

Crazy…

Oh, yeah. Dee…

I wonder if she ever called.

Jack woke up in a hospital bed. Karl sat beside him. "Where's Abbey?" he asked, as soon as he felt able to speak.

"Here," the police commissioner said. "Downstairs."

"Downstairs?"

"There's a morgue," Karl said, looking down and away.

Jack blinked, and tears ran down his cheeks. A great weight pressed against his chest, stifling the beat of his heart and making it nearly impossible to inhale again.

Karl gestured to the bathroom. "I had the staff bring over some clothes for you."

"Get out, Karl. I don't want you here."

"I know you don't, and I don't blame you, Jack."

"I said, get out."

"You're angry, and you have a right to be. But you're going to need friends now, to help you—"

"Friends?" Jack blurted a laugh through the tears. "Are you kidding me?"

Mike arrived at the coffee shop and got in line behind an eager newspaper reader wearing an "I Love NJ" T-shirt. The headline of the guy's *Post* read: *Trial by fire!* The headline sat over a picture of the Stranger, holding a limp child in his arms. The subheading: *Abbey Molinaro dead. "Stranger" under arrest.*

"No way," Mike said aloud. "What the hell happened?"

The guy from Jersey said, "Where have *you* been—solitary confinement?"

The line inched forward. The guy turned to page three.

A photo of Terry Stone? Mike read over the Jersey guy's shoulder. Stone had been interviewed and quoted.

"Iced mocha frappé," the customer at the head of the line said.

"Name?"

"Sonny."

"Get it at the bar, Sonny. Next."

The line inched forward.

Mike strained to read some more.

"Yo, get your own, cuz," Jersey said. "They're right over there."

"Sure," Mike said. "Hold my place?"

The guy nodded.

Mike grabbed the day's papers off a rack. The *News* and the *Times* had the same front page, more or less. He got back in line.

"Next?"

"Red-eye," Jersey said.

Terry Stone, the article read, *says there was no bomb, except the one the terrorists had already defused. The Stranger did not retaliate. He did not resist with violence.*

Terrorists? Mike said to himself. He turned the page, read about Beheshti and the suitcase bomb and the execution of the young Iranian boy. Mike looked up from the paper. Everyone seemed calm. Just another day in New York City.

"Can I help who's next?"

"Yeah," Mike said. "I'll have the same."

"Same what?"

"Red-eye. And pound cake. And the name is Mike." He paid and stepped to the bar and read some more. "Heaven itself rejected the violence brought to its door," Stone had also been quoted as saying. "It simply pushed everyone back. No one was hurt. No one was even injured. You have to understand. Time doesn't even exist in there."

Jesus, Terry, you sound like a crackpot.

"Mike?"

"Yup." Mike carried his coffee and bag of carbs to the counter where a line had formed for milk. He shoved his folded paper under one arm and poured. Wow, he thought. I can't believe it. I'd better call Connie and see if she wants me to—oh shit. I forgot about Dee!

Denny Brandt stood outside the door of Tom-Tom's apartment. On the way over, he'd thought twice about coming over personally, but he'd run through the decision in his mind. He couldn't trust this guy to anyone else, not with so much on the line. God only knows what he might say if I'm not in his face, he'd thought. Now he called Tommy's cell phone again, and this time he heard the phone ringing inside the apartment.

Is he in there or not?

Only one way to find out. Brandt used his key. He'd made one just in case.

Always thinking ahead. That's why I am where I am.

Okay, he thought, stepping inside. Door's not bolted. Probably means he's not here. Stupid bastard went out after I told him not to leave.

Shit!

Brandt wandered into the living room.

I'll just wait.

Brandt thought about his driver, double-parked in front of the building. Might scare little Tom-Tom off if he sees the car and knows I've come for him. Pathetic little prick. Probably panic and run. Brandt called down just in case. "Hey," he said. "Park around the block and tell the security detail to get back in the car and stay put. I'm going to be a while." He hung up and shoved his cell phone in his pocket. He walked around some more. Half the press in the world is looking for me, he thought, and I'm in this dirtbag's apartment.

He kicked something.

A roll of duct tape.

"Place is a shithole," he said.

Is that blood?

He bent closer.

Still wet?

And now, on the kitchen counter: a shotgun.

Oh, for the love of God—

A squeak from behind a door down the hall spun Brandt around. "Hello?" he said. He picked up the shotgun and went slowly toward the slightly open door and silently pushed it open some more, with the barrel. "Oh, no," he said softly.

A woman with bright-orange hair, naked and bloody and taped to a chair, stared at him, eyes wide as saucers. He pushed some more with the shotgun barrel, and a hand shot out and grabbed the barrel and tugged. Brandt came forward forcefully, off balance, and that sharp pain seized his gut again, even as he felt a strange sense of relief, and release, finding himself face-to-face with his one-eyed prop. "Ta-tom…Tom?" he said, curiously choking on the words, coughing them out in his own, new stutter. And now he tasted blood. And now the pain…staggering. "Oh, my Go…Ohhhh!" Brandt slid his hand to his side and felt something hard, something sharp inside of him, tearing at him, ripping him open.

Tom-Tom pulled him closer, jerked up the blade, and pushed him back, and now a flash of light on polished steel caught Brandt's eye above him.

"Don't you ca-call me that," Tommy sneered, and his lone eye brightened with rage, and he brought the blade down fast and jammed it into Brandt's neck. "Na-never again."

Brandt convulsed and collapsed to his knees and let go of the shotgun and grabbed for his neck.

Tommy, knife in one hand, still holding the shotgun by the barrel in the other, bent over him and said, "What the hell are you da-doing, coming in here like that…Da-da-da-denny?"

Brandt fell to his side at the bloody feet of the bound and naked woman.

"Ain't so funny now. Is it, big shot? My na-name ain't so fuh-funny now."

No. Not funny, Brandt thought. You…

Made…

A mistake…

Counselor…

Miscalculated.

Brandt curled into a tight fetal position and closed his eyes and tried hard not to fade out.

Footsteps.

He's leaving…me to…

Die…

The rise and fall of Brandt's belly as he struggled to breathe became less and less pronounced, and pain drove him to spasms.

It's not…fear.

It's death…

Coming…

For me.

He fought it, opened his eyes. The peeling white paint on the ceiling and the sunlight streaming through the window turned the entire room cloudlike. And now the soft whiteness began to turn a dirty gray, like truck smog stalled in a stifling hot garage. Poisonous. Choking.

He began to wonder who he was, and *what* he was.

Am I to become…

Something…

New?

The naked woman's muffled cries for help stirred him, as if from sleep, but then again he drifted toward an enveloping darkness.

The feeling of floating overtook him.

Yes…floating…on a vast red sea now.

A sea of blood.

He went a great distance away from the sensations of being alive and in a body, and he did so in no time at all, and yet the voice of a man, very far off and clearly filled with panic, came across the vastness of the crimson sea and entered his consciousness.

And the man said, "Oh my God, Dee!"

And floating became drowning.

Jack had left his necktie in the bathroom, and his top button open. His suit jacket felt oddly casual. His shoes, tight. His wallet, still damp in his pocket and clammy against his leg, reminded him how recently everything had happened.

The elevator doors opened at the B level, and the smell of lemon-scented ammonia cleanser stung Jack's nostrils, making him nauseous.

He needed a drink.

The morgue attendant nodded as if expecting him, and Jack froze for a moment before entering the room. Karl, who'd insisted on coming along, took the lead. He pushed through the double doors and held one for Jack.

Inside, the fluorescent lights in the ceiling buzzed.

"What about my wife?" Jack asked.

"She's at the Dakota. Unharmed. I mean, no one was hurt, really."

"No one?"

"I'm sorry. Except for Abrianna."

"Where's Brandt?" Jack asked.

"He's dead, Jack."

"What?"

"An hour ago. Breckenridge killed him. Ex-con. Rap sheet as long as your arm. We picked the bastard up leaving his apartment. That guy, Mike, the cameraman from NY1, he went there looking for Dee Weiss, and—"

"How?"

"Breckenridge stuck a knife in Denny's belly first, and then, for fun, he nearly tore his head off. Cut him ear to ear. Dee's alive. Apparently she went there with a shotgun to kill Breckenridge. Obviously didn't know what kind of an animal she was dealing with. For that matter, neither did Denny, I guess. Or any of us."

Now Jack understood why Karl had come to the hospital. To make amends. To get back in his good graces now that his bene-factor, the governor, was gone and the jig was up. "What about the Stranger?" he asked.

"Surrendered. In Bellevue. Denny had him taken there before all of this shook out. Feds are going to do a psychiatric evaluation, then move him to God knows where. At least, that was the plan. Who knows now?"

Karl led Jack to a wall of drawers, about waist high.

"Have they—" Jack choked on the words.

"No. No autopsy," Karl said. He reached for Jack, held his arm. "No one will ever know, Jack. I promise you."

"Know what?" Jack pulled away, baffled and frustrated and angry, yet somehow instinctively full of fear.

Karl stood stone still and stared into Jack's eyes for what seemed an eternity. But he didn't speak. The hairs on the back of Jack's neck stood up, and a chill rose from his ankles to the top of his head. He'd recalled now that Abbey had looked untouched by the fire when he saw her in the Stranger's arms. But the smoke, he thought. It had to be the smoke.

He turned to Karl. "Exactly how did she die?" he asked, but again, Karl did not speak. He looked as if he could not.

Jack pulled the drawer open, about halfway, and a black rubber bag lay before him, zipped closed. He began to tremble as he reached to open it.

Karl said, "Wait. Please."

"To Hell with you," Jack blurted. "How did she die? From what?" He tugged the zipper and slowly opened the bag until Abbey's eyes, doll-like and lifeless and framed by her golden curls, stared at him. He steadied himself against the metal drawer.

"I thought you knew. My God. I'm begging you, Jack. No more. Just—stop!" Karl grabbed hold of Jack's wrist with one hand.

Jack did, and he faced Karl.

And now Karl removed a small plastic bag from his breast pocket and held it out.

Jack's brow furrowed as he tried to focus on the silver, mushroom-shaped stone inside the plastic. He took the bag, held it nearer his eyes, and examined the stone more closely.

"A slug? You found the dog?"

"Not the dog, Jack."

Jack's insides went hollow, as if his very soul had left him.

"I'm sorry, Jack. I thought you knew. I really thought—" Now Karl pulled a black pistol from his suit jacket pocket.

"Joe Black's pistol? The one I took over there and gave to Saragossa?"

"It doesn't matter. Right? I mean, it was an accident," Karl said. "Nobody knows. And nobody has to know."

"No," Jack said, shaking his head, his voice cracking, his mind overcome by an irresistible flood of emotion. "That's...*not*...what killed her."

"I'm sorry, Jack. I'm so sorry."

"No!" Pain, deep self-pity, self-hatred, and denial took Jack over, and into his mind rushed an image of the single shaft of light that had streamed out the Stranger's structure immediately after Saragossa had fired Joe's weapon, and the sound of the dog, the yelp as the animal had leaped at him. The bullet. It had hit the dog. Passed right through. Right through! And now it came back to him as if in slow motion. In black and white and hot, glowing orange: The Point. The dog. The flames. The Stranger's structure. The hole in it. The single shaft of light. Again. The Point. The dog. The flames. The Stranger's structure. The hole in it. The single shaft of light. "'Daddy,'" he said. "She called out to me, Karl. To warn me. 'Daddy,' she said! She was in there, and the bullet, it went straight through that dog, and—"

The Point. The dog. The flames. The Stranger's structure. The hole in it. The single shaft of light where the bullet went in and killed her in the instant she'd returned to bodily form.

Jack buckled.

His tears rained and spattered on the rubber bag.

He shook and choked and convulsed. "It's too much…" Jack said. "I can't. I—ca-can't know this…"

"I'm sorry, Jack. So sorry."

"It's too much…I killed my baby! I killed my own little girl!"

CHAPTER 20

WE SCREW IT ALL UP, TERRY STONE THOUGHT. WE IGNORE GOD'S law and make our own laws and have things our own way. We exercise our free will and buy weapons for self-defense, and things go wrong, and innocent people suffer, and little children die. And then we blame God and ask, why did you let this happen, Lord?

Then we want intervention.

Deus ex machina.

We want a reset switch to undo everything we've done wrong.

But that's not possible.

Not in the real world.

Not possible...

He faced his brother, Cezar. The wooded peninsula, where the Stranger had lived for a few precious days, poked into the lake directly across from where they stood. Believers now knew it as Abbey's Point.

On Stone's right, a passerby fiddled with the lens of his camera. Behind him, the Angel of the Waters rose out of the circular fountain on the expanse of red bricks. Bethesda Terrace. The broken heart of Central Park.

Red Cross tents were pitched on the hills surrounding the Point again. The crowds were back, but smaller. Thousands of sick and dying still needed help. A miracle. And they still believed the Stranger would come again. But many thousands more had gone home.

It had been two days since the tragedy. The charcoal-colored tree trunks and ghostly shrubs and the very earth itself still smoldered. Around the base of the fountain, hundreds of flowers and wreaths now replaced the weapons that had been surrendered there.

"I can't believe he's gone," Cezar said. "The Stranger, I mean."

"He's not gone," Stone said. "He's in a mental institution." God is going to jail, he thought. His gaze drifted to the green hills, the boathouse, and the weeping willows. And now he spotted a Marine, in full dress uniform, bending to touch the lake, as if its waters were holy. The war had spread to ten countries now. It would spread across the world and cost many lives, perhaps even the life of the young man who had caught his attention. Perhaps it would lead to the end of all human life.

"Why do you think we did it?" Stone asked.

"Did what?"

"Enlisted," Stone said. "I mean, we were raised to fear God. We went to Sunday school. We learned the lesson of M-39. Turn the other cheek. How could we ignore it?"

"We wanted to serve, I guess."

"Did we?"

"I did," Cezar said. "And a college education."

"Like those guardsmen? And the men who started that fire?"

"Look, you recruited me, remember? What the hell are you asking me for?"

"Yeah. You're right. I'm sorry," Terry Stone said.

"Yeah," Cezar said. He held out the stump that had once been an arm. "Me too."

Stone knew Cezar had looked up to him, trusted him, and followed him into battle out of love, kinship, and respect. Just as he had followed others, leaders who'd told him things that sounded noble and honorable—politicians and lawyers, priests and TV pundits, people whose actions and laws stood in stark opposition to God's laws. They'd made their way of thinking sound patriotic, and their actions look heroic, and that had allowed him to ignore "love thy enemy" and "turn the other cheek." Somehow he had become a tool in their hands. "I helped them," Stone said.

"Helped who?"

"The men in power. The rich. The ones who sent us, and still send the poor, the opportunity starved, those who need a sense of worth or an education…"

"I'm as responsible as you or anybody else for what happened to me."

"No. You're not. That's just more hero, I-am-the-master-of-my-fate bullshit."

"Okay. Go on. Get it off your chest, if it'll help."

"You want to know why we went? Why men and now women volunteer? Why women now demand an equal opportunity to kill, as if they're being deprived of something good by being kept out of combat? It's because we never question those in power. We never ask, how can this be right and just? How can it be that I am a hero for doing this if God says no? And if we do ask, we're told, 'We know better than you do what's right and wrong, good and bad, what the scriptures do and do not say.' And that's all it takes. We're persuaded to kill, so that corporations run and owned by the rich can have open shipping lanes and secure oil fields. So that the entire structure of rich on top and poor on bottom can remain secure. We do it so the 1 percent can have yachts and private jets and mansions and Bentleys, and maybe, just maybe, throw us some crumbs. We're stupid! The actions we take aren't even in our own interest. Not spiritually. Not economically. Not in the long run. Not at all. We do their bidding and arrest one another when hunger drives one of us to steal. We shoot one another over the drugs we take to cope with the desolation of life as it is. We police and guard ourselves while the rich sleep safely in palaces made with our sweat and blood, and we go home to our slums—or, if we're lucky, if one of them does throw us some crumbs, we make it to the suburbs, and we hope and pray we won't get found out and fired."

"Okay, Mr. 99 Percent. So what?"

"So: 'The destruction of life is not an act that tends to improve it; it's suicide.'"

"True."

"Tolstoy said that. Over a hundred years ago, and nothing's changed. Doesn't matter what you call the form of government or the kind of economic system you live under. It's always the same. The poor are sold a lie, and they buy it and follow their leaders like lambs to the slaughter. And you know what hurts me the most?"

"What, pray tell, my Marine brother?"

"The deceit," Stone said. "The sheer and absolute deceit by those behind all the most shocking of crimes: the executions of foreign leaders, the midnight invasions, the drone murders of innocent civilians, and the smart-bomb carnage. The killing of hundreds of thousands of women and children noncombatants. All that shit done in Christ's name by people who claim to be born again, and who justify their own unholy, ungodly acts. The Republicans who hate the Democrats more than they love our country. The Democrats who laugh at those who love God, see us as 'simple-minded fools.' Acts of violence Jesus clearly abhorred, and gave his life to condemn, done in our name, and condoned by *both* parties."

"As if it's for God and country. Yeah. I hear you."

"Oorah."

"In a word." Cezar nodded. "The funeral is tomorrow afternoon. For Abbey Molinaro."

"You going?" Stone asked.

"Can't," said Cezar. "I'm headed to the new front lines."

"What?"

"Yup. Going in as a new kind of Christian soldier. Going to suit up, M-39 style, and protest at NRA HQ."

Stone smiled. He stared across the lake again. Bare, charred, lifeless black trees creaked. A fireman shoveled dirt onto a pile of smoking leaves.

"You blame the mayor for the little girl's death, don't you?" Cezar asked.

"Ruthie warned him to stay out of the lake. Jeremiah warned him too."

"And that means it was his fault?" Cezar asked.

"What I see is that the same bullshit story that lured me into the Marines lured him out there. Going into the fire to be the big hero again. Save a poor, helpless child when God was already on the scene."

"That's being pretty hard on him, man," Cezar said. "What was he supposed to do? Let her burn?"

"Not saying that. Going in to help is one thing. Going armed, that's another. That's all. You go armed, and innocent people get killed. You don't go armed, and maybe the dog doesn't even bark at you. Pretty clear if you look. Gun in act one, somebody's dead in act two. Pretty damn clear."

"You mean like, over three hundred and fifty thousand innocent women and children killed by us while we were 'liberating' them in Iraq?"

"A lot more people dead than that. But, yes. Just like that."

The brothers walked across the terrace, through a potted forest of lovely blooming roses and lilies and impatiens and wreaths with ribbons that read *God Bless the Stranger of Central Park* and *God Loves Abbey Molinaro*. They sat on the edge of the fountain, surrounded by the fragrances and colors, and the sounds of birds, and the hum of cars in the distance helped create a perimeter, a feeling that this was a sanctuary, a holy place, though one beside an insidious Hell.

"So, what now for the great Terry Stone?" Cezar asked.

Stone pulled out the note Jessie had given him, the note from Katie she'd found in Jack's drawer. He read it, shook his head, and turned to the Point again. "I don't know. I mean, Jessie told me this was important. She said I should read it, but what can I do? It's not up to me."

"Let me see it," Cezar said. He read it aloud: "'Dear Jack, before the end of the year, you will be president of the United States of America.' Damn. Well, you said it was in your dream too."

"It was, and Jessie—she was with me, and…ah, hell, man. So much for that." Terry Stone wadded up the note and tossed it to the bricks.

"Maybe, if it's not true, it just means it's not finished," Cezar said. "So it's just not true yet."

Stone smiled. "My eternal optimist."

"Hell yeah," Cezar said. "And I'll leave you with that."

A petite brunette in a red, V-neck sweater caught Stone's eye as she descended the stairs on the right side of the terrace. She'd caught Cezar's eye too, Stone noticed. She crossed the terrace, clutching a burgundy leather attaché case in one hand and holding it close to her body.

"Mr. Stone!" The woman now shouted and waved. "Terry Stone?"

"Ahhh, fame. Wish I was you," Cezar said.

"No, you don't," Stone said.

"Love ya, bro," Cezar said, smiling. "See you in Heaven."

Stone stood and embraced Cezar and watched as he walked away on one leg of flesh and another of steel. "M-39!" Stone shouted.

Cezar raised a clenched fist into the air.

And now on the far shore, on the crest of the ridge where the Stranger's structure had stood, Jack Molinaro appeared, wearing a crumpled, gray suit. The wind tossed his hair as he wandered the charred landscape and kicked at smoldering embers and wandered some more. And now Jack bent, and then he rose again and brushed smudges of dirt and ash off the small brown teddy bear he'd pulled from the ash. He held it gently to his heart.

A tear fell from Stone's cheek onto his own hand, and then it splattered onto the bricks. "Damn."

"You're Terry Stone, right?" the brunette said, close beside him now.

"Yeah," Stone said.

"The lady at the television studio said I'd find you here. Connie."

"Okay. What's this about?"

"I have something for you," she said. She handed him the attaché case. "It's from the governor. You know, Denny Brandt. He said if anything happened to him, if he got…like…killed or anything, I should give it to somebody, somebody um…reputable. Yes. That's it. Reputable. And I saw you on TV lots and lots of times, and I think you are."

"Reputable," Stone said. He couldn't help but laugh aloud. "Okay…well, I'll take it." He opened the case and slid out a thick file and read the initials penned on its cover in black Magic Marker. "RJ," he said, suddenly overcome by an indescribable heaviness. "As in, the president?"

The brunette shrugged. "I guess. Denny told me not to read it. So I didn't."

Stone thumbed through the pages quickly.

"Holy crap," he said.

"This yours?" The brunette asked. In the palm of her hand sat the crumpled note.

Stone turned to the Point. Jack was gone.

Four hours later, in the Oval Office, Stone stood staring at a photograph of Abraham Lincoln. "Peace through strength has not worked, Mr. President," Stone said. "Perhaps it's time we try strength through peace." He'd taken the first train to DC, read the file twice on the way, and stuffed it in a locker at Union Station after telling Connie his plan.

"So, that's your demand?" the president asked. "In exchange for Denny Brandt's files, all you want is world peace?"

"No, sir. As I've explained, I am not making any demands. I am simply suggesting that Denny Brandt's files and the details of your affiliation with organized crime will be a lot less interesting to me, and the country, if you resign—say, due to bad health. You know, after appointing a good man as vice president."

"Does Jack Molinaro know what you're demanding?"

"Sir," Stone said, "the choice of a successor is entirely yours."

"No one knows, Jack," Karl had said at the hospital as he closed the drawer with the body of Jack's child inside. "So it's up to you what happens next. I'll do whatever you want."

"I do," Jack had said. "I know. And I'll always know."

Back home in Gracie Mansion now, Jack sat on Abbey's bed, and every time he thought of his child alone in the ground for eternity, he lost all control.

He took no calls, nor food, nor sleep. He allowed no one in the house, though many came or called to console him. He could not stop the war of confusion in his mind, the roaring litany of self-recrimination and self-hatred. The loop of events playing over and over. He needed help, the kind of help that had once come from earnest prayer, from confessing and doing penance. And so he found himself on his knees, in a church confessional, though he had no recollection of going. "Please help me, Father," he said now. "It's been so long. I don't really recall how to do this anymore."

"Worst things first," the priest said. "But start with, 'Bless me, Father, for I have sinned.'"

"Yes. Of course," he said. "Bless me, Father, for I have sinned. It has been many years since my last confession." Jack flooded emotionally, but somehow the frightful words came out of him like some thick, black poison. "I killed…my daughter. And I've hurt many people, and lied and cheated, and—oh God…"

After a moment, the priest said, "Your child…was it an act of rage, done in anger?"

"It was an accident."

"God does not judge us for accidents, my son."

"No. It's a lie. It was pride and anger. I—I didn't trust. I didn't listen."

"Pride…yes. Well, pride may be conquered by acts of humility. Bow down daily before God. Begin your days on your knees. Bow your head to the floor so it is lower than your heart. Always keep your heart above your head—figuratively, at least. Pray for humility and forgiveness. From now on, treat everyone you meet as if they were the temple of the Lord and bow to them, internally, serve them, and forgive them any harm they do to you. Be a peacemaker."

"Why did it take this? Why did she have to die for me to see my arrogance and stupidity? My sins?"

"Spiritual blindness is like physical blindness. The physically blind, though told for years by loving family and friends what it's like to see, still do not really know. For some who are physically blind, there is the hope of a surgery, but until they've gone under the knife, and been cut deeply, and personally come out of the darkness for the first time to see the world with new eyes, they cannot understand. Until then, they simply cannot even imagine.

So too it is with spiritual blindness. You have been cut deeply, and now you can see."

"She was innocent."

"And we were warned: The sins of the fathers shall be visited upon the children. Did you think you were an island, that you could sin and then confine the damage done to only your own self?"

"Yes."

"We are one human family, my son, tied together by the One within us. No one can harm another without bringing harm to all. Sadly, it takes the selfless act of an innocent, one willing to die that we might see, to bring us to the light. This is the story of our Lord and Savior."

"How can I pay for this sin?"

"You can't. But the spiritual debt is paid for you. You have walked through an open gate by coming here and confessing with a broken and contrite heart, and that is the key. However, as I am sure you know, you must still live with the consequences of your actions and pay any earthly penalty for your transgressions. Spiritual absolution does not release you from the laws of cause and effect, nor can it help you escape earthly justice."

"Yes," Jack said. "I understand…and I am so sorry."

"I believe you, my son. And I am sorry it has taken so much pain for you to realize the error of your ways. The physically blind are blessed to realize their need for help, and so they go out on the arm of another, and by doing so they learn trust. You did not know your blindness, and so you could not ask for help or lean on others. But God saw your need. And perhaps because your soul is more important than your body, or even the body of your child—because your soul was too important to lose—God intervened. We can never know for certain why what happens does happen. But we can trust. Let the remainder of your life be your penance. Be present to the spiritual opportunity of every moment. God has brought each moment to you. See him working through you, even in times of trial and pain and tribulation, and you will be a light unto the world…"

"And for my lack of trust, and my willfulness?"

"Surrender. Say: Thy will be done."

Jack fell silent.

"And you have lied?" the priest asked.

"Yes."

"To yourself and others?"

"Yes."

"And have you found the truth?"

"No."

"Then you must continue to seek it. And you have had an affair?"

"Yes."

"Did you love the woman?"

"I thought I did. I don't even know who she really is. Or was. Maybe I projected onto her the attributes I wanted to see. But it doesn't matter. She betrayed me in the most despicable way. I can't forgive her."

"Then you cannot be forgiven. Do you not see her actions as merely the reflection of your own?"

Jack paused a long while before answering. "Yes. It's true."

"Then forgive her. And if you are to love her again, love her not as a form or object, not even as a woman, for you are married and have taken vows that are sacred. Love her as you would love a person: as a beautiful soul, alive with the same essence as the essence of your soul."

"Yes."

"And what of your wife?"

"I don't know. She wanted to reconcile. But now…I fear she will never forgive me when she learns that I was responsible for the death of our child."

"Lean on the risen Christ until you merge with him, until you realize he is the vine and we the branch and leaf. Live as one with the One who is one with the Father. Offer the world unconditional love."

"Unconditional love?"

"This is why Jesus overturned the tables of the merchants at the temple. Love your wife for love's sake alone. Do not make the love of God or the love of others a transaction. When you want only the happiness of your beloved, your love will be pure. Your words and your friendships will also be true. Only such love is worthy of a Christian, and a true husband."

"Yes, Father. Thank you."

"Let us make the sign of the cross now and pray for absolution and forgiveness, for strength and faith, and for the wisdom to know lies from the truth."

On his way home, Jack wondered: What is the truth?

He recalled the Book of Romans: There are none righteous. No, not one. None understand. None truly seek God. None do good.

None.

We're merely human. Weak. Fearful. We trust nothing. No one. Least of all, the unseen, unknowable, all powerful Lord. We have very little faith. So how can we turn the other cheek if the reason for doing so is that we believe we'll be rewarded in an afterlife?

We can't because we don't believe!

How can we resist the temptation to strike back when struck? Forgive when offended?

How can we be kind to those who mock us? Pray for our enemies?

Who can turn the other cheek and watch while their own child is being harmed?

Who can witness a wife or daughter or sister raped and resist it not?

I cannot.

So shall I be damned?

Is that the message of M-39?

Will we all be damned if we cannot go like lambs to the slaughter?

Is that the truth?

No. It is not. It cannot be.

Mercy must then be the true and overarching message. We cannot do as commanded. Our frailty prevents it. It is against our human nature to submit to death rather than fight. So we must seek mercy. And forgiveness.

And self-forgiveness is the start to all forgiveness, Jack told himself.

That is true.

And we need humility too.

We need humility because we know all about our own weaknesses, shortcomings, and failures. We may deny we have them to others. But we know all about them.

Yes.

This is truth. And it means few are worthy of the name *Christian*. Few should claim it.

Rather, we should try to live up to it fully, and, until we can do so fully, we should, at best, refer to ourselves as apprentices.

Carpenter's apprentices.

Christians in training, perhaps. But not Christians.

Not fully Christian until we can actually do as commanded.

Yes, humility until then.

And then, if we can someday achieve that great summit, if we can actually *be good Christians* and follow M-39, we won't need humility anymore, for we shall *be* humility personified.

Like him.

Like the Stranger.

Lord, please, Jack now prayed, even if the lessons I learn from failing to heed M-39 are too salutary to regret, I beg you: please, spare me any more tests!

Deliver me from evil instead of making me face it, for I am too weak to face it well. Too self-interested. Too fearful that the death of my body or the bodies of my loved ones is the actual end of them.

Oh, give me a sign, Lord, for I have no faith!

None.

I am not worthy of your name.

And my God, if it is *you* who leads me into temptation, as the Lord's Prayer implies, I pray: lead me not toward a fate that has me facing a choice that I cannot make well. Rather, Lord, God, deliver me from evil, for I may become one with the evil I face, even as I attempt to face it as you command: by turning the other cheek.

Even Jesus, while in a human body, feared of his trials and cruel death.

Even he, in the Garden of Gethsemane, prayed that the bitter cup of physical agony might pass his lips.

Even he prayed to be delivered from the cross.

May we all be so delivered, Lord. Please!

Though, like him, I say: Thy will be done, Lord.

Thy will be done.

Jack blessed himself.

He paused a moment and reflected on the need to do something, even if he could not do everything the Stranger commanded. And now he prayed again: Please, Lord, if it be thy will, allow me to work toward bringing the Kingdom of Heaven to its fullness on Earth. Allow me to do so, Lord, and I pledge to you that I will work to make sure the choice men face will no longer be between watching evil happen and resisting it by force. For, by your grace, I will work to prevent evil *before* it happens, before the choice of whether or not to resist it arises. I will do so by following *all* the commandments of

Jesus Christ, and working also to see to it that many, many others know that this is something we all *must* do.

I will love my neighbor as myself.

I will help the poor.

I will lift up the needy.

I will.

I will work to create a society that has fewer and fewer broken, fewer and fewer deprived, fewer and fewer needy, sick, hurt, angry, and suffering souls.

I will.

I will.

For this even I can do. And by so doing, perhaps I can help make M-39 a choice we face less often.

Yes, I will try Christianity.

I will. By thy grace.

I will truly and fully try Christianity as the Lord himself taught it. As God intended it—M-39 is the ideal, and any denial of it as the ideal is not the truth. But it is also true that until we can be truly Christian, we must do what we can, even if we fall short of the ideal.

Amen.

Terry Stone had just come from Bellevue. He had asked the president for one more thing: access to the Stranger. And the president had provided it. Stone had been welcomed in and shown to the room where the Stranger was being held. However, when he arrived, the officer assigned to stand guard outside the room said, "You're too late." He reported that he'd been on duty earlier, when suddenly a great flash of light had streamed from the cracks around the door, blinding him and forcing him to kneel. He could not speak or call out for help. When he'd finally opened the door, the

Stranger was gone. He'd opened it again in Stone's presence and led Stone inside the cell.

"When did that appear?" Stone had asked, pointing to a dark silhouette on the wall.

"Right after he—after the light—went away."

Stone had stepped farther back in order to make sense of the image. "I saw something like it once, in pictures of Hiroshima. Shadows, engraved," he'd said. "From a flash, like the light in the park. See there?" He'd pointed to the outline of a human form, in shadow, on the wall. "That's the Stranger. And there…that's the figure of a child."

"Abbey Molinaro?" the guard had asked.

"Yes," Stone had said.

An hour later, Stone stood outside Katie Molinaro's hospital room, and he felt oddly happy when a nurse said, "About two hours ago, her body just vanished in a flash of light."

Stone rushed out and grabbed a cab.

Jack's black Town Car came to a stop on Fifth Avenue, across the street from the *Atlas* sculpture in Rockefeller Center, and in front of the grand Roman Catholic cathedral named for Patrick, the patron saint of all excluded people.

Atlas.

He had defied Zeus, the god and ruler of the ancient pagan gods, and sided with the Titans against Heaven itself. As punishment, Zeus had condemned Atlas to bear the weight of the entire world—indeed of the celestial Heavens too—on his own shoulders.

Like the all too heavily burdened mythological Atlas, Jack had shrugged off any divine suggestions about how to live his life. So now he too had to bear the weight of his world alone.

If you want things done your way, not even God can help you, he now knew.

Jack had, only too late, seen the folly of his "selfish" and self-isolating Randian hubris.

He turned to the cathedral and reflected now on his earthly heritage: Italian and Irish. *So I am a little like Saint Patrick too, in a way,* he thought. *If only by lineage.*

Patrick, who'd been expatriated from his home in Ireland, was enslaved in Rome as a child. There he had received a vision in his sleep, experienced a miracle, and escaped his terrible early fate, later becoming one of the truly beloved of the world. Patrick had done so by the power of his faith. *His acts of selflessness inspired others to join Christianity,* Jack told himself now. *And to act according to its precepts. That's how Saint Patrick did it. Not by politics, nor the accumulation of power, nor the exercise of free will. Not by the selfish pursuit of individual interest justified by the assertion that a rising tide lifts all boats, for such platitudes ignore the fact of the masses stranded on the shore.*

No.

By serving God's will, whatever the cost.

He, unlike me, Jack told himself now, *is truly worthy of the great title* Christian.

And once again, self-recrimination and spiritual desolation began to overtake him.

Three days had passed since Saragossa had fired a weapon at his command, and the bullet that had been meant to enable him to save his child had torn through her tiny heart.

One night had passed since he'd gone to confession, and then kicked at embers on the Point, and later wandered the city streets, clutching the teddy bear he'd found in the rubble. He held it now, as he sat thinking over all this. He'd brought it because he knew Abbey would not be able to rest, would not sleep, even in Heaven, without it.

He'd pulled the stuffed bear from the black, smoldering earth and walked home, past people who had recognized him, pointed, and whispered about his terrible loss. But they did not know what he knew. They did not know that he had killed his own baby, and their pity deeply shamed him.

And here they were again, surrounding his car, alongside the haters, the self-righteous, the men and women who judged him for the speck in his eye, though they had beams in their own. Only Jack could not claim a mere speck. No. Blood, he told himself. Abbey's blood. That's what's in my eyes.

Exhausted, mourning his loss, and his sins, he could not get out of the car.

Not yet.

I cannot face myself, much less God.

The shadows of buildings stretched long on the sidewalk, cast by the late-afternoon sun. The press, cameras, and microphones, held poised and at the ready, awaited him like the weapons of a firing squad.

"Saragossa," he said to himself, taking pity on his accomplice as the young police officer walked past the car without looking up. She's broken, he thought, by the death of Abbey. Completely broken. And she doesn't even know the truth of it all. At least not yet.

Sophia, wearing black head to toe, her face in shadow behind an onyx-colored lace veil, passed too, zombie-like in grief, and climbed the cathedral steps.

She will truly hate me, he thought. When she learns I did this. I killed our daughter.

And my life will last too long now.

Too long.

He took a deep breath and forced himself to exit the car.

Uniformed officers in blue with bright brass buttons and white gloves rushed to his side and shielded him from the pressing crowds.

He ignored the reporters and their shouted questions. He ascended, still clutching Abbey's little stuffed bear.

At the great doors, he struggled against his fear. He stepped in, made his way down the wide aisle between the wooden pews. Great stone walls stood to his left and right, bulwarks of a common sepulcher of the living. A repository for lost and broken souls, carved from stone. He stood as if at the bottom of a great gorge or canyon: tiny, meaningless.

The coffin looks so small too, he thought.

And the pews are so full.

People from all over the world had come. They'd come for Abbey.

The walk to her coffin seemed endless, each footfall a hollow chop at the present moment, and a reminder of his future: A life without his baby.

The stained-glass windows, a kaleidoscope of the power of faith, did not comfort him.

The organ pipes, a vibratory dirge of low and enervating sound, deepened his mourning.

The shiny copper-colored box, cold and confining and now very close, provoked only one thought: What an awful abode for a child, for all of eternity.

The fragrance of roses, and smoldering frankincense and myrrh, wandered into his consciousness. And now the minor chords of the grand organ gained volume, the people stirred, and their hushed gasps and stifled weeping on seeing the small, torn, burned bear hanging from his hand sent yet another pang of self-loathing into his heart.

Jesus, lifeless, on a sculpted golden cross that stood on a high altar behind Abbey's closed coffin, seemed suspended between Heaven and Earth.

As am I, Jack thought. I belong neither here nor there, but in Hell. And, in time, I shall surely go.

Surely.

The music stopped.

Jack stopped.

To his right, on the aisle, beside Terry Stone, sat Karl Kastleman.

Karl, who had betrayed him.

Karl, who had then covered up the truth of what had happened without ever being asked to do so.

Karl, who even now kept the secret, the real cause of the death of Abrianna Molinaro, from the world.

The truth? Jack wavered. Oh, yes. That again.

He did not deserve the chance, he now decided, to do what good he could do with the remainder of his life. To do what good he could if he could not live up to M-39.

Why?

Because, learning about Becka betraying him with Brandt had driven him to the brink of madness, and, at least in part, it had driven him to what he now had to admit was an act of pure ego-inspired depravity: taking a gun to Denny Brandt's head.

Taking a gun to the Point.

Yes, in that same moment, he had feared for Abbey's safety. But it was not that fear that had sent him onto the lake or rushing into the flames on the Point to save her. Hatred of a political rival who'd beaten him, his own crippled pride at the humiliation of losing, and the need to be seen as the hero again had driven him to it.

Yes. He had felt the need to win in the park that night. To take control of his own destiny. To assert his power. To defeat Brandt at something. Anything. No matter what the cost.

And to defeat God. To circumvent God's will if God's will did not align with his own.

That is truth, he confessed now.

Truth.

Ego, his ego, and pride had killed Abbey, and so he could not rightfully call it "an accident."

At the end of the wide aisle, when he could no longer stand being between the real truth and the lie he'd been living with for three days, with everyone behind him and no one before him except his unseen, lifeless child in a burial box, he turned and confessed in a loud, clear voice: "It was me!"

Neither shame, nor fear of popular judgment, nor even the instinctive desire for self-preservation could hold back the words now. The entire world would turn against him for what he'd done. Yet, he turned to the left and the right and confessed it again, over and over, so everyone could see him saying it, so that all assembled could hear: "It was me!"

He pointed to his child's coffin. "I did that! Not Denny Brandt. Not the Stranger." He turned to Sophia. "Me! It's my fault! Abbey is dead because of *me*!"

"It was the smoke!" Karl stood and shouted. "The fire! It was no one's fault!"

"No!" Jack shouted. "That's *not* the truth. She was shot! Shot, I tell you! And I am to blame!"

A collective gasp of horror filled the cathedral.

Saragossa stood. "No," she cried. "Please. No!"

"Yes!" He turned to Saragossa. "But it's my fault. Mine! I ordered it. You did what I told you to do. You shot the dog, but the bullet went right through. Right through!" Tears streamed down his cheeks, and he turned back to Sophia. "And it killed her. It killed our baby girl!"

Sobs and shrieks of pain echoed off the cathedral walls now, and Jack turned again to Saragossa. "I'm sorry. So sorry. We tried to…save…Abbey…but we killed her." He dropped to his knees. "I killed her."

And now the doors at the back of the cathedral flew open and a great gust blew, and an unnaturally bright light streamed in.

Jack shielded his eyes, strained to see.

Someone stood in the midst of that light. A woman. She approached, glowing even more brightly as she came to the altar and the coffin.

"It's Katie," Terry Stone shouted. "Oh!"

"How?" Jack asked. His sister. Alive. New. In a body of light, like...the Stranger.

She reached him and lifted him to his feet, and they held one another in a deep stare. "A miracle," he said. "It's a miracle!"

Katie kissed his cheek and gently guided him back onto his knees. She turned and gestured, and everyone in the church knelt too. And now she moved beside the tiny coffin and turned to face the gathering. "My brother," she said, "is right. And he is wrong. It is his fault. And it is our fault too. All of us. We live by the sword, and our children die by it. Our lack of faith and our inability to trust God kills our children. Our defiance killed this beautiful, innocent little girl." She gestured to the coffin. "Our desire for self-defense killed her. Our deceitful, ironic willingness to kill in order to preserve life killed her. It kills thousands of men and women and children, day after day. But now it is time to stop this madness!"

And the word *madness* echoed off the walls of the cathedral and into the city streets: *madness!*

Madness! Madness!

Madness! Madness! Madness!

When the echoes faded, and another moment passed in silence, Katie too knelt before the coffin. She prostrated herself low, pressed her forehead to the floor, and prayed in whispers. And when she finished, Jack broke his silence. "God," he said in full voice again, "oh Lord, my God, I am so sorry." He came high onto his knees now, and with arms outstretched he pleaded to the crucified Christ on the cross. "Please!" His body shook, and his words came out in sobs and fits and starts. He closed his eyes. "Take me. But please! Spare my child. Spare my baby!"

After a moment, Katie rose to her feet. She touched Jack's shoulder, and through his tears he saw her nod and smile. It seemed so strange to Jack that she would. But she did.

Some idea, unfathomable to him, had clearly overtaken her.

And now she turned to the altar and raised her arms to Heaven, and in that instant a golden light flashed and spread in a widening circle around the crucifix. The light grew in intensity and spread until it touched the floor, until it became a single ball of unfathomable, blinding light, tinged at the edges with sapphire and emerald and pink, filling the sanctuary.

And the light moved toward the coffin and parted.

And in the midst of the light stood the Stranger.

No one could speak. And no one could stand.

Katie stretched out her hands, opened them, palms forward as if to receive. And in her palms, she bore the stigmata, the wounds of the crucified Christ.

Jack could not fathom what had happened, what Katie was or had become. And now the Stranger's halo emanated from his sister too, and Katie's voice rose as if from Heaven. And Jack shook with fear when she spoke, for her voice filled the cathedral with the name of his child.

"Abrianna!" Katie shouted. At her word, light suddenly streamed from the little metal box, streamed from every seam of it. And now Katie said, "Come out!"

Another great gust of wind swirled, and a sound like a chorus of angels rose and filled St. Patrick's Cathedral. The earth shook, and the lid of the coffin opened and released a flood of golden, sparkling, blinding light.

Katie pulled Jack to his feet. She led him forward, squinting, shielding his eyes again, toward the open box. There Jack paused in awe. He turned to Sophia. She lifted her veil, and her eyes met his. He shook his head, but he could not speak, could not answer her unspoken query, and could not even fathom what was happening.

Jack turned again to the coffin.

He took a step closer.

He squinted and blinked and bent and tried to be sure of what he beheld, for what he beheld astonished him: the cushioned red velvet bed inside the copper-colored box was empty.

Katie smiled at him once more.

Jack staggered backward. "My God," he said. "My God."

And a small, warm hand slipped into his.

ABOUT THE AUTHOR

"Love and Serve."

From early on, James Patrick Dillon found the world to be a place of contrasting experiences. Some life events engendered feelings of inspiration, awe, and wonder. However, others, abusive and humiliating, were not only very unpleasant in real time, but they also replayed over and over in his mind and eventually led to a feeling of "spiritual desolation."

While still in high school, James found Saint Ignatius of Loyola had aptly described this condition in *The Spiritual Exercises*: "darkness of soul, disturbance in it, movement to things low and earthly...without hope, without love...as if separated from his Creator and Lord."

James felt moved by the saint's teachings, especially by the fact that someone else had so aptly described his personal suffering. He dove into studies of the Bible, pored over the works of other saints, and read everything he could find about the early Christian church and, of course, about Jesus Christ. Eventually, following his love of learning, James earned a bachelor's degree in literature and writing from Columbia University.

Along the way, James concluded the cause of his ongoing spiritual disquietude was not just the injustice of his own childhood abuse but also the pervasive, systemic injustice he witnessed in the world. The fact of wanton cruelty, endless war, avoidable famine, and untreated diseases plagued him. He watched the strong, the powerful, and the privileged routinely victimize the poor, the weak, and the underprivileged. Worse yet, he saw that they often got away with it. This continued to provoke the question: Why does God permit such suffering and injustice?

James turned to the East for answers, and he received initiation and training in Transcendental Meditation™ as taught by Maharishi Mahesh Yogi. He also completed the Self-Realization Fellowship study of the teachings of Paramahansa Yogananda and earned an Aquarian Teacher certification as a Kundalini Yoga instructor in the school of Kundalini Yoga as taught by Yogi Bhajan®. James continued to study religion, spirituality, the occult, philosophy, Theosophy, yoga, Advaita Vedanta, and Christian mysticism. In December of 2008, Hindu spiritual leader Mata Amritanandamayi Devi accepted James, a lifelong and still devout Christian, into a guru-disciple relationship. Amma, as she is known to the world, most definitely helped heal his soul and inspired him. Yet, he has still found no satisfying answer to that one burning question: Where is God and why doesn't he intervene?

It was not until James fell in love with Julia, his one true soul mate, that he finally understood that the pursuit of the answer to that question would never bring him peace.

Through my love of Julia, I have found God among us, and I reap the first fruits of a continually emerging apperception of the One Divine Lord. Only now do I know the stunningly simple truth: It is only in pure, selfless, unconditional, and nontransactional love that we may behold the face of the Eternal Divine. And only in such beholding may we realize that the question is not: Why does God allow bad things to happen to good people? The question is: What do good people do when bad things happen?

I now know that when good people experience or witness suffering, they must not waste time asking, "Why is God allowing this?" Instead, they must take action themselves. They must jump in. Help. Love and serve.

Through the example of my wife, Julia, I have experienced this. By her actions, with kindness, patient and loving persistence, and forgiveness, she has taught me what a thousand books could not.

I now fully apperceive that if I truly love, all questions of "I, me, and my"—including "Why did this happen to me or others?"—will be dispelled as light dispels the darkness, without the need of an answer as to the cause. For the cause of darkness is always merely the absence of light, which is to say, love. So, when the question arises, simply respond with love, and the darkness shall vanish. For true love heals. It seeds the desire to serve. In serving lovingly, we reap and sow again all the love we have ever received, and by so doing, we increase it ten thousand times, and our love may give off a light that dispels darkness everywhere, forever.

I can say this with certainty only because I have found the one whom my soul loves, and in so doing, I have had all my questions quieted, all my longings sated. In my Julia's loving embrace, I finally possess peace and can truly share love.

I now know: God is not an object to be studied. God, conceived of thusly, will ever remain an enigma.

Rather, God must be apperceived within all things and all beings, which is to say recognized, realized, and consciously perceived with full awareness and a conviction that is deep and essential in the soul, as being here, there, and yes: everywhere!

Pull back the opaque veil of self-centeredness, and you will find God!

This apperception yields a peace beyond cognition and understanding. It provokes, at long last, the joyful, soul-shouted exclamation: God is!

Julia, my love, revealed God's love to me in her very being-ness.

It is my prayer that each reader of this work, and every reader of each of our shared works—Julia's and mine—shall find such a love too. And share it!

Thank you.

May God richly bless you with the desire to love and serve.

Contact James Patrick Dillon at JPD@enlightenedlittlesouls.com.